# PRAISE FOR *DEEP STATE*

Editor's Choice, *The New York Times*

"Hayley Chill is one of those preternaturally talented solo operatives skilled in every endeavor, from her physical stamina to her administrative competence to her Jason Bourne–like cool in the face of near-death experiences. She also figures in one of the more surprising double-reverse plot twists I have seen in some time."

—*The New York Times Book Review*

"*Deep State* is a propulsive, page-turning, compelling fragmentation grenade of a debut thriller."

—C. J. Box, #1 *New York Times* bestselling author of *Wolf Pack* and *The Bitterroots*

"The plot of Chris Hauty's *Deep State* rings eerily true in a novel that will keep you turning the pages well into the night."

—Jack Carr, former Navy SEAL and acclaimed author of *The Terminal List, True Believer,* and *Savage Son*

"Hauty provides a fresh twist on the American patriot. Hayley Chill has what it takes to carve out her place in today's thriller scene. She's shrewd, fierce, and always lands the blow that puts her on top."

—Kyle Mills, #1 *New York Times* bestselling author of *Lethal Agent* and *Total Power*

"Jarring . . . intriguing . . . The ending seems pulled directly from a movie."

—*Booklist*

# DEEP STATE

### A THRILLER

★ ★ ★ ★ ★ ★ ★ ★ ★

# CHRIS HAUTY

POCKET BOOKS

New York   London   Toronto   Sydney   New Delhi

Pocket Books
An Imprint of Simon & Schuster, Inc.
1230 Avenue of the Americas
New York, NY 10020

This Pocket Books paperback edition November 2020

POCKET and colophon are registered trademarks of Simon & Schuster, Inc.

For information about special discounts for bulk purchases, please contact Simon & Schuster Special Sales at 1-866-506-1949 or business@simonandschuster.com.

The Simon & Schuster Speakers Bureau can bring authors to your live event. For more information or to book an event, contact the Simon & Schuster Speakers Bureau at 1-866-248-3049 or visit our website at www.simonspeakers.com.

Interior design by *Erika Genova*

Manufactured in the United States of America

10  9  8  7  6  5  4  3  2  1

ISBN 978-1-9821-2659-9
ISBN 978-1-9821-2660-5 (ebook)

*For George and Jackson*

# DEEP STATE

A lady asked Dr. Franklin, "Well, Doctor, what have we got, a republic or a monarchy?"
"A republic," replied the Doctor, "if you can keep it."

—Anonymous, from Farrand's *Records of the Federal Convention of 1787*

# PROLOGUE

★ ★ ★ ★

Leaving her air-conditioned quarters and stepping into the thick Texas summer night with less than forty minutes before the start of her bout, she begins to run. Humidity and air temperature persist above ninety despite the late hour, and she breaks a sweat before crossing Tank Destroyer Boulevard. Her footsteps hardly make a sound as she jogs the deserted, orderly streets of Fort Hood. Anyone who isn't already jammed into the fitness center for the monthly smoker has departed for lives off base. In this way she can enjoy the extravagance of being alone with her thoughts.

She's avoided warming up inside the venue since the beginning of her amateur career, preferring exercise outdoors until the last minutes before being called to the ring. Running clears her mind of all thoughts except those regarding the contest to come, removing her from the crowd's roar and its profanity. Rain or shine, day or night, she jogs alone at a steady pace wearing the same clothes she will wear in the ring. With this solitary pre-fight ritual, Hayley Chill prolongs an imperfect control over her world before the chaos and violence to come.

She can remember every fight. Whether childhood brawls back home in Green Shoals, West Virginia, or organized bouts as an amateur fighter since enlisting in the army, physical combat is the fierce memoir of a hardscrabble life. The oldest of six children—her single mother laid low by multiple cancers—Hayley defended herself and her five siblings with sav-age determination. Losing her first four fights, she absorbed hard lessons with each defeat. Eight victo-ries followed those early routs, a dozen fights in total before graduating first in her class from high school. Hayley has fought as many times as an army boxer and remains undefeated. Tonight, she defends her regi-mental title.

After thirty minutes of steady jogging, her muscles have become elastic beneath a sweat-drenched T-shirt and shorts. Her thoughts are as measured and orderly as her heart rate. Barely winded, Hayley stops and checks the time on a Citizen Eco-Drive Nighthawk Black Dial watch she took off an army pilot who chal-lenged her to a barroom arm-wrestling match. At her feet is the loose stone and gravel of the construction site for a new PX. Hayley bends down and picks up one of the jagged rocks, clenching her fist tightly around it. The stone's sharp edges send jolts of pain through her body, acute and clarifying. She maintains the intensity of this clench for ten seconds, then twenty more. Finally, Hayley takes a deep breath and drops the stone to the ground. Studying the palm of her hand with clinical detachment, she sees blood seeping from multiple quarter-inch lacerations. There is nothing to fear. Blood has been drawn. Now she can fight.

Hayley turns, reversing course, and begins running again, faster, in a final push to accelerate her heart rate. Two blocks distant, the concrete-and-glass fitness center crouches under LED vapor-tight lighting.

---

HAYLEY, WEARING MANDATORY headgear and gloves, follows her trainer, Master Sergeant Stanley Oakes, as he leads her toward the boxing ring at the center of a raucous crowd of mostly drunken fight fans. Oakes roughly deflects the outstretched hands of Hayley's supporters, carving a path through the throng with gruff authority. The fighter stares straight ahead, eyebrows furrowed, and fixates on the boxing ring, where her opponent calmly waits.

She leans forward and speaks into Oakes's ear, loud and firm. "What do we know about the replacement?" she asks as they press forward through the crowd and finally arrive at their corner of the rudimentary boxing ring erected on the basketball court.

Oakes scans a piece of paper given to him by organizers of the smoker when informing him that

Hayley's scheduled opponent had withdrawn. He's been working the military boxing circuit for enough years to know his fighter has been set up. Her streak of twelve straight wins is celebrated throughout ARSOUTH. A ringer is just the ticket for an upset and the ensuing wagering windfall.

"Marcela Rivas, First Armored Division, Fort Bliss. Two-time Golden Gloves champ from Camden, New Jersey. Straight puncher, like Roy Jones Jr. A lock to turn pro soon as she discharges."

Hayley doesn't react, her gaze focused on Rivas dancing lightly at the center of the ring. The Jersey fighter stands six feet, one inch and weighs 145 pounds. Without a hint of fat on her immaculate frame, she is all muscle and pride. Even the most casual, boozed fan can see Rivas is a warrior.

"Don't wanna bullshit you, HC. This beast could knock out half the men on base. No shame in a forfeit," Oakes consoles her.

Hayley smirks. Oakes, a natural born worrier, always has had an odd way of motivating a fighter. The crowd erupts as Hayley climbs three steps and ducks under the ropes. Something less than five feet, eight inches and weighing 125 pounds, Hayley is every bit as lean and exquisitely muscled as her opponent, with nearly as much experience in the ring and probably more out of it. Training and prefight ritual have been rigorously observed. And, as always, she possesses an unflinching will to prevail in a just cause, in this case the honor of thousands of men and women in the Sixth

Army across the entire ARSOUTH. All these factors must be folded into the calculus of predicting the fight's outcome.

But Marcela Rivas is pure boxer, destined to win a gold medal in the Paris 2024 Summer Olympics before turning pro, as Oakes predicted. After a stellar professional career in which she suffers only a single loss in eight years, Rivas will be a shoo-in for induction into the US Boxing Hall of Fame. Retiring from the sport that rescued her from indiscriminate poverty, she will buy a gilded multimillion-dollar home on the water in south Florida and raise three daughters, all of whom will also fight professionally one day.

If Hayley has estimated her slim odds in the handful of seconds before the first of three rounds, she doesn't show it. With clang of bell and howl of the crowd, she moves forward, workmanlike, on light feet and absorbs a fist that seemingly materializes in the void three inches from her face a half fraction of a second before breaking her nose.

---

SITTING ON THE stool Oakes has placed in her corner of the blood-spattered ring before the start of the third and final round, Hayley must concentrate to register the words Oakes shouts urgently into her ear.

"One more round, HC! Just keep dancin'! You've done better than anyone could expect of you!"

Hayley spits her guard into Oakes's hand and accepts the water he squirts into her mouth. Oakes starts to work on her nose, stanching the flow of dark blood with a cotton swab soaked in adrenaline hydrochloride and then pressing an ice-chilled enswell to the bruised area. While he works, Hayley stares doggedly at Rivas, who hasn't even bothered to sit between rounds. The future Olympian is treating the bout as an extended sparring session.

Hayley's powder blue eyes clock all of this. After the punishment she has sustained, no one could predict Rivas's eventual induction into the Hall of Fame better than her. If she guts out a final round, ARSOUTH will undoubtedly survive the defeat with pride intact. Amplified by time and alcohol, the tale of Hayley Chill's valiant stand against the future welterweight champion of the world would be told again and again in barracks and officers' quarters across the US Southern Command.

But Hayley has no affinity for noble defeat. The notion of coasting to certain failure is an indignity she would never voluntarily swallow. In her entire life, the West Virginian has never backed down before a homegrown tyrant. She fights at full pitch, relentless until victory or defeat. There is no middle ground.

"She just thinks she's going to win." Hayley's soft, West Virginia drawl belies the frenzied and dire situation, recalling lazy haze-shrouded hills, sweet tea, and rusted-out pickup trucks.

Oakes can't believe the words he's just heard. If Hayley's trainer didn't fear the ensuing riot, he'd throw in the towel then and there given his fighter's apparent derangement.

"There're never any knockouts in your weight class, kid, not with headgear." Hayley glances at Oakes with an inscrutable expression. He presses the point. "It's over. Rivas has the points. She'll cruise the last round if you do."

An old bromide admonishes a boxer in the ring to pay attention to her opponent, not herself. Hayley has always been a connoisseur of detail. In the first two rounds of the bout, she analyzed Rivas's technique and watched for patterns. The Jersey girl is an absurdly talented fighter. Her superb conditioning is the result of a religious dedication to physical preparation. But even the most skilled and committed boxer repeats herself, despite all best attempts to camouflage those patterns.

With the bell commencing the third round, Hayley surprises Rivas, Oakes, and everyone in attendance by jetting to her feet and hurtling across the ring to confront her startled opponent. The prior two rounds were lopsided affairs, bookended by Hayley's broken nose in the first round and a brutal knockdown at the conclusion of the second. Only a fool or masochist would further antagonize her tormentor after ten minutes of such punishment.

Hayley's frenetic punches fail to land solidly. Rivas could deflect these furious haymakers and off-tempo jabs in her sleep. But the dispassionate expression she has maintained throughout the fight shifts to one of irritation and anger. What's this white girl's problem, anyway? The rapturous crowd howls in misguided delight, magnifying Rivas's annoyance. She gives Hayley a violent push backward and, departing the fight plan carefully devised by her trainer, launches an unnecessary attack.

Jab, right, left hook, right uppercut, left hook, and right cross. Jab, right, left hook, right uppercut, left hook, and right cross. Jab, right, left hook, and Rivas steps into the perfect position for Hayley's best and purest punch, a devastating phantom left hook thrown from the bottom of her feet that connects with the right side of Rivas's head as if painted by Michelangelo.

Shocked spectators fall silent. Somewhere to the side of the vast room a vending machine dispensing cold drinks rumbles to a start. Hayley steps back a pace or two and watches Rivas crash to the canvas, out cold. The partisan crowd erupts, drivers as distant as Battalion Avenue hearing the delirious celebration taking place inside the fitness center. Hayley makes no acknowledgment of the riotous acclaim. She moves forward and takes a knee beside her opponent, whose eyes already begin to flicker open. Within moments, Rivas's trainer joins Hayley and roughly pushes her away as he tends to his fallen fighter.

Hayley stands and, for the first time since it was broken, puts fingers to her nose. The subsequent pain brings her surroundings more sharply into focus. Rivas on her back. The frenzied crowd. A man in a blue suit standing just inside the entry doors to the arena, strangely expressionless and removed from the merriment. But processing it all eludes Hayley. Only the fight's result seems concrete and quantifiable.

From that day forward, the subtle crook of Hayley's nose remains as silent testimony of that momentous and bloody night when the Sixth Army welterweight champ rose from near death to deliver a stunning victory.

Oakes wraps his arms around Hayley from behind and lifts her a half-foot off the ground. The crowd roars even louder, if that were possible. Hayley relinquishes a brief smile and pushes down on Oakes's arms, demanding release, and he sheepishly complies.

"How the hell . . . ?" The question catches in his throat. With twenty-three years in the sport, both as fighter and trainer, Oakes has never been so shocked by a bout's result.

Hayley grins and grimaces simultaneously. Her musculoskeletal structure has suffered terrible abuse; a constellation of muscles, bones, joints, tendons, and ligaments are pummeled and overtaxed. That collective pain is only now being registered by the microscopic nociceptors and neurons in her skin. She will wake up the next day suffering from a cascade of physical agonies. With a few Advils and a full breakfast, she will nevertheless report fifteen minutes early, at 6:45 a.m., for a regiment-wide, three-day open-terrain training exercise.

Winded and sweating copiously from her exertions, Hayley reveals to her trainer the secret of her impromptu strategy. "May 15, 2004. Antonio Tarver beat a heavily favored, straight-punching Roy Jones Jr. with a counter left hook." Hayley mimes the same left hook that put her opponent down on the canvas. "Tricky part was bringing Rivas to the punch."

She dips her chin slightly, a nod of her head that seems to acknowledge simply a job done well. As Oakes marvels at his fighter's intelligence, the uproarious carnival continues around them, seemingly without end.

————————

SOUTHWESTERN COACHES SITS at the corner of East Avenue C and Fourth Street in Killeen, Texas. The August sky above is cloudy and threatens a summer rainstorm. The occasional passenger car or pickup truck glides past the bus depot, but otherwise the streets at midafternoon are empty and forlorn. Without the military's presence, Killeen would have dried up and blown away a long time ago. The perpetual nightmare plaguing boosters is an intermittent threat posed by budget cuts in Washington that would shutter the army's massive installation on the edge of town.

Four weeks to the day since her improbable victory, Hayley stands outside the terminal's door with Stanley Oakes and waits for Greyhound's 2:41 p.m. bus to Houston. The master sergeant stares across Fourth Street, his gaze fixed on J.R. Boxing Club, a storefront gym with yellow lettering affixed to the display windows: MALES-FEMALES-CHILDREN. BOX-ING TRAINING. AMATEURS-PROFESSIONALS. An enve-lope taped to the door is stuffed with handwritten flyers that flutter in a wind that blows unobstructed across the Great Plains, all the way down from cen-tral Canada.

"Guy who runs that joint is beyond clueless." Oakes pauses to spit. "Couldn't train a dog to lift its leg to pee."

Hayley glances toward the gym across the street and says nothing in response to Oakes's random dec-laration. She has mustered out. Leaving the army is a life-altering event. Her worldly belongings are in the duffel at her feet. All goodbyes but this one have been made.

Oakes is plainly unhappy, his hands shoved into his pockets as if he might punch himself from self-pity otherwise. He doesn't know what to say but knows he must say something. "Wish you'd recon-sider, HC. Army could use a stealth left like yours. That's a fact."

Hayley answers without deliberation. "Military was a way out, Master Sergeant, never the destination."

Oakes can't mask his hurt feelings. "What, then? Taking a year off to figure it out is not a plan."

The warmth in Hayley's eyes reveals the gratitude and affection she has for her trainer. "Don't take it per-sonal, Stan."

"Personal? Hell, the military invested a shit-ton of money in your skinny ass. Isn't just about you. What you achieved means something, in a broader way. Ain't the boxing."

"It was never about the boxing," Hayley promises him.

Oakes frowns. As a boy growing up in Detroit, near Highland Park, he had been caught with several friends throwing rocks at cars from the Wyoming Street bridge over Interstate 96 and spent one tumultuous year in juvenile hall. He understands the impetus of escape and identifies with this twenty-four-year-old blond white girl from West Virginia in ways that often astonish him. With her sudden and surprising decision to leave the army, Stanley Oakes now sees in Hayley the road not taken. That awareness gnaws at him, at the implacable gristle of regret and insecurity.

Oakes's expression softens. "Okay, then. Have it your way." The marvel of military life is unlikely pairings, geographic and ethnic boundaries erased by a cohesive necessity. He slowly nods as the Greyhound bus appears from around the corner on Avenue C and lumbers into the depot's driveway. He gestures toward the bus with his chin.

"Make 'em pay, champ," he says gruffly. In this way grown, childless men conceal their emotions and say goodbye to someone they've come to love like their own flesh-and-blood daughter.

Hayley retrieves the duffel bag with her left hand and briefly lays her right on the side of her trainer's cheek. "Thank you, Stanley Oakes. For everything."

She moves toward the waiting bus driver, who takes her bag and deposits it in the storage compartment under the coach. Hayley pauses on the steps leading up into the bus and turns to offer Oakes a wave.

He nods in appreciation. "When you figure out a better somethin' to all of this, you be sure to let me know. Never too late, even for old war dogs like me!"

Hayley busts a sly West Virginia grin, and then disappears inside the bus. The doors close soon enough, and a melancholic Oakes stays to watch the bus depart the brick depot.

In the years that followed, before Oakes officially retired from the army, he often thought about the best fighter he ever trained. It was easy to be reminded of Hayley's achievement. A framed picture of her in the ring with Rivas snapped by the base newspaper's photographer hung ceremoniously in the fitness center lobby. After a few visits to the bottom desk drawer where he kept a bottle of Old Grand-Dad, Oakes often found himself standing in front of the photo and musing on Hayley's improbable victory on that savage August night.

But when Oakes finally does leave the army, twelve interminable years on, and moves back north, to Detroit, he thinks less and less often about Hayley Chill and her powder blue eyes. Rarely does he dwell on that golden time, until another decade hence, when one Sunday afternoon he will be caught in gang-related gunplay, as if by a sudden April shower, and takes

undergone in the fifteen months since saying goodbye to Stanley Oakes at the Killeen bus depot, it has transformed Hayley Chill into an accurate facsimile of a DC worker bee.

It is 7:08 a.m. in late November and the weather clings stubbornly to Indian summer. Passing sights they've seen hundreds of times before, all other passengers on the bus are engrossed by handheld devices or asleep. But Hayley has ridden the 38B only once before, one week earlier, on a test run after signing the lease on a studio apartment just across the Potomac in Rosslyn, Virginia. Despite having grown up only a six-hour drive from Washington, DC, the city and its monuments are entirely new to her. She gazes out the window, gathering impressions of the passing city with the keen attention of a cultural anthropologist.

As the Metrobus eases to the curb at the southeast corner of Farragut Square, its last stop, Hayley disembarks with a dozen other passengers. The familiarity of another workday is etched on the bored faces of those stepping off the bus. Only Hayley moves with a surplus of energy and a brisk, five-minute walk south on Seventeenth Street brings the President's Park into view. She pauses on the sidewalk to take in the iconic sight. The White House, partially obscured by fern-leaf beech, American elm, and white oak, impresses her as both splendidly grand and surprisingly modest at the same time. She knows the building's original architect was Irish-born. She has memorized the names of every senior aide and their phone extensions. Somehow she has even ascertained what flavor ice cream the president is said to prefer. Unsurprisingly, Hayley Chill has arrived for her first day of internship at the White House completely and thoroughly prepared.

A gatehouse opposite the EEOB controls entry into the White House complex, and Hayley joins the long queue there. The majority of staffers waiting in line have green badges on lanyards. Many fewer, including Hayley, possess blue badges. The young officer from the Secret Service Uniformed Division who performs the initial screening accepts her driver's license and checks it against her badge. He has warm eyes and a folksy grin.

"West Virginia, huh? I grew up in Lewisburg." His voice possesses the familiar twang of Hayley's tribe.

She nods. "Lewisburg. Sure. Nice."

"Blue badge," the officer remarks with surprised regard. He hands her ID back and gestures behind him, toward the White House complex. "Ready for the viper pit?"

Hayley laughs. "I hope so!"

The policeman waves her through the gate. "You have yourself a pleasant day, Ms. Chill."

She offers her hand. "Hayley, but you already know that."

He nods, shaking her hand. "Ned." Hayley continues forward as the line of people waiting for ID check lengthens behind her.

Once cleared through security screening, she and other arriving personnel are waved through an aggressive, final series of barriers and frowning Secret Service uniformed officers. As instructed by email, Hayley passes through the Eisenhower Executive Office Building and continues outside, onto West Executive Avenue. Nearly all interns receive green badges, designating their access as being limited to more prosaic confines of the Eisenhower building. Hayley's blue badge allows her to breeze past the Secret Service uniformed officers monitoring access between the EEOB and the White House's West Wing.

Hayley enters the West Wing through a door on the ground floor. She is older than the typical White House intern by at least five years. Her serious expression is evidence of a life lived without favor or entitlement. Self-delusion is a luxury she could never afford. Even as an eight-year-old sitting on the lap of a Charleston department store Santa reeking of Camel cigarettes and boiled onions, Hayley could tell a fake beard when she saw one. Nor is she unduly overwhelmed here, within these historic walls of the president's house.

Hayley pauses just inside the entryway to get her bearings, the plastic encasing her blue badge shiny and unscuffed. A passing man, cowboy handsome and wearing a dark suit, perceives Hayley's plight. "New intern?"

"That obvious, huh?" Hayley's demeanor is friendly and matter-of-fact. The Secret Service agent knows from experience that most new interns are like kindergartners on their first day of school, breathless and wide-eyed. For that reason alone, this young woman impresses him. He gestures toward her credentials.

"They teach us how to decipher those doodads, oddly enough."

"I feel safer already," Hayley says, smiling.

"Whose office?"

"Peter Hall."

"I've heard of him," he responds sarcastically. He indicates a nearby stairwell door, but his hazel eyes remain on Hayley. "One flight up, go right, then right again. First door on your left. Can't miss it."

Hayley nods curtly, signaling she's got it from here. The Secret Service agent is disappointed their encounter is over so quickly but covers with a wink, continuing on his way.

There have always been pretty boys on the periphery of Hayley's life. Back home in Lincoln County, a roundelay of aggressive suitors vied for kiss, grope, or better from the most desirable girl for miles. Charlie Hadden, All-Conference quarterback and proud possessor of a cherry 1964 Pontiac GTO, hung in long enough to earn the mantle of Hayley's high school boyfriend but too much Smirnoff and a hairpin curve on Sproul Road ended his tenure, and he died before she could gain what she had at long last decided to take. Hayley wore black for two months, fetchingly so in the opinion of would-be replacements.

Enlistment followed high school graduation by twenty-four hours, a day in which Hayley relinquished her virginity to a twenty-eight-year-old drifter who wrote love songs, had a mutt dog with a face like Bukowski, and played a pretty wicked twelve-string guitar. After that underwhelming initiation to the world of sex, Hayley had chosen to never attach herself to a steady mate. Her priorities were other than romantic love, namely seeing that there was a roof kept over the heads of her younger siblings and food on the table. Nearly every penny of her army pay was sent back home. Pay scales are higher for infantry soldiers, all the inducement Hayley needed toward becoming one of the first eighteen women to earn her blue cord.

Once she's climbed the stairs to the first floor, Hayley finds herself in a carpeted corridor that muffles the footsteps of dozens of staffers and personnel hustling to and fro as if the nation's business really is important work. None pay the slightest notice to the new intern. Hayley threads her way along the corridor, dodging other staffers, and stops outside a door like all the others. On the wall to the left is a surprisingly unostentatious placard that identifies the office as belonging to the White House chief of staff.

Pushing the door open, Hayley ventures into the suite's reception area. No one is inside the compact room. The single, curtained window boasts a commanding view of the North Lawn and Lafayette Square beyond. An oil painting of a three-master blasting through a white-capped tempest hangs above the couch. Lights blink silently across an impressive phone console on the receptionist's desk. With no receptionist to offer guidance, Hayley is unsure what to do. She hears voices drifting from the partially open interior door.

Crossing the room, Hayley stops just inside the doorway leading into the suite's primary office and observes sixty-three-year-old Peter Hall, wearing a suit jacket and tie, sitting behind a large desk and surrounded by a nervous litter of aides and assistants. The White House chief of staff has a black phone receiver pressed to his ear, barking into it as he scans papers held before him by his courtiers. In jarring contrast to his august work space, Hall's voice possesses the timbre of a high school football coach from west Texas, which in fact he once was before running for the state's Twenty-Third Congressional District and winning in an improbable landslide.

Representation of a mostly Hispanic constituency of five hundred thousand souls offered only modest horizons for an idealistically charged, ambitious former All-American tight end and only son of a Korean War veteran. Over the years, however, Peter Hall paid his political dues and amassed influence extending far beyond the dusty Twenty-Third district in Texas, stretching to every corner of the nation and beyond. But there are limits to power and prestige even for one of the highest-ranking politicians on Capitol Hill. Congress makes laws. The executive branch makes history.

Hall's salvation came in the form of Richard Monroe's stunning victory in the previous year's presidential election. The president-elect yielded to Hall's persistent lobbying and plucked him from the House of Representatives, installing him as chief of staff of a West Wing in need of congressional expertise. The president, an actual war hero, was the embodiment of the electorate's craving for change in Washington and possessed senator into submission, one of his aides glances in the direction of the doorway, where Hayley stands. Karen Rey, midthirties and furiously raven haired, with a master's in English literature from UVA and a Bedlington terrier back home named Churchill, reacts with outraged expression to the unknown young woman's presence in the gaping doorway.

Rey stands fully erect and darts across the expansive office, a Scud missile headed directly toward Hayley. She confronts the White House newcomer, and her question is neither gentle nor rhetorical. "Are you insane or just stupid?"

Hayley's gaze is unwavering. Her voice is firm and clear. "Hayley Chill, ma'am. I'm interning for the chief of staff's office."

Rey sizes up Hayley with an incredulous gawk; the intern's West Virginia drawl is often mistaken by some as a sign of slow-wittedness and unsophistication. Rey thrusts out her hand.

"Let me see your paperwork," she snaps.

Hayley complies, retrieving the pertinent documents from her backpack. Rey briefly peruses the paperwork, arching her eyes in mild surprise.

"Military veteran?"

Hayley is used to such reaction to her military status. With her trim build and pretty face, she could easily be mistaken for a performer with Disney On Ice or a retired beauty queen. "Third Cavalry Regiment, ma'am. Forty-Third Combat Engineer Company," she informs the White House aide and intern wrangler.

"No college degree?"

"Two years at Central Texas College, ma'am, on the Active Duty Montgomery GI Bill."

Rey looks up from Hayley's paperwork and offers it back as if it were drenched in biohazard.

"The West Wing operates at a grueling pace, Ms. Chill, especially with this administration. No disrespect to your community college, but perhaps the First Lady's office would be a better fit." Her condescension is not gratuitous. Peter Hall's persecution of the slightest incompetence is of DC lore. Hayley's first significant flub would be on Rey's head.

"Thank you, ma'am, but I believe I'm up to the task. Mr. Hall must think so, too." Hayley flips to the last page of her sheaf of papers and offers it for Rey to see. "That's his signature right there."

Karen Rey's expression goes flat. She silently leads Hayley back into the reception room and to the entry door. Stepping out into the corridor, she points toward the near stairwell as if casting a fallen angel from the heavens. "Interns live, work, and die downstairs." Pronouncement issued, Rey turns and retreats back inside Hall's office suite, closing the door behind her with an emphatic push.

---

HAYLEY ARRIVES BACK where she started, on the West Wing's ground floor, and locates the correct office door, a handwritten sign designating it as "CoS Support." Entering, Hayley discovers a room not much bigger than a janitorial closet, which in fact it was until only a few months before. Peter Hall wanted his interns close at hand, located in the West Wing, and being the chief of staff, that's exactly what he got. Four desks are jig-sawed into the claustrophobic space, three of which are occupied with sharply dressed young people. The fourth desk, Hayley's apparent work space, is heaped with files and binders, an impressive and disorderly pile two feet high.

The other interns, two-week veterans of the West Wing, regard Hayley with cold suspicion. CoS Support has been their exclusive domain, and Hayley is an unwelcome addition. What possible good could come of her joining the team? At best, the blue-eyed, blond-haired young woman wearing an off-the-rack Dress-barn cardigan represents an annoyance. At worst, she is potential competition. The goal of any White House intern is to be noticed, achieving special recognition at the expense of the several dozen other young people toiling there. A glowing personal recommendation from a powerful DC player is of incalculable value in scor-ing admission to Ivy League graduate programs, entry positions at Goldman Sachs, or further advancement in Washington.

Luke Charles, the only male in CoS Support, is a junior at Georgetown with the obligatory major in political science. His father, a fantastically wealthy hedge fund manager, hopes Luke's interest in politics is a phase his son will soon leave behind. In the elder Charles's view, politicians follow while money leads.

Luke will indeed come to this same conclusion in the coming year. The grubbiness and panhandling that defines every politician's life doesn't escape the notice of the sufficiently bright Luke. After graduation from Georgetown and an MBA from Harvard, he will join his father's firm and notch his first seven-figure annual bonus before he's thirty.

Sophia Watts, her desk abutting Hayley's, is barely receiving the required grade point average to avoid expulsion from USC, having spent much of her first two college years trolling Los Angeles's hottest clubs. In Sophia's second sophomore semester and still an undeclared major, she had a two-week-long Tinder fling with an aide of a Los Angeles councilperson. Landon was a sweet and fun-loving boy who infused an impressionable Sophia with a passion for government. Given this newfound purpose, her father, a successful film producer of cacophonous superhero movies, used his clout to score his only daughter a highly coveted internship at the White House. Sophia's future love child with a Senate minority leader will result in moderate infamy and a best-selling memoir, a literary sensation that, synergistically, will be adapted by her movie-producing father into a scorching independent film. Daughter will join father onstage at the Oscar ceremony for a Best Picture acceptance speech.

The third intern in the room, commanding the biggest and best-positioned desk, is Becca Byran. With a lion's mane of dirty-blond hair, she is a recent graduate from NYU under an accelerated program. Her father owns a small print shop in Queens, on Myrtle Avenue.

Her mother is stay-at-home, taking in neighborhood toddlers for day care. Burning deep within Becca is an obsession to rise above these modest origins and apply her fierce drive to amassing power in whatever form it might exist. In seven years' time, she will be the founder of a rapidly expanding, quasi-religious "commune" located in Vermont. Within the decade, Becca Byran will begin an eight-year stretch at FCI Danbury for bank fraud, money laundering, and tax evasion.

"What's your name?" Becca demands of the newcomer, weaponizing that brief, normally innocuous sentence.

"Hayley Chill."

Becca slides a look toward the other two interns seated at their respective desks. Her expression is difficult to gauge. Sophia takes a stab at decoding the alpha intern's judgment of the new addition to CoS Support.

"Can't be for real, right?" Sophia asks. Becca shrugs in response.

"Where is that accent from? Kentucky?" Luke asks Hayley.

"West Virginia." Hayley indicates the desk nearest to the door, currently being used as a file dumping ground. "Guessing this is where I sit?"

Becca is again regarding Hayley with cool, analytic precision, taking measure of the threat level posed by the newcomer and how she might be manipulated to personal advantage. "We're under a lot of pressure, if you didn't notice. Sit there if you must, but don't mess any of that stuff up."

Hayley doesn't respond. The unfriendly and unwelcoming attitude of the other interns doesn't much bother her. The other interns just seem to be kids, not worth her time or energy. Hayley places her bag on the floor and, ignoring Becca's admonition, begins to organize the mess of folders and papers on the desk.

"You look kinda old," Sophia tells Hayley. "Where do you go to school?"

Hayley continues to work as she answers Sophia's prying question. "Two-year community college in Texas, near where I was stationed." Their blank faces prompt her to add, "Believe me, you've never heard of this place."

The three other interns exchange a communal look of bewilderment.

"Stationed?" Becca demands clarification with distaste.

Like most civilian Americans, none of the other interns have had any personal interaction with an actual serviceperson, let alone set foot on a military installation. That ignorance does not stop them from forming the near-universal bias against military personnel. This prejudice prompts all three college-educated interns to share an opinion that a US Army veteran, particularly one who enlisted, is of subpar intelligence, backward thinking, and perhaps psychopathic. Why else join the military if not a hopeless loser with mental issues?

Hayley has encountered this sort of prejudice since her earliest days in the army. Typically, she wouldn't bother justifying to anyone what was a profoundly transformative life experience. But, in this instance, encouraging the cooperation and affinity of her fellow interns strikes her as important. "Enlisted out of high school, discharged about a year ago," she tells the others. "And here I am."

"But I thought . . . ?" Sophia's question dies in mid-sentence.

Becca lays it out for the USC girl's benefit. "White House interns must be a current college student, recent grad, or veteran with high school diploma." With that explanation, the judgment of the intern kangaroo court is final. Hayley is nothing but a carbon-based organism taking up valuable space and time. On first sight, Luke had privately mused on the potential of fucking Hayley, her sex appeal undeniable. Knowing what he does now, however, the Georgetown student decides to keep his focus on the brighter sparkle of Sophia. Luke instinctually assesses that his dad would have a shit fit if he took up with this baby-killing white trash from West Virginia.

As Hayley continues organizing her work space, the other interns utterly ignore her. Not one says another word to Hayley the entire day. Luke departs first, at four thirty, for an appointment with a personal trainer at an Equinox on NW Twenty-Second Street. Sophia and Becca leave together at 6:05 p.m. for a double drinks date with two congressional pages at Black Jack near Logan Circle. Hayley's workday, therefore, ends peacefully and gloriously alone. She finishes organizing the pile of documents on her desk, then turns to other stacks of position papers, memos, and briefing binders stacked throughout the cluttered office. At eight forty-five that night, her work is finally complete. The CoS Support office has been meticulously organized. Hayley puts on her jacket, turns off the lights, and begins her commute via the 38B Metrobus to her modest intern housing at the Henry House.

———————————

AFTER A WEEK and a half in the West Wing, Hayley has yet to leave the former janitorial closet. History may be made in the White House, but the real action might as well be happening on Mars for all Hayley knows. Her primary duties and responsibilities have consisted of maintaining the organization she had brought to the interns' office and preventing it from sliding back into a persistent chaos. Becca, Luke, and Sophia are perfectly satisfied with this new arrangement. The West Virginian's diligence has allowed them to cherry-pick assignments while receiving glowing performance reports for work actually done by the newcomer. In effect, Hayley is the interns' intern.

Karen Rey occasionally drops by for a few minutes but deals exclusively with Becca, who has achieved this elite status through sheer force of personality and Machiavellian cunning. Luke and Sophia never really had a chance. Since their first encounter in Hall's office suite, Rey has exchanged only a few desultory words with Hayley. Confined to the CoS Support office, the West Virginian toils in abject anonymity, a real-life Cinderella. If there's a silver lining to her exploitation, it's that the other interns rarely include Hayley in their feckless chatter.

Their immediate task on this particular morning is responding to emails sent to POTUS, electronic missives that range from outraged condemnation to idolizing approval of administration accomplishments, real and imagined. Whatever the category, each email receives the same cordial and appreciative reply. Even messages threatening harm toward the president are given respectful response while simultaneously being forwarded to the Secret Service. The volume of these disturbing missives fluctuates, depending on the news of the day and latest presidential statement or action. The record for actionable emails was set one week earlier, after Monroe gave a speech at a national VFW meeting in which he attacked NATO as a relic of twentieth-century geopolitics having no relevance to a twenty-first-century world. In proposing an alternative, eastern European alliance reflective of the new world order, Monroe generated a total of thirty-five active threats in the span of twenty-four hours, all of which were meticulously investigated by the Secret Service.

But answering emails isn't met with abundant enthusiasm. Becca, in particular, is feeling underutilized, her ambitions roadblocked. Frustrated, she shakes her head in disbelief as she types. "Freaking morons are driving me crazy! This lady wants POTUS to help her son get a liver transplant. What does she expect Monroe to do, invade Mexico and harvest some?!"

"That's actually not such a bad idea," Luke muses, already attuned to exploitative opportunities in every facet of human existence. He doesn't know it yet, but he'll prove to be an even more successful hedge fund manager than his dad.

Sophia is more cursory in her response to the emails, with replies reading more like Zen koans. Some of these marvels of epistolary brevity have been printed and tacked to the office bulletin board. "Sir, the President appreciates the concerns of every citizen of this great country but cannot discern exactly the nature of yours. God totally bless the United States of America" was an early example. In straightening up the interns' office, Hayley had considered taking down Sophia's little gems, but even she had to appreciate their value as morale boosters and left them in place.

"I might as well be doing product support at Apple and actually get paid for my talents," Sophia surmised, resisting a habit of reminding the others that her semi-famous father once hosted Steve Jobs for dinner. On that occasion, the Apple founder gifted a ten-year-old Sophia with the first model iPhone before the device's official release, an event Sophia naturally mentions in telling the story.

"It's either this or studying for the GREs. Frankly, I'll take this," confesses Luke, reflecting his country-club work ethic.

Becca glances toward Hayley, who has been quietly loading briefing binders. The job is not without its significance, and the other interns have come to rely on the flawlessly conscientious military veteran to handle the job.

"What about you, G.I. Jane? What's your plan B?"

Hayley is surprised to be included in the discussion. Her response doesn't require meditation. "Long as I can serve my country, I'm good."

The other interns exchange a look, barely restraining their guffaws. Before one of them can get off a snarky remark, however, there is a quick rap at the door, and it's pushed open, revealing White House Chief of Staff Peter Hall. Without his suit jacket, Hall is in roll-up-your-sleeves work mode.

Becca, Sophia, and Luke freeze, not quite believing their eyes. The chief of staff has never stopped by the ground-floor support office. As a matter of fact, none of them have exchanged more than a few words with Hall besides expected pleasantries. He certainly doesn't know any of them by name.

"Staff's jammed. Need someone for fifteen minutes," Hall announces, needlessly adding, "not another second more than that, I promise."

Luke, Sophia, and Becca all stand in unison, but the NYU grad finds her voice first. "I'm available, Mr. Hall!"

Hall glances around the room, ignoring Becca's declaration. "Which one of you is the army vet?"

Hayley raises her hand to half-mast. "That's me, sir. Hayley Chill."

Hall's normally fierce demeanor instantly softens when he turns his gaze on Hayley. "Chill? Sure. How the hell could I forget a name like that? Fort Hood base commander wrote your letter of recommendation. Among the first females to gender-integrate the infantry. History making, General MacFarland said. Hell of a boxer, too."

"Yes, sir. Honored to serve in any capacity."

Hall fancies himself an ear for regional accents, not without justification. "Kanawha County, West Virginia?"

Hayley grins. "Pretty close, sir. Green Shoals, Lincoln County."

Watching Hayley interact with the chief of staff, Becca knows she has lost a major battle here, though the war is far from over. Sophia and Luke's game is strictly two-dimensional, and they don't even realize the contest is over for them. Becca now understands that this was a two-man race from day one of Hayley's arrival. Underscoring that point, Hall's focus remains exclusively on the West Virginian.

"Your father, he made the ultimate sacrifice?"

"Yes, sir. Bravo Company from Marine Corps Reserve's First Battalion, Twenty-Third Regiment. Second Battle of Fallujah. Killed in action at Blackwater Bridge, sir, when I was eight. My mom raised us six kids slingin' grits and black coffee at a Shoney's in Charleston, up until she got sick herself."

Hall nods, sagely, recognizing the backstory. "Monroe people," he assesses approvingly.

"Yes, sir. The president is very popular back home."

Without a glance toward the other three interns, Hall crooks his finger and tilts his head toward the door. "Let's go. Not enough hours in the day to save a country."

Hayley stands and follows Hall out the door, leaving Becca, Sophia, and Luke to exchange looks of stunned misery.

Hall leads Hayley up the stairwell and down the corridor to his office suite. The reception area is empty except for his primary assistant seated at her desk, running traffic control on the office phones. "No calls or interruptions for fifteen minutes," Hall barks at his assistant as he strides past. Hayley follows him into his office.

She gestures behind her. "Door closed, sir?"

"Leave it." Hall picks up a sheaf of papers from his desk and thrusts the papers at Hayley, indicating a chair opposite his desk. "Sit."

Hayley takes the pages and briefly scans them.

"The president's speech in Ohio Saturday on national security," Hall informs her, sitting on the corner of his desk with arms folded across his chest. Through the window behind his desk, the Washington Monument looms. "Read. I want to hear it."

Hayley glances down at the pages for no more than five seconds, then looks back up to Hall.

"'This is a time, my fellow Americans, when we must reach within ourselves and discover the essential strength of our convictions. We must recall the lessons taught to us by our elders, ones that spoke to ideals that once made this great country—'"

Hall raises a hand, stopping her recitation. "Bullshit."

"Sir?"

Hall gestures for the speech transcript impatiently. Hayley hands the pages back to the chief of staff.

Hall asks, "Photographic memory part of army training now?"

"Fortunately, sir, my recall has always been pretty good."

As a child, Hayley did not begin to speak until the age of two but then spoke in complete sentences and was reading by the age of four. It was her second-grade teacher who first discerned Hayley's photographic memory. On a field trip to the local park, Hayley had flawlessly recited the birthdays of every student in class by recalling the dates written on a homeroom poster. As it developed, Hayley realized her eidetic memory wasn't limited to visual aspects of memory but also included auditory memory and other sensory stimuli associated with a visual image. Sensitive to the freakish nature of this gift, she downplays its significance to the point of obscuring it unless exposure is absolutely necessary.

"Fantastic. How good are you at forgetting it?" Hall unceremoniously dumps the pages into the garbage can. "Speechwriters we hired couldn't write a thank-you note without a fucking thesaurus. I'll write the damn thing myself."

"A field general is only as good as his EO, sir."

Hall nods in agreement, his impression of this army veteran from West Virginia only getting better by the minute. With four grown sons, he has always lamented having no daughters. In the car later that evening, after a long day, Hall will recall these few minutes with Hayley and consider fixing up his youngest son with her. After Hall's wife, Carol, died from cancer three years ago, Paul has been the most attentive in helping his dad through the dark, lonely times. Next time his youngest is down from New York, Hall makes a mental note to invite the new intern over to the house on Kalorama Road for brunch.

"No one expected him to go all the way. No one even saw Richard Monroe coming. Ninety-nine percent of Washington figured him for just another war hero with a book deal at Simon and Schuster," Hall informs her. "I saw a chance for national redemption."

"It was a good book, sir. Read it twice," she relates.

"And its author actually wrote it! Words like hand grenades and napalm for ideas. How else to win a political war for the ages? Obliterate the status quo and take no prisoners."

"Yes, sir, but as Bismarck said, politics is the art of the possible."

Hall scoffs. "The art of the next best? Nice try, Ms. Chill, and kudos for being better read than all of your Ivy League colleagues combined. But don't underestimate the forces mobilized against us." He pauses for dramatic effect, hinging at the waist as he leans his face toward hers. "They want us dead!"

"Sir . . . ?" Hayley protests.

Hall cuts her off with an index figure pointed to the ceiling. "The president or me. Dead! And don't be surprised when it happens. They'll do anything to stop us. Trust no one."

"Who is 'they,' sir?"

"The people who actually control this town, the shadow government, or 'deep state.' Call it what you will, they are a hybrid association of elements of government joined with parts of top-level finance and industry that effectively governs the United States, and without consent of the electorate. They're afraid of what Richard Monroe might do to the precious power they've accrued over decades of entrenchment. These elements are mortally afraid of an end to a status quo of their creation and will preserve what they believe is rightfully theirs through any means necessary."

Hayley remains quiet, Hall's words hanging in the air.

"We, as a country, think we're so different, that we're better than all of that. But we're not better. We're not all that different from anyone else. This country was founded in blood. Blood is our heritage, just like every other country on the planet." The chief of staff gives Hayley a sidelong look, a wry grin on his face. "But I'm not telling you anything, am I, Ms. Chill? You've seen something of the real world, unlike your fellow interns."

Hayley's face remains impassive. "Yes, sir."

Hall nods, satisfied with this meeting of like minds, however disparate their professional positions. He casually gestures toward the door, as if the dire threat he had just mentioned was simply part of the job. "Don't have much time to bang this out. Appreciate your time."

"That's all, sir?"

"For now." Hall seems to consider saying more but decides against it.

Hayley dutifully rises to her feet and strides toward the door.

"Keep close, Ms. Chill, and stay alert. Your country needs you," he calls after her.

"Thank you, sir." Hayley quietly leaves the room.

———————————

WASHINGTON'S DELIGHTFUL INDIAN summer ended with finality three weeks after Hayley started her internship. Balmy temperatures and blue skies were replaced overnight by a low ceiling of gunmetal clouds and air temperatures in the midthirties, with snow flurries in the forecast. Disinclined to join one of the budget fitness centers in town, Hayley begins every day before daybreak with a five-mile run through the District's dark streets. She follows that cardio workout with a series of basic calisthenics in her studio apartment, a condensed twenty-minute workout comprised of multiple sets of pull-ups, push-ups, woodchopper squats, and sit-ups. Six days a week, without deviation, Hayley's workout is the same.

After a shower, Hayley dresses and then ducks back into the tiny bathroom. Studying herself in the partially fogged mirror, her self-assessment isn't gentle. Since she was thirteen, Hayley has judged her lips too thin and nose too wide. The issue here isn't one of attractiveness or imperfection so much as competence. If you can't fix your own face, then how capable can you be? She opens her makeup bag and contours her nose, skillfully narrowing with concealer. Next, lips are over-drawn with liner and then filled with lipstick and gloss. After she has finished and carefully studied her work, a dissatisfied Hayley removes all of the makeup with a quick wash and leaves the bathroom cosmetics-free.

This process of brutal self-appraisal, application of makeup, and then reversal of all her work is com-pleted within only a few minutes and is clearly a famil-iar ritual. After a hurried light breakfast of fruit over instant oatmeal, Hayley catches the 38B bus a block from her building. The other commuters are bundled up with down jackets, scarves, and knit hats, but Hay-ley wears only a simple navy-blue peacoat. After disem-barking at Farragut Square and making the short walk down Seventeenth Street to the Eisenhower Executive Office Building gate, Hayley presents her ID to Ned, the Secret Service uniformed officer.

"Sorry about the weather, Hayley." Ned's crush on the intern really doesn't know where to go.

Hayley rewards him with a generous smile. "Thanks, Ned, but I don't mind it at all. You've obvi-ously never spent a summer in central Texas." Their brief exchange represents the only words spoken in the gatehouse. The other personnel in the queue, cowed by the change in weather, pass through security screening wordlessly.

The energy inside the West Wing on this cold morning is also muted and workmanlike. With no international incidents requiring a response from the leader of the free world and nothing on the president's calendar rising above the routine, operations today are strictly paint-by-number. Peter Hall maintains an iron grip on administration staff and personnel. Naysayers, malcontents, and bunglers have all been long since expelled from the premises. The Monroe administration is a marvel of discipline, speaking with a single voice and operating at a high level of efficiency.

As Hayley makes her way along the ground-floor corridor, toward the CoS Support office, she sees the handsome Secret Service agent approaching from the opposite direction. There had been only rare occasions in the prior three weeks in which Hayley had seen him from afar—walking with other agents up the White House driveway or across the crowded commissary in the EEOB—but there was never opportunity to pursue what she has come to recognize as romantic interest in the man.

It has been more than a year since Hayley last had sex. She had two lovers while stationed at Fort Hood, neither of whom were anything but physical attachments. In the time since leaving the military, Hayley hasn't found within herself that particular urge to become intimate with another human. But the Secret Service agent has awakened something in her. What draws her isn't his obvious physical attractiveness but the simple connection with a lightness in his eyes and warm, unostentatious smile. She intuits in him a man in whose company she will feel safe and relaxed.

As Hayley and the Secret Service agent draw

abreast, both stop, seemingly in tune with a mutual desire to connect again.

"You don't seem lost anymore," he observes.

"Guess I'm starting to get the hang of things." She smiles easily. "Thanks for helping out the other morning."

The suit-clad agent offers his hand. "Scott Billings."

Hayley accepts his hand with hers. "Hayley Chill." Their handshake lingers, as does their gaze.

"Ex-military, I understand."

"Have you been asking around about me, Agent Billings?"

Scott smiles guiltily. Of course he'd asked around about her. In his defense, his inquiry into Hayley and her background could've taken far more invasive proportions with the investigative tools available to an agent of the US Secret Service.

"Nice to meet you, Hayley Chill. See you around the shop." Reluctantly, they release hold of each other's hand. Scott gives Hayley the briefest, flirty salute as he continues on his way.

―――――――――

A FEW MINUTES before ten in the morning, the interns in CoS Support have just about finished prepping briefing binders for a cabinet meeting, hastily called by Peter Hall only an hour earlier. Because of the short time frame, all four interns pitched in to finish the job in time for the meeting, scheduled to begin at 10:15 a.m. Disbursement of the binders is a desirable job, affording the lucky intern the opportunity to escape the jani-

torial closet and gain face time with administration big-
wigs. As self-anointed queen of CoS Support, Becca
decides who gets the disbursement job. No one is more
surprised than Hayley when she gets the nod.

"It's your turn, after all," Becca rationalizes.

"Sure. Okay. Thank you." Hayley hasn't had an
assignment outside of the janitorial closet in the whole
time she's been in the West Wing. Neither Sophia nor
Luke is happy with Becca's unexpected decision, but
they don't dare speak up.

Becca clocks Sophia and Luke's unhappiness and
artfully ignores them. "Did you double-check the contents of every binder?" she asks Hayley. "It's your ass if
they're incomplete."

Hayley had assembled the binders with the others
and can attest to their completeness. "I went through
them before my break."

Becca shrugs and sits, checking her phone for messages. It's apparent from her frustration that cell reception is an ongoing issue. "You'd think the most powerful
country in the world could have halfway decent Wi-Fi."

"Dead zones all over the building, but this office
seems to be the worst," Luke offers.

The NYU grad levels a sneer in Luke's direction.
"Thank you so much for that."

Hayley wants no part of their sniping and points
the pushcart toward the door.

There is more than bad cell coverage in explaining Becca's persecuted mood. On a limited budget like
Hayley, Becca was walking to work that morning when

she saw Luke dropping off his Maserati at the W Hotel valet on F Street, as was his custom. The White House parking garage is off-limits to interns and clerical staff. The thirty-five-dollar charge at the W Hotel is chump change for the hedge fund scion, and the Salvadoran who delivers the car again in the late afternoon can always expect a hefty tip.

But it wasn't Luke's extreme wealth that was gnawing at Becca. She has surrounded herself with wealthy people since her first year at NYU. What galled her this morning was seeing Sophia sitting in the seat next to Luke, sufficient evidence she and Luke were fucking. Becca has no sexual desire whatsoever for Luke. Point in fact, the soccer-loving, Imagine Dragons fanatic with unrepentant cowlick and lingering odor of AXE White Label Dry Spray mildly disgusts her. Nevertheless, losing any contest, even one of such meager stakes, to a second-rate SoCal nitwit like Sophia is a burden too great to bear without retaliation, however indirect. Sophia and Luke are easy targets, and their usefulness has not yet been expended.

Hayley is another matter. Complete and total annihilation of her potential rival is just what Becca needs to brighten her day. Once Hayley has pushed the cart laden with briefing books out the door and disappeared, Becca withdraws a folder from under a pile of papers on her desk. "Oh, wait! You forgot an insert," she calls after Hayley many moments too late.

After riding a service elevator up to the first floor,

Hayley pushes the cart down the corridor, passes Peter Hall's corner office, and approaches the hallowed grounds of the Oval Office. Several aides and uniformed military personnel are gathered in a clutch just outside the doorway. None of them except a wary Secret Service agent Hayley has never seen before pay any attention to her as she shuttles past with the mail cart.

She continues down the corridor a short distance, turning for the open doorway leading into the Cabinet Room. Entering, Hayley sees a few of the less important cabinet members standing at the far end of the room in a tight scrum, speaking in hushed voices. Respectfully minding her own business, Hayley begins to disperse the briefing binders. She takes care to place a binder exactly in the same position before each of the sixteen identical chairs at the table, one briefing book for heads of fifteen executive departments and the vice president. An extra-large chair is situated at the exact midway point of the table. Before the president's seat, Hayley places a special, leather-bound briefing book.

As she is just finishing up her careful work, the remaining cabinet members filter into the room. Peter Hall herds the late arrivals inside with typical brusqueness. "Let's go, people! The president needs to be on Marine One in forty-five minutes. Time's wasting." No matter their prestige and importance, all cabinet members respond obediently to Hall's badgering. Hayley moves to leave the room, pushing her cart toward the far door. Hall catches sight of her.

"Park that rig in the corridor and get back in here, Ms. Chill," he bellows from the opposite end of the room. "Want you here in case we need anything."

Hayley does as directed, depositing the mail cart outside and returning to take a position standing in the southwest corner of the room. A hush falls over those in attendance, as if everyone's radar simultaneously picks up the imminent arrival of a Man of Significance. Those instincts are fantastically accurate, as within moments Richard Monroe enters through the north doorway with a gale force of extreme charisma, accompanied by his vice president, Vincent Landers.

As America's warrior hero, Monroe carries a well-known résumé, having held rank everywhere from the army's Second Battalion, Seventy-Eighth Field Artillery to US Army Pacific Command. A career soldier before winning his first and only political campaign as president of the United States, Monroe is a West Point graduate who led a thunderous tank charge across the sands of Kuwait in Operation Desert Storm and later, as a major general and commander of the First Armored Division, drove the tyrant Saddam Hussein from Fortress Baghdad in Operation Iraqi Freedom. With chiseled features and hawklike profile, Richard Monroe was then and continues to be an iconic presence, the natural born leader America sorely needs in rancorous and divisive times.

Everyone stands in respect for the president's entrance, the electricity in the room supercharged. Though nearly all members of the cabinet are themselves powerful and accomplished individuals, no one's light comes even close to shining as brightly as Monroe's. He offers only the slightest of gestures. "Thank you, everyone. Please, sit."

All take their seats. None dare breathe a word until spoken to by the president, who pauses a moment to scan the papers on the table left for his attention. After a moment of silence as he reads, Monroe squares the pages and then looks up, addressing his cabinet.

"Thank you again, everyone, for coming on short notice. We've been under the gun here, getting our affairs in order for the upcoming trip. Excuse the disorder." Few commentators would use the word "disorder" to describe Monroe's administration. The West Wing runs with the steady beat of a Roman slave galley.

Vice President Landers, seated across the long table from POTUS, is perennially cast in the greater man's shadow and is therefore eager to be heard. "As always, Mr. President, we are all so grateful for your leadership." Other cabinet members start to talk all at once, similarly anxious to flatter the destroyer of tyrants. Monroe only grins slightly, benignly tolerant. Peter Hall loudly clears his voice. "Sir, you've got wheels up in less than an hour."

Monroe nods and fingers the pages in front of him. "Our trade policy with China. I wanted to get everyone on the same page before I make my speech tonight in Columbus. Obviously, a unified voice in terms of these proposed tariffs would be best, yes? Let's have a look."

The cabinet members, the vice president, and POTUS all open briefing binders in near unison. Land-

ers is the first to notice a problem with the briefing materials. "Hold on. Where's the transcript of Yii's address?"

Other cabinet members and Monroe are flipping
through the pages and sections in their binders. Monroe looks to his chief of staff with eyes that don't suggest
leniency. Hall leans over the back of Landers's chair,
inspecting the binder for himself. "The translated transcript of Yii's address, Peter? It seems to be missing."
The president's cool agitation snaps like a whip, with
Hall seeming to cringe from its lash. Sensing weakness,
Landers leaps into the fray. "Jesus, Peter, without that
transcript, this whole meeting is pointless!"

Hall is temporarily at a loss for words, a rare condition for the infamous verbal gladiator. Unaccustomed
to making mistakes, he finds himself in the middle of a
very public fuckup, and that exposure has paralyzed him.
Hayley discreetly materializes at the chief of staff's elbow.
"Mr. Hall, you excluded the complete transcript because
a *Washington Post* article under Tab Four summarizes
President Yii's speech with annotations, explaining some
of the more arcane Chinese linguistic idiosyncrasies."

"Yes," the chief of staff manages to get out, "only so
much time in the day."

It's not lost on Monroe what has just transpired.
The president regards the young woman in the $49.99
blazer with frank admiration. "With interns like this one,
we just might get something done in this goddamn city."

Cabinet members voice their agreement. A few of
them—secretaries of education, veterans affairs, and
human services—even applaud. Hayley acknowledges

their appreciation with bowed head and retreats to the far corner of the room, alert and ready for however next she might be of service.

Less than thirty minutes later, after the cabinet meeting has ended and POTUS is aloft in Marine One, Hayley pushes the mail cart back into the CoS Support office. The other three interns silently observe her entrance, studying Hayley for signs of emotional trauma or devastation. They are disappointed in that hope. Hayley is her usual confident, well-balanced self. Becca takes her failure to kill off Hayley particularly hard.

"Where have you been?" the NYU grad asks. "You've been gone almost an hour."

"Mr. Hall asked me to stay after I'd distributed the briefing binders," Hayley tells her matter-of-factly.

"You stood in at the cabinet meeting," Luke asks incredulously, "for, like, the whole time?"

"It was a pretty short meeting," Hayley offers as modest comfort to the other interns.

Before Becca, Luke, and Sophia have had the time to regain equilibrium, the door is pushed open, and for only the second time in his tenure as White House chief of staff, Peter Hall pokes his head inside the repurposed janitorial closet. "Nice recovery, Miss Chill." Hall then turns to address the other interns. "Can't have any more screwups like that."

"Sorry, sir. Won't happen again," Hayley assures the chief of staff.

Hall disappears again, as abruptly as he'd materialized. Hayley sits down at her desk to resume work, seemingly ignoring Becca, Sophia, and Luke as they gape at her. Only after a loaded pause does the West Virginia native slide a quick glance in Becca's direction, just to let her know she's fooling no one. As an accomplished boxer, the West Virginian recognizes a well-delivered body blow. Hayley's opponent is still standing, but the fight has been knocked out of her.

Dejected and defeated, Becca requests to leave work early, soon after lunch. She cites an upset stomach as the reason. Karen Rey is displeased, but Becca is her favorite intern in the complex, and so she reluctantly acquiesces. With the coast clear, Luke and Sophia take turns revealing to Hayley not only Becca's sabotaging of the briefing binders, but also her numerous other transgressions and general abusiveness. Hayley expresses no interest in the gossip, working quietly as the others talk. Failing to make an alliance with the new queen of the CoS Support office, Luke and Sophia turn to making their dinner plans. They depart at four thirty p.m. and, as is their custom, leave Hayley to complete their half-finished tasks.

---

NOT LONG BEFORE seven p.m., Hayley finishes all CoS work and leaves the office, turning off the lights as she does so. A short walk up the corridor of less than thirty seconds takes her to the ground-floor exit and out onto the exterior grounds. Dusk has fallen, and the air temperature is below freezing. Hayley has neglected to retrieve her coat from a hook on the back of the office door and is considering returning for it when she hears a voice.

"Cabinet-level save. Pretty heady stuff for a hillbilly from West Virginia."

Scott Billings has just finished his shift and was about to head over to the garage to retrieve his vehicle when he caught sight of Hayley exiting the building. In order to intercept her with his quip, he had to backtrack nearly twenty-five yards. Despite her many physical attributes and obvious intelligence, Scott is surprised by the intensity of his attraction for Hayley. Seducing women has always been a trivial matter for the handsome Secret Service agent, with the real problem being choosing one or two from the several.

Hayley stops and turns toward the approaching Secret Service agent. "Kind of ironic, coming from a Division Three quarterback who bombed his combine."

Scott is momentarily thrown for acceptable comeback. The sensation of being one-upped by a female is neither familiar nor pleasant. Intelligence and wit is one thing, but how the hell did she learn about his disappointing performance in Indianapolis? Clocking his distress, Hayley simply grins.

"Interns know shit, too, Mr. Billings."

Her smile has its intended effect. Whatever hurt feelings Scott may have suffered are vanquished by the glow of Hayley's countenance. The collision of emotions she engenders in him is a new experience. Scott struggles to regain footing and deploys a tried-and-true bit of charm.

"I'm armed, you know. Call me Mr. Billings again and I might have to shoot you."

Again that smile and a nod of her head in agreement, but Scott is no longer looking toward Hayley but intently off, over her shoulder and beyond. She pivots to see what has distracted him, when Scott starts running in that direction.

Two figures—too distant to ascertain race, gender, or age—are running across the North Lawn, toward the White House. Video surveillance tapes reviewed after the fact will reveal the "jumpers" scaled a fence in the northwest corner of the Treasury Building, immediately adjacent to the White House, and activated a sensor alarm in the Treasury moat. But the Secret Service uniformed officer in charge of monitoring that particular alarm, among others, had stepped away from his station to use the restroom without securing a replacement. Consequently, the two intruders were able to trespass on White House grounds without being noticed.

Numerous individuals have illegally entered the White House grounds by scaling the fence in recent decades. They rarely venture far, although there have been significant exceptions. In November 1975, Gerald Gainous roamed the grounds for more than two hours and approached President Ford's daughter outside her car. The year of 1991 saw the highest number of jumpers, with a total of seven intruders. Between 1995 and 2005, there were none. In 2017, Curtis Combs jumped a concrete barrier on the outer perimeter of the south

grounds and was arrested. He was dressed in a Pika-
chu suit. It's easy to forget that until the Second World
War anyone could enter the premises and knock on the
front door.

As Scott Billings races to intercept the two intruders, he shouts so there's no question of his voice being
picked up by a Motorola handset in his suit jacket
pocket. "Unauthorized entry! North Lawn, east side!
Seventy-five meters from residence! Closing fast!"

The two jumpers apparently realize Scott has seen
them and immediately split up, one of them veering
east. With no other agents currently in sight, Scott
makes the spot decision to stop the intruder nearest
him, doubtlessly leaving the other jumper to reach the
building unhindered. Only then does Scott glance to
his right and see Hayley also running, moving to intercept the second intruder. Without slowing, he waves
emphatically at the intern. "Stay back! Stop!"

Hayley Chill, one of the first women to success-
fully gender-integrate infantry training, does not stop
running. Maintaining a strong, steady pace, she tracks
the intruder's course perfectly and brings the six-foot-
three, twenty-seven-year-old man to the ground. A
Schrade SCHF10 Survival knife, with 5.3-inch black
blade, pops from the intruder's hand and he reaches
to retrieve it. Hayley scrambles behind the big man's
back, shooting a forearm across his neck, her left hand
gripping her right wrist, and executes a sneak choke
from armbar position with shocking efficiency. The

intruder's grip on his knife falters as Hayley applies steady pressure against his windpipe, critically reducing oxygen and blood to his entire system.

Hayley's subduing of the second intruder has taken approximately twenty seconds, enough time for Secret Service agents to converge on the scene from every direction, weapons drawn. Two of the agents drop to their knees and assume control of the intruder's arms as Hayley eases off the armbar and then slides out from underneath the man. She gets to her feet, putting one hand on her White House credentials for emphasis. The nervous, hyperventilating Secret Service agents aren't entirely certain who the hell Hayley is and what she's doing here. One agent keeps his submachine gun trained on her as he quickly scans her ID.

"It's all right! She's okay!" Scott comes running over from where he had held the first intruder, restraining him until the cavalry arrived. Seeing Hayley being braced by his colleagues quickened his pace. He arrives and puts a comforting hand on her shoulder to signify Hayley's legitimacy.

The more-senior Secret Service agent lowers his P90 machine gun, glancing from the male intruder on the ground in handcuffs to Hayley.

"Who the hell is *this*?" the incredulous senior agent asks Scott, gesturing.

"Hayley Chill," Scott tells him. "She's a White House intern."

# 2

★　★　★　★

## KALORAMA ROAD

**H**ank's Oyster Bar on Q Street off Dupont Circle is behind an unmarked door, an appropriate entry for a tavern that's dark and doggedly traditional. Whether actually old or simply designed to appear that way is of no concern to Scott Billings. He's had drinks here with other Secret Service agents as well as numerous dates. The joint suits him well. As he sits at the corner of the bar with the intern at his elbow, he takes quiet measure of Hayley's reaction to their surroundings and her degree of contentment. Does she like her drink, a shot of Fortaleza Reposado over ice? Is she tired or, worse, bored? Are the staffers from the Commerce Department at the other end of the bar making too much noise for her liking? And why is he worrying about such trivialities? His job is one of the highest national importance. What exactly is the fucking deal?

He raises his glass, their second round. "To White House interns stealing Secret Service jobs."

Hayley raises her glass to clink Scott's. "Thanks, but skinny ties and dark sunglasses aren't really my thing."

Scott pretends hurt feelings. "What's that say about my chances?"

"Chances for what?" Hayley asks with a straight face.

They drink. Hayley's gaze roves over the interior of the singles hangout. This evening is the first time since leaving the military that she has stepped foot in a bar. In the time since then, she has had exactly five alcoholic drinks. With her workload, there had been very little time for socializing or recreation. Sleep. Eat. Work. Repeat. Day after day, month after month. Now Hayley is sitting in Hank's, brought here by the cowboy-handsome Secret Service agent with a body like Nureyev. Life is strange, never moving in a straight line. She recognizes the agent is becoming more anxious by the minute, fretting over her interest in him. His insecurity, while foreign to him, is familiar to Hayley. She has this effect on potential sexual partners. There's nothing to be done. The sex always seems to sort itself out. In a brief lull of their conversation, Hayley recalls she failed to do a full twenty-minute strength workout in the morning. She owes herself five sets of bicycle crunches before going to bed.

"Almost feel sorry for the other interns, having to compete with the likes of you," Scott muses.

"I have an unfair advantage. I've seen more of the world than the others."

"But that's not all. You've got the inside game."

"I don't even know what that means."

"The fact you'd say something like that means you've got the inside game." He takes another pull off his drink, straight-up whiskey. "You're wasted down there, sitting in that broom closet."

"Janitor's closet," Hayley corrects him.

"Pardon me. Janitorial closet," he says with a flourish. "Most people I can read like a book, their ambitions and aspirations. You're different. This is all a stepping-stone to what?"

Hayley shrugs. "Hard to say."

Scott grins but is privately frustrated by her caginess and reserve. Hayley perceives his impatience.

"What about you? Just another young gun for the US Secret Service?" she helpfully inquires. People just love being asked about themselves.

"Ten years protecting presidents and I can write my own ticket in corporate security. Settle down," he says, then continues, grinning, "watch my wife raise a family."

Hayley laughs, adding wryly, "Just because you make an obviously sexist comment doesn't mean you're not sexist."

Scott lifts his glass to his lips and drains it with a tilt of his head. He gives her that moment-of-truth look.

"Well, Hayley Chill, which way is this thing going to break?"

"That's it? That's your pitch?" She had expected something more artful from him.

"Pretty much," he has to admit.

Hayley takes a moment to consider the notion of going home with the Secret Service agent. It occurs to her that accepting Scott's rather blunt proposition will mean she doesn't have to knock off those sets of crunches when she gets home.

Hayley looks him level in the eye, meeting his gaze so intently that Scott instinctively looks away. "As long as I'm able to deliver the overnight brief to Peter Hall at 0500, then we're good to go."

Scott reacts, impressed all over again. "How did you snag that gig?"

"The other interns gladly delegated the task to me, and hated me for it all the same. For most college kids, sleep trumps access."

Scott nods and checks his watch, a black-faced Rolex Daytona 6239 given to him by his mother on the occasion of his father's death, the timepiece all that was left intact of the old man after a plane crash in Milwaukee back in 2002. "Six hours ought to be enough time, I think."

Hayley drains her drink. "Let's hit it," she tells Scott as she slides down from the bar stool.

After they have had sex three times in the ranch-style home in suburban Virginia—on the kitchen counter, living room floor, and, as if by obligation, in his bed—Scott and Hayley rest. Hayley wears one of his Ohio State T-shirts. He wears a pair of boxers. She senses that he wants to talk, and avoids making eye contact. What they had done together and to each other is precursor of so many unwanted side effects. She wishes she could put it all in a box, like a soon-to-be forgotten keepsake or carnival Kewpie doll, without consequence or attachment. Hayley knows this dire mistrust of real intimacy is the hard guarantee for a life of solitude. But she has never felt more than an intermittent loneliness and long since determined that separateness is the better course for her. In her observations, love is annihilation of self and the ultimate declaration of insanity. As these broodings tumble through her consciousness, Hayley gratefully takes note that her lover, only minutes before a dervish of fornication and amorous calisthenics, has succumbed to a monumental physical fatigue and fallen into a deep, satisfied sleep in his bed.

———————————

WHEN THE ALARM on Hayley's phone sounds at 4:30 a.m., she is already up and getting dressed. Scott stirs. As with all other areas of the house, his bedroom exists in a high state of dishevelment, the detritus of an ex-jock and inveterate single guy scattered everywhere. Fully awake now, he indulges in the timeless joy of watching a woman get dressed at the foot of his bed after a long night of very good sex. Scott wonders if such a pleasure has been similarly appreciated throughout the history of man, all the way back to the days of the Neanderthals. Did Neanderthal woman even wear clothes? He cracks a smile at the absurdity of his random musings.

"What?" Hayley asks.

"Nothing." His silly speculations don't complement the persona of a grave Secret Service agent he strives to project. "One for the road?" he proposes.

Hayley shakes her head. "I need to go. Home, then work."

Scott accepts her refusal good-naturedly. But he is already eager to see her again and is relieved they both work in the White House complex. What the hell is happening to him? he wonders, rising from bed. Hayley isn't above admiring his physique as much as he had hers. As sexual partners, they fit.

"This fits," she admits to him out loud.

He envelops her in his arms and kisses her. But despite this connection with Hayley, shockingly fast and somewhat terrifying, career comes first. "We might want to keep this on the down low," he advises.

"Yes," she agrees. "That would be wise."

———————————

THE REDBRICK GEORGIAN mansion on Kalorama Road squats close to the street, constructed in 1754, and in that pre-motorized era conveniently sited. The proximity to public roadway and subsequent lack of privacy today seems expensively anachronistic. One would expect to see candles burning in the windows or a horse-drawn carriage in the drive. Only the rich and powerful can afford the inconvenience of such a relic. Look closely. Triple-pane windows and instead of candlelight, there is the faint glow of amber LED on the panel of a sophisticated alarm system down below window level at the northeast corner of the stately home.

Snow drifts down from an opaque sky, leaving a tentative, sugary coating on scattered surfaces. Accumulation seems unlikely. The temperature is just below freezing. But these early flurries are a harbinger of the winter to come.

Cloaked in this haphazard dusting of snow, the mansion is dark and graveyard silent. The street and sidewalks are empty. Six figures emerge from shadows, materializing like *yūrei* of Japanese folklore, clad in tight-fitting dark clothing, knit caps, and stealth duty boots. Each man—self-evidently special tactics operatives—carries a stuffed duffel or backpack.

Taking care to stay on the gravel bed that frames the home's perimeter, the operators stop under a window off the northeast corner of the mansion. One of the men, code-named "Lawford," attaches a suppression device to the side panel of the home security system. The LED light on the console briefly flickers and then resumes a steady glow. The suppression device boasts its own LED light, verifying the device is jamming signal flow to the security console from sensors placed throughout the residence. With a gesture from Lawford, a second man, "Bishop," slides open the window left unlocked in an earlier intrusion. A third operator withdraws a white full-body contamination suit from his duffel and slips it on. Code-named "Sinatra," he is the unit leader.

After making what appears to be the sign of the

cross, Sinatra clambers through the open window without making a sound as the other operators slip on their contamination suits. Each man follows the other through the open, first-floor window. The operators, six in number, regroup inside a formal dining room, where they pause, awaiting a signal from Sinatra. The faint sound of a television tuned to a cable news channel is now detectable, drifting into the darkened room from elsewhere on the lower level of the mansion. The unit leader gestures to Lawford, who immediately proceeds to one of two doorways leading out of the formal dining room.

Meanwhile, a fourth operator, "Martin," withdraws a peculiar device that only superficially resembles a small-size syringe and hypodermic needle. Manufactured with a resilient, boron-nitride nanotube attached to one end of a glass pipette and coated with a micro-thin layer of gold, the injection apparatus is a nano-needle capable of penetrating the membrane of a living cell for targeted delivery of one or more molecules into the cytoplasm or nucleus. Injection with nanoneedle is virtually impossible to detect. Sinatra watches Martin prepare the apparatus, awaiting his go-sign.

In the mansion's modest kitchen, Peter Hall sits at a butcher-block table on a hard-backed chair perusing the morning paper while a television murmurs in the background. He had managed to sleep only a few hours, at best. Resistance to the administration's agenda from his own party in Congress has been relentless, to say nothing of the opposite party's near hysteria. On trade issues, relations with China and Russia, and ongoing tensions with allies in Europe, Monroe has advocated a consistent course of disruption. Such was his mandate in winning the election, a victory that few had predicted. The chief of staff lost several friends, both personal and professional, over his early support of Monroe's presidential bid. In fact, Hall's oldest son had broken off all contact with his dad over these political disagreements. But losing sleep and relationships is all part of the bargain in attempting to save the country from ruin. Hall's lifelong custom had been to wake at five a.m. Since Carol's death, this morning routine has gained even more traction. Sleep is the happy indulgence of the less burdened.

Turning the page of the front section of the *Washington Post* and eagerly awaiting arrival of the morning's State Department security briefing package to be delivered by the impressive intern in his support office, Hall looks up to see three men clad in white contamination suits standing silently in the kitchen doorway. With their presence now revealed, the men respond by moving forward, in apparent choreography, toward a startled Peter Hall. Only the briefest grunt escapes the White House chief of staff's lips as Sinatra and another operator, code-named "Davis," take hold of Hall, restraining him while Bishop swiftly inserts the tip of a small squeeze bottle into one of his nostrils and pumps three bursts of its contents into the victim's sinuses. Hall continues to struggle against the men, who immobilize him for the few seconds before he goes completely limp.

Sinatra and Davis gently ease Hall's head and upper torso down onto the kitchen table as Martin appears with the nanoneedle. Working with the aid of a Keplerian Loupe, which magnifies the insertion area, the operative threads a micro-thin wire through the nanoneedle and into Hall's jugular vein and feeds the length of it down the vein, into the right atrium of the chief of staff's heart.

Satisfied the wire end has found its intended target, Martin attaches the other end of the wire to a battery amplifier. Once all is in order, he gives Sinatra a look. On that cue, the unit leader and Davis place their hands firmly against Hall, pressing him against the tabletop. Sinatra gestures to Martin to proceed. Without emotion, Martin flips a switch on the amplifier.

Hall's body seizes. Sinatra and Davis continue to lean on the spasming chief of staff. After a few moments, Hall becomes still. Martin already has a stethoscope in hand, and he checks their victim for heartbeat. Finding none, he nods to Sinatra.

"Dead," Martin declares.

Sinatra nods, businesslike and without expression. They have exactly fifteen minutes before the intern normally arrives with the daily brief. As Martin and Bishop begin to clean up and stow the apparatus, Sinatra turns and walks out of the kitchen, followed by Davis. In the hallway, they encounter Lawford and the sixth man, "Lewis," standing at the open door of a hallway closet. Inside the closet is an array of security and surveillance equipment. Lawford has removed the security system's hard drive and is just about finished replacing it with another drive of the same exact specifications and manufacture.

"We're done," Sinatra informs Lawford.

Lawford nods, replacing the system console's cover and screwing it closed again.

"Done here."

Lewis scans their work area for contamination as Sinatra and Davis return toward the kitchen, where Martin and Bishop have completed staging of the scene. Hall has been placed flat on his back, a spilled cup of coffee halfway across the floor just beyond his outstretched fingertips. He looks exactly like a late-middle-aged man who has suffered a massive and fatal heart attack while perusing the morning paper at his kitchen table. Martin and Bishop stand by as Sinatra makes a thorough inspection of the dead man and the surrounding area. He finds nothing amiss.

"Good," he pronounces, gesturing to the other operators to head out.

All six men regroup in the formal dining room. Sinatra takes a poll by leveling an index finger at each man. They all nod their heads or mumble their assent. No problems have been encountered. No trace of the operation has been left behind. All mission objectives are complete. "Let's go," he instructs them.

Sinatra is the last man out the window, joining the others on the gravel path that serves as drainage for the structure's exterior and foundation. The earlier flurries have stopped, but the sky has yet to lighten with sunrise. There isn't a sound except for a city bus accelerating on Connecticut Avenue two blocks distant. The others have already stripped off their coveralls and stowed them in packs. Within seconds, Sinatra is also ready to go. He leads his team up the gravel bed, merging with the shadows beyond. Martin, at the rear, nearly stumbles into Bishop in front of him, and his left foot goes slightly wide of the gravel bed. As he regains his balance and falls in lockstep again with the others, he fails to notice the boot print he has left in the light snow coating a brick walkway adjoining the gravel path.

---

WHEN HAYLEY EXITS Scott's house in Falls Church, an Uber is idling at the curb. The Secret Service agent had offered to drive her home to her apartment in Rosslyn, but she had rebuffed him, wanting to be alone. She can't remember the last time she spent an entire night with a man. Escaping the house for the cold night air, light snow falling from the abyss above, Hayley feels a surge of renewed well-being and confidence. She has sensed Scott's intensifying feelings for her and begins to devise a strategy to keep his emotions from outpacing hers. As long as she can remember, Hayley's relations with men have been a management issue.

Her Uber driver is a middle-aged Egyptian man in the US for more than ten years. Hayley engages him in conversation, asking several questions about that country's current political situation and the relative safety of an American visiting there. Egypt has always been a source of interest to her. When Hayley was seven years old, she dressed up as Cleopatra for Halloween. One of her mother's favorite movies was the 1999 version of *The Mummy*, which supplanted *Stargate* as the family's top flick. What any of these preoccupations had to do with the reality of present-day Egypt, of course, amounted to exactly zero. Nevertheless, in the idle moments of her ride from Falls Church to her studio apartment in Rosslyn, Hayley fantasizes about a trip to Abu Simbel temples, Karnak, and Colossi of Memnon. In the chaotic days that follow, Hayley will intermittently recall these quiet moments in the back of the two-year-old Ford Focus and the kind, sonorous voice of her Egyptian driver.

Once home, Hayley quickly showers and changes into a fresh outfit and dashes out again after hailing another Uber from her apartment. A young Salvadoran immigrant drives her in a Honda Civic to the State Department on C Street, only a few blocks from the White House. Its proximity to his office in the West Wing notwithstanding, Peter Hall likes to peruse the daily briefing binder at the earliest hours of the day in the comfort of his home.

A State Department aide one bump higher up the Washington food chain than Hayley meets the Honda Civic at the corner of Twenty-First and C Streets. Coatless and hugging himself against the cold, he passes the binder through the Civic's rear window to Hayley. "You look different today," the twenty-three-year-old prematurely balding young man informs Hayley. She doesn't respond but checks the binder for all anticipated sections. "Did you get laid last night?" the guy asks, making the common joke.

Hayley looks up from the binder, satisfied her State Department counterpart has done a sufficient job. "A few times," she answers, gesturing to the Salvadoran. "Let's go." The Uber driver obliges by burning a few micrograms of rubber pulling away from the curb.

The Civic stops outside Hall's residence on Kalorama Road and Hayley steps out with briefing binder in hand. Before she closes the rear door, she bends down to address her driver. "I'll just be a minute," she promises.

Hayley ignores a brace of cold wind and opens the wrought iron gate leading to the brick steps and mansion's front door. Binder in hand, she presses Hall's doorbell and waits. In the two weeks Hayley has performed the task, returning to her apartment afterward to start her run, she has been accustomed to Hall answering the doorbell within fifteen seconds. Taking the briefing binder from her, the White House chief of staff would typically grunt and start reading before he had shut the front door again. After a half minute, she presses the doorbell again. Hall still fails to appear.

Hayley glances over her shoulder, back at the Civic waiting at the curb. She gestures to her driver to wait and steps off the porch, moving along the front of the structure toward the northeast corner. As she progresses, she looks inside each first-floor window she passes. There is no sign of Hall or any activity within the residence. Her facial expression betrays her concern. She has never known Peter Hall to be anything but precise, consistent, and predictable. His failure to appear at the door telegraphs, by her calculation, a high probability for an emergency situation. Consequently, Hayley's attention to detail and keen observational skills increase to a high degree.

Rounding the northeast corner of the structure and looking into the formal dining room without seeing any sign of her boss, Hayley continues up the gravel drainage bed. Glancing down to her left, she sees a fresh boot print in the thin coat of melting snow covering the brick path. Hayley stops and stares at the boot print, then looks up and through a pantry window that offers a view into the kitchen. From that vantage point, Hayley can see Peter Hall's body sprawled on the kitchen floor, his coffee cup upside down just a few inches from his outstretched hand. Breathless, Hayley looks down again at the fast-disappearing boot print in the snow. Judging by the crisp outlines and micro-ridges, the print cannot be but a few minutes old. Whoever left the print walked here less than five or ten minutes before Hayley arrived. There isn't an explanation for its existence other than one that is highly suspicious. Hayley retrieves her cell phone from a coat pocket, selects the camera app, and quickly snaps a photo of the boot print.

---

WITHIN THE HOUR, the mansion on Kalorama Road is overrun with uniformed police, FBI agents, MPD detectives in suit jackets, and overly curious neighbors. TV news vans are kept at bay by yellow-tape barricades at either end of the block. Temperatures have risen to the high thirties. The dark sky overhead threatens rain.

FBI agent Helen Udall takes a sip of her Sugar Shack coffee, deliciously warm and familiar. The doughnuts at the Sugar Shack are arguably the best in town, but Udall has been following a weight loss program requiring denial of pretty much everything she loves. Udall's motivation for losing weight is a cute accountant who works for the Commerce Department and lives in the condo just down the hall from her. Since the start of her campaign to win Carl's heart, Udall has seen a commendable reduction of twenty pounds. But, sweet Jesus, she craved one of Sugar Shack's signature maple bacon doughnuts on this particular morning worse than life itself. Consequently, depriving herself has spoiled Udall's mood.

Standing with Hayley Chill in the entryway of the redbrick mansion on Kalorama Road, the FBI agent regards her witness through eyelids that are half-closed not because of a lack of sleep the night before or for intimidation value, but because Helen Udall was born with congenital ptosis. In grade school, her nickname was "Sleepy." In high school, it was "Droopy." At the Hoover Building just off Pennsylvania Avenue, the moniker given her by other agents is "Half-Mast," but never to her face.

"In your time at Mr. Hall's residence, before arrival

of MPD, did you notice anything out of the ordinary?" Helen asks Hayley. "Anything irregular?"

Hayley pauses before answering the FBI agent. When she was thirteen and earning extra money babysitting for the town's general practitioner, the good doctor's wife had made a hearty demonstration of treating Hayley like one of the family. The care of twin toddlers was a trial, requiring Hayley's presence from the end of a school day until long after the doctor returned home from his office late in the evening. The doctor's wife bought birthday and Christmas gifts for Hayley and insisted she sit with the family during meals. She confided in the teenager, relating the frustrations of her marriage and disclosing details of a mostly barren sex life. To friends, and in Hayley's presence, the doctor's wife would refer to their babysitter as being like an eldest daughter.

Late one evening, when his wife had run out to the store, the doctor cornered Hayley in the entryway, pressing his six-foot frame against her and forcing his tongue into her mouth. Forcefully pushing the slightly inebriated man off her, Hayley locked herself in a downstairs bathroom until she heard the familiar sounds of a car's return. Hayley met the doctor's wife in the driveway and, in tears, relayed everything that had just transpired. Instead of reacting with outrage or indignation directed at her husband, as the young teen undoubtedly expected, the doctor's wife violently shoved her babysitter to the ground with a curse. Hayley struggled to her feet, and the wife pushed her down again, accusing the thirteen-year-old of viciously slandering a virtuous husband. Threatened with increasing physical assault, Hayley scrambled to her feet and ran all the way home.

Ever since that dismal night, whether she realized it or not, Hayley has embraced a more Emersonian attitude. "Wise men put their trust in ideas and not in circumstances." The circumstances in which Hayley currently finds herself are exceedingly unreliable. Hall's death by sudden heart attack in and of itself would not necessarily incite undue suspicion. His temper was volcanic and stress levels extreme. Leftover barbecue was his idea of the perfect breakfast, and he carried at least forty pounds of excess weight. By any medical analysis, the man was a prime candidate for myocardial infarction. But the boot print in the dusting of snow on the walkway next to Hall's residence, long since vanished in the rising temperatures of the day, undeniably suggests a conspiracy of some magnitude. Even greater reason for caution was the chief of staff's admonition to Hayley in the privacy of his office that continues to reverberate, "Trust no one." What if Hall's death was not from natural causes but the handiwork of a deep state conspiracy? She makes her decision within moments of Udall's most important question.

"No, ma'am. I saw nothing out of the ordinary until discovering Mr. Hall's body," Hayley informs the FBI agent.

Helen Udall has interviewed hundreds of witnesses and suspects. How a person says something is equally important to what is said. Hayley's pause before speaking was noteworthy, blatant as the lipstick on her ex-husband's collar. "Anything at all, Ms. Chill. No embarrassment in stating the obvious." The words say one thing, but Udall's hard expression says another. Hayley is being told in certain terms: "Stop screwing around, young lady, this is the F-for-fucking-B-I and you best tell me what you know because I am grieving here, inconsolable over the maple bacon I denied myself, so speak up!"

Hayley meets the FBI agent's gaze, Udall's brown eyes partially hooded and prison-yard lifeless. This isn't the first time in her life Hayley has dealt with the law. There were at least six interactions with the sheriff's department or state police back home in Lincoln County. Even during her honorable and lauded career in the army, Hayley had occasion to be questioned by military police, but always as witness and not possible suspect in wrongdoing. As long as she can remember, her world has been one of checkered reputation, frequently requiring police intervention or official investigation. Consequently, Hayley does not intimidate easily in contact with law enforcement personnel. In her experience, it's no different than an exchange with the local baker.

"Ma'am, there was no answer at the door. I went to the side of the house, persisting because Mr. Hall demanded the briefing binder be hand-delivered to him every day without fail." She pauses, waiting for Udall to catch up with her furious note taking, then proceeds.

"Looking in, through the pantry room window, I could see the chief of staff on the kitchen floor, lying there motionless on his back. I called 911, returned to the front porch, and waited there for EMTs to arrive."

Udall finishes jotting down on her notepad and then slides a look toward the scrum of investigators observing the interview from a few yards away. Her failure to gain anything of use from the witness, a mere intern, has soured her mood even further. "Enjoying the show?" she cracks to the spectating detectives, who take the hint and disperse. Udall looks back toward Hayley, unwilling to let go. "And what about before this morning?"

"Ma'am?"

"Your relationship with Mr. Hall, what was that like?" Again the FBI agent's facial expression preloads her words with meaning beyond their dictionary definition.

"Nothing inappropriate, if that's what you're asking, ma'am," Hayley calmly assures the FBI agent.

Udall releases Hayley from the interview with an emphatic slamming shut of her notepad. "Okay, well, obviously, I'll be speaking with more people there, in the White House."

---

GIRARD STREET PARK, in Washington's diverse Columbia Heights neighborhood, has long resisted all attempts at gentrification. With shade trees, picnic tables, playground, and a full basketball court, it possesses the basic amenities of urban refuge and nothing more. The neighboring streets of Girard and Fairmont provide a reliable clientele of panhandlers, addicts, gangsters, and petty criminals in addition to a few brave, less subterranean types. "Public" in the extreme sense of the word, the park isn't pretty.

Since a midday shootout cleared the playground a few years before, few parents allow their children to visit the area. On this chilly November morning, the sun rarely peeks through roiling, dark clouds. Even the bums and criminals have shunned the grimy square for a warmer and drier indoors. The only person in the park is a man sitting alone on a bench. Bearded and wearing a navy-blue duffel coat and astrakhan cap, the man watches a pair of sparrows tussle over a dead, desiccated beetle.

Sinatra materializes from behind the Bearded Man's shoulder and takes a seat on the bench. The Bearded Man had been anticipating Sinatra's stealthy arrival and doesn't react in the slightest. The operative, dressed in jeans, wool shirt, and down jacket, smokes a cigarette and watches the birds in mild combat.

"Haven't you heard?" the Bearded Man asks, gesturing to the cigarette dangling Jean-Paul Belmondo–style from Sinatra's lips. "Those things will kill you."

"Sitting with you on this bench, in broad daylight, has a higher probability of killing me than cancer," Sinatra retorts. "Let's talk about your hat."

The Bearded Man doesn't have a self-conscious bone in his body. The cap sits atop his head with aplomb. "'Astrakhan' is the Russian word for the pelt of a young Karakul lamb, a breed of sheep native to Central Asia," he explains. "Harvesting at birth, when the wool is still black, soft, and very tightly coiled, it creates a pleasurably dense mat." The Bearded Man gives Sinatra a wink. "Popular among Soviet Politburo members back in the day."

Sinatra is spectacularly uninterested. Then again, he had asked about the damn thing. He flicks the cigarette a dozen yards away, where it rolls to a stop against a curbstone. "Why am I talking to you?"

"I want to hear there were no errors made on Kalorama Road. Your lips, my ears."

Sinatra sighs, a wheeze of petulant arrogance. "Peter Hall died of a massive heart attack. Dead before he hit the floor," Sinatra relates. "Read about it in the *New York Times*."

"Your men performed to expectation, then? No mistakes."

"I was first in and last out. The team's execution was flawless."

The Bearded Man nods approvingly. "Excellent." He checks his watch.

"That's it?" Sinatra appears both surprised and annoyed.

"Well, I don't want to take any unnecessary risks with your safety." The Bearded Man stands.

Sinatra also rises, eye-to-eye with him. "Our man inside 1600 requires direction."

The Bearded Man levels an irate look toward

Sinatra, disappointed with an operative who had been selected by another member of the task group less particular than himself. If it had been up to him to choose a candidate for the job, given the targets, he would have looked offshore. His fellow Americans can be such outrageous brats, spoiled children weaned on a steady diet of network television and McDonald's hamburgers who never really ever grow up. The Bearded Man is grateful he was raised well before the Internet age and ubiquitous handheld devices. He's doubly grateful not to have children himself.

"He is to do what he's been ordered to do and nothing more."

"Damocles?" Sinatra presses.

"At the present time, there is no need for further action," the Bearded Man reiterates.

"At the present time," Sinatra restates pointedly.

"Should the situation change, I'll be in touch. In the meantime, your man is to remain in ready position, and that is all."

Sinatra nods, message received. He finds himself staring at the battling sparrows. The partially masticated beetle lies between them on the damp concrete, not three feet from where rival gang members had exchanged close-quarter gunfire.

The Bearded Man follows the other man's gaze. "*Anthus rubescens.* American Pipit."

Sinatra clearly doesn't know what the Bearded Man is talking about. His mind is elsewhere. What if the job on Kalorama Road wasn't error-free? What if he or one of his team had made a mistake? There would be no escape or avoidance of consequence. He and every man on his team would be the most wanted men on earth. It's a dreadful and terrifying thought, and Sinatra can feel a thunderclap headache coming on.

"What?" he mumbles, eyes blinking.

The Bearded Man makes a dismissive gesture. "Never mind. We'll be in touch." And he walks off, wrapped in his duffel coat and astrakhan cap riding jauntily atop his head.

---

IN THEIR GROUND-FLOOR office of the West Wing, the four interns spent most of the morning in confused idleness. With Peter Hall's death and the entire White House shell-shocked, demand for intern services is at low ebb. In the first three and a half hours of the work-day, not a single call comes down to the repurposed janitorial closet. Sophia and Luke pass the time with heads pressed together in intimate conversation. Becca chats on the phone with friends who aren't really friends but means to an end. Unlike the others, Hayley keeps silent and still, replaying in her head the sequence of events at Kalorama Road over and over again.

Finally, just before noon, a tearful Karen Rey appears in the doorway. "That's it. Everybody go home. Unless someone calls to tell you otherwise, come back tomorrow at the usual time."

"Are we being let go?" This coming from Luke with

a somewhat hopeful tone that he isn't clever enough to hide.

"Internships are the last thing we're trying to deal with up there," Rey replies haughtily. Peter Hall had been her best and most cherished mentor. Losing him has created a mosh pit of emotions in Rey, the most impassioned of which are fear and bitter frustration. Few of her tears are shed out of sadness for a human life snuffed out at too young an age.

After Rey departs, the interns begin to gather their things. Sophia and Luke make a plan for lunch at Zaytinya. "Do you like Mediterranean?" the USC junior asks Becca.

Becca makes a face and shakes her head no. Actually, she absolutely loves roasted branzino but can't afford splurging on such an extravagance. Her savings are running alarmingly low. Kept secret from the others is the fact that she goes to Taco Bell every day and fills up with a five-dollar Triple Melt Burrito Box. Many years later, after Becca has amassed a personal wealth of several million dollars as head of her own secular church, and before her incarceration in federal prison, she will occasionally slip away from her small army of assistants and sycophants, driving to a Taco Bell one town over from her own to briefly relive those delicious, bad old days.

Sophia looks to Hayley next but says nothing, refraining from extending a lunch invitation to the West Virginian. After these few weeks sharing a work space with Hayley, Sophia has decided that class divides really do exist in America. The naturally occurring barriers that segregate one income group from another actually matter. Hayley's experiences growing up in near poverty and her time in the military are utterly foreign to the Los Angeles native, whose primary and college education will generate nearly a million dollars in tuition expenses. The army vet is so strange, so alien and unapproachable. The fact that Hayley is prettier than Sophia makes their incompatibility even more pronounced. Until this hillbilly showed up, Sophia ranked herself hottest woman in the West Wing.

Rather than lunch at Taco Bell or Zaytinya, Hayley eats her peanut butter and jelly sandwich sitting on a bench on the Mall. By 12:30 p.m., the temperature has risen to the high forties or perhaps even the fifties. Hayley has spoken very little since her interview with the FBI agent, rebuffing the other interns' gossipy inquiries regarding what she saw on Kalorama Road. Leaving the White House complex, Hayley had encountered Scott Billings. He was completely sympathetic to her circumstances and anxious to console her. But Hayley didn't need comforting. Death was not an abstract and therefore did not disturb her all that much. Peter Hall was a man who had extended to her a measure of kindness and respect. Now he was dead, and only that. What Hayley did in fact require was time to think and devise her best course of action with the scant evidence in her possession.

There's no question of telling Scott what she saw

beneath Hall's pantry window, no matter how good he is in bed. Ideas, not circumstances, right? By every measure, Scott Billings is pure circumstance. A man with a penis and the skill with which to use it is not a man whom she should automatically trust. That he's a Secret Service agent doesn't necessarily instill confidence, either. Plenty of conspiracy theories about JFK's assassination suggest involvement by members of his Secret Service detail. "Trust no one," Mr. Hall had cautioned. If there's one thing Hayley has been trained to do, it's to follow orders.

Eating her peanut butter and jelly sandwich on the Mall and studying the nation's obelisk in the thin mid-Atlantic sunlight, Hayley recalls reading somewhere that between the years 1884, when it was completed, and 1889, the Washington Monument was the tallest man-made structure on Earth. It astounds her that such a world, where 555 feet was the pinnacle of man-made achievement, could have existed. Nothing lasts forever. People die and for all kinds of reasons. But what cannot change is her primary assignment, no matter the danger or risk involved. Service to country is a privilege, one that must be based on impeccable moral foundations. She will keep her own counsel for now. Only when she knows more will it be safe to approach the authorities. Hayley finishes her sandwich and decides against the bus, walking home instead.

That evening, after a long run, Hayley makes a pot of spaghetti and meat sauce, a meal she had prepared for her siblings hundreds of times. After cleaning up the kitchen, she sits down at the dinner table and opens her laptop. A television across the room is tuned to CNN, which reports heightened tensions over Russia's buildup of forces on its border with Estonia. She accesses her phone and brings to its screen the photo she had snapped that morning of the boot print. The particular details of its sole—linear x's and dashes above an array of squares—are extensively visible in the dusting of snow on brick pavers.

Placing the phone on the table next to the laptop, Hayley begins cruising the web, entering search requests until she arrives at a page she desires. It strikes her as faintly ridiculous to be engaged in this futile Internet search, but to do something—anything—feels good all the same. An army surplus website favored by ex-military types and survivalists offers dozens and dozens of special tactic boots, listed with photographic renderings of their soles. Hayley carefully scans each selection, page after page, in meditative search of a match of the boot print in her cell phone photograph. What she would do with a match, she really has no idea, but in this way she slows her racing thoughts and begins to think of sleep as a real possibility.

---

ON THE FOLLOWING morning, Hayley arrives at the White House complex at her regular time of exactly 7:45 a.m. Typically, the other interns in the CoS Support office report later, drifting in sometime between nine and ten a.m. Sophia didn't come in until after lunch twice in the last month, citing doctor appointments. Hayley finds these hours before her coworkers arrive to be her most productive. Within fifteen minutes of settling down at her desk, a little more than twenty-four hours after Peter Hall's shocking death, Karen Rey appears in the doorway.

"Minute of your time?" the White House aide inquires flatly. Rey doesn't seem happy about whatever business is at hand. As Hayley gets up to follow her supervisor out the door, she wonders who she has managed to piss off. Maybe in some outrageously unfair way, she is being blamed for Peter Hall's death. If only Hayley had arrived a few minutes earlier, Hall would have risen from the kitchen chair and answered the doorbell. He may have collapsed in front of her, allowing for possible medical intervention. Has the FBI already determined Hayley had spent the night before at Scott's house? Outlandish speculation might suggest that had Hayley not had sex with the Secret Service agent, the White House chief of staff would be alive today, recuperating in a hospital bed at Walter Reed hospital.

"Is there a problem, ma'am?" she inquires, following Rey up the corridor. But the intern wrangler is mute, pointing for Hayley to enter the cafeteria.

Though the Navy Mess and CoS Support office share the same floor in the White House's West Wing, interns are not supposed to eat at that exceedingly convenient location. Instead, they and other low-ranking support staff are directed to use the much larger and more utilitarian cafeteria in the Executive Office

Building. Until this moment, Hayley had never set foot inside the cozy, well-appointed Navy Mess, reminiscent of a country club dining room. Rey gestures to Hayley, indicating a table across the room where a bespectacled black man in his late thirties sits. Kyle Rodgers, the deputy chief of staff, has just started eating a breakfast of fruit salad, Denver omelet, and coffee infused with sugar-free Red Bull.

He gestures to a chair. "Have a seat, Hayley."

"Thank you, sir," she says, sitting. Rey also takes a seat.

"Hungry? Can I order you something?"

"No, thank you, sir."

"Coffee? Red Bull?" Rodgers motions to a passing waitperson for more coffee in his own cup.

"I'm good, sir. Thank you."

Rodgers doesn't ask Karen Rey if she wants anything. Gunning for Rodgers's job as deputy chief of staff, Rey has engaged in guerrilla warfare to further that goal. Rodgers is well aware of her pedestrian machinations—floating rumors, talking to the press, critiquing Rodgers to his boss—but doesn't really consider her much of a threat. A gladiatorial in-fighter with a dozen scalps hanging from his blood-soaked shield, the deputy chief of staff can handle Karen Rey.

"Do you know who I am, Hayley?"

"You're Kyle Rodgers, deputy chief of staff. You worked in Mr. Hall's congressional office before following him here to the West Wing. Your White House telephone extension is seven-four-four-three."

Rodgers exchanges a look with Karen Rey, then turns his focus back on Hayley. "I get it now."

"What's that, sir?"

"Why POTUS knows you exist," Rodgers explains, spearing a fat mushroom with his fork and popping it into his mouth.

A modest Hayley says nothing.

Karen Rey finally speaks, abruptly. "Given these unfortunate events, it's been decided that CoS internships will be terminated for this quarter. The new chief wants only paid staff in his office."

Kyle Rodgers clears his throat like cocking a shotgun, dissuading further interruption. He looks to the intern again, privately relieved Hayley isn't the one gunning for his job. "The president is keen to keep you on, Ms. Chill."

"Apparently, helping save his life is a way of getting on his good side," Rey adds snidely.

Hayley looks to her supervisor with a mild expression, utterly unnerving. "Thank you, ma'am, but the only life I saved that day was the intruder's."

Rodgers cannot fathom why Karen Rey is making this more complicated than it needs to be. He gestures with his fork in Hayley's direction. "White House Operations. How does that suit you?"

Hayley nods. "Thank you, sir. It would be an honor."

White House Operations is easily the best posting inside the West Wing an intern can possibly obtain. Adjacent to the Outer Oval Office, where the president's personal secretary controls access into the inner sanctum, it is at the epicenter of West Wing activity. The primary role of WHO is serving the clerical needs of POTUS and his personal assistant. Typically, low-paid, junior aides are assigned White House Operations, not interns.

Before reporting for duty up on the first floor, Hayley stops back in the office of CoS Support to retrieve her backpack. The other three interns have arrived by this time and are packing up more extensive personal belongings.

"That's it. We've been let go," Sophia announces to Hayley.

"No biggie. We can still put the internship on our résumés and B-school applications," Luke reminds the others.

"What's that?" Becca demands to know, pointing at a WHO orientation packet Karen Rey had given Hayley.

She tells them what the folder contains. The news Hayley has been assigned to WHO is met by stunned silence. The military veteran has not only prevailed but sailed higher than they could have ever dreamed for themselves. Becca makes the only assumption her brain can possibly formulate. "Who the hell did you blow to land White House Operations?" she asks.

"It's the military thing," Luke theorizes. "Welcome to Fort Monroe."

Hayley finishes the short work of collecting her things. Hooking the backpack over her shoulder, she turns to face her fellow interns. "Thanks, guys. It was fun."

Only Sophia can muster the social graces to stand and give Hayley a companionable hug. "Good luck up there, Hayley." Luke is already staring into his phone, muttering about the lack of Wi-Fi signal. Becca stares long knives at her nemesis. It's not easy admitting defeat. "Fuck off," she tells Hayley, more out of resignation than anything else.

---

WHITE HOUSE OPERATIONS is at least three times as large as the CoS Support office, with higher quality furnishings and lighting. But, like the ground-floor work space, it's still a windowless box. A young man with sandy-blond hair, wearing a starched white shirt, tie, gray suit pants, and black Aldo oxford dress shoes, sits on the floor with a large moving box before him. The box is filled with new-in-the-package smartphones. More phones, removed from their boxes, sit in a small pile next to him. Asher Danes is on his personal phone when Hayley appears in the doorway, backpack slung over her shoulder. Smiling, he waves her inside. Hayley enters and, with another gesture from Asher, sits on the floor opposite him.

"She's here. I've gotta go," he announces to whoever is on the other end of the call, disconnecting. Asher, looking younger than his midtwenties, holds his arms out wide. "Yes! Our hero arrives! You have no idea how much fun you're going to have!"

Hayley smiles, appreciating a much friendlier reception than she ever enjoyed downstairs. She gestures at the dozens of boxed and unboxed cell phones. "What's with the phones?"

"White House Operations is essentially 'floater' support, assisting any office needing an extra pair of hands. Today we're helping the Scheduling and Advance team, who leave tomorrow for Japan to prep the president's trip next week. Staff's existing phones don't work internationally. Therefore, somebody has to program seventy-five new smartphones each with seventy-five new phone numbers."

Hayley retrieves one of the boxed devices from the moving carton and examines the packaging.

"Blackphone? Never heard of it."

"Most secure phone on the market. So secure no one can figure out how it migrates data," he grumbles, reaching for another boxed phone.

Many hours later, Asher and Hayley are still programming smartphones. Conversation between them is easy. "My dad contributed five million bucks to Monroe's campaign. How dare you get this gig by sheer dint of your exceptional competency and work ethic?" he asks Hayley in mock outrage.

"I'm an intern. You're an actual, paid White House aide."

"Who will need more than one hundred and sixty-three years to repay his father," Asher rejoins. "Money only means something in terms of campaigning. No one comes to the West Wing to get paid."

"So why are you here? You don't seem like the résumé-polishing type."

"Political aspirations. I plan to be the first gay president," Asher confides. "Openly gay president, that is."

"And you just wanted to try the Oval Office on before buying?"

"Exactly. Imagine enduring the dreary humiliations and eternal horseshit of a presidential campaign only to realize all of your ties clash with the wallpaper?"

"Very sensible," Hayley has to agree.

Asher pulls another boxed Blackphone from the shipping carton for programming.

"Have you seen it yet? The Oval?"

Hayley shakes her head no.

"You wanna?" Asher asks, smiling.

"Yes, I do," Hayley manages through her grin.

Asher tosses the unprogrammed Blackphone aside and pops to his feet. "C'mon."

Hayley remains seated cross-legged on the floor. "We can't!" she protests.

"Of course we can. We're White House Operations, dammit!"

Hayley doesn't budge. "You're talking about just barging into the Oval Office, Asher!"

He just grins, heading for the door. "POTUS left for Camp David two hours ago."

Without further debate, Asher exits the room through the doorway that connects with the Outer Oval Office. Hayley jumps to her feet to follow after her new coworker.

In the Oval Office, Asher is seated in the president's chair with his feet insouciantly up on the *Resolute* desk when Hayley enters. She is horrified to see him there.

"Asher!"

Laughing, he gets up out of the seat and brushes off the desk where his feet had been.

"Good as new."

Hayley stops in the middle of the room and spins 360 degrees on the balls of her feet. "It's bigger than it looks in the movies and on TV." She is in awe.

Asher indicates the phone console on the president's desk. "You want to call the British prime minister? Or the space station?"

Hayley approaches the desk, a piece of furniture of considerable historical significance. She traces her fingers across its polished surface.

"Try not to bomb Moscow or someplace," Asher warns her.

Hayley smiles out of politeness. She privately muses on the unlikelihood of a person with her background finding herself in a place such as this. When she was twelve years old, Hayley wrote a report on the White House for school. Her teacher liked it so much he had it published in the school newspaper. A spiteful Tyler Johnson, who had considered himself something of an authority on politics and was the class president from grades four through eight before drowning in an abandoned mine pit, punched her on the playground during recess. Hayley won that fight, too. A little more than thirteen years later, she's standing in the real Oval Office recalling that funny little school paper.

Hayley walks past Asher, to the floor-to-ceiling windows just behind the desk. Through the trees on the North Lawn, she can just barely make out demonstrators in Lafayette Square. Asher joins her at the window.

"Resist!" He mockingly raises his fist.

"I saw one of them try to kill another, using an American flag like a spear."

Asher shrugs. "What passes for political discourse these days."

"You shouldn't treat the country's flag that way," she reminds him.

Asher levels Hayley with a flat look. "You're kind of intense, you know that?"

Hayley stares at him, not quite understanding his point. Asher makes a face and gestures for her to follow. "Let's go. The fate of the free world hangs in the balance, and we've got phones to program."

# 3

★ ★ ★ ★

## GAMMA-HYDROXYBUTYRIC ACID

She wakes up well before dawn lying in bed next to Scott. He has been awake for almost thirty minutes now, simply watching her.

"What?" she asks him.

"Trying to come up with a label for this. You and me."

"Cardio?" Hayley suggests. He reacts with a hurt expression, and she regrets her glibness. But it's only been a week. What's the rush to give it a name? Scott opens his mouth to make his case, but she stops him with a gesture.

"Don't. Your words for it might be different than mine, and then where will we be?"

"Okay," he concedes, but it's obvious he won't let it go. Hayley has seen this look before, with her other lovers. The clock starts ticking down, only a matter of time now before she'll end it with him. This need men have to own a thing rather than simply experience it. They convince themselves it's love they're feeling, but Hayley knows better. What they actually have is property lust, craving something around which they can build a wall. Following the death of her father, Hayley had had a front-row seat to her mother's exploitation and abuse by a series of ever-worsening boyfriends, witness to a lifetime's accumulation of lies, harangue, and deception. Even before she was twelve years old, Hayley had promised herself never to cede control of her life to any man. How refreshing would it be to reveal these thoughts to Scott without his defensiveness or recrimination? Hayley has yet to meet the man capable of handling who she really is and the limitation of her needs. Without further conversation, Scott gets out of bed and leaves the room to make coffee.

Scott's kitchen is brightly lit, the windows like black mirrors in the predawn hours. Hayley sits at the Ikea dining table as Scott serves the breakfast he has prepared for them and takes the opposite chair. Hayley seems taciturn, even for her.

"You okay?" he asks her.

"I'm fine. Why?" Hayley could've scripted this scene before it unfolded, a replay of prior encounters.

"You seem a little preoccupied," Scott tells Hayley.

She regrets their brief but significant exchange in bed. Up to that moment Hayley had sufficiently enjoyed Scott's company and the physical release of sex. Though they have little in common besides a physical compatibility and mutual respect, she had hoped they might maintain a relationship parked somewhere between committed and casual. It would have been nice to rest at this place with Scott awhile and pursue a less solitary life. What would it be like to have just that level of companionship? But after their awkward talk only minutes before, all of that seems impossible. She feels Scott's gaze on her. He expects a response.

"My boss died. I found his body. It was unsettling."

"Of course. Right." Scott starts eating. Hayley watches him for a brief moment.

"So are you married or anything?" she asks, already knowing the answer. Hayley had clocked the indisputable evidence in the two visits to Scott's home. A lamp no man would purchase and therefore inherited in the separation. Same with the food processor gathering dust on the counter. The entire place smacked of hodgepodge, the grim and depressing vibe of man-child recently and involuntarily set adrift. Someone as observant as Hayley would not miss the artifacts of a failed marriage.

Scott's fork freezes in midair, just below his chin. "Is it that obvious?"

"Yes, it's that obvious."

"Separated two years," he concedes.

"Why not divorced?" Hayley presses.

"Losing a three-year-old to leukemia wasn't punishment enough?"

Hayley bites her lower lip. One of her younger siblings had had asthma that nearly killed her. Inhaled nedocromil managed the problem. Poor Harper deals with the effects of that awful disease to this day.

"I'm sorry," Hayley tells Scott.

"I know."

Scott grabs his tablet. The device sports a Rolling Stones "tongue and lips" decal. So Scott. Such a bro. He inputs the device password and accesses a photo of an adorable toddler. Offers the tablet to Hayley for closer inspection. "Max," he tells her.

"Beautiful," Hayley acknowledges.

Scott says nothing. Outside the window, the sky has gone from ink black to the most cobalt of blues. Another day is just beginning. What wasn't said continues to weigh between them.

Later, driving into the city with Scott, Hayley performs familiar calculations in her head. Barely a fling, their affair has run its course. When is the best time to break it off with him? Now? They have plans for dinner after work this evening. Would it be more humane to do it then? The interior of the black BMW 335i is over-the-top messy, like the bedrooms of the least reputable frat on campus. There are scuff marks on the dash, and garbage is thick on the floor. The clutter is almost childish, suggestive of Scott's vulnerability. Hayley's conviction fails her. Dinner. She'll have the talk with him then.

The silence that developed between them in the house persists in the car. Hayley strives to alleviate that unease with mild banter. She indicates the confusion of empty coffee cups and fast-food packaging at her feet. "My brother hunts out of his car and manages to keep it cleaner than this."

"What about the city bus? Clean or less clean?" Scott asks her, grinning widely.

He has no idea it's over between them. He thinks this is only the beginning. Recognizing these facts makes Hayley increasingly uncomfortable, and she suffers the self-recrimination that accompanies any failure of willpower. Why had she let herself be pulled into this mess? It occurs to her she might have some personality disorder, a terror of real intimacy, but just as quickly banishes the thought. There's no time now for therapeutic response, if in fact she has a problem. Looking out her passenger-side window, she sees a crowd of protestors in Lafayette Square. The group is much larger than she has seen there before and more demonstrative. DC Metro and US Park Police confront the protestors, who carry signs decrying Russia's interference in Estonia.

Leaving the car parked in the White House lot and walking toward the West Wing ground-floor entrance, Scott discreetly takes Hayley's hand and gives it a squeeze before releasing it. "Eight o'clock?" he asks her. Hayley nods. They diverge then and continue in opposite directions.

When Hayley arrives at White House Operations, she joins Asher and Karen Rey watching CNN on one of the office computers. Senator Taylor Cox is being interviewed in the marble corridor outside his senate office. Cox, the minority leader and ranking member of the Committee on Foreign Relations, appears genuinely agitated and not merely grandstanding.

"There's a difference between disruption and destruction. What the president proposes in creation of a new European alliance, a kind of NATO-lite, is nothing short of a gold-plated invitation to Russia to do as it pleases, whether meddling in democratic elections around the world or military invasion of its neighbors, like Estonia," the senator tells the CNN reporter.

"The president feels the greater threat is China, Senator," the reporter needlessly reminds Cox. "Can you really so easily dismiss the military assessment of a man who spent nearly his entire adult life in the army?"

The senator swallows an obscenity. How can they be so blinded by the man's wartime exploits? He composes himself and responds with controlled anger. "No one is dismissive of the president's military service. But let's not confuse the manifestation of power, which is the essence of military might, and policies and long-held political ideals of the United States of America. We must uphold a long-standing commitment to protect our allies, no matter on what hemisphere. Let me speak frankly. President Monroe is taking this nation down a perilous path. To be honest, I'm worried for our country and for the world."

"Thank you for your time, Senator," the reporter tells him as Cox turns and walks away. The reporter faces the camera. "Strong words from the Senate minority leader this morning."

Rey reaches for the computer's keyboard and mutes the volume. "Okay. Let's get back to work."

Asher glances to Hayley standing next to him. "Ever get the feeling you're a henchman rather than a sidekick?" Hayley keeps her opinion to herself. Asher feels the senior aide's hard gaze on him. He throws up his hands in mock appeal. "Just kidding!"

Karen Rey is in no joking mood. Work in any West Wing is an incredibly exhausting endeavor, but a job in the Monroe administration multiplies that stress by a factor of ten. She hasn't taken a vacation in God knows how long. Hired to work on the Monroe campaign early in its formation, Rey has ridden the wave from unexpected election victory to today, eleven months into a confrontational presidency. Because Monroe's political philosophy and agenda is essentially Peter Hall's political philosophy and agenda, Rey can be categorized as a true believer. She isn't in this for post–West Wing riches. Rey believes POTUS really can make America America again.

When Rey turns away from the computer screen, she sees a middle-aged black woman in her forties blocking her path out the door. "Who the hell are you?" the White House aide demands of a deadpan Helen Udall.

---

FBI AGENT UDALL and Hayley have Peter Hall's office on the first floor to themselves. The new chief doesn't arrive for another day. As a courtesy to the bureau, Kyle

Rodgers has given his okay for Udall to conduct interviews there. The FBI agent sits at a small worktable in one corner of the office, next to a large window overlooking the North Lawn. Hayley sits across from Udall, hands folded calmly on the tabletop.

"Polymorphic ventricular tachycardia. Fibrillation, followed by cardiac death. Open-and-shut, right?" Udall asks Hayley.

"I wouldn't know, ma'am."

"It's the sort of thing that happens to otherwise healthy men and women countless times a day." Udall snaps her fingers. "Just like that."

Hayley is expressionless, giving the FBI investigator nothing. Udall continues, doling out information like chum. "What's different here, atypical it would seem, is the fact that a very minute trace of GHB was discovered in Mr. Hall's blood. Gamma-hydroxybutyric acid." Hayley still says nothing but is interested in every word the FBI agent has to say.

"GHB is the 'date rape' drug. What's a date rape drug doing inside the president's chief of staff?"

"I don't know, ma'am," Hayley replies. "What does any of this have to do with me?"

"You were the first person on the scene."

"I didn't enter the residence until after the police and EMTs had arrived, ma'am," Hayley reminds Udall. "I saw Mr. Hall's body from outside the house, through a window, and from an adjoining room."

Every investigative muscle Udall has developed over twenty years in the business tells her the White

House intern is withholding information. Exactly why Hayley isn't more forthcoming is anyone's guess, but Udall is more determined than before to crack the West Virginian's walnut-hard shell. "If you saw anything unusual, Hayley, the FBI wants to know about it."

Hayley shakes her head, seemingly helpless to give her interrogator what she wants. "Sorry, ma'am. Sure wish I could be more help."

For the next several seconds, the FBI agent stares at Hayley with a blank expression, communicating silently her suspicion the intern isn't telling the truth. Hayley doesn't waver or rattle, coolly meeting Udall's gaze.

"Ma'am?" she asks Udall after this long silence, giving the FBI agent all the room she needs to pursue the interview.

A thoroughly stymied Udall offers Hayley her card. "Call me. With anything."

Hayley doesn't accept the agent's card. "You gave me one of your cards yesterday, ma'am. Remember? I still have it."

Udall unsmilingly continues to offer the card. "Take another. Got tons of 'em. The FBI has a deal with somebody."

After Udall leaves, Hayley returns to the White House Operations office. Karen Rey had been assigned the task of doing the spadework vetting the new chief of staff before his selection is made public tomorrow. She then delegated that tedious chore to Asher. He and Hayley spend the next ten hours performing much of the necessary background research. Did the candidate actually receive the advanced degree he said he did on his résumé? Did he pay taxes for his nanny? What is the real status of his marriage, not just the legal one? Countless phone calls and follow-up emails are made. By eight p.m., they've worked through most of the vetting checklist. Asher leaves, citing utter exhaustion, and drags a promise from Hayley to leave by nine p.m. They can finish the job by noon tomorrow, as demanded by Rey.

Once Asher has left and Hayley has the office to herself, she pushes the CoS candidate file to one side of her desk and opens her Internet browser for more quixotic searching of a match of the boot print in the snow at Kalorama Road. Manufacturer sites and whole-sale sellers display their offerings in great photographic detail. Hayley methodically peruses each site, comparing boot soles to the photo of the print. So far she has found nothing that suggests an exact match.

Hayley is so engrossed in her work she doesn't hear Scott enter the office and walk up to just behind her.

"Ready?"

Hayley reacts with a start. "I didn't hear you come in," she tells him, somewhat embarrassed.

Scott indicates the computer screen and display of boots.

"What's this all about?"

Hayley picks up her phone and dumps her keys in her backpack, slinging it over her shoulder. She pointedly ignores Scott's innocent question. "Let's go," she announces as she heads for the door, for the first time since this morning remembering the unpleasant task that lies ahead. Like anyone in her situation, Hayley wonders how Scott will react to being dumped.

A car breakdown at the Virginia Avenue on-ramp to Interstate 66 has jammed traffic there. Scott steers the BMW sedan west on Pennsylvania, transitioning to M Street in order to cross the Potomac on Key Bridge. Rain has been falling since lunchtime and the roads are slick, reflecting city lights. Scott had suggested a Thai place near his home in Falls Church. The food quality is only average, but they're guaranteed not to run into anyone from work.

During much of the ride, Hayley remains preoccupied and mostly quiet. In her head, she runs the lines she will deliver to Scott. This breakup shouldn't be too big a drama given how long they've been seeing each other. Hayley ponders the expression "seeing one another," such a useless and overtly benign euphemism. Whoever can truly see another person? People wear so many masks they can't even see themselves, let alone their significant other. She and Scott have been fucking each other for less than a week. Easier to think of their relationship in those more accurate terms, given what she is about to say.

"Sure you're okay?" he asks her.

Hayley shrugs and plays a card she's dealt before.

"The FBI interviewed me again today."

"I heard they were on the premises. Questioning you?" he asks with some surprise.

"Peter Hall," she tells him, nodding. "Wanted to know if I'd noticed anything odd or out of place."

"Did you?"

"No. But Udall thinks his death might be foul play. They found traces of anesthesia in Hall's system."

"Okay. So the FBI can worry about it."

Hayley says nothing. She finds herself staring at the BMW's black faux-leather dash in front of her. Among the scuff marks there, she sees a dusty imprint of the boot, an exact match of the print she found in the snow outside Hall's residence, down to the distinctive linear x's and dashes above an array of squares.

Scott sees Hayley gaping at the boot print on the dash. In that instant, he links this fixation to her inexplicable Internet search for boots just a half hour earlier. At the time he had thought nothing of it. Now she's similarly transfixed by the presence of a boot print on his dash. "What?" he asks.

"Nothing," she responds. "The whole business, it's just upsetting."

"Must be," Scott responds, but his voice has gone strangely hollow and vacant. He focuses on the road ahead as the vehicle begins to cross the Key Bridge.

Hayley feels time elongate, stretching like taffy between the present and an unreliable future. Each heartbeat thuds with anticipation and dread. The game is up. No longer a question of breaking off a brief love affair, this is a stark matter of survival. She is in the jaws of the lion.

Without announcement, Hayley unlatches her

seat belt and reaches for the door handle. She has managed to push the door halfway open when Scott reaches across her and pulls it closed again. Then, with the same hand, he withdraws a combat knife from an ankle sheath and thrusts, with the intent of driving it deep into his passenger's chest. Hayley raises her backpack, which she had in her lap, and blocks his attack. The knife's blade pierces the pack's fabric and becomes hung up when Scott tries to withdraw it for a second attempt. Armed only with her fists, Hayley smashes her balled-up right hand into Scott's face, bringing a constellation of stars to his vision.

The BMW sedan veers right and crashes through the masonry balustrade on the north side of the bridge. Flying off the span as if choreographed by stunt artists, the vehicle arcs elegantly through the air and splashes into the Potomac, front bumper first. It floats for a moment, but water quickly floods inside through a shattered windshield. Within seconds, the BMW sedan has submerged and sinks toward the riverbed.

Scott and Hayley continue to fight as the car fills with water. Holding her breath, Hayley reaches again for the door handle in the dark murk of the Potomac water. She is halfway out the open door when Scott grips her arm from behind and hauls her back inside. With his other hand, he tries to undo his own seat belt and succeeds, but the retracting belt becomes ensnared around his neck. He must release his grip on Hayley in order to free himself. Unencumbered, Hayley pushes off from the car seat and jets out the open door, swimming toward the glimmer of lights above.

Hayley comes to the surface underneath the bridge, choking and gasping for breath. The current carries her south, away from where the car entered the water and on the opposite side of the bridge from where people have gathered to observe the aftermath of the accident. No witnesses interviewed later by the authorities recall seeing anyone surface from the submerged vehicle.

She swims the few dozen yards to the river's edge and clambers onto the bank, water dripping from her clothes, face, and hair. Both shoes are missing, but otherwise she is completely unhurt. There isn't a bruise or cut on her. Checking the inside pocket of her jacket, Hayley retrieves her phone. Miraculously, it remains fully operational.

---

THE RECENTLY BUILT condos at 3303 Water Street, in the words of its promotional materials, are "modern to a T." They're also extremely expensive, on the highest end of condo valuations in the District of Columbia. Prices hover between two and three million dollars, with $3,000 a month HOA dues, for 2,200 square feet of above-average construction and "ultra-luxury" fixtures with a panoramic view of the Potomac River. The majority of residents are lawyers and lobbyists. There is only one low-level White House aide residing at 3303

Water Street, Asher Danes, whose father purchased the condo as an investment. Sparing his only son the indignities of lesser accommodations was the primary consideration, however.

Asher eats his takeout dinner from Tono Sushi delivered to his door by Uber Eats and watches the emergency vehicle lights flashing on the Key Bridge, prominently visible through floor-to-ceiling windows that define the living space. A television nearby is tuned to MSNBC at a low volume. Getting home from another grinding workday, Asher prefers to tune out. Eat, a little reality TV, then sleep. It's the same routine every day. On weekends, if he isn't at the White House, Asher is sleeping, recharging for the week coming up.

He has become disillusioned working in the West Wing, his unhappiness so acute he's considered quitting. Sure, Asher would like to be the first (openly) gay president. He loves politics as much as ever, motivated by a keen desire to help people and change the world for the better. His problem with the White House is its current occupant. Asher was an early supporter of Monroe but has become disenchanted with the administration's agenda as it evolved into actual policy. In his time since working there, Asher has exchanged exactly zero words with the president. He suspects Monroe is homophobic.

Asher isn't sure what he would do if he quit and moved back to Greenwich. No doubt his parents would love to have him home. Eventually, he will get hired by some random political candidate to help with his or her campaign for some random congressional seat or another. But Asher really would prefer not to take that easy way out. He craves a more dynamic and directed confrontation of his dissatisfaction. Gifted with a prodigious intellect, good looks, and an effortless wit, Asher Danes perceives he has coasted through life without breaking a sweat.

In this moment, while idly picking at the remnants of his sushi dinner and watching the hectic activity on the distant Key Bridge, Asher decides to run for political office himself. He doesn't know where exactly. New York, where his father is a high-powered lawyer? Or Connecticut, where he grew up? Either place provides possibilities for a state senate or congressional seat in the next two years. In this way emotionally reinvigorated, Asher calculates a timetable for declaring his political intentions.

All of it will require considerable research, of course, a time-consuming endeavor that would be impossible while also working in the West Wing. If he's serious about any of these ideas, Asher must quit his job at the White House. He muses on the potential of making a declaration of his resignation. Can it be spun as a protest of Monroe's policies? All of this speculation gets Asher's blood moving, passionate again for the first time in weeks. He doesn't worry about upsetting his parents. Prone to bragging about their son, the White House aide, they'll be undoubtedly even happier to boast of their son, US representative from New York's Seventeenth District.

The condo's landline phone buzzes, snapping Asher from his reveries. He goes to the phone mounted on the wall between sleek, open kitchen and the entryway.

"Miss Chill in the lobby to see you, Mr. Danes," the doorman informs him over the phone.

"Thank you, Hector. Please send her up."

Asher is surprised by Hayley's unexpected visit. In the few days they've worked together, he has come to enjoy her company and assistance immensely. Asher has found the West Virginian to be a refreshing change from the previous interns sent to help him out in White House Operations. Intelligent and hardworking, she has proven to be decent company as well. But Hayley comes from a vastly different world than Asher. Her values seem extraordinarily traditional, which might explain a rather odd otherworldliness. All things considered, Asher isn't displeased she has chosen to stop by. He had given Hayley his personal contact information because she seemed so excruciatingly trustworthy. Asher is curious, however, why the intern has come to his residence at this time of night. He guesses it must be something very important as he goes to answer her knock at the door.

On the small video screen of his entryway console, Asher sees Hayley is clearly in both physical and emotional duress. "Holy shit!" he exclaims. He yanks the door open wide, revealing Hayley soaking wet and bedraggled on the other side. "Oh my God, what happened?"

A shivering Hayley steps inside, checking over her

shoulder as she does so. Her skin is blue tinged and eyes wide with shock. "Car accident," is all she can manage to get out.

Asher looks over his own shoulder, through the condo's windows, at the accident scene still unfolding on the bridge. "On Key Bridge?" he asks incredulously.

Hayley nods.

"You went over the side? Into the Potomac?!" Asher presses, not entirely registering what has happened.

"I didn't get caught in a rainstorm." No smile accompanies her small joke, betraying slight irritation with Asher and his prattling.

"But how? How did it happen?! Oh my God! Are you okay? Are you hurt?" His questions come in rapid fire, his dismay and anxiety goading the other on.

"I'm fine," she assures him, adding with genuine concern, "Lost my backpack and house keys."

"But you're okay? That's what's important." Asher finally clicks into action mode, taking Hayley by the shoulders and steering her toward another part of the expansive condo. "C'mon, let's get you in a hot shower and dry clothes."

Hayley allows herself to be guided down the hallway by Asher. Never in her life has she felt so vulnerable and frightened as in these earliest hours after the accident. When Scott attacked her, Hayley's training kicked into gear. The same could be said about her escape from the submerged car and swim to safety, within sight of Asher's condo building at 3303 Water Street. But once safely on shore, with the realization she had

escaped uninjured, the impact of what had just transpired landed hard. With every minute that followed,
the implications of those events—Hall's death, seeing
the boot prints, Scott's shocking attempt on her life—
exploded in a mushroom cloud, expanding far beyond
her ability to rationally process them. Paranoid fear took
grip. It was a small miracle that Asher's residence was
within a three-minute walk from where she crawled out
of the cold, dark Potomac. If there was ever a time in
Hayley's life she needed a friend, however tenuous, it
was in these hours after the incident on Key Bridge.

"What about the police, Hayley?" Asher asks her as
they reach the second-bedroom bath. "Who's car was
it? A ride share?"

Hayley shakes her head no. "One of the Secret
Service agents. He was driving." She pauses, then continues, "I don't think he made it out."

For her sake, Asher masks his shock. "Hot shower,"
he responds, pushing her into the bathroom. "I'll get
you something to wear, then we'll sort all of this out."
After she has closed the door, Asher wallows in the anxiety he'd hidden from Hayley. This shit is insane! What
the fuck has he just invited into his house? Hearing the
shower, he goes back into the front area of the condo
and picks up his cell phone. He dials 911 and listens
for one ring and then another. An operator comes on
the line and asks what emergency is being reported.
Hearing her voice, Asher changes his mind, mumbles
an apology for accidentally calling, and disconnects.
Despite only knowing Hayley a very short time, she has

become a friend. Asher won't call the police, at least not just yet.

---

HAYLEY SITS ON the couch, skin red from a near-scalding shower, wearing Asher's sweatpants and I ♥ SOUTH BEACH T-shirt. The sound of her clothes tumbling in a dryer behind a discreet utility room door drifts from across the large open-space living room. Asher sits in a Jean Prouvé chair opposite the off-white Edward Wormley couch, where Hayley is perched. If this political business doesn't pan out, Asher demonstrably has a future in interior design. Hayley takes a sip of tea from a cobalt-blue Limoges bone china demitasse cup with encrusted rim in twenty-four-karat gold, serenely unaware of its multi-hundred-dollar cost.

"Better," she pronounces in regard to her general well-being.

"All right. So. You guys were seeing each other, I take it?"

"Something like that," she tells him. Then adds, more definitely, "Yes."

"The cowboy? Dark hair, heart-melting, Elijah Wood–blue eyes?"

Hayley nods. "Scott Billings."

Asher marks a box in his mental checklist. Emphatically, he tells her she needs to call the police. She shakes her head no.

"Seriously. The man is dead. You were in the car." He pauses and then asks, "It was an accident, right?"

Hayley ducks the question. "You know what my high school girl friends are doing now? They're mothers on some form of public assistance, strung out on opioids, or both. Do you have any idea how hard I've worked to escape all of that? How do you think a messy scandal involving a dead, married Secret Service agent plays out for me?"

"This thing with you and Scott, it was a secret?"

Hayley nods. "And no one needs to know. What would it accomplish?"

Asher broods on it for a moment and decides Hayley is right. "It's not like you've committed any crime."

"Not one I know of."

He has an awful thought. "Your backpack!"

Hayley had already calculated these odds. "With any luck, it's been swept clear of the site by the river's current," she says. "If not, well, then I'm screwed."

"Is that a plan?" he asks skeptically.

Hayley says nothing, staring into the blue teacup. She hasn't exactly enjoyed the beverage. Back home, folks drank Dr Pepper, Tab, and coffee. Drinking bottled water, hot tea, or Pepsi was considered suspect. In the years since she left home, Hayley has endeavored to broaden her culinary horizons but still can't abide the taste of Pepsi. Sometimes, you really just have to draw the line.

"Not *the* plan," she tells Asher, who becomes anxious all over again.

SCOTT BILLINGS'S RANCH-STYLE home is shrouded in shadow, not a single light glowing from within. The street and surrounding houses are quiet. Moderately strong winds cause trees in the neighborhood to swirl and gyrate in a frantic, unsyncopated dance. Asher's Prius is parked across the street, lights and engine off. Hayley sits beside Asher, behind the wheel. They both stare at the Secret Service agent's house in silence, neither one of them wishing to speak but for different reasons. Finally, Hayley breaks the loaded silence.

"Five minutes. Just a few things I left inside," she assures Asher.

"Be a hero and make it three."

Hayley ignores the crack. Swaddled in Asher's gray long coat, she grips the door handle and exits the vehicle, striding across the street and up Scott's walkway.

Asher watches her disappear around the far corner of the house and grips the steering wheel with white-knuckle anxiety. Maybe Hayley hadn't broken the law before, but what would you call this latest activity? Only now he is her accomplice.

Hayley must trust Asher Danes out of sheer necessity. On the surface, at least, he seems utterly without guile. But she can't predict how her coworker would react if he was made aware of the suspicious evidence surrounding Peter Hall's death or the very concrete fact that Scott tried to kill her. Hayley can't afford Asher freaking out completely and running to tell whichever authority he can find first. What she knows as truth is the existence of a conspiracy directed at the Monroe presidency, if not the president himself. Until she knows more, Hayley is determined to protect that information as if it were the crown jewels.

Judging by Scott's reaction when he realized she had an inkling of the conspiracy, Hayley can deduce certain reliable assumptions. First, Hall's death was the result of foul play, most likely at the hands of special-operation-trained individuals. Second, with the exception of Scott, no one suspects she knows anything about Hall's murder. And because Billings now lies at the bottom of the Potomac River, her secret remains safe. Will the FBI be suspicious of Hall's death or merely go through the motions of an investigation? Was Scott a genuine Secret Service agent? How trustworthy is that organization? The identity of players and their agendas remain unknown, but Hayley, though only a lowly intern, is determined to influence the game's conclusion.

Having entered through a rear kitchen door where she knew Scott kept a key under the mat, Hayley creeps through the darkened house and searches for items that would suggest her existence to his coconspirators. She doesn't expect to find much unless the Secret Service agent had notated her contact information somewhere besides his phone, which is with him in the river and hopefully inoperable. What she's really looking for is evidence pertaining to the bigger conspiracy against the president. She finds nothing of interest in the living room or the kitchen, only the clutter of a single man who apparently cared little for cleanliness or domestic order. The mess appalls Hayley, and she wonders how she even spent two nights in this place. Searching methodically, she moves toward the bedrooms.

Waiting in the car, Asher becomes increasingly nervous the longer Hayley is inside the residence. Scott's house remains dark and tomb-like from his vantage point, no sign of Hayley inside. The thought strikes him that being accomplice to the break-in of a dead Secret Service agent's house in Falls Church is an inauspicious start to his future political career. How has he fallen under the intern's spell? Or is he simply sabotaging his grand ambitions before they even have the chance to congeal? Not always completely trusting in himself, how can he put so much of his own well-being in the hands of this redneck military vet? Asher wishes he'd never quit smoking.

An SUV with blacked-out windows rounds the corner at the opposite end of the block and slowly approaches. His stress levels spike as the SUV stops and parks in front of Scott's house. Asher watches all four of the SUV's doors open and men exit the vehicle, moving en masse toward the house. He has the unavoidable sense his life has become a movie, while simultaneously acknowledging a perverse pleasure in that realization.

"Oh, fuck," is what he says.

Inside the house, Hayley gives Scott's bedroom an efficient toss. It's impossible to discern where she has scattered items or not, the natural state of all things inside Scott's bedroom being upside down and disorderly. Hayley has yet to find anything of informational value in her search, but then hits pay dirt. Nestled in a pile of dirty laundry on the bedroom floor, just inside a shallow closet, Hayley finds Scott's tablet. In this same moment she hears the front door open.

Sinatra leads other members of his team into the house. Lewis hits the lights, illuminating the entryway and living room.

"What a fucking slob, this guy," Martin observes after brief inspection of the home's interior.

Sinatra is in no mood for casual conversation. Scott's death is like an iceberg adrift. There's no telling of the impact and ramifications hidden beneath the superficial fact of his demise. Was it really an accident? Who drives off a bridge? Could a mere tire blowout cause such calamity? Certainly there is more to the story and probably none of it is good. Sinatra wishes like hell he'd refused the job. Operations overseas, while perilous for other reasons, are always preferable. This business is far too close to home, practically in his backyard. But the money was beyond tempting, an even million for a maximum three months' work with the guys under him collecting $250,000 each. A man would have to be a fool to turn down that kind of money, no matter how distasteful or risky the job. After losing his house in Alexandria in a truly gothic divorce, Sinatra hopes to remake his life with the money from this gig.

"Bag the personal belongings. Leave the rest," he instructs his team. They don't exactly snap to the housekeeping task at hand. "Let's go!" Sinatra barks. As they begin to work, he checks his phone for emails from a real estate agent who is hot on the trail of a new-construction five-bedroom on King James Place. He is determined to buy a home larger than the one his ex-wife has moved into with her new husband, never mind the fact there is no one in his life to fill those extra four bedrooms.

Martin leaves the ugly mess in the kitchen and living room to the others, hoping the master bedroom is in better shape. He carries two black plastic contractor bags with a forty-two-gallon capacity, figuring they ought to be sufficient for the job. When he enters the bedroom and flips on the lights, Martin can see he had underestimated Scott's ability to amass clutter. Muttering a curse, he staggers through the piles of clothes and empty bags and boxes on the floor, moving toward the closet with accordion-style, louvered doors.

Hiding inside, Hayley can see Martin approach through the louvered slats. The operator is clearly going to inspect the closet's interior, the only uncertainty being how she plans to react when he does. If she is taken hostage by these men, they will kill her and dispose of her body before the new day dawns. Searching for an accomplice, they will undoubtedly find Asher and kill him, too. Doing nothing is not an option. In this case, the best defense is offense. The moment the man opens the closet door, revealing her admittedly unimaginative hiding place, Hayley decides she will attempt to kill him by punching him in his trachea and then defend herself from the others in the house, however many there might be, by arming herself with whatever weapon the dead man might be carrying. In the few seconds it takes the man to reach the closet, Hayley calculates her odds of survival at 25 percent, give or take three percentage points.

Martin has put a hand to the closet door pull when a car alarm begins to sound outside, its blare shattering the neighborhood's calm. The operator releases his grip on the door pull and backtracks out of the bedroom. After a short pause, Hayley exits the closet and goes to the single window in the bedroom. Trying to slide it open, she discovers the sash is painted shut. With diminishing options available to her, Hayley turns and walks to the open door. Peering down the hallway, she sees five or six men—it's hard to discern exactly how many from her vantage point—converging in what she knows is the home's living room. Hayley hears the men's voices, discussing the car alarm, as all of them apparently head outside the house. Risking that none of the men have remained inside, Hayley walks quickly up the hallway, through the living room, and into the kitchen, where she knows there is a back door.

Sinatra waits on the front porch as Bishop and Lewis walk across the front lawn, to their squawking SUV. The vehicle's lights flash, illuminating the street with false emergency. As Martin appears on the porch, he uses the car's remote to silence the alarm. Sinatra and the others look up and down the block, suspicious of the alarm's mysterious activation.

"It didn't just 'go off,'" Martin tells Sinatra, who definitely didn't need to be told this assessment. "What do you think?"

Sinatra's posture is rigid. His intuition tells him the alarm was a diversion. He pivots on the balls of his feet and stares inside the house, seeing nothing amiss there. But then, he wouldn't see anything amiss if the alarm was indeed a diversion. They would have already been scammed. He turns again and surveys the dark lawns and dimly lit street of his immediate surroundings. A clandestine operative for most of his adult life, Sinatra now has the very real sensation of being watched. But hanging around Scott's house any longer than is absolutely necessary and potentially arousing the curiosity of neighbors would be unwise. He gestures silently to his men, and they troop back inside the house.

The incidents of the last few hours have convinced Sinatra that the operation is dealing with a counter-agent of not insignificant talent and skill set. This revelation will require an alteration of tactics at every level, in addition to a demand for a 15 percent increase of his fee. As the realization takes hold, Sinatra begins the process of adjusting each and every future action and operational decision.

Escaping from the home through the kitchen door, which she was careful to lock on her way out, Hayley crouches in the dense shrubbery between the houses and watches the hit team investigate their vehicle alarm's activation. Six in number. All male, between the ages of thirty and forty-five. All fit, with rigorously athletic frames. Hayley knows the species well. Even a casual observer could see the unit is composed of military or former-military personnel. The man who remains on the porch most certainly is in charge. His dark, wavy hair and melancholic expression strike Hayley as oddly attractive. As he disappears inside the house with his men, she wonders what it would be like to kiss him. She wagers he's a good fuck, his sadness a reservoir from which he draws an off-kilter passion. She quickly dismisses the thought with a self-reprimanding urgency. No more sleeping with the bad guys.

After the men have withdrawn into the house, Hayley scampers from the bushes into the neighbor's yard and heads toward the rear of the property. A dog barks frantically as she passes through the backyard, but dogs are always barking in any neighborhood. Hayley isn't concerned about alerting the hit team. She finds the Prius parked on the next street over. The vehicle's lights and engine are off, but Asher's silhouette is visible inside. Hayley watches him watching her approach. She opens the door and climbs inside.

The expression on Asher's face is similar to the spouse whose partner has returned home at two a.m., stinking of well bourbon, stripper perfume, and regret. "Talk," he demands.

---

SHE HAS ASKED for help only three times in her life. Growing up in Lincoln County, you learn to swim or you sink. For some, opioids are the answer, but Hayley refused to take that way out. With a mother sick and in the grinding process of not quite dying, responsibility for the family fell on her shoulders. But even an independent and fiercely capable Hayley Chill might find herself in a predicament so intractable, so excruciatingly relentless, that a stranger's charity is her only hope. Three times the need has arisen, and in each occasion, unexpected assistance was her salvation.

Among the numerous medical ailments Hayley's mother suffered, one of the most problematic was angioedema, painful swelling of the tissues beneath the skin, and neither state nor county was willing to foot the bill required for treatment. With Cinryze costing well into the six figures, relief for Linda Chill was absurdly beyond the family's reach. Watching her mother writhe with pain and waste away, a desperate twelve-year-old Hayley asked anyone she could for help. The only person to respond was the sixty-year-old corner grocer, who had once called the cops on Hayley's next youngest sister when caught shoplifting in his store. Childless and a widower, the man paid the entire cost for one year's medication and essentially saved Linda's life.

Another occasion arose in Hayley's first year in the army, when an unusually brutal master sergeant, wanting sex from the recruit and rebuffed, made life a living hell for her. The military is the ideal social environment for abuse of authority. There was nothing Hayley could do to escape the sergeant's harassment short of going AWOL or physically retaliating. Going above her abuser, to a commissioned officer, would

look. Asher adopts a different but no less skeptical tack. "So who's behind this mysterious plot of indeterminate nature? The *deep state*?" he asks, as if about the Easter Bunny.

Hayley ignores his incredulity. She only needs Asher's assistance, not his affirmation of what she knows to be true. "I don't think Scott Billings was actually Secret Service." Again she ignores his arched eyebrows and sidelong look. "If they were willing to kill Peter Hall, what's to stop them from assassinating the president?"

"And why am I hearing about this now?" he asks with some justification.

"I was trying to protect you, Asher. I'm sorry."

"Oh, save your apologies. It's not like my feelings are hurt or anything. It just surprises me someone of your intelligence wouldn't see the need of collaborators. I mean, you *are* just an intern."

"Thanks for reminding me," she grinningly tells Asher. "Hiding in a closet with that military-trained assassin seconds from opening the door, I almost forgot."

"Who the hell are these guys?"

Hayley shrugs. "I was kind of hoping you might help me figure that out."

Previously in Hayley's life, when she had made the rare appeal for help, assistance was given without comment or complaint. There is something about her demeanor that suggests the request is genuine and of great urgency. When Asher had been sitting in his car waiting for Hayley to emerge from Scott's house, he had brooded on this aspect of the intern's character, on what had compelled him to step out of his comfortable life and into hers. Asher Danes, Harvard grad and aspirational presidential candidate, wanting for nothing and able to go wherever he pleases, contemplates putting that extraordinary freedom at risk.

"Of course I'll help you," he tells her. "But need I remind you of our worrisome lack of qualifications for the job?"

Hayley reaches into her jacket and withdraws Scott's tablet, with its signature Rolling Stones decal.

"Whose is that?" Asher asks her, already knowing the answer.

"What were you saying about qualifications?"

"You're crazy!"

"Maybe," Hayley confesses.

"That thing better be turned off," Asher warns her.

Hayley rolls her eyes. "Turned it off inside his house."

Asher reaches for the ignition. "Are we done here?"

Hayley nods. Despite their unequal status within the West Wing hierarchy, she has quickly established dominance in their relational dynamic. "We're done."

Powered up, the Prius pulls away from the curb and silently zips up the dark residential street. He waits until he's gone a couple blocks before he dares turn on the headlights.

Later that night, Asher walks through the mostly dark condo on Water Street, switching off lights and checking the entry door's dead bolt. Outside the condo's enormous windows, limited traffic has resumed across the Key Bridge. Once Asher has finished buttoning up his place for the night, he pauses to watch Hayley sleeping under a blanket on the couch. Her breathing is slow and steady, a fact that seems to please the nurturing side of her host.

He leaves the living room and walks down the hallway of polished concrete to the master bedroom. This room also boasts a lush view of the river and Key Bridge. A Savoir No. 2 bed—favored by Winston Churchill, Bram Stoker, Marilyn Monroe, and John Wayne, to name a few—dominates the expansive room, which is otherwise sparsely furnished. Generously proportioned twin walk-in closets contain an extensive wardrobe. Asher goes to the window and gazes out at the bridge. Reaching into his pocket, he retrieves his phone and places a call.

"Hello?" an older man answers.

"Hi, Dad," Asher responds, his voice suddenly sounding very young.

"Hey, bud, what's up?" Asher's dad seems genuinely pleased for this unexpected call from his only son.

"Not much. Same old thing, you know. I just wanted to check in." Asher's need for comfort, familiarity, and reassurance is unabashedly laid bare.

"Sure, of course. I'm glad you did. Great to hear your voice, son."

Asher allows himself an almost imperceptible sigh of relief. It's good to have loving parents.

Approximately two miles away from 3303 Water

Street, the executive mansion at 1600 Pennsylvania Avenue is similarly dark at this late hour. Few lights burn within. In the second floor of the executive residence, Richard Monroe is asleep in the president's bedroom, overlooking the South Lawn. His wife of forty-one years rarely stays in the White House, preferring their thousand-acre estate in upstate New York. Monroe's best-selling memoir, covering the entirety of his illustrious and colorful military career, brought him many things, the least of which was the home in Woodstock on Ohayo Mountain Road. The president misses Cindy's company tremendously, but such are the sacrifices one must make for country. Never once in his life suffering the torment of insomnia, POTUS sleeps soundly.

On the ground floor of the executive residence, a sole Secret Service agent exits the entrance leading into the Diplomatic Reception Room and stops in the empty driveway. He withdraws a pack of cigarettes from his pocket and matches from another, lighting up and taking a luxurious pull of tobacco smoke. The rain from the day before has moved to the east, and a near full moon occasionally appears from behind the fragmented clouds scuttling low across the night sky, illuminated like feathered showgirls by the city's lights.

# 4

★ ★ ★ ★

## THE BEARDED MAN

Vehicular traffic across the Key Bridge remains closed in the morning, creating commuter delays on both sides of the Potomac. Recovery of a vehicle from the river normally would have been performed the night before, just within a few hours of an accident, but jurisdictional squabbles delayed the operation. Who would pay for the recovery was the primary though not only disagreement. The border between the District of Columbia and Virginia is drawn on most maps on the Virginia shoreline with the river, but DC city officials were able to obtain maps that suggested a different boundary line down the middle of the Potomac. Because Scott's car was reported by witnesses to have gone over the bridge just past midway of the span, with the broken balustrade as obvious proof, those same budget-minded city officials argued that recovery was the Old Dominion's responsibility. Virginia State officials were forced to appeal to the District's nonvoting representative in the Congress to calm emotions and determine the ultimate outcome.

Now, at the District's expense, a twenty-ton truck-mounted crane with 33.5-meter-long boom has been moved into position as dozens of city transportation officials, police, and US Secret Service agents and authorities look on. Divers in the water have attached steel cables to the BMW sedan. With a signal from a hard-hat-wearing transportation official, the crane's operator throws controls inside the cab that begin to raise Scott's car from the river's bottom. The vehicle quickly appears, water cascading from its cracked windows. The crane gracefully swings the car over to just above the bridge's deck and gently lowers it to wheels down.

Four city detectives approach the sedan, Scott's body plainly visible behind the wheel and still entangled in the seat belt. Two senior Secret Service agents accompany the homicide detectives. Because of the freakish nature of the accident, it had been the decision of the police that Scott's body, carefully inspected by police divers the night before, would be removed only after it and the vehicle were thoroughly investigated by detectives. That decision, as well as delay in recovery of the BMW sedan, is fated to be reported in minute (and embarrassing) detail by reporters from the *Washington Post*, a relatively minor incident that exposed deficiencies in DC governance and, again later, in a much bigger political exposé.

Almost at the same time Scott's body is being photographed dozens, if not hundreds of times, inside his drenched BMW 335i sedan, seat belt wrapped tightly around his neck like a noose, Asher is driving to work with Hayley. They had stopped first at her place in Rosslyn so she could get some clothes, prevailing upon the building's resident superintendent to use his duplicate key to get inside her studio apartment. Wearing her own clothes and heading to work brings a sense of well-being and orientation to Hayley that is almost intoxicating.

"You know, I'm not the world's biggest Monroe supporter," Asher said, making his confession warily.

"I suspected as much." In fact, Hayley has been shocked by how many people inside the West Wing seem to be soft in their support of the man for whom they all worked.

"Is that a problem?"

"No. But wouldn't it make more sense to work for one of his political opponents? Why work for him if you oppose his agenda?" Hayley asks the obvious question.

"Exactly."

"You're thinking of leaving?" Hayley asks Asher.

"Almost since my first day," he admits to her. "What he said he stood for during the campaign and what he's actually trying to do while in office are completely different. Monroe's rolling back every progressive initiative made in the past seventy-five years!"

"Apparently, the majority of the voters support those rollbacks."

"Electoral majority," Asher corrects her.

"This is the democratic system our country has espoused since its founding. Regardless of personal beliefs, my priority is the service and protection of that political system, not the man," Hayley says.

"Did you have that written on an index card or something?"

She ignores his remark, prompting Asher to ratchet up the cynicism.

"Don't forget, Hitler was democratically elected."

"Richard Monroe isn't Adolf Hitler," she reminds him calmly.

"Correct. No mustache." Asher places two fingers under his nose, clownishly mimicking the German fascist. "The man's a danger to the nation, and I'm beginning to wonder if removing him from office isn't the only way to save it."

"A little shrill, don't you think?"

"No. Not really."

Hayley sighs, striving for patience. After all, she needs his help. "What if the shoe was on the other foot, Asher? What if forces were arrayed, behind the scenes and from within our own government, to undermine or remove a president whose agenda you supported? What would you call a movement like that? A coup d'état?"

Asher can think of no easy response to Hayley's hypothetical. Without much effort, she has boxed him into his own hypocrisy. Brooding as he steers the Prius into the parking garage two blocks from the White

House, he says nothing and thereby concedes the point. It's five minutes past seven in the morning. The state of the union, by all appearances, is sound.

---

THE TOWN OF Shady Side, in Anne Arundel County, Maryland, is famous for nothing. Prior to the nineteenth century, the area was known as the Great Swamp, if that says anything. Today, something slightly more than five thousand souls live within the town's borders, and few inhabitants want anything other than to be left alone. It is an insular and clannish town on the western Chesapeake Bay as unpretentious as a trim from Supercuts and about as attractive. Steamy and dank in the summer and frigid cold and dank in winter, the town is mostly ignored by day-trippers and tourists. An F-150 Ford pickup is the preferred chariot in Shady Side, and if there's any reason at all for a brief visit, it's Andy's Crab House.

The Bearded Man eases his 2016 Buick Regal TourX into the gravel lot that serves as Andy's parking lot. He could afford a more expensive car and one that carried with it more status, but the Buick suits the Bearded Man just fine. He is frugal, and the amount of money his fellow citizens spend on their automobiles has always struck him as juvenile, a surrender of common sense to marketing and peer pressure. The other vehicles crowded into the lot are uniformly black and evenly divided between expensive European sedans and gargantuan luxury SUVs. A few of these other vehicles come with drivers, middle-aged men in cheap dark suits who stand in a tight cluster behind a looming Escalade, smoking cigarettes and gazing into their smartphones.

The Bearded Man parks and exits the Buick, heading across the grass lawn toward the low-slung restaurant. Comprised mainly of a wraparound, screened-in porch, Andy's Crab House has a fine view of the bay, the gentle shoreline not thirty yards away. Everyone must already be here, the Bearded Man thinks as he draws nearer to the screen-door entrance. There's no overestimating the significance of today's meeting, as evidenced by the perfect attendance.

The Bearded Man grew up seventy miles as the crow flies from where he stands, and twice that far by automobile. Crisfield, Maryland, on the Chesapeake's eastern shore, is a crabbing town, and he is, appropriately, the son of a crabber. The crab man's life wasn't easy, the hours brutal when crabs were in season and the drinking even more brutal when they were not. The Bearded Man's father beat him close to every day of his life, until the age of thirteen, when the beatings stopped and were replaced with verbal abuse. The Bearded Man, in hindsight, preferred the physical stuff. His father, especially when inspired by the twin muses of vodka and beer, wielded a lancing wit.

Salvation came in the guise of the sweetly named Belle, a churlish hurricane that thrashed the Delmarva Peninsula on August 9, 1976, and overturned the thirty-two-foot boat the Bearded Man's father had taken out, against his own better sense and advice of all his peers, to run his traps despite storm warnings. Whether his father had been simply drunk, pressed by mounting unpaid bills, driven by dumb bullheadedness, or some combination of all three, the Bearded Man was liberated from his tormentor at the age of fifteen.

As he pauses before entering the crab shack, the Bearded Man glances at the flat light bouncing off the slate-gray bay that swallowed up his father. He can almost believe he loves the Chesapeake and that he yearns to return for a life here, to build the home he has designed to the last dormer in his imagination. His grandkids will visit him and his wife at this house. The Bearded Man imagines how he will teach them how to crab by hand, with string and raw chicken leg, and how to break apart their shells after steaming and extract all of the succulent meat from inside. He will grow old in a rocking chair on the porch of the fantasy house, watching the sunrise across the bay.

He smiles to himself and shakes his head. He wonders why he's been succumbing to these absurd musings of late. Sit on the porch and watch the sunrise? Good God, he'd rather blow his brains out. And crabs? He hasn't been able to stomach the meat of those vile, spindly creatures in decades. Memory of countless hours spent teasing out the meat from cracked-open, razor-sharp shells and stuffing it into plastic containers for the tourist trade are almost too painful to recall. Washington is where he belongs, he reminds himself. That's where he can be useful.

He enters the crab shack. Its proprietor, Andy, knew the Bearded Man's father back in the old days. His discretion is guaranteed. With the end of the season, the crab shack never opens before five p.m., if at all. The Bearded Man and the six men seated at one of the long picnic-style tables on the screened-in porch have the place to themselves.

He greets the proprietor with warm embrace. "Hello, Andy. How are you?"

Responding to the pleasantry seems a cross too heavy to bear. Andy pours his newest guest a cup of awful coffee, refills other cups, and then retreats back into his beloved kitchen, his sanctuary. As the Bearded Man takes a seat by pulling up a cheap plastic chair to the end of the picnic table, the others look at him expectantly. All of the men are white, except for one who is black. All of the men are in their fifties or sixties. One of the men is the senator interviewed by CNN outside his office, Taylor Cox. They are all conspirators.

After a moment's pause, he brings their meeting to order with a simple announcement. "Confirmation came in an hour ago. Positive identification was made. He's gone."

"Assessment?" one of the conspirators asks.

"This man was a significant piece. We have other assets inside, of course, but purely intelligence-gathering players. Nonoperational. Our action team is formulating a revised plan, should it come to that."

"What details do we have about his death? What do we know right now?" another conspirator demands.

"The police have only begun their investigation, but they believe a second person was in the vehicle and that a struggle occurred inside the vehicle prior to it going over the bridge." The Bearded Man pauses, troubled more than the others might guess by the following piece of information. "The operative's combat knife has not yet been recovered."

"How do we know he was even carrying his knife?" asks a third conspirator.

"The empty sheath was strapped to the man's ankle," he replies dryly.

"What about his cover?" the first conspirator asks with concern.

The Bearded Man pauses, barely hiding his impatience. "Scott Billings wasn't undercover."

"He actually *was* Secret Service?!"

They've covered these general aspects of the operation many times before, but the Bearded Man explains again, this time more tolerantly. "We have allies at every level of every agency in the federal government, and beyond," he assures them.

"Except for this mysterious 'second person' in the car apparently," Senator Cox reminds them, speaking up for the first time. It's clear his voice carries weight among the men gathered around the table.

"We're pursuing that inquiry independent of the police investigation, collecting incidental surveillance cams and eye witnesses. If and when this individual makes himself known, we'll be there to control the situation."

The senator nods in approval. "The president is golfing on a day Russia's Northern Fleet has moved its flagship Kirov-class battle cruiser twenty miles off the coast of Estonia. Time is clearly of essence," he adds, speaking gravely.

"Is playing golf after Labor Day now a treasonable offense, Senator?" a fourth conspirator asks.

"Is sitting at this table?" the first conspirator interjects before Cox can speak.

The senator clears his throat, an unsubtle signal to the others. If there is a leader of this cabal, it is Taylor Cox. "Argue all you want, but there is no question the country is in grave danger." He speaks by rote, as if giving a speech. "That's why we've assembled this group, is it not?"

The others voice their unanimous agreement. The Bearded Man gestures for order.

"Peter Hall was Monroe's fixer. No one else in the West Wing even knows how to make the toilets work on Capitol Hill. Hall was Monroe's guy. Now Hall is dead. Without him, he's just an icon with a noble profile. God willing, the need for additional measures has been alleviated. Time now to just watch and wait."

Throughout the meeting, the phone or electronic device belonging to each man has intermittently vibrated or alerted a new message. That these notifications have been unanimously ignored is testament to the meeting's importance. But then, all of a sudden, the devices of everyone at the table begin to simultaneously signal incoming calls, emails, or text messages. This barrage is too much to disregard, and within moments everyone at the table, including the Bearded Man, is peering into their respective electronic device.

---

WALKING PAST THE Secret Service agents stationed on West Executive Avenue, Asher and Hayley detect an emergency, all-hands-on-deck vibe as they approach the ground-floor entrance of the West Wing. Asher reacts warily. "All of this excitement isn't because a Secret Service agent dumped his BMW into the Potomac, is it?"

"I don't think so," Hayley surmises. They both retrieve their smartphones to see what's going on.

Entering the building, Hayley and Asher encounter a frenzied atmosphere. Staffers move up and down the corridor at a half jog, unmindful of anyone in their path. Asher and Hayley pause inside the doorway, avoiding the trampling herds. Karen Rey, her expression drawn tight with anxiety, strides past and pulls a double take on seeing her young staff members taking cover in the doorway. She pauses briefly to have a word with them.

"POTUS due in fifteen minutes! I need you up in Operations, now!" Rey starts to move off again, no time for discussion.

"What about the Japan trip?" Asher asks after her.

"Canceled," the senior aide informs them. Their blank expressions inform Rey they haven't heard the news. "Cyberattack on Estonia. Banks. Government. Infrastructure. All down."

Asher and Hayley try to process the revelation. It doesn't happen fast enough for Karen Rey.

"Get to your desks and stay the hell out of the way!" Rey turns and hurries up the corridor.

Hayley follows Asher to the stairs. The scene on the first floor is no less frantic. They take refuge in the windowless White House Operations support office, just off the Outer Oval Office. Asher immediately picks up the television remote and turns on CNN. The news channel carries a live feed of Marine One landing on the South Lawn, the white edifice of the Washington Monument in the background. Monroe immediately disembarks, greeted by a saluting Marine in dress uniform, and heads across the still-green grass, grim faced, toward the executive mansion.

"Never fails to freak me out, watching this business on TV when it's all going down just on the other side of that door," Asher observes.

Hayley doesn't respond but instead withdraws Scott's tablet from a tote bag.

Asher has taken note of this action. "What do you think you're going to do with that?"

"We're running out of time. I'm not sure, but the threat against the president may have just increased dramatically." Hayley can see she has failed to convince

Asher, so she adds, "We need to know if POTUS is a potential target."

Asher gestures at the tablet as if it's a two-headed venomous snake. "Turn that thing on and you're no longer the X factor. Go live and you're real-time and highly GPS-able."

"Is there a more secure and controlled location on the planet than the West Wing of the White House?"

"I saw those guys, Hayley," he says emphatically. "That was a hit team!"

"So you learned at Harvard what a 'hit team' looks like?"

"I've seen every Jason Bourne movie in existence. I can even tell them apart."

"That puts you ahead of all CIA case officers combined," she jokes, standing up and heading toward the door, tablet in hand.

"I'm serious, Hayley. Don't power up that machine."

"The ground floor is one, big fat Wi-Fi dead zone. There's zero cell coverage in CoS Support office."

"Intermittently a dead zone!" Asher corrects her.

In actuality, Hayley's plan is to try the Room That Is Not To Be Mentioned (RTINTBM), next to the Situation Room and on the same level as CoS. Impervious to wireless eavesdropping and swept twice a day for listening devices, the RTINTBM is a kind of secure phone booth, designed specifically for personal communications. Included in the security packet of everyone who receives West Wing credentials is a sworn oath never to disclose the existence of the Room That Is Not To Be Mentioned. Hayley isn't even certain what exactly is inside the room. Is there a table and chair, at least?

In the weeks Hayley has been in the West Wing, she has yet to see the RTINTBM in use. It's also usually locked and secure from unauthorized entry. If Hayley were to mention her plan A to Asher, then he really would have good reason for outrage. Better to lead with the slightly less dumb plan and not even mention unauthorized use of the RTINTBM. She puts her hand on the doorknob, turning to face Asher, who sits in his chair with arms defiantly folded across his chest.

"If Rey comes around, tell her I'm in the bathroom."

"You're forgetting she can go check for you in the women's lavatory," Asher reminds her. But Hayley ignores this comment and disappears out the door.

───────────────

THE ROW HOUSE on W Street is remarkable in its utter un-remarkableness. Sinatra had been able to rent it furnished and on a month-to-month basis. All of his guys are from out of town, and he prefers keeping them together and under close supervision. They're bored, sometimes spending whole days without leaving the generic, little clapboard row house, but they're also being well compensated for doing nothing. Operations really are like life while on active duty in a war zone, long stretches of doing nothing followed by short bursts of intense combat and hair-raising action. Except for the hit on Peter Hall, which went flawlessly, Sinatra and his team have done nothing but wait for orders.

While some of his men are sleeping, watching television, or playing video games (Bishop absolutely rules at *Counter-Strike*), Sinatra checks Redfin on his tablet for new listings. His agent has emailed him late the night before that an offer on the house on King James Place had been accepted by the seller, which distressed Sinatra more than was really appropriate. Scrolling through the listings in and around Alexandria, Sinatra recognizes his manic house search is just compensation for how much he misses his ex-wife. This kind of thinking often devolves into robust self-loathing, and when his cell phone vibrates, Sinatra welcomes the distraction from his own obsessions.

"Hello," is all he says in answering the phone. The caller ID tells him it's the Bearded Man calling.

The Bearded Man drives his Buick in moderate traffic on the northbound side of Interstate 395, exiting at Fourteenth Street. He can't explain the vague depression he has felt since leaving the meeting at Andy's Crab House but surmises the place brings back unpleasant memories of his father. Andy's dad had been a drinking pal of the old man. No doubt Andy bears some of the same emotional scars. The Bearded Man recalls gossip regarding Andy suggesting a stint in state prison. Remembering this lifts the cloud hanging over him. Life could've turned out a lot worse. It's important to count one's blessings. Always. Placing the

"The FBI is still pushing the Hall investigation." Sinatra pauses before revealing this next piece of news, but then plunges ahead. It's not like the Bearded Man won't find out anyway. "They found trace Xylocaine in the autopsy."

If there's a silver lining of this call with Sinatra, it's that it came after the meeting at Andy's Crab House.

"I'm working on a fix. Adjusting dosages," Sinatra promises him.

"A little late for that, don't you think?" The Bearded Man's cold fury comes over the phone line like an Arctic blast. "Anything else?"

"One more thing. We didn't find our man's computer at his house. We're thinking it was lost in the accident. If not, we'll have a location the second it's turned on." With a brave burst of optimism, Sinatra adds, "It might be just the lead we need to find the passenger."

"Who must suspect something amiss. Otherwise he or she would've gone to the police by now."

"How do we know the passenger isn't halfway to Alexandria, swept conveniently downstream?"

"That kind of blue-sky thinking will put your ass in a federal penitentiary, as well as mine. Let's assume we're dealing with a trained counter-operative and act accordingly."

Sinatra detests being patronized like this, but he holds his tongue. The soothing cigarette smoke expanding in his lungs helps him stay calm and keep his emotions in check. But he truly does hate this job.

"Roger that."

"Keep me informed." Saying that, the Bearded Man curtly disconnects the call as he's pulling up to the White House's southwest gate. The Secret Service uniformed officers manning the security kiosk there have checked him through numerous times in the past, but protocol remains the same. Everyone receives a thorough identification inspection upon each arrival. The Bearded Man has his federal ID and passport available on the seat next to him and passes it through the open window. Within moments he's driving up the White House driveway to an available parking space, exclusively for VIP visitors.

———

HAYLEY COMES DOWN the stairwell linking the first floor with the ground floor two steps at a time. Entering into the ground-floor corridor, she finds a much calmer scene than just thirty minutes before when first arriving for work. Aides and support staff must be huddled in their respective offices, allowing for Hayley's unobserved passage through the rabbit warren of corridors and small offices that define much of the entire West Wing. With this brief window of opportunity, Hayley scoots up the hallway, jogging past her old office space and the entrance to the Navy Mess, devoid of customers in this moment of international crisis, and stopping just short of the next corner leading to the always guarded Situation Room, at an unmarked door.

Of course, Hayley has never been inside the Room That Is Not To Be Mentioned and has no idea what lies within. But Becca, in her ongoing effort to pump up her own self-importance, made a point of telling Hayley all about the RTINTBM because secrets are a narcissist's currency of influence and manipulation. Spilling insider knowledge was the NYU grad's first play in a long game of gaining power and control. In this moment of need, Hayley appreciates Becca's obnoxious tendencies. She only can hope it pays off.

Fully expecting the secure room to be locked up tight, Hayley puts hand to doorknob and, to her amazement, is able to turn it. Looking up and down the empty corridor, she pushes the door open and steps inside, finding herself in a relatively small room, walls covered with signal-blocking Faraday. The Bearded Man, a Northrop Grumman SCS-100 integrated brief-case communication system opened before him on a desk, is startled to have a visitor. He glares at Hayley with irritation.

"Yes?" the Bearded Man demands with a tone of voice that would make most men cower in response.

Hayley doesn't express anything but sincere apology, masking her disappointment. "I'm sorry to disturb you, sir. Wrong door."

Wondering who the visitor might be, Hayley back-pedals out the door, closing it firmly behind her, and heads back up the corridor toward the CoS Support office. The man seemed more like college professor than DC insider. Whoever he is, he must have top security clearance to have free rein of the RTINTBM. Pressing forward with plan B, Hayley guesses correctly the former janitorial closet will be empty. Soon as she has pushed the door closed, she checks her Blackphone for Wi-Fi or cellular signal. There is nothing. The phone is a plastic brick.

Hayley places Scott's tablet on her old desk and sits. Closing her eyes, she recalls the morning a few days earlier in the Secret Service agent's kitchen and, from an upside-down perspective "sees" Scott tap a four-digit PIN on the tablet's screen, gaining access. Grateful for her eidetic memory, Hayley opens her eyes again and types the pass code into the computer. Access is granted. The interface displays Scott's tablet homepage, containing the usual jumble of folder icons and files.

"Shit!" Hayley exclaims, analyzing the tablet screen. The cellular icon in the top right corner of the desktop suggests the faintest of connections.

Working quickly, Hayley taps the settings icon and shuts off Wi-Fi and cellular connections on the device. She doesn't delude herself. If the bad guys were anticipating their fellow conspirator's device to be activated, they've made its location within only a few moments of triggering. The damage is done.

Hayley returns to the tablet's desktop screen and begins searching folders, quickly closing one and opening the next after quick review. She finds nothing of particular interest. Stored on the Secret Service agent's device is the exact sort of data one would expect to find. For a moment, Hayley is stumped. She stops searching and broods on it.

On a hunch, she goes to the tablet's display settings and deactivates the Reduce Transparency option. Returning to the desktop, Hayley sees that a previously hidden folder titled DAMOCLES has appeared there. She clicks on the folder, revealing dozens of files with random, alphanumeric names. Hayley hovers the cursor over one file, chosen unsystematically, and clicks it open. The file contains a log of Peter Hall's personal schedule for the week past, down to the minute, with specificity that could have only been created through intense surveillance.

Hayley closes the Hall file and randomly selects another file. It contains a detailed blueprint of Hall's residence on Kalorama Road. She closes that file and chooses another, revealing the doctor's report of the president's latest physical examination, a document that isn't supposed to be seen by anyone but Monroe or his wife.

Hayley pauses to reflect on the confirmation of her suspicions. Without a doubt, the president's life is at risk. She guesses the plan is for Monroe to suffer a "heart attack" similar to Hall's. Timing for the potential attack remains a complete unknown, however. Hayley's reverie is interrupted when the door is abruptly pushed open, revealing an unhappy Karen Rey on the other side. Hayley closes out the Monroe file without taking her eyes off the White House aide standing in the doorway.

"Ma'am?" Hayley asks innocently, aware she has no valid excuse for hiding in the CoS Support office.

"I've been looking all over for you!" Rey exclaims.

"Ms. Rey, I'm—"

But her supervisor cuts her off with a hand gesture. "No time for that. Follow me," she orders Hayley, disappearing from the open doorway.

Hayley powers down the tablet and sees on its dark display a profusion of her fingerprints. Alarmed, she swipes the tablet glass with her shirtsleeve and hurries to catch up with Rey in the corridor, halfway to the stairwell.

"Oval Office briefing in three minutes. POTUS asked specifically that you be on hand to support," Rey explains as she walks. "Don't ask me why," she adds with a cutting look back at Hayley.

———————

THE BEARDED MAN closes the briefcase communications unit. He's due in the Oval Office in seven and a half minutes. As CIA deputy director, Office of Intelligence Integration, one of James Odom's responsibilities is daily communication with the National Counterterrorism Center, back at McLean. Without a clear directive from the White House regarding ongoing election meddling by the Russians, among other active campaigns of international espionage, Odom has made it his personal mission to direct the NCTC to conduct clandestine countermeasures against Moscow. Several levels of the US intelligence community, above and below, support his efforts. Were they to become public or made known to the administration, Odom would be fired. With the CIA's powers under assault by a hostile executive branch, he doesn't see that termination as much worse a fate.

Odom exits the West Wing ground-floor-level secure room and hurries toward the stairwell. The Russians' cyberattack on Estonia demands immediate response from the West, and the CIA deputy director is determined to convince the president to lead that action, despite Monroe's bewildering hard-on for Russia. Charging up the stairs to the first floor, Odom reminds himself to maintain respect when speaking with Monroe. It will be no small task. Though the president's military record is to be commended, the man is completely ill-suited for the office he holds. His election is the strongest evidence for the ultimate failure of democracy and certainly puts the future of the United States as perennial superpower in doubt. As he strides into the Outer Oval Office and is greeted by the president's personal secretary, Odom can only worry about his children and grandchildren. Who knows what the United States of America will look like in twenty-five years?

The CIA deputy director is ushered into the Oval Office, where he finds one of the West Wing's dozens of aides as well as the young woman who had barged into the secure room downstairs, an intern, judging by her young age. The more senior aide fusses after him in the manner to which Odom is accustomed, far too obsequious for his taste.

The intern, in contrast, displays a cool nonchalance in his presence. As evidenced by their earlier, accidental meeting, the young woman does not fluster easily. Odom is impressed with the intern's poise. He knows from experience such a character trait cannot be learned. The CIA deputy director makes a mental note to follow up with inquiries regarding the young woman, after the current crisis has been resolved. The agency is always on the lookout for potential recruits, and this intern with the pleasant southern twang just might make an ideal candidate. Who knows? Maybe she could be a deputy director one day.

---

As HAYLEY FOLLOWS Rey up the stairwell, to the West Wing's first floor, she processes the evidence she has gleaned from Scott's tablet, fighting against the panic welling up within her. Everything she has experienced in life has conditioned her to control fear and compartmentalize it. Properly handled, fear can serve primarily as motivation, fuel for the fire necessary to act. To be brave.

Whom to trust is the question that looms large. Asher Danes is a helpful ally but hardly possesses the necessary skills or facilities to roll back a threat to the president. The Secret Service is clearly not the answer, not while it remains unclear whether Scott was an authentic member of that organization or covert operative. Perhaps the FBI is where she can turn. Agent Udall appears genuine in her investigation of Peter Hall's death, but Hayley decides it's too soon to reveal her findings. Doing so makes herself a target. Her best defense remains her anonymity. She has a hunch the conspiracy is currently in a holding pattern, waiting for further international developments or corresponding actions by the president. By the time Hayley follows Rey into the presently unoccupied Oval Office, she has soothed her anxieties and resumes being in full control of her emotions.

"Unnoticed and unseen. Listen only for a direct request from the president or myself," Rey instructs Hayley as she surveys the large room for anything amiss.

"Yes, ma'am," Hayley tells her. "Will do."

Rey sees the tablet in Hayley's hand. "Give me that thing!"

Rey abruptly snatches the tablet from Hayley just as the door leading from the Outer Oval Office opens. With no other options, given the obvious time crunch, Rey stashes the tablet on a side table and turns to greet James Odom as he strides into the room.

"Deputy Director Odom! Welcome to the White House, sir!" Rey exclaims to the CIA official, hating how loudly she has said it.

Odom makes no move to shake Rey's hand and barely acknowledges her even with a glance. Instead, he surveys the room, his eyes falling on Hayley standing to one side and recognizing the intern from the interruption downstairs just twenty minutes before. The West Wing really is an awfully cramped space, with people practically working on top of one another.

Hayley feels the deputy director's eyes on her but

simply nods, meeting his gaze with a neutral expression. She briefly entertains the notion of seeking his help in combating the conspiracy against the administration then dismisses the idea. How could she ever approach an individual of his stature even if he could be trusted? She might just as well shout it from the rooftops. It's ludicrous to even consider.

Rey, meanwhile, continues to flutter around Odom like a nervous bird in search of bread crumbs. "Some coffee, Mr. Odom? Or hot tea?"

Odom dismisses the offer with a shake of his bald head and points at the couch. "Here?" he gruffly asks Rey.

"Yes, sir. That's perfect."

As Odom sits, the door leading into the president's private study opens, and Monroe strides into the room like MacArthur storming Blue Beach at Luzon, trailed by Deputy Chief of Staff Kyle Rodgers, Vice President Vincent Landers, and the president's wonkish national security advisor, Albert Seretti.

Monroe's eyes find Hayley before anything else. "Ah, our intruder-defying intern."

Hayley responds with only the most demure smile. "Good morning, sir."

James Odom has risen again to his feet. He is respectful but not reverential. "Mr. President," he says as he extends his right hand to Monroe.

The president shakes Odom's hand. "Thanks for swinging by, Jim." There is no warmth in their greeting, only business.

The vice president lurches into the uncomfortable

pause in the conversation. "Can you believe these fucking Russians? The president tries to go over to Japan for alliance building in the Far East, and Fedor unleashes his cyber-monkey horde on the soft underbelly of NATO. The Second World War wasn't painful enough for these crazy bastards?"

No one in the room quite knows how to respond to the vice president's outburst. Monroe sits on a chair presidentially placed before the fireplace. Odom takes his seat again on the couch. The vice president and Al Seretti take seats on the opposite couch, while Kyle Rodgers joins Karen Rey standing against the far wall.

Monroe stretches his long legs before him, sliding down into the chair, hands thrust into his pockets. "In his own way, the vice president raises the essential question, Jim. What are we to make of this? Are we sure Moscow is behind it?"

Odom glances toward Hayley, hesitant to begin the briefing in front of someone clearly without even a whiff of security clearance. Monroe nods impatiently.

"How about a grilled cheese from the mess, Ms. Chill?" He looks to his guest. "Jim? Anything?"

"No, thank you, Mr. President."

With a nod from Karen Rey, Hayley turns and quickly exits the door leading into the Outer Oval Office.

"Okay. Let's hear it," Monroe tells Odom.

"In short, sir, it's the opinion of the Central Intelligence Agency and the intelligence units of our cooperating allies that these cyberattacks by Moscow are a debilitating precursor of a full-scale military invasion of Estonia." Odom pauses for a reaction from the president and gets none. Monroe stares at Odom without expression. The CIA deputy director continues. "This is the Russian playbook, sir. It represents the final trip wire, a test of US and NATO resolve to intervene on behalf of an otherwise defenseless member nation."

"But they've launched a cyberattack against Estonia before," National Security Advisor Seretti interjects.

More than ever, Vice President Landers is anxious to display his grasp of the issues. "In 2009, I think. Tiff over some old Soviet memorial the Estonians wanted to move."

But no one in this room is going to outperform James Odom. He addresses the vice president with a slightly patronizing tone. "It was 2007, Mr. Vice President. The Bronze Soldier of Tallinn." Odom turns back toward Monroe. "Last night's attack was fifty times broader in scope than 2007 and, at this hour, continues to intensify. Digitally speaking, sir, Estonia is operating this morning at a pre–Industrial Age capacity."

Monroe doesn't seem terribly concerned. "Could be worse. One ICBM from Yoshkar-Ola and the entire country would be eating dog food from a can."

Odom remains stone-faced, keeping his emotions in check. He knows he must choose wisely the perfect time in the meeting to go on the attack. He only gets one chance.

Seretti elbows his way into the discussion. "Isn't it problematic to attribute a DOS attack like this to a government entity? Could just as easily be a few nationalist-minded Estonian teenagers with mad love for Fedor Malkin."

Odom feels his phone vibrate with an incoming text. He discreetly checks the phone while Seretti continues with his pedantic blather. He sees a text from an unidentified caller, reading: *connected ten mins ago*.

The president sees Odom checking his phone and isn't pleased. "Something more important on your phone than a meeting with your president, Jim?"

Odom looks up from his phone on the couch next to him and gives his full attention to Monroe. "Our hackers are better than their hackers, despite what you hear. We know who did it, sir. Russia attacked Estonia. Sanctioned in full by Moscow."

As he finishes addressing Monroe, Odom feels the phone vibrate again. Fortunately, Seretti launches into another long-winded monologue, and the CIA man has the opportunity to glance quickly at his phone again.

The second text from the unidentified number, presumably Sinatra, reads *inside WH*.

While Seretti drones on, with the vice president occasionally interjecting in order to prove his usefulness, Odom looks up from his phone and glances around the room. With a jolt he sees that the only tablet in sight is Scott's, as clearly described to him by Sinatra, on the side table where Karen Rey had left it.

With an economy of movement, Odom taps a response to Sinatra's texts: *need diversion*.

The meeting with the president and the need to

convince him of taking action against Moscow has now taken a back seat to recovering the tablet. Odom cannot take his eyes off the device as Seretti and Vice President Landers get into a low-grade beef, each trying to impress Monroe with their incisive analysis. The president, for his part, doesn't seem interested. His decision regarding a response to the Russian aggression was undoubtedly made before the meeting even started. Odom waits for his moment.

─────────────

WHEN HAYLEY REACHES the "to go" window of the Navy Mess, Leon Washington, white hair matching his chef's uniform, is just about to cover a piping hot, beautifully grilled cheese sandwich, presented on a stainless-steel room-service-style tray. She is surprised to find the food already prepared, and the cook, in his early sixties, reads her expression.

"How else you think I keep this job goin' on twenty-five years now?" he asks her.

"Obviously by being very good at it, sir."

"Don't 'sir' me," he orders Hayley, extending a hand. "Leon Washington."

Hayley accepts his hand. "Hayley Chill, Leon. Good to meet you," she says, feeling his close scrutiny. "What?" she asks.

"You an intern? Haven't seen you around down here before."

"Yes. I'm in White House Operations. Discharged almost two years ago."

"Veteran? Yeah, I thought so. You smell like army."

"I hope that's a good thing."

"Oh, yes, it is. I'm a retired navy man myself. Now I'm here. Guess you could say I've been military all my life."

Hayley nods with sympathetic understanding. Leon continues to study her.

"If anybody asked for my opinion round here, I'd tell 'em to bring on nothing but vets. White House could use more adults."

"You couldn't get any more military than POTUS, Leon."

"Brass hat," the chef says in response, using the army slang for colonels and generals. He doesn't say it nicely.

Hayley declines to comment. Leon smiles broadly, instantly won over by the intern. "Yeah, it's probably best you not say a damn thing." He produces a can of Diet Coke and a clean glass from under the counter and places them on the tray. "You best get going or we'll both be out of a job. The president likes his cheese sandwich hot!"

Hayley slides the covered service tray off the aluminum counter top and takes it in hand. "It was nice meeting you, Leon. See you around."

Leon winks at her. "You know it, doll. So long now."

---

A BLACK SUV with tinted windows stops on L Street, just behind the Capitol Hilton and only a few blocks from the White House. Traffic is light. There is no one on the sidewalks. The location has been scouted previously and selected as one of several swap-out sites, devoid of incidental surveillance video cameras on the surrounding buildings. It's becoming increasingly difficult to find such CCTV-free sites in the District of Columbia, which is threatening to join London and Beijing as the most spied-upon cities in the world. At last count, the UK's capital had 420,000 CCTV cameras in the city's center.

Martin and Bishop emerge from the rear passenger doors of the SUV, which immediately pulls away and disappears down the street. The two mercenaries approach a white delivery van parked at the curb. Both carry large black duffel bags.

Martin unlocks the vehicle's doors with a remote. They load the duffel bags into the rear of the van and head to the front. Martin climbs in behind the wheel as Bishop enters on the other side. Within moments, the delivery van pulls away from the curb, executes a U-turn, and speeds away in the opposite direction from where the SUV had gone.

# 5

★ ☆ ★ ★

## SHELTER IN PLACE

H ayley reenters the Oval Office, carrying the take-out tray from the Navy Mess. The smell of the grilled cheese instantaneously fills the room. Richard Monroe breathes in the scent, inciting Proustian memories of his youth and his mother. His was nearly an idyllic childhood, spent mostly on military bases all over the US and the world. His father had been career army, and one of Monroe's fondest memories is sitting down to the rare lunch in which his dad was home from his duties on base. His mother would make the most wonderful sandwich of rye bread; grated Jarlsberg cheese; and hot, yellow horseradish mustard, preferably Zakycoh, a Russian concoction his father secured from God knows where. One might think the president of the United States could get a decent horseradish mustard in the Navy Mess, but apparently, this has been too much to expect. Nevertheless, the boys down on the ground floor have been putting together a pretty good sandwich with the materials at hand.

"Have you ever smelled anything so good in your entire life?" Monroe exclaims as Hayley places the tray on the coffee table in front of the president. Eschewing the glass, he snatches the can of Diet Coke, which Hayley had carefully opened just prior to entering the Oval Office, and takes a long, satisfying draw of its artificially sweetened contents.

As Hayley turns to exit the room again, Rey anxiously hurries to place a coaster on the coffee table next to the service tray where Monroe has placed the Diet Coke. The president regards the coaster with disdain.

"West Virginia's not coaster country, is it, Ms. Chill?"

Hayley pauses halfway to the door. "Not typically, sir."

"Drink straight from the can back home. Leave a ring on the coffee table if that's your preference."

"Coffee table, sir?"

Monroe laughs boisterously at Hayley's mild joke. Odom twists around in his seat on the couch and regards the intern with even more interest than he had before. There is no doubt in his mind this remarkable young woman is a force to be reckoned with.

---

THE INTERSECTION OF Seventeenth Street and Pennsylvania Avenue is busy, with a US post office occupying the southwest corner and the northwest corner of the White House grounds directly across the street. The sidewalks are wide and traffic lanes four across on Pennsylvania before being forced either north or south with the avenue closed to vehicular traffic east of Seventeenth Street. Police from five different departments are on patrol at any given time. Pedestrians in the area, mostly federal employees from the various buildings in the immediate vicinity, feel safe in these confines. About the worst thing that can happen around here are protestors from Lafayette Square invading the restrooms at the local Peet's Coffee shop.

Martin steers the delivery van east on Pennsylvania, approaching Seventeenth Street. Bishop, sitting shotgun, has retrieved an HK MP7 submachine gun from a backpack. Both men pull on lightweight SWAT balaclava tactical face masks as Martin speeds toward the intersection. Bishop presses a button on the vehicle's low-grade radio, tuning in a classic rock FM radio station. The Beach Boys' "I Get Around" bounces off the bare steel of the van's cab.

It's 11:47 a.m. The surrounding buildings haven't yet disgorged their occupants for lunchtime, and therefore the sidewalks are relatively empty. There isn't a cloud in the sky. Temperatures have risen to the low fifties. A US Park Police patrol car is parked, engine off, just across Seventeenth Street, in the pedestrians-only portion of Pennsylvania Avenue to the north of the White House complex. Inside the patrol car, two Park Police officers are in the middle of a spirited discussion regarding the relative merits of Amy Schumer's latest movie.

The white delivery van, approaching at high speed from the west, blows the red light at Seventeenth Street, only to slam to a stop at dead center of the intersection. Bishop leaps out of the vehicle and, shielded from view of the patrol car across the intersection, fires a long and steady burst into the air, empty brass shells flying in a graceful arc to the pavement. Without muzzle suppressor, the weapon's report echoes across the urban canyon, an unmistakable racketing of automatic gunfire. Traffic screeches to a stop in every direction. A young woman who has just exited the post office having delivered a package for her boss at Office of the US Trade Representative screams horror movie–style. The US Park Police officers in their patrol car on Pennsylvania Avenue jump-start their response after a brief delay from shock with the driver hitting the ignition while his partner is calling on the radio for backup.

Bishop walks to the front of the delivery van. About eleven seconds have transpired since the initial outburst of gunfire, and four seconds since ceasing. He lowers the machine gun and takes aim on the patrol car, slightly more than two hundred feet distant, and pulls the trigger. High-velocity, armor-piercing, copper-alloy-jacketed lead-core Fiocchi rounds obliterate the patrol car's grill and shred its front tires. Both cops drop below the dash, with the one officer shouting his panicked report into the radio. After approximately twenty-two seconds outside the delivery van, Bishop backtracks and reenters the vehicle. Martin takes his foot off the brake and stands on the accelerator, rear wheels smoking as the vehicle fishtails out of the intersection, heading south on Seventeenth Street. For three blocks around, pedestrians lie prone on the ground or cower in doorways. Traffic is stopped, haphazardly, as if in a post-apocalyptic tableau.

---

EVERYONE PRESENT IN the Oval Office, including Hayley, freezes at the sound of the close-in gunfire. There is a moment of silence and utter stillness, then both doors burst open and Secret Service agents flood into the room. In their rush, the protective detail shoves Hayley roughly aside, as well as Kyle Rodgers and Karen Rey, converging on the president who has half risen out of his chair. James Odom and Seretti are held down in their seats on the couch by agents as four other Secret Service men take both Landers and Monroe by the arms and hustle them toward the door leading to the president's private study. Within ten seconds of the agents barging into the Oval Office, Monroe and his vice president have been whisked away to only the Secret Service knows where.

Kyle Rodgers picks himself off the floor, where he had been pushed. For a moment, everyone in the room remains in place, unsure of what to do next or what had just happened. More Secret Service agents appear in the doorway leading into the Outer Oval Office.

"Shelter in Place order is in effect. Everyone out! Now!"

Despite the emergency, Al Seretti is his usual combative self. A scrappy shortstop on the University of Oklahoma baseball team and an occasional abuser of steroids, his temper is hair-trigger. "If we're sheltering in place, aren't we supposed to stay in place?!"

"Oval is restricted, sir," the Secret Service agent responds with dry sarcasm and little patience. He moves deeper into the room to ensure that all present have evacuated. Standing near the northwest door leading into the Outer Oval Office, Hayley turns to retrieve Scott's tablet from the side table across the room. Her way is blocked by the six-foot-four Secret Service agent.

"Out! Let's go!" he shouts into Hayley's face. He leaves no room for discussion, pushing Hayley toward the door.

After Hayley, Karen Rey, and Kyle Rodgers have been ushered out of the room, the agents focus on the remaining occupants. A rattled Albert Seretti goes meekly enough, but James Odom brusquely shakes off an agent's guiding hand. "That would be unnecessary," he tells the agent with a lacerating tone. Odom steps around the temporarily immobilized Secret Service agent and retrieves Scott's computer from the side table. Only then does the CIA deputy director allow himself to be shown to the door.

---

THE WHITE DELIVERY van hurtles south on Seventeenth Street, weaving through stopped traffic and blowing through intersections as police sirens wail in the distance. Both operators inside the van keep their masks on as Bishop stows the machine gun in one of the duffel bags. Martin steers the van right, onto New York Avenue, getting snarled in stopped traffic there briefly, before regaining speed again as New York transitions to E Street. By the time the van turns right on Twentieth Street, both Martin and Bishop have removed their face masks, though each keep hospital gloves on their hands. Midway between F and E Streets, Martin pulls over to the curb, parking behind a familiar black SUV.

Their location is another quiet block, chosen for the fact there are absolutely no CCTV surveillance cameras for two blocks in every direction. Martin and Bishop exit the van and walk up to either side of the SUV, which they enter. The SUV immediately lunges away from the curb and continues north on Twentieth Street. A moment later, smoke begins to pour out of the open windows of the delivery van. Within ninety seconds, the entire vehicle is engulfed in flames. It will take more than seven minutes for a DCFD fire engine to arrive on scene and extinguish the vehicle fire, leaving only a charred hulk of its chassis.

In the weeks that follow, Metro and Park Police departments will investigate the mysterious and violent incident at the intersection of Seventeenth Street and Pennsylvania Avenue. The perpetrators will never be identified, much less charged. Motivation for the shooting, which left no injuries, is assumed by FBI and MPD investigators to be a diversion for another

the Secret Service or Karen Rey. Eliciting the aid of the president's personal secretary is probably the best course of action. Madison Smith has been with Monroe since the president retired from the military. In her late fifties, Madison is also from the South. Recognizing the benefits of such an ally within the hothouse atmosphere of the West Wing, Hayley has done nothing to discourage the older woman's offer of casual friendship. She has no doubt Madison will facilitate recovery of the wayward tablet from the Oval Office.

Moments after coming up with this plan to retrieve the tablet, Hayley catches sight of the device nestled under the arm of the visiting CIA deputy director, the telltale Rolling Stones sticker clear identification enough. Odom was his name, right? Hayley masks her shocked reaction, aware the man is actually studying her at this very second, as if reading her mind and taunting her with his possession of the incriminating device. Hayley pretends to look past the powerful CIA official, her wildly spinning thoughts seeking traction. What is James Odom doing with the tablet? Why is he staring at her? Is the CIA involved in the conspiracy? Do they know she is aware of the plot, however dimly? Hayley wishes Asher were there and able to talk over all of these startling developments.

---

ODOM IS AMONG the last to join the herd of West Wing staffers in the Cabinet Room, finding a place to stand under John Singer Sargent's monumental portrait of

Theodore Roosevelt at the north end of the room. The atmosphere is not unlike the disaster drills he remembers from his grade-school years. It's all such a ridiculous waste of time. The fact that he is responsible for orchestrating gunplay that prompted the shelter in place is no comfort. Between his everyday duties as deputy director overseeing the Office of Intelligence Integration, the emerging crisis in Estonia, and managing a clandestine Operation Damocles, Odom finds even his herculean time-management skills being put to an extreme test. He is due back at Langley in twenty minutes and highly regrets being thwarted in his plan to lock horns with Monroe in the debate over US policy regarding relations with Moscow. Recovering the agent's tablet, however, goes a long way toward mitigating that disappointment.

Gripping the SCS-100 briefcase communication system in one hand and cradling the retrieved tablet in the other, Odom considers the next sixty minutes of his day. Once the shelter in place ends, he will proceed directly to his vehicle parked less than five hundred feet from where he presently stands and text Sinatra from there. They will have to be careful in the transfer of the tablet, but Odom understands the operative has preselected drop sites throughout the city and can communicate to him a location for the closest one. Then it's off to Langley and the daily briefing at the National Counterterrorism Center. He plans to order a response in kind to the Russians' cyberattack, with or without Monroe's permission. The NSA has the appropriate tactical units necessary for untraceable offensive cyber actions. He will contact his liaisons at Fort Meade from the car. There is no time to waste. Moscow will up-phase their actions against Estonia within hours minus robust response. If this isn't war, James Odom doesn't know what is. For only a brief moment, he feels the fatigue of an old man who has run too many races. Odom wonders if willpower is a kind of psychology muscle that can atrophy with age.

As he's musing like this, Odom's gaze falls on the young female intern from the Oval Office. Without a doubt, the president favors the girl. Knowing as much as Odom does about Monroe, there is no question the president's attention is anything but platonic. Nor is it unwarranted. The young woman is unmistakably intel-ligent, possessing rare poise for a person her age. Again Odom feels the long-forgotten urge to recruit, a skill he hasn't employed since his days long ago in the field. Assuming he has a few more wasted minutes cooped up in the Cabinet Room, the CIA deputy director decides to act on his impulses. Leaving his position under the Roosevelt portrait and threading his way through the restless throng inside the room, Odom makes his way toward the intern standing with others at the opposite end of the room.

---

HAYLEY SEES THE CIA deputy director making his way across the room, clearly with the intention to interact with her. Odom had been staring at her for the last two minutes. Hayley cannot imagine what he wants to say to her and braces for anything, including outright accusation. With some relief, Hayley sees Odom smile slightly as he draws nearer to where she stands.

"Never a dull moment, right?" He gestures at the windows and French doors looking out on the Rose Garden. "Like sheltering in a veritable fishbowl."

"Yes, sir. Hope everyone is okay out there." Hayley keeps her breathing as normal and steady as possible, aware of her own heartbeat racing.

"The president seems to have a real affection for you. I can see why." He extends a hand. "James Odom."

Hayley takes his hand in hers and shakes. "Thank you, sir. Hayley Chill. Sorry about walking in on you downstairs. I was confused by the doors looking all the same." She pulls off a fairly admirable job of appearing helpless.

"Perfectly understandable. Place is a rat's maze, in more ways than one, right?" He says this with a conspiratorial grin, seeking connection necessary for recruitment.

"Yes, sir, I suppose some might think so." Hayley stops there, denying Odom her collaboration. Her eyes briefly glance toward the tablet under his arm but not long enough to arouse suspicion. Clearly Odom expects more from her. "I'm an intern in Operations," she adds helpfully.

"You look too old for college, Ms. Chill."

"Discharged about a year ago, sir."

Odom nods. Of course! She's ex-military. Why hadn't he assumed as much in the first place.

"Happy here?" he asks, zeroing in.

"Very grateful to be serving my country, sir, in any capacity," she answers, deflecting his inquiry with a canned line.

Odom nods again. Without even trying, this young woman is a stone-cold pro.

"After you complete your internship here, come see me at Langley." He produces his business card and hands it to Hayley. "Our country suffers from a dire shortage of adults."

A Secret Service agent pokes his head in the doorway that leads out into the corridor. "All clear, folks. You're free to move about the complex."

Odom winks at Hayley. "We live to fight another day."

Before she can respond, the CIA deputy director exits the door leading out into the Rose Garden and takes Scott Billings's tablet with him.

Hayley looks down at the card Odom had given her, which is stunningly spare.

## JAMES ODOM
202-589-1212

She places the business card in her jacket pocket with conflicting emotions. Scott's computer and all of its resident data are lost to her. Contained in its storage mediums is indisputable proof of a conspiracy to attack the administration, if not POTUS himself. Nevertheless, Hayley has gained two irrefutable facts with its loss. First, the CIA deputy director has revealed himself to be party to the conspiracy, if not its leader. Secondly, Odom's friendliness toward her suggests the conspirators have no idea Hayley suspects anything. She is an important factor in the game, and none of the other players know it.

The intern follows the others through the door, into the first-floor corridor. Looking over her shoulder, she sees two Secret Service agents walk past on the West Colonnade outside the Cabinet Room doors, carrying P90 submachine guns but chatting casually. It strikes Hayley the agents carry themselves with a swagger, like they own the place.

---

THE METROPOLITAN POLICE Department boat, one of two and more typically used as a sobriety checkpoint for inebriated recreational boaters, remains anchored just south of the Key Bridge. Police divers occasionally emerge from the depths with debris they've gathered from the river bottom. Uniformed officers in the boat collect the mud-covered items from the men in the water and lay them on tarps spread out on the deck. Tires, baby carriages, fishing rods, dozens of beer bottles, and an artificial leg, among other items, have been collected. Their relation to Scott Billings and the accident remain unsubstantiated. Nevertheless, the divers make repeated trips to the river's bottom with their collection sacks.

Asher and Hayley watch the police boat and divers at work from the balcony of his condo. It is not quite five p.m. Because of the unexplained gunfire and ongoing investigation, all but the most essential West Wing staffers were sent home early. The sun is setting to the west. Asher has a vodka and tonic in hand. Hayley holds a glass of water.

"It's like they know your backpack's there and just haven't found it yet," Asher worries aloud.

"They don't know it's there. They're just being thorough," she responds, earning a dubious look from Asher. Hayley adds, "People in the military and law enforcement, they're thorough."

"I get the distinct feeling I'm being patronized."

"That's because you are being patronized."

"A White House intern turns on a computer, and half the government shuts down," Asher reminds her.

"And confirms POTUS is an active target in a conspiracy headed up by a CIA deputy director." She pauses as another thought occurs to her. "Hell, I wouldn't be surprised if Odom didn't orchestrate the shelter in place."

Asher involuntarily howls. "Oh, then what's to worry?" His sarcasm doesn't seem to affect her in the least. "Hayley, you were one of six people in the room where Odom found the tablet. Your fingerprints are all over that thing! As a recruit, yours have to be in the database."

"Which is why I wiped it down." Hayley dismisses his concerns with a gesture. "Three dozen different people in the West Wing could've left that tablet in the Oval, including Scott."

"Why are you doing this? And spare me all that 'duly elected' business. You're an intern, and I'm barely a White House aide. What's so terribly wrong watching all of this play out from the sidelines?"

"James Odom doesn't get to decide who stays president. And if it doesn't piss you off he thinks he can, then we don't have a whole lot more to talk about."

Hayley turns and exits the balcony, heading back into the condo. Is she angry with him? Asher can't say for sure. He pauses a moment to stare back out over the river and the police boat, bobbing on the flowing Potomac, then turns and reenters the condo.

"Hayley . . . ," Asher calls after her. But Hayley keeps walking toward the entry door. In fact, she is angry. Asher's diffident attitude is so contrary to her personality it gets under her skin. If Asher can't see the imperative to act, then why waste any more time on him?

"Goddammit, Hayley—stop!" Asher calls out after her. She stops and turns toward him.

---

CLYDE'S OF GEORGETOWN is exactly what you'd expect of an insider hangout without pretensions. Brick walls, framed lithographs and a long pine-wood-topped bar with Tiffany lampshades overhead, the vibe is Everyone Knows Your Name at a price. Whether well-heeled lobbyist impressing a would-be client that he or she is regular people who can still enjoy the modest eighteen-dollar hamburger or agency staffer celebrating a birthday with office mates, Clyde's has been packing them in seemingly since the dawn of time, and this evening is no different.

Thirty minutes after Hayley had nearly walked out in a huff, Asher disconnected a call and turned to her sitting on the couch. "He'll meet us for drinks after work."

"You're sure it's safe to talk to him? He can be trusted?" Keeping her secret to themselves has been keeping them alive.

"Homer is a family friend and a Pulitzer Prize–winning journalist. If we can't trust him, then we might as well quit and kiss democracy goodbye," Asher had assured her.

Hayley wasn't convinced, but what choice did they really have? If she'd learned anything today, they potentially have the entire deep state arrayed against them in a conspiracy to destroy Monroe's administration. Powerful allies are a necessity. Her gut was in a knot. It'd been hours since Hayley had had a bite to eat. Eight hours of uninterrupted sleep seemed like an impossible luxury. Without telling Asher, she had wondered if she ought not arm herself. Buying an unregistered weapon in Washington is as easy as purchasing a new pair of shoes. In infantry training, Hayley scored thirty-nine out of forty targets and earned an expert badge. Skills like these are hardly superfluous given the highly critical situation.

Now, just another hour later, Asher, Hayley, and Homer Stephens are crowded into a leather-upholstered booth built more comfortably for two. The bar area is crowded with Washington worker bees in suits and business skirts, blowing off steam after another day pushing forward the nation's business. Hayley and Asher had arrived earlier and had finally eaten. Now their guest enjoys an after-dinner Scotch whisky.

Homer Stephens is a middle-aged man who dresses with Tom Wolfe panache, unsurprisingly, since the novelist was Homer's all-time favorite. With that more famous writer, Homer shares a disinclination for the traditional values of journalistic objectivity. He doesn't shrink from injecting himself into any reportage, digging down deep into a subject and his own psychology with equal enthusiasm. These sometimes cartoonish efforts have been lampooned by his journalistic peers, but when he was younger and perhaps more rigorous in originality, Homer secured his Pulitzer in 1985 with a feature series on the Scientology movement run by the *Post*. Despite his diminished stature today, Homer is well-informed if not completely respected. To this day, he serves a vital function in town. His connections to powerful figures, past and present, are multitudinous. Information in Washington is a commodity, and Homer Stephens is the Wall Street of its transactional exchange.

Homer's expression is best described as dubious as he sits across from Hayley and Asher crammed into their side of the shallow booth.

"Peter Hall suffered two heart attacks within the last seven years. A third, fatal attack is hardly a bolt out of the blue."

"Sir, the FBI found trace Xylocaine in the autopsy," Hayley reminds Homer, respectful but persistent.

"Do you have any idea how many people in this town indulge with recreational opioids and narcotics on a routine basis?" he counters.

Hayley doesn't hide her frustration with the journalist's dismissive, condescending attitude. "How many of those routine drug users are the White House chief of staff?"

Asher kicks Hayley under the table. Homer levels only a baleful look. She dials it down. "Sir, Scott Billings tried to kill me because of what I'm doing here tonight, raising the alarm." She pauses for emphasis. "I saw what I saw on his computer."

"And yet, similarly to the disappearing boot print, neither Mr. Billings nor his tablet are available for inspection." Homer wears his disapproving frown like a ball gown. See me. Hear me. I am prettier than you. "I'm sorry, but without actual proof, there's not much here that rises to the level of 'story.' It's really all quite fantastical."

Asher finally jumps into the fray, with beseeching expression. "Homer—"

Stephens cuts him off with the stern look and outstretched palm of a traffic cop.

"Dear boy, your father spent an awful lot of money to get you a job in the West Wing. I doubt highly a bit part in *Three Days of the Condor* was what he had in mind for you there."

But Hayley won't be dissuaded. "Why did James

Odom take that computer, sir? I saw it under his arm with my own eyes. Is the Central Intelligence Agency that hard up with their budget that a deputy director needs to steal computer equipment?"

The journalist has heard enough, gesturing with his index finger as if to a panhandler. Hayley's persistence grates on his nerves, her intensity an affront to his taste for frivolity and informed wit. He is determined to humiliate her in front of Asher, for whose welfare Homer is now concerned.

"What's the point?" he asks Hayley sharply. "Do you even know why the CIA's deputy director of Intelligence Integration would be involved in a plot to kill the White House chief of staff and, if I'm understanding you correctly, the president of the United States? Before you start lobbing accusations, you'd best understand the motivations."

Hayley reacts with some surprise, startled by such a simplistic and obvious question. "James Odom and others in the government don't agree with the president's policies and agenda. They think he's selling out the country to the Russians."

Homer makes a face like he just drank spoiled milk, with a denigrating chuckle as chaser. "How little you understand Washington massively undercuts your credibility, darling."

Hayley is genuinely insulted, but not completely certain that the journalist is wrong in his assessment of her. "Sir?"

Homer leans closer across the table, toward Asher

and Hayley, speaking in an undertone. "Let's say you're one hundred percent correct. James Odom and all of his deep state brethren are in a conspiracy to take down the Monroe administration, even if that means assassinating the president himself. All horrifically true. Why would they do such a thing? Over contrary policies and agenda? That's a hoot! Power, my dear, is the currency in this town, not policy. Our heroic warrior/president has been undercutting the intelligence community with quiet, relentless consistency. At this rate, in six more years of a Monroe presidency, the CIA, NSA, House and Senate intelligence committees will have all the power in this town of a 30-watt lightbulb. If there's any reason to kill that bombastic buffoon, it's that. Forget about Russia."

Hayley is uncharacteristically quiet. Homer's effort to make her appear ignorant in front of Asher is a success. With some embarrassment, she must concede the journalist's point. "Yes, I see what you mean."

Homer continues, falling in love not for the first time with the sound of his own pontificating. "Presidents come and go. The men and women who run federal agencies and departments, they survive in one capacity or another from one administration to the next, clinging to the same position sometimes for decades, accumulating power and influence like casino chips. Threaten to claw back some of that power, and you've got a war on your hands."

But Asher is confused by the journalist's frank assessment of the infamous deep state. "And so, judging by what you've said, maybe these people really are gunning for Monroe."

"Maybe, maybe not. Who knows? But who's to stop them if they are? The deep state *is* the US government." Homer sits back in his seat and takes a self-satisfied sip of his twenty-year-old bourbon. "Why would James Odom take a tablet from a side table in the Oval Office? Haven't the foggiest. Perhaps we should call him and just ask. I've spoken to Jim off the record a few times in the past."

Hayley reacts with alarm. "You can't do that, sir. You mustn't do that!"

Homer raises his arms in mock surrender. "Fine. I won't call him. But I'll need much more from you to take a run at this. Just being honest." He retrieves his wallet, withdraws three twenties, and throws them on the table. Addressing Asher directly, "Stay in touch, my boy. You have an excellent mind and enviable prospects. Just don't be careless with that future."

He stands up out of his seat at the booth, briefly letting his gaze fall on Hayley. "Pleasure, Ms. Chill." Without further ceremony, the journalist strides out of the neighborhood restaurant with the gait and bombast of a Roman emperor.

Asher orders more drinks after Homer has left. The journalist's sixty dollars will easily pay for a second round, especially given Hayley's tonic and lime. She processes all of what Homer has said and attempts to formulate their next move. For his part, Asher is a bit weary of the business. He hopes Homer doesn't contact his father. Life is good at 3303 Water Street. If the money spigot is turned off, God knows what Asher would do. Get a *real* job? "Are you still close to your family?" he asks Hayley, hoping to take her mind off plots and assassinations. "What about your mom?"

A distracted Hayley takes a drink of her tonic and lime, eyes on Asher's straight Patrón Reposado over ice. Up until her enlistment, she had been an enthusiastic and joyful drinker. You don't get elected prom queen by being abstinent, at least not in Lincoln County, West Virginia. Hayley reflects on those days that seem like a different lifetime ago. "My mother died while I was stationed at Fort Hood. Base commander let me attend the funeral on a three-day bereavement leave. It was the first and last time I returned home since joining up. I felt no connection there anymore. Had no idea what to say to old friends, my brothers and sisters. It was all very awkward. Most of my friends never escaped."

"God, I can't even imagine. My childhood and family life was embarrassingly normal and happy."

"You were never rejected . . . ?" Hayley awkwardly fails to finish the question.

"Because I'm gay? God, no! You want rejection in Greenwich, Connecticut? Bring a quarter pounder with cheese to a picnic with your friends."

"That's Thanksgiving dinner where I come from," Hayley remarks dryly. A void has yawned open within her. Her past and its misery-infused incidents suddenly loom large, rising up from the darker recesses in her consciousness where she had relegated them.

What she had said was no joke. When Hayley was ten years old, her mother did serve them McDonald's for Thanksgiving dinner.

Oblivious to the shift in Hayley's mood, Asher continues with his cheerful recitation. "Gay or not, I've always been the good son, keeping it between the white lines. A regular gay Eagle Scout. I still send my mother a Valentine's Day card every year! Embarrassing, I know, but I love my mom and dad."

"No shame in having good parents, Asher. You're lucky," she tells him with flat expression. She abruptly drains her glass, signaling a desire to leave.

"What's wrong?" Asher asks. Hayley walks off without answering.

Asher catches up with her on the sidewalk out front. "Wait. I'm confused. Did I say something to offend you?"

Hayley burns with a renewed fire to act. Her frustration is obvious. "Your journalist friend wasn't much help," she tells Asher accusingly.

"I'm sorry. What did you expect, a story above the fold in the *Washington Post*? Who's going to play you in the movie, Hayley? Amy Adams?"

"Fuck you, Asher."

He is understandably perplexed by Hayley's attitude. "What did I do but try to help?!"

"Help better." She starts to turn away but then stops to face Asher again. "Must be nice. Loving parents? Nice. Multimillion-dollar condo on the Potomac? Super! Sexy job in the White House. Why not? Hell, you're even gay with privilege and entitlement. Thing is, rich people don't even know how to be angry. They just get *pissy*."

Asher stares at Hayley in disbelief. "You're. Not. Being. Fair."

Hayley dismisses him with a flip of her hand. "I don't have time for fair." She turns and stalks off.

Within thirty seconds of leaving Asher in front of Clyde's, Hayley regrets losing patience. Asher was an easy target and Hayley knows it. By the time she has reversed course, rounded the corner again, and returned to the restaurant entrance, her friend and coworker is gone. She considers messaging him but decides a texted apology is lame. Better to call Asher when she gets home. If he refuses to accept her apology, then Hayley will be once again on her own. It won't be the first time.

She starts walking east, passing the usual collection of higher-end retail franchises that have all but erased the neighborhood's original character, heading toward Wisconsin to catch the bus there. Glancing over her shoulder, she clocks a late-model blue Taurus that seems to be keeping pace with her. She feels her heart rate accelerate slightly and focuses on remaining calm and prepared. With normal traffic on M Street, the Taurus should pass her quickly. Hayley faces forward again and maintains a steady pace for ten seconds, then looks over her left shoulder again. She sees the Taurus has pulled over to the curb and parked. Her suspicions were nothing more than paranoia. No one is following her.

A stop for the Arlington-bound 38B Metrobus is only a half block away. Hayley crosses the street and stands at the curb just short of the intersection with Wisconsin Avenue. After only a few moments, she sees the blue Taurus leave its parking place across the street and cruise past at far too deliberate a pace for her comfort. In the evening's gloom, Hayley cannot make out any defining features of the two individuals inside the vehicle. The Taurus turns right at Wisconsin and drives out of her view.

Later, when Hayley steps off the bus on Wilson Boulevard at Oak Street in Rosslyn, she looks up and down the block for the Taurus and sees nothing. The streets are quiet. With quickened pace and alert, Hayley walks up Oak toward her building three blocks north. In addition to marksmanship, her army training included hand-to-hand combat skills. But Hayley must concede that two armed men, with the element of surprise and cover of night, could easily abduct her or worse. As she approaches the intersection of Key Boulevard and Ode Street, her footsteps echo up and down the silent, residential block. The houses are buttoned up tight for the night. Will her screams be heard through those closed windows? But after a minute of more walking, there is still no sign of the Taurus. Hayley silently upbraids herself for succumbing so readily to useless fears.

Breathing easily for the first time since leaving Clyde's and her heart rate slowing to a more normal speed, Hayley reminds herself as she turns right on Ode to call Asher. Her apartment building is the second one north from Key Boulevard and, with most lights inside ablaze, seems cheery and inviting. Glancing to her left, Hayley sees the blue Taurus parked directly across the street, with the lights off and its occupants plainly visible inside.

Hayley doesn't react in the least. She hasn't changed her pace in any way since first noticing the vehicle tailing her. She continues to the walkway leading to her building entrance and turns right, approaching the entry door with her keys already in hand. She artfully adopts the mien of the typical commuter, home from work and happy hour drinks. Hayley reaches the door to the building and enters. Once inside the entry vestibule, she senses the Taurus passing by out front and just manages to catch sight of its taillights. Peering out the closed entry door, Hayley sees the Taurus turn left at Key Boulevard, heading east. Letting out a long breath she had held since walking up to the front door, Hayley leans her back against the vestibule wall and drops her chin to her chest. The thought occurs to her she might be in wildly over her head.

———————

HOMER STEPHENS, WEARING his favorite silk robe and hedonistically enjoying a late-night second glass of his favorite bourbon, watches CNN on his computer screen. Nothing surprises him, not anymore. The cable news anchor is relaying the news, in the typical shrill manner, that the White House has confirmed reviewing long-standing treaty guarantees, including Article 5, all on the eve of a visit from Russia's president. Though many in Washington had predicted that President Monroe, with the death of Peter Hall, might retreat from a possible realignment of European alliances, it is now recognized by most pundits across the political spectrum there will be no shift in the administration's policy.

Homer chuckles and takes another sip of his marvelous bourbon, savoring its sharp bite. No one really cares about Europe, and that goes double for Estonia. It's the relationships, stupid. As Monroe keeps stumbling around, blindly obliterating those very valuable connections between players in their respective countries, he's undercutting individual power alliances that have existed for decades. The US intelligence community has invested God knows how much money, time, and energy in relationships with allies and overseas assets that will take generations to rebuild. This is a power struggle of the ages, one in which the parties involved are playing for keeps.

The Pulitzer winner toggles down the volume with the keyboard. He broods on the events of the day and his drinks meeting with Asher and his friend earlier. The girl had obvious intelligence and grit but is inexperienced. What cannot be easily dismissed is the fact Hayley Chill had seen something of significance at Hall's residence on Kalorama Road. And what is there to make of her wild and completely unsubstantiated tale of her near murder? Homer considers himself a wily interviewer. He knows how to get subjects to reveal themselves without even realizing they're being questioned. Why not give the CIA deputy director a call? Perhaps the old warhorse might inadvertently disclose something that will be the seed of a story. If even just a fragment of what the West Virginia girl alleges is true, then conceivably there might be a second Pulitzer in Homer's future!

Across town, James Odom is preparing a midnight snack in the kitchen when he sees his phone on the marble counter top light up and vibrate like those ridiculous gadgets restaurants hand out to patrons waiting for tables. Curious who might be calling at this late hour, he snatches up the phone and accepts the call. Phone pressed to the side of his head, he utters a single word that lands with the thud of an artillery shell. "Odom."

---

HAYLEY EXITS HER building before sunrise, dressed for her regular morning workout. Unable to afford the sort of gear on which civilians spend hundreds of dollars, she wears the PT uniform issued to her in the army: black pants with US Army star logo on the left thigh, black long-sleeve shirt with gold ARMY lettering on the front, black jacket with gold chevron across the chest and back. Her running shoes came from a discount sports outlet in Silver Spring, on sale for $24.99. It was her drill sergeant who coined a phrase that sticks in her head to this day. "Physical fitness requires minimal expenditure and maximum sweat."

She did not expect to see the blue Taurus on the street and is correct in that assumption. Hayley pondered on it overnight and reasoned Odom was only testing anyone who had had access to the Oval Office yesterday. It would not surprise her if three dozen people in the West Wing were similarly tailed in such a blatant manner. Hayley credits her military training to maintain composure in high-stress situations for passing this blunt-edged test. She is positive she in no way betrayed incriminating behavior when Odom's goons executed their drive-bys.

Regardless of having fooled her adversaries, Hayley knows she is operating on borrowed time. Whether by connecting her to Scott Billings or his tablet, Odom will identify her as a witness who cannot be allowed to exist. Without knowing the full reach of the conspiracy, Hayley is prohibited from raising the alarm. It would be like putting a target on her back. As she jogs at a strong pace through the dark streets, Hayley resists the urge to despair. Leaving town would be as simple as buying a train or bus ticket. All of her worldly belongings can fit in her one duffel bag. Surrender would be almost too easy.

But Hayley will not leave. Consideration to do so is a passing fantasy, having the life span of a yawn. Imagining James Odom's possible success makes Hayley seethe with anger, especially given the CIA deputy

director's self-interested motivations. Without thinking, Hayley increases her running tempo, channeling
her deep-seated rage into a furious pace. Feet barely
seem to touch the ground. There is no traffic in the
street to impede her. Desire for action surges through
her body. Odom and his cabal just *think* they're winning. She imagines how their arrogance would only
increase if they knew their opponent was a mere intern.
She is undeterred, feeling more impactful than ever.
"Believe you can is halfway there." That was another
favorite saying of that legendary drill instructor at Fort
Benning.

By the time Hayley has finished a forty-five-minute
run and stopped again in front of her building, she has
settled on a next step. The first attempt at convincing
Homer Stephens was not a total failure. The journalist
was not completely dismissive of Hayley's allegations. A
second attempt must be made to convince Stephens to
join with them and lead a professional investigation of
the so-called Operation Damocles. Excited to share her
thoughts with Asher, Hayley hurries inside to shower
and get ready for work, having decided to forgo the
remainder of her daily workout routine. Her coworker
had never returned a voice mail from the night before,
but Hayley would be shocked if Asher still harbored any
ill feelings regarding her moody acting-out at Clyde's.

---

KAREN REY EXITS the ground floor of the West Wing with
a colleague, Harriet Cohen, the deputy chief of staff

for Policy. They're due in the EEOB in five minutes for a morning staffer. The intern wrangler sees Hayley passing the Secret Service Uniformed Division checkpoint dividing West Wing from Eisenhower Executive Office Building and heading in their direction. Rey turns to confide conspiratorially to Cohen. "You can't be too aggressive dealing with a bright, young thing on the rise. Next thing you know, she's in the Oval and I'm planning luncheons for FLOTUS."

Cohen follows her friend's gaze to Hayley approaching from across the narrow plaza. "What? The intern? I've heard about her. How the hell did that hillbilly get out in front?"

"Making the evening news in her first week didn't hurt. Don't make the same mistake I did and let appearances fool you. Hayley Chill is smart, disciplined, and extremely capable."

"What's your play?"

"Surgical removal," Rey responds, grimly determined.

"Fair enough. When?"

Rey frowns. Hayley is only one of innumerable problems currently facing her, and certainly not one of highest priority. "Unsure. Timing's got to be right," she admits.

Hayley comes abreast of her superior and offers a polite smile. "Good morning, ma'am."

Rey merely nods curtly in response. Walking a few more steps before glancing over her shoulder to see Hayley disappear through the entrance of the West

Wing's ground floor, the White House aide shakes her head with bitter resignation. "As if we don't have enough shit hosed into our faces every day."

———————————

HAYLEY BOUNDS UP the stairs to the first floor, eager to smooth over Asher's hurt feelings and then conspire together how best to take another run at Homer Stephens. Surely they can gather evidence sufficient to win the journalist's interest. Though no longer employed by newspaper or journalist organization, Homer has the contacts to pitch the story as a freelancer. If he still refuses to throw in with them, perhaps he can recommend someone of equal stature who will.

Entering the White House Operations support office in her usual rush and with her speech to Asher fully rehearsed, Hayley stops in her tracks the moment she clocks her coworker's expression. Asher looks not only morose but scared.

"What?" Hayley asks warily.

He says nothing, seemingly unable to talk.

"Asher, what is it?" Hayley repeats herself, more emphatically.

"Homer Stephens was shot and killed outside his brownstone. Mugged." He continues incredulously. "Eight in the morning, off Dupont Circle? They're saying he resisted the mugger's demands."

Hayley processes the news. "They tried to snatch him. He wouldn't go, so they shot him."

Asher slams his palm on the desktop. "Fuckers!"

Hayley stands motionless in the open doorway. Homer Stephens is dead. Forces terrifyingly larger than her are at work, gigantic spheres of power and influence that will crush any opposition in their path. Her newfound optimism to reach out again to Homer Stephens seems now, with his murder, to be puny and futile. What's to be done? Contrary to her earlier assessment, the bad guys are winning . . . if they haven't already won.

# 6

★ ☆ ★ ☆

## ASHER

The Russell Senate Office Building is a Beaux-Arts marble edifice of unique grace and dignified stance. To score an office here, the thirty-five senatorial occupants have outlasted dozens of political opponents within and outside their party, won reelection a minimum of four times and achieved the kind of status in Congress only the very biggest lobbying dollars can buy.

A franchise player in the intelligence community and defiantly above the consumer-grade political fray, James Odom would be welcomed through any door in the building. Several senators and senior aides signal for a private word with the CIA deputy director as he strides down the grand corridor, but he waves off all such invitations. He's too busy for glad-handing and steps through the open doorway leading into the office suite assigned to Senator Taylor Cox. An aide greets Odom and immediately shows him into the senator's expansive office. Cox, seated at his glossy-topped desk, gestures to his man. "That'll be all, Michael."

The aide silently retreats from the wood-paneled sanctum, closing the big, heavy oak door behind him. Odom takes a seat opposite Cox behind his desk. "Are we on mute?" he asks as a precaution.

The senator nods. "Not encouraging news last night."

"We've been ordered to sit on satellite images indicating forward units of Russia's Sixth Army have engaged with Estonian forces at the border."

"The IC assessment?"

"Moscow knows they have a pass. Striking while the iron is hot. Use any platitude you want, but Monroe will play to his base and the rest of us can take a flying fuck. You know any Estonians? Is your mother-in-law Estonian?"

The old senator frowns. "Proverbial bull in a china shop. He can't *not* break things. Fucking amateur." Cox trembles with rage, hand too shaky to keep a grip on a thousand-dollar Meisterstück Solitaire Blue Hour ball-point pen. "Your boss?" he asks, already fearful of the answer he anticipates.

"What do you think? Monroe installed him. I've lost more than forty percent of my funding, with more reappropriation to come. Early retirement has been muttered into my ear by his retinue of flying monkeys more times than I care to remember."

"Maybe something we both should consider? Take our chips off the table," Cox suggests, adding, "while we still can."

"I grew up on a crabbing boat. Not ready to die on one, thanks."

The senator sighs. He has no desire to exit the political stage, either. Colleagues who have disappeared from public life are exactly that: disappeared. Useless and inconsequential. Once you've tasted real power, willingly giving it away is nearly impossible. No one voluntarily leaves Washington. You're either voted out, fired, or you die. Without his senate seat, Cox must admit, he is quite literally nothing. His wife dead now seven years, kids grown up with their own families, Cox's entire reason for being is the US Senate. The perks aren't half-bad, either.

"We're inching precipitously close to jump off, James," the senator warns his longtime DC ally. Both of them came to the capital in the same year and came up the ranks together. A bond like theirs is gold. They have each other's back, that is, up to the point of self-preservation.

Odom nods somberly. "Yes."

"The vice president—"

"Can be contained." Odom has never been reluctant to finish Cox's sentences for him.

The senator nods, concurring.

"There's something else. A finite degree of exposure," Odom admits to his friend.

"Finite degree," Cox repeats, obviously finding the phrase unsettling.

"One or more individuals in play against us. They have the broad outlines only, if that. Making efforts to learn more. To stop us."

"The infamous Second Passenger."

Odom nods. "I'm thinking low profile. Bit players who attempted to solicit Homer Stephens's assistance, who then called me."

Cox reacts with alarm. "Stephens was shot and killed outside his house this morning!"

Odom's expression is studied and mild. "No kidding?"

Cox panics on hearing Odom's response but masks it as best he can. The effort to counteract the president's reckless behavior in office has spun wildly out of control, in Cox's private opinion. But there is no retreating now. The damage is done. As Cox stands abruptly, gesturing toward the door, he really wonders if his old friend has lost his mind. "Keep me posted, James. Thanks for stopping by."

Odom stands and follows the senator to the door, well aware Cox is shrieking in silent, abject terror. It's laughable. Some men simply aren't equal to their office or standing. "More as it comes into focus," he glibly tells Cox as he glides past him.

Odom strides through the office antechamber, ignoring the respectful salutations of the senator's staff, and enters the marble-lined corridor. The thought strikes him the Russell Senate Office Building would make a wonderful residence. These weird and random thoughts he's been having lately amuse him more than worry. Like imagining a leap from the subway platform as a train hurtles into the station, his daydreams are trifles of an overactive mind. Who doesn't occasionally indulge in such fantastic speculations?

Leaving restricted parking at the Senate Office Building, the CIA deputy director calls Sinatra at the W Street safe house. Odom dispenses with small talk in dealing with Sinatra, who seems to prefer it that way. "What did you learn from analysis of the computer? Fingerprints?"

"Yours. Whoever used it last wiped it clean."

Odom's impatience and frustration get the better of him. "Nothing?!"

"Someone brought the device to the White House after the accident. Accessed minutes before you arrived at the West Wing or concurrently."

"Data?" Odom asks guardedly.

"Not everything, but he had enough on there to cause problems."

"How secure?"

"Impossible to crack, for an eight-year-old." The silence from Odom communicates his disgust. Sinatra walks it back. "Not a fatal leak, just damaging. Suggestive."

Odom mutters a curse. "What are the names of possibles on your list?"

"Put tails on all of them. Had to hire a dozen more guys. Nobody jumped and ran."

Odom sighs. This minor annoyance is fast becoming something much more than that. "Your team was at the residence two hours after the guy's car went off the bridge?"

"Someone set off our vehicle's alarm while we were inside the house. In hindsight, clearly a diversion." Sinatra ruefully admits, "Whoever we're looking for was inside the residence while we were there."

Odom broods, mentally shuffling the jigsaw pieces available to him and seeing if any of them fit together to form a recognizable image. Blurry outlines of a hypothetical scenario come to him.

"Your guy was fucking someone. She was in the car, had to erase her presence at his house."

"First I'm hearing about it," a defensive Sinatra is quick to confess.

In the privacy of his vehicle, Odom sneers. "Sit tight," he orders his operative. "I'm digging deeper."

"You're going to hit up another asset in the West Wing." Sinatra's educated guess is more statement of fact.

"You know, for a psychopath, you've got a fine, analytical head on your shoulders." Odom disconnects the call.

---

THE MIDAFTERNOON CROWD in the Starbucks on Stuart Street in Arlington, Virginia, is overwhelmingly underemployed adults of diverse ages exploiting unlimited Wi-Fi access for the price of a cup of coffee. Odom enters and makes a face, finding the acrid smell common to the franchise an affront. Such are the sacrifices one must make in defense of the country, he muses. Odom continues toward the rear of the store, where Asher Danes is waiting for him at a small table against the wall.

"Asher, my friend, how are you?"

The low-level White House aide is feeling a good deal less bonhomie than the older man. "All things considered, I'm grandly fucked. Thanks for asking."

Odom sits opposite Asher. "These are trying times for sure. Defending our freedom and democracy isn't a trivial matter." A dark look comes over the White House aide. "What?" Odom presses, clocking Asher's every mood swing.

"Is that what you call murdering the White House chief of staff?" Asher has assumed he was only providing privileged information to the president's adversaries within the government and not playing a role in any active conspiracy aligned against Monroe. Having been swayed by Hayley's intense convictions, Asher is finding it difficult to play both sides of the fence and requires assurances from the older man.

Odom seems uncomprehending enough. "Murder? What are you talking about?"

"Peter Hall. Kinda convenient him dying and everything."

Odom smiles wearily at Asher in the way one would to a puppy that has just peed on the kitchen floor. No damage done. Just needs the quick swipe of a paper towel.

"Peter Hall died of a massive heart attack. Your suggestion I had anything to do with his untimely demise is paranoid and baseless."

Asher isn't so easily mollified. "The FBI came around to question the intern who found Hall's body. *They* seem to feel the cause of death is worth investigating. Drugs were detected."

Odom appears aggrieved by Asher's persistent suspicions. "Asher, when I first asked for your help, I explained with complete candor and transparency the nature of our effort. We all share an acute concern over the danger Monroe represents to our nation and a singular interest in legal avenues of diminishing that threat. Murder is not in our toolbox. Information is our best weapon to wield against the ongoing disaster of the Monroe administration."

This gentle pushback seems to have its intended effect. Asher says nothing, settling for a disapproving frown. Odom rolls forward, unimpeded. "We haven't heard from you in more than a week. Besides these irrational fantasies, is there anything wrong?"

Asher dials back the petulance. "I'm fine."

"Anything to report?"

Asher shakes his head. "Nothing that isn't in the news. I have the clearance level of a White House usher, holed up in the Operations office doing mostly administrative stuff."

"Have you been worried about any kind of personal exposure?"

Asher dismisses Odom's solicitousness with an emphatic shake of his head. He hates to be treated like a baby even if he's acting like one. "No. I told you, I'm fine. No one in the West Wing suspects I'm a rat." Asher pauses and then tries a different tack. Probing. "Was that Secret Service agent working for you, too?"

"Yes, he was," Odom admits matter-of-factly.

Odom's confirmation of what Asher knows to be fact only magnifies his indecision and paranoia. Could Hayley be wrong after all? But why would Scott Billings attack her? Was it, in fact, only a lovers' quarrel? What does he really know about Hayley anyway? One verifiable fact only gives birth to a dozen more questions.

The CIA deputy director seems only too happy to discuss the dead Secret Service agent. "Mr. Billings was a second set of eyes and ears in the West Wing. We regret his death terribly. Such a tragic accident." Odom pauses, and then asks innocently, "Are you aware of any personal associations the agent might have had in the White House, Asher? Any romantic entanglements?"

Odom isn't the only proficient dissembler. Asher makes a creditable display of pondering the question. "None that I know of," he tells the CIA deputy director.

"Are you sure, Asher? This is important."

"Why is it important? You said he died in an accident. What difference does it make if he was seeing someone?"

"We need to know if Mr. Billings had confided in a third party, of course. Monroe is a vengeful and vindictive man. If he became aware of our intelligence gathering—"

"Spying, you mean," Asher corrects him.

"As you will, but surely you can see the need for confidentiality." Odom pauses, gazing more intently into Asher's eyes. "You've been completely discreet, haven't you?"

"Yes, of course."

"What about Hayley Chill?" Odom persists.

"The intern?"

"Yes. Was she involved with Mr. Billings?"

Asher gestures emphatically. "Hayley? No way."

"Anything strike you as odd about Ms. Chill? Is she unusually devoted to the president? He certainly seems to favor her."

"I haven't noticed anything out of the ordinary, no more so than you'd expect from a relatively unsophisticated and uneducated military vet."

Odom nods, grateful for Asher's seemingly candid assessment. "Not that we doubt your intuition and representations, but we might have a chat with Ms. Chill."

A flash of panic crosses Asher's face, despite his effort to maintain neutral composure. Of course, Odom notices the younger man's anxiety.

"You wouldn't mind that too much, would you, Asher? If we speak with your friend?" Odom's words are intended to rattle Asher, but the White House aide has had time to recover his poise.

"Why in the world would I mind?"

Odom only shrugs, as inscrutable as Buddha. He smiles blandly and stands to his feet. "Keep up the fine work, Asher, and thank you. Your country appreciates it." He raps the tabletop with a knuckle. "Stay in touch!"

Asher watches the CIA man hustle through the crowd forming a ragged line at the counter and out the door. Should he call Hayley and warn her? He wouldn't put it past Odom to have his phone bugged. Asher wonders if his condo isn't bugged as well. Maybe the cabal already knows everything about his friendship with Hayley and her allegations. If Odom was willing to kill Peter Hall and attempt to kill a White House intern, what's to stop them from killing him? How did he ever find himself in this crazy situation anyway? With a sensation not unlike a gut punch, Asher recalls how it all started.

He met Daniel on a rainy afternoon in February, not quite a month after the inauguration. Asher had started at the White House less than a week before. Though he had moved to Washington in January, having been hired by Karen Rey in those giddy first weeks after the election, almost all of his spare time had been spent looking for someplace to live, working with his dad to purchase the condo at 3303 Water Street and the long but enjoyable process of furnishing his new home. Asher was grateful for the enormous amount of work required in making the condo an expression of his own exquisitely good taste and character. Having that activity helped stave off the crushing isolation he felt in the odd duck of a city that is Washington, DC.

Once he had started in the West Wing, Asher thought his loneliness would abate somewhat but such was not the case. Hours were brutal in the Monroe administration, with limited socializing. And it wasn't as if there were other young people (or older) who really him for the daughter of an Oscar-winning actor. Asher adopted a more cautious line following that flameout, hooking up when the need and opportunity arose but his desire for committed companionship remained at low ebb.

He had always dreamed of a boyfriend like Daniel, and miracle of miracles, he materialized as if the universe had decided that Asher had suffered long enough. With Daniel's job at the Department of Health and Human Services, a darling flat on Riggs Place just off Dupont Circle, and a rescue dog that was the spitting image of Zeus from a childhood favorite, *Zeus and Roxanne*, Asher was more than ready to ordain him as The One. Daniel, blue eyes and all, seemed happy to accept this designation. After three months of exclusive dating, Asher booked a summer's long-weekend trip to Connecticut so he could show off his new boyfriend to the parents. Unmentioned to Daniel was Asher's private fantasy they would "just happen to" bump into the lacrosse champ, who had accepted a job with a Greenwich hedge fund after graduation.

In fact, the problems began right around that aforementioned three-month mark. From the outset of their relationship, Daniel had engaged in a low-grade but constant criticism of Richard Monroe. Sometimes their political discussions would devolve into argument, with Daniel upbraiding Asher for being on the president's staff. But these tiffs would always quickly blow over, followed by wonderful, amorous reconciliations that made the disagreements all the more worth it. As the weeks passed, Asher found himself increasingly in agreement with Daniel's hostility toward Monroe. The man who was once a political hero to Asher was transformed into false prophet. The arguments ceased. Happiness between them again reigned supreme.

Daniel introduced him to James Odom on a Saturday night in June at Mayahuel, where the couple had gone to celebrate Asher's twenty-eighth birthday. Odom had been dining with a colleague at a table next to the one where the hostess seated Daniel and Asher. Odom's jack-o'-lantern smile seemed to fit right in with the grinning skulls and colorful Mexican Day of the Dead decor. He insisted on buying the birthday boy and his date a round of twenty-five-dollar tequilas and instantly connected with Asher by regaling him with thrilling stories of espionage and foreign intrigue. Indeed, Odom made no secret of his job at the CIA. He was the opposite of what Asher romanticized as "spy material." Odom seemed more like an oddball professor of anthropology at Georgetown than anything else. Daniel vaguely identified the older man as a family friend. Of Odom's dining companion, Asher had no memory.

The twosome became a threesome, in a strictly friendship way, of course. Odom would take the young men on expensive junkets around town or field trips where they might get a privileged view into the machinations of the US intelligence apparatus. It was heady stuff. All the while, Odom and Daniel put forward a constant and persistent case attacking the president's character, judgment, and agenda, with Asher serving as appreciative, agreeable audience. The strongest argument made against the president occurred one Sunday afternoon when Odom brought Asher (Daniel couldn't make it because of other commitments) over to Langley and the offices of the Defense Clandestine Service. Odom encouraged Asher to have a peek of a top-secret dossier compiled by allied intelligence operatives overseas that more than hinted at some bizarre and disturbing connections between Monroe's campaign and Moscow.

Two days after Asher's Sunday visit to the deserted DCS offices, without warning or preamble, Daniel announced at dinner he felt suffocated by the relationship and needed out. Asher was more than floored. Had Daniel ripped off a mask and revealed himself to be Quasimodo, it would've been less of a shock. Asher was gobsmacked. No amount of pleading or angry demands would dislodge one word of explanation from his lover. Within an hour of his appalling announcement, Daniel was gone from Asher's life completely. Texts and telephone calls went unanswered. Asher had been irrevocably ghosted.

James Odom called a few days following the breakup. Asher told him the news and received sympathetic support from someone who had evolved into something of a surrogate father. Lunches, events at the Kennedy Center, and invitations to parties flowed at a steady pace. Asher felt as if he would never fully get over Daniel, but the friendship and understanding

Odom offered him went a long way toward making that emotional pain bearable. Agreeing to Odom's casual request for inside information from his lowly perch at the West Wing seemed like small compensation for all the CIA man had done for him. But that request for hallway gossip became discussions overheard in cabinet meetings and finally actual documents sneaked out of the White House. Before Asher truly realized it, he was Odom's mole in the Monroe administration. Then Hayley Chill walked into White House Operations, and Asher's world shifted once again.

————————————

IMPROVED RELATIONS WITH Russia had been a top priority with the Monroe administration, included in the campaign speech boilerplate from the beginning. Throughout his long and storied military career, the president had come to respect Russia for its soulful endurance and national strength. A lifetime student of military history, Monroe was particularly interested in the Soviet Union's horrific experience in the Second World War. With perhaps as high as twenty-seven million military and civilian dead, no other country suffered worse in that conflict than Russia. And yet, unlike many other European countries, the Russian people never capitulated. Despite horrendous losses and the Wehrmacht's overwhelming military superiority, Russia persevered. There was much in that country's monumental will to survive that Monroe had always admired.

An alliance of Russia and the United States, in

Monroe's unshakable belief, was the only way to compete with the historical merging of a Chinese communist dictatorship with rabid, unchecked capitalism. The president's earliest warnings on the subject, dating back a quarter century, had indeed proved to be well-founded. In the last decade, Beijing has edged closer and closer to assuming a position as the world's greatest superpower, eclipsing the United States by every measure except military. It had been too easy for US political leaders to overlook the steady advancement made by the Chinese while seemingly more urgent flash points around the world drew Washington's focused attention. ISIS, al-Qaeda, Iraq, Russia, Syria, Mexico had all been massive commitments, pulling attention and resources away from a far graver threat to US power and prestige.

In Monroe's estimation, after China achieved economic hegemony, inevitable within years and not decades, their logical next step would be to realize military dominance as well. In other words, once economic supremacy is established, the game is essentially over. Or so President Richard Monroe had long suggested, to a rising chorus of fellow believers. The president's exemplary military career has given weight to his argument, though pundits early on dismissed his theory with patronizing counterarguments. But growing numbers of Americans, experiencing a falling standard of living, began to see it Monroe's way. China's astounding economic success and lightning-fast development, while being home to the world's largest population, had created real fear in the United States. The country needed

The five-hundred-million-dollar Russian-built upgraded Voronezh IL-96-300PU long-haul jetliner lands at Andrews Air Force Base about the same time James Odom sits down across the table from Asher in the Arlington Starbucks. Traveling with a police escort of significant size and extravagance, complete with MRAP (Mine-Resistant Ambush Protected) vehicle, Malkin's motorcade travels directly to the Embassy of the Russian Federation on Wisconsin Avenue, north of Georgetown, where a sizable throng of mostly Estonian protestors is waiting. Assembled on the sidewalk across Wisconsin Avenue from the embassy complex, the impassioned Estonians carry signs decrying Russia's hostile actions toward the much smaller country and call out Malkin specifically for his tyrannical ways.

The Russian president's armored limousine enters the complex through a secured gate and stops at the embassy entrance. More than three dozen bodyguards, dressed in dark suits and carrying an assortment of weapons, create a human barricade, shielding the Russian leader from the protestors, more than seventy-five yards away from the embassy entrance. As Malkin emerges from his vehicle, he looks to the Estonian protestors across the street and then gestures toward his head bodyguard, whispering into his ear over the din raised by the demonstration.

The bodyguard nods, then turns to have words with the men in his charge. Within seconds, the entire contingent of Russian bodyguards head toward the embassy gate as Malkin disappears inside the building.

Sensing impending attack, the unarmed Estonians begin to disperse in the face of an advancing phalanx of Russian bodyguards.

DC police on the scene, numbering less than a dozen, are unable to stop the bloodbath that ensues. Numerous protestors, males and females, are clubbed over the head with truncheons and then kicked after falling to the ground. The beatings continue for ten minutes, until the grim-faced bodyguards run out of potential victims. Police reinforcements arrive on the scene only after the Russians have already crossed Wisconsin again. Dozens of stunned Washingtonians in their cars, stopped in traffic lanes, watch the thugs troop back through the embassy gate.

When asked about the incident an hour later, a White House spokesman suggests the Estonian protestors had incited an admittedly too extreme response from the Russian security personnel when rocks were thrown at Malkin's car. In the later days and weeks, no witnesses, except those connected with the embassy, could attest to seeing any objects hurled at the barricade. All in all, five Estonians were hospitalized, two of them with serious injuries.

———————

IT WASN'T FEAR Hayley experienced learning Homer Stephens had been murdered, but impotent rage. The unfamiliarity and rawness of this emotion twists her guts into a knot and only diminishes her ability to devise an alternative plan. While she dawdles and remains inactive, her enemies become more entrenched. No amount of exercise or other diversions alleviate her roiling thoughts. She has been useless in the office, second only to Asher's distraction. An impenetrable fog has descended on both, isolating them from each other.

Hayley arrives home well after eight p.m., her usual bus having broken down. Once inside her apartment, she shucks off her coat and collapses into a chair. There's a knock at the door. Annoyed and wanting only to disappear for a few moments from her life, Hayley goes to the door but hesitates opening it.

"Yes? Who is it?"

"Secret Service," comes the voice through the closed door, neither friendly nor officious.

Hayley checks the peephole and whatever she sees is enough for her to unlock and open the door partway. Bishop stands at the threshold, wearing jeans and an expensive-looking leather jacket. "Hayley Chill? Jim Christie, US Secret Service," he tells her, holding out his credentials for her inspection.

She is on guard. Thoughts, questions, and hypotheticals careen inside her brain. Trust no one, Peter Hall said. It is impossible to miss the Sig Sauer P229 in the man's vertical shoulder holster. Without checking, Hayley recalls a knife left on a cutting board in the tiny kitchen area behind her back. Her military instruction in Close Quarters Combat included scenarios in which an attacker is armed with a handgun. Hayley factors into the equation her estimation the man hasn't been as diligent with his training as she has been.

"Yes? What is it?" Hayley retains cool detachment, betraying nothing.

"May I come in? Just have some questions for you."

Hayley hesitates.

Bishop offers a seemingly genuine smile. "It'll only take a few minutes, Ms. Chill. I promise."

Hayley holds the door open wide for Bishop to enter. She leads him toward the small dining table at the other end of the cozy studio apartment, beside the kitchen alcove. In choosing a seat, Hayley takes the chair where she will be within arm's reach of the knife on the cutting board. Bishop sits opposite her, taking a moment to gaze around the studio and its modest furnishings.

"Cozy place," he offers.

Hayley remains silent, staring evenly at the operator.

"My apologies for intruding like this, Ms. Chill. Approaching you at home seemed like the better choice. Security reasons, you understand."

"Security reasons?"

"It would appear a job at the White House is becoming a deadly proposition. In only the last week, the chief of staff and a Secret Service agent, both dead."

"I thought those were both accidents. Are you saying Mr. Hall and Scott Billings were murdered?"

"Still under investigation, Ms. Chill." As if an afterthought, he adds, "That's why I'm here."

Hayley won't be rattled. "Isn't the FBI leading those investigations, Agent Christie?"

"We take care of our own," Bishop fires back. Sitting back in his chair, he places his right ankle across his left knee, in the process exposing the sole of his right boot. Linear x's and dashes above an array of squares, she is only slightly surprised to see in a glance.

"What does any of this have to do with me?" she asks without any different modulation of voice or tenor.

Bishop gets to the point. "Did you have a relationship with Agent Billings?"

"Why would the Secret Service be interested in my romantic life?"

"Our sworn duty is to protect the president of the United States. That makes us extremely interested in any person who comes in contact with him, including Scott Billings and, by extension, you, Ms. Chill."

"I believe the oath prospective agents take before service is to support and defend the Constitution of the United States." As she finishes, Hayley checks the distance between her hand and the knife, estimating she can have it in hand within two seconds.

Bishop's eyes seem kind enough but behind them is an impulse to throttle this young woman with his bare hands. "We can finish this at H Street. Makes no difference to me."

"I had no personal relationship with Scott Billings. He was a nice guy in a blue tie, dress shoes, and dark suit who I said hello to in the West Wing."

Bishop scrutinizes her face, boring in with his intense gaze. "What about Homer Stephens? Any contact with him?"

Hayley doesn't flinch. "Who?"

Bishop lets it go, standing. The intern had failed to be flustered by his off-tempo questioning. "Of course, after we've had the opportunity to examine Mr. Billings's phone, we'll be able to gauge the veracity of your statements to me tonight." He turns for the door.

"Is my life in danger, Agent Christie?"

He stops, looking back toward Hayley. "Any reason why you think it would be?"

Hayley shrugs, playing it noncommittal.

"Have a good night, Ms. Chill."

In a few minutes, Bishop rejoins Sinatra in the SUV parked outside Hayley's building. The cigarette smoke roils in a thick cloud inside the vehicle. Bishop waves his hand in front of his own face, repulsed.

"Jesus!"

Sinatra really couldn't care less about his man's discomfort. How many bodies has he piled up to earn the right to smoke in a mission vehicle if he wanted? It would be difficult to come up with an exact number. He should've put it all on QuickBooks a long time ago when he first started. Too late for that now. For these purposes, a ballpark figure will have to suffice. Twenty-two bodies, directly by his hand, is a good estimate. Surely twenty-two notches earns one the right to smoke when and where one pleases.

"Well?" he asks Bishop, gesturing with the crown of his head toward Hayley's building.

Bishop makes a show of deliberation. This is his first job with Sinatra, and he's been careful not to antagonize his unit leader. Everyone on the team agrees that Sinatra is odd stuff. His rampant Catholicism is the source of much speculation. Some of the guys wonder if he is a lapsed priest. Sinatra is certainly creepy enough to suggest such an irregular past. Special Operations draw the highly strung and hard-to-read from the military ranks. Not much different from serial killers, Bishop muses, we just like getting paid for it.

"She doesn't know shit," Bishop tells Sinatra, referring to Hayley.

"What makes you so sure?"

"I can just tell. Unless she's a better covert operative than just about any I've met, this intern is a non-actor. She's Walmart white trash desperately trying to claw her way out of Oxy-Appalachia."

"You can just tell," Sinatra murmurs dubiously.

Irritated and maybe a little frightened of Sinatra, Bishop again waves the cigarette smoke away from his face.

"Look, man, what did you send me in there for if you don't trust my judgment?" Bishop jerks his thumb toward the building he had just exited. "She doesn't know shit!"

Sinatra stares placidly at his man with an expression that is impossible to read. After a long moment of regarding an increasingly anxious Bishop, he touches the screen on his phone a few times and then lifts it to his head. He never takes his gaze off Bishop as he does so.

"It's me," Sinatra says into the phone. After a brief

pause, "The intern isn't involved." Another pause. "Yes, we're sure."

He disconnects the call and lowers the phone. Eyes are still on Bishop.

"You know that I pray, correct?"

Bishop nods. "Yeah. I know you pray."

"But do you know what I pray for, Bishop, or whatever your real name is?"

Bishop shakes his head. "Haven't a clue."

"I pray you're right about the intern. I pray for that in the very worst possible way."

Bishop says nothing. He's having a difficult time meeting Sinatra's gaze.

"Would you like to pray with me? Shall we do that together? Let's pray that you're right about this 'Walmart white trash' intern."

Petrified, Bishop can barely nod his head okay. His eyes are like a steer's before slaughter, peeled back and unseeing. Sinatra, without warmth, offers his hand. Bishop takes it, flinching slightly at the other man's tight clasp.

Sinatra bows his head and closes his eyes. "Our Father, who art in Heaven, hallowed be thy name . . ."

Bishop can scarcely believe this is happening. But, not wanting to take any chances, he bows his head and closes his eyes, too. With Sinatra, he joins in recitation of the Lord's Prayer. "Thy kingdom come, thy will be done, on earth as it is in Heaven."

HAYLEY'S ALARM GOES off at five a.m., waking her from a night of restless sleep. While showering after her usual workout, she finds herself recalling the Sunday afternoon her mother packed all six kids into the dilapidated Buick and drove up to Charleston for a visit with their grandmother. These trips were bright moments in an otherwise monochrome childhood, highly anticipated by Hayley and her siblings. Their grandma lived in a modest two-bedroom house on a tree-lined street. After a lunch of fried chicken and ice cream, Hayley and the other children would go outside to play while the women visited. Only many years later did Hayley realize the trips to Charleston were occasioned by her mother's need for cash, grudgingly dispensed by a former public school teacher on a fixed income.

Their favorite game at the time was hide-and-seek. As the oldest, it was Hayley's role to play referee. The middle girl, seven-year-old Sadie, had hidden behind bushes below the open window of a next-door neighbor but fled this perfect spot within seconds and approached Hayley with a frightening observation. Sadie reported hearing strange sounds coming from within the house. Hayley went to the window in order to investigate and, peering through a rip in the pulled window shade, saw something that both mystified and terrified her. Only after she joined the military did Hayley realize what the man was doing to his wife was a form of torture known popularly as "waterboarding." Hayley, eleven years old, only recognized the intense terror of a middle-aged woman, sadistically abused by her husband.

squeezed and squeezed the rock, so hard that when she unfurled her fingers, Hayley saw blood welling up from several cuts in her palm. Emboldened by the sight of her own injury, the pain banishing all fear, she stood to her feet and threw that rock through the window of the neighbor's house, startling the man. Hayley remained rooted in place just outside the window, even when the man came thundering over, boots cracking broken glass scattered across the wooden dining room floor, and spewed a stream of vile obscenities at her.

Two police cars, lights ablaze, pulled to a stop in the middle of the street where the man had cornered Hayley between two parked cars. The cops were able to throw him to the ground, rescuing Hayley, after he had only managed to hit her twice. Later, when her grandmother was treating the rock cuts in the palm of Hayley's hand with iodine, the woman who lived next door appeared at the back door. Cleaned up and wearing dry, freshly laundered clothes, she hardly resembled the woman who had undergone such a horrific ordeal only two hours before. The woman offered nothing in the way of reward for Hayley's help except for tearful thanks. "You are a gift sent from God" is exactly what the woman told the eleven-year-old Hayley. "You are a guardian angel."

If this is who she is, Hayley ponders as she dries off from her shower, then this is who she must be. The solution had come to her in the middle of the night, when she had woken up with the realization that she must speak directly with the president. She must tell him everything she knows and in that way save his life. This is her duty. Certainly, buttonholing the president will cost Hayley her internship, if not get her arrested. She is completely willing to make that sacrifice. The real problem will be getting close to the president. There is no other way to convey her message. Hayley must speak to Monroe himself before Odom or any of his henchmen determine she has knowledge of their crimes.

She is just putting on her coat to leave the apartment when her phone rings. Hayley considers not answering it, being a few minutes late, but connects after the fourth ring. "This is Hayley."

Karen Rey's voice emerges from the pinhole speaker in Hayley's cell phone like marbles poured from a tin can, clattering and scattershot. "Hayley, it's Karen Rey. I wanted to catch you before you left for work. My apologies for calling you so early."

Hayley glances at her watch. It's 7:05 a.m., more than fifteen minutes later than she usually got out the door on work mornings. She must speak to the president today. The sooner she can get to work and get her hands on Monroe's schedule, the sooner she can begin devising her plan. It would be best to speak to the president privately, but Hayley knows this is next to impossible. The fewer people who hear her message to POTUS, the better.

Rey continues, "We're shifting you over to the Library of Congress for the remainder of your internship program, Hayley. You can report over there straightaway this morning. Ms. Spellman is expecting you. She's a supervisory archivist with the library."

Hayley is stunned. She has neglected to factor her supervisor's obvious hostility into her equations. The transfer has caught her completely flat-footed, having been too focused on the bad men with guns to notice a bureaucratic, middle-management assassin right beside her. Hayley can scarcely believe her own stupidity in overlooking the enormous threat Rey represented. Buried in the Library of Congress, Hayley might as well be in Lincoln County.

"Ma'am?" Hayley is able to say.

"I'm sorry. I simply don't think it was an ideal fit, Hayley. Best of luck to you."

Rey disconnects the call to Hayley with a musketeer's flourish and turns to her confidant and coworker, Harriet Cohen. "With Fedor Malkin in town, POTUS will never know she's gone," she tells Cohen, but really only assuring herself.

---

ASHER ARRIVES FOR work just after seven thirty a.m. The White House complex swarms with additional security personnel drawn from all of the usual law enforcement and US government entities. Russian security personnel are also present, distinguishable from their American counterparts only by the quality and cut of their business suits. Beyond the gates, demonstrations and assorted protestors have been kept farther away from the White House complex perimeter than usual.

Traffic is diverted off Seventeenth Street for three blocks in either direction, and new portions of Pennsylvania Avenue are cordoned off as well. No chances are being taken with the very important person visiting the White House on this special day.

Making his way through the crowded and hectic corridor on the first floor of the West Wing, Asher enters the White House Operations office and stops in the doorway when he sees a petite young woman who is definitely not Hayley sitting at her desk. She smiles pleasantly at Asher, who continues to gape at her.

"Who are you?" he asks her in an unfriendly way.

"I'm Charlotte," she tells Asher, offering him her hand.

He doesn't take her hand. "Where's Hayley?" he demands to know.

"Who?" she asks innocently. Charlotte had been interning in the scheduling office located on the second floor of the EEOB, and this morning is the first time she has set foot in the West Wing. An assignment with White House Operations is more than she had imagined in her wildest dreams, and she has already group-texted nearly all three thousand names in her contact list with the news. Having heard stories about Asher told by other White House interns, she is intimidated by him. Nevertheless, Charlotte is determined to perform above expectations. Her dad, a huge fan of Monroe, would kill her if she fails to score a selfie with the president.

Asher's phone buzzes before he can say anything

unkind to the new girl. He walks over to his desk and sits in order to answer it.

"It's me," Hayley tells him. She is seated at a small metal desk in the subbasement of the James Madison Memorial Building on Independence Avenue. The library's stacks are silent and still as a mausoleum. Every other bank of overhead fluorescent lights has been turned off to save energy costs, casting even more gloom.

Asher is relieved to hear from his friend. "I've been trying to call! Where are you?"

"I turned my phone off. They're all over that. They suspect I might know something."

His eyes fall on Charlotte across the room. "There's some strange person sitting at your desk. Why aren't you here?"

"I'm at the Library of Congress. Karen Rey transferred me."

Asher is stunned. "What? Why? Oh, God, is she part of all this, too?"

"No, at least I'm pretty sure she isn't. This was just office politics."

The awareness of his own complicity in the plot hangs over Asher like a noxious cloud. "But are you okay?"

A gap yawns in their conversation. The question strikes Hayley as odd. "Asher, did you know one of Odom's guys came to my place last night?"

"Wait, what? One of them came to your place? When?" His alarm and dismay is genuine.

"Last night. Right after I got home." Asher doesn't respond, the words stuck in his throat. "It's okay," Hayley assures him. "He just asked a lot of questions and left. But I'm pretty sure they'll still be following me."

The silence from Asher continues. Everything has gone so dreadfully wrong, his betrayal of Hayley carving a pit out of his gut and filling it with anxiety. He no longer is frightened, just terribly fatigued. His willpower has deserted him to the extent he doubts whether he can summon the energy to retie the lace on his Ted Baker suede desert boot. All the beautiful objects with which he has adorned his existence now seem garish and wasteful. Self-loathing brings bile to his mouth. What would his parents think of their golden child now?

"Asher? Are you there?" Hayley's voice is soft and kind, her West Virginia accent like a warm, comforting hand on his cheek.

Asher can barely marshal the words for a response. Quietly and filled with regret, Asher tells Hayley, "I can't do this."

His confession does not surprise her. She accepts it without argument. What point would there be in trying to dissuade him? Asher's trepidation is a danger to her mission. Better he bows out now, before inadvertently getting them both killed. "Okay, Asher. You can only do what you feel is right for you."

"This just isn't me. Know what I mean? I'm not cut out for this shit." He resists crying, but the emotions pent up inside him threaten to erupt.

"It's okay, Asher. I understand." She worries he might break down in the office, in front of the new intern. "You have to go home, Asher. Leave work now and go home."

"Go home," he repeats. "Back to Greenwich."

"Yes. It's not safe in Washington. Go home to Greenwich. Be with your parents." Hayley catches a glimpse of someone at the end of a long row of bookshelves. Distracted, she warns him again, "It's not safe here."

With a shell-shocked expression, Asher disconnects the call. He experiences the peculiar sensation of floating, his brain buzzing uncomfortably. Tears sting his eyes. He is a man on the verge.

Charlotte, the new intern, looks at Asher with the apprehension of a young person who has really experienced nothing but juvenile setbacks and triumphs. His breakdown is alien and excruciating to witness. She wishes he would just get it together. "Is everything all right?" she asks tentatively.

Asher ignores her. Lurching into action, he stands and quickly starts loading all of his personal belongings from the desk into his Tumi Alpha Bravo backpack. More than ten months of artifacts, every last item with any kind of personal connotation to him, he stuffs unceremoniously into his bag, a time capsule of his year in the West Wing. The desk empty and cleared, Asher exits the office without another word, leaving the bewildered intern teetering on the edge of her seat.

# 7

★ ★ ★ ★

## MONROE

ayley lowers the phone after her call with Asher and sits perfectly motionless, listening to the footsteps echo from the other end of the stacks. She stands and, treading as silently as possible, keeps pace with whoever is on the floor with her. She catches a glimpse of the figure in the half darkness as the footsteps stop. Hayley is chasing a ghost, more paranoia-fueled apparition than man.

"Hello? Who's there?" she defiantly calls out to the specter.

With a scuffle of footsteps, the shadowy figure darts out of sight. Hayley hears the door of the opposite stairwell open and slowly close. Her visitor has vanished. Total silence returns to the library subbasement, catacomb of tens of thousands of books that will never

THE RUSSIAN PRESIDENT'S motorcade winds its way around Washington Circle then resumes its journey on K Street, heading east toward the White House. At the outset, demonstrations are scattered only at major intersections along the route, but as the motorcade reaches Farragut Square and turns right onto Seventeenth Street, the number of protestors explodes. District police keep the mob at bay, but emotions are running high. Not only are the crowds opposed to Russia's threatening posture toward Estonia and other neighbors, but also the assault on demonstrators the previous evening by Malkin's security forces has made this a very personal struggle. It's one thing to act like a bully on their own turf, quite another to bring that thuggish behavior to the United States.

Lafayette Square, just north of the White House complex, is jammed with raucous, overstimulated demonstrators carrying signs and banners protesting Malkin's visit. As the Russian president's motorcade passes the park to the west, the throng erupts in a single great howl of rage. Park Police struggle to keep the protestors from surging into the otherwise empty street. Russian security personnel, in their vehicles, are on edge, fingers draping trigger guards on their weapons. Malkin, seated in the rear of his armored limo, regards the protestors dispassionately through five-inch-thick bulletproof windows. In the Oval Office, senior aides join Monroe as they gaze out the windows behind the *Resolute* desk, staring apprehensively at the mob of protestors on the opposite side of the North Lawn, their bellowing outrage filtering into the serene office of the president.

Karen Rey shakes her head, clearly stunned by the size and vehemence of the demonstration. "Maybe an official visit wasn't such a good idea after all."

Monroe slowly pivots his head so that a hard stare known well by his army subordinates across numerous military campaigns falls directly on Rey. "Maybe keeping you around wasn't such a good idea, either."

Rey swallows hard and says nothing. She exchanges a look with Kyle Rodgers, who backs away from his subordinate like she's cancer while checking his watch. With an itinerary that is scheduled down to the half minute, he knows there is zero leeway in timing. "How about a little focus here?" the deputy chief of staff prompts his aide.

Eager to be useful, Rey turns for the southwest door leading to the Outer Oval Office. Passing Madison Smith at her desk, juggling a half-dozen tasks simultaneously with not so much as a furrow in her brow, Rey continues to the door leading into the Operations office. Flinging open the door, Rey is aggravated to find Charlotte, Hayley Chill's replacement intern, alone inside.

"Where's Asher?" she barks at Charlotte. "Malkin arrives in three minutes."

The fearsome intern wrangler intimidates the new girl. "I think he left," Charlotte responds meekly.

"Left? Left for where?" Rey demands to know.

"Connecticut . . . I think," Charlotte offers, relieved to be of even this modest assistance.

Rey growls with frustration and turns to exit

the office, slamming the door behind her. Charlotte remains seated, hands folded in her lap, beginning to have serious doubts if she will snag a presidential selfie after all.

---

HAYLEY JOGS UNDER the shadow of the Capitol building and through the Botanic Garden, veering northwest to Jefferson Drive, which traces the length of the National Mall. Running is second nature, her pace effortless and each footfall seemingly preordained. Past the Air and Space Museum, then the Hirshhorn and the baroque Smithsonian Castle, past national monuments buzzing with the usual swarms of tourists and school groups. None of them knows what she knows, blissfully ignorant of the dark forces roiling behind closed doors to undermine a benign democracy they take for granted. Hayley's pace is strong and steady. Running is as easy as breathing, effortless whether in work clothes or PT gear.

The Washington Monument looms to her left as Hayley tacks right at Fifteenth Street, jogging north. She has yet to see anything not normally witnessed every weekday on the nation's front yard. Tourists mix easily with the District's worker bees. Vehicular traffic in the streets flows steady and unhindered. But as she runs diagonally across the Ellipse to Seventeenth Street, just south of the White House complex, Hayley encounters the fringes of the enormous anti-Russian rally. As she continues running north on Seventeenth, devoid of the normal vehicular traffic, she hears the demonstration before seeing it. An intensifying howl strikes her as bestial, snarling and angry. Soon enough, with the EEOB behind her to the right, Hayley can see Lafayette Square and the throng of protestors corralled by police there. Turning then to her right, Hayley observes, through trees that have shed all of their leaves and stand bare under the clear sky, Malkin's motorcade pulling up to the door of the Diplomatic Reception Room at the south side of the White House.

Withdrawing her White House credentials from her pocket and draping them around her neck, Hayley advances toward the Seventeenth Street gate outside the EEOB. The Secret Service uniformed officer at the gate entrance recognizes Hayley and smiles, despite the circumstances. "Hi, Hayley. Crazy day, huh?" Ned remarks.

Hayley, only slightly out of breath from her three-mile run, grins, opting for nonchalance. "Ned, how are you?" She gestures in the direction of Lafayette Square. "Makes you miss home a little, doesn't it?"

He grins and shrugs. "Not really."

Hayley laughs, nodding. She grips her credentials hanging from the lanyard around her neck so the policeman can easily see and inputs the four-digit code she has always used. The computer response display on the screen is clearly not what Ned had hoped to see. "Looks like you're not cleared for today, Hayley."

She was prepared for this obstacle. "Must be some mistake. I was due in Operations thirty minutes ago. Going to be crazy in there this morning."

"Sorry, Hayley. Can't let you through. Maybe you can call Ms. Rey?"

"Karen Rey is going to be way too busy to deal with this right now, Ned." With a beseeching smile, she adds, "Come on. You know I'm not a terrorist, right?"

The officer reluctantly frowns and shakes his head. "Can't do it, Hayley. You're not entering the complex today."

Hayley acknowledges Ned's reluctance to disappoint her with a brave smile and pivots, walking north on Seventeenth Street. Having taken her shot and failed, she is now unsure what next to do. Perhaps Asher hasn't left the grounds yet. If not, she can enlist his effort to get word to the president. Dialing Asher's number, she realizes now supporting his decision to leave town was a mistake. As she waits for him to answer, Hayley stares through the fence surrounding the complex. The exterior of the Oval Office is within sight. It might as well be on Mars.

Her call goes to voice mail. In the past, he has always picked up. Asher Danes's phone is as vital a part of him as his heart. She assumes he is ducking her call, wanting to be done with the whole business. Hayley doesn't bother to leave a message but disconnects and starts to walk in the direction of Lafayette Square with no clear purpose except to lose herself in the crowd.

---

ASHER HAD ALREADY cleared Baltimore and was approaching the exit for Abingdon off I-95 when he saw Hayley's call light up his phone on the passenger seat next to him. He reluctantly picked up the phone to answer but then thought better of it and tossed the phone on the seat again. What more is there to say? He's left Washington and is unsure he'll ever be back. The notion of running for Congress now seems an embarrassing and juvenile pipe dream. His father, a graduate of Harvard Law School, has quietly lobbied for Asher entering the legal profession. Certainly there are worse fates.

The unappealing thrum of the Prius hybrid motor fills the vehicle cabin. Asher had pointedly not played music over the sound system. The less stimulation, the better. Perhaps his thoughts make for bad company, but Asher masochistically inflicts them on himself. First and foremost are his stifling feelings of guilt and self-loathing. He had quite obviously been played by Odom, who used Daniel as honeypot to draw Asher into a conspiratorial web. He no longer trusts a single thing Odom has told him in the past, and with that conviction comes a realization that he has the blood of at least two men on his hands.

Thoughts like these continue to tumble inside his head, a free-for-all of contradictory ideas and paralyzing uncertainty. What if Monroe and his agenda really are bad for the country? Perhaps James Odom and his mysterious cabal are patriots willing to sacrifice everything for the nation's sake. Has he abandoned the effort just in its eleventh hour? Daniel ghosted him, but does that necessarily mean everything they discussed about the Monroe White House is to be rejected as well? In that case, no atonement needed. Maybe a degree from Harvard with the goal of a career in environmental law is the most productive course of action.

Oh, God, the eternal back-and-forth! As he drives north, toward the comfort and familiarity of his parents' home, Asher falls deeper and deeper into despair. The bland interstate pavement unspools beneath the tires of his car. In the abnormal silence of the vehicle's cabin, he falls prey to the master of torture that is his hyper-educated mind. Who will dispose of his many beautiful objects in the condo at 3303 Water Street? Who will ever love him? Who is Hayley Chill? And, finally, the question he keeps asking himself over and over again, who is Asher Danes?

---

IN THE OVAL Office, the two world leaders strike a pose for the clutch of press pool photographers. Sitting in twin armchairs before the fireplace, Malkin and Monroe reach toward each other, clasp hands, smile widely, and make self-deprecating jokes to their respective aides backstopping the photographers. The mood in the room is lighthearted. Friendly relations between former adversaries are a win for planet Earth and its eight billion inhabitants.

The photo opportunity continues for an awkward duration. The two world leaders would release their grasps on each other's hand, but senior aides from both countries encourage their bosses to continue. The visit is going well, despite the unfortunate incident yesterday outside the embassy and the thousands of protestors massed outside in Lafayette Square. If only the press and hostile pundits could be convinced to embrace the concept of an allied Russia and United States.

A reporter standing to one side of the room calls out loud enough to be heard over the clatter of camera shutters. "Mr. President, did you and President Malkin discuss Russia's threatening stance toward Estonia and possible US intervention in the crisis?"

Monroe and Malkin let go of each other's hand so the US president may address the reporter directly. He looks magnificent in his blue suit and red tie, a profile that instantly commands respect and awe. The unfortunate Russian president, with a diminishing chin, receding hairline, slumping shoulders, and too short legs, seems not quite the same species in comparison. He looks to Monroe with keen attention and what seems like real affection as the US president thoughtfully considers the question.

"We did discuss the situation in Eastern Europe, and President Malkin was most helpful in clarifying Russia's case and intentions. These are long-standing disagreements by two sovereign countries with a history that goes back centuries and that, by simple geographical measure alone, don't involve the interests of the United States."

A chorus of questions erupts from the pool of reporters corralled by the southeast door leading directly out to the West Wing corridor. Monroe gestures for quiet and immediately receives it from the respectful White House correspondents.

"NATO is more than seventy years old, formed in a different time when the partner countries had just emerged from the horrors of the Second World War. Today, we witness a new Europe, a new Russia, and a new and vital United States, one that welcomes innovative and powerful alliances in its fight against terrorism and, even more importantly, in confrontation with an emergent Chinese threat."

The reporters have a dozen follow-up questions, but White House aides brusquely show them out the door as the two world leaders stand up from their armchairs and stretch their legs. Malkin leans in close to whisper in Monroe's ear. No one hears what the two world leaders say to one another, but the US president grins in response to the Russian president's jovial aside.

———————————

No ONE IS more surprised that Richard Monroe sits in the Oval Office swapping jokes with the Russian president than Richard Monroe. The book that launched his candidacy wasn't even his idea, but his wife's. From the beginning, the plan had been to end his military career with the Joint Chiefs of Staff, culminating with elevation to chairman or vice chairman. He could not have imagined a finer way to cap his long service career.

That plan unraveled in a single afternoon, with the visit of a freelance journalist to Fort Shafter, headquarters for US Army Pacific Command. Doing a story on the oldest military base on Oahu, the journalist was given relatively free access. She happened to be within earshot when Monroe, shooting the shit with some of his junior officers, was overheard criticizing the current administration's appeasement of the Chinese juggernaut. This being private confines on a US military base, all in attendance, including General Monroe, used salty language. Later that night, the journalist wrote a story that was picked up by the *Los Angeles Times* and, within a few hours, by every other news organization in the country. When army officials questioned the veracity of her reporting, tapes were made available that confirmed everything in her article.

Monroe was immediately summoned to Washington. After a brief meeting with the president in the Oval Office, during which he reiterated a "clean" version of his taped allegations, the much-decorated general submitted his resignation and thereby ended a forty-year career with the US Army. The popularity of America's Warrior wasn't diminished in the slightest by his defiance of his commander in chief. In fact, many of his fans thought more highly of him for it. But Monroe downplayed this acclaim, anticipating nothing but a quiet retirement with his loving wife in their beautiful home on Poipu Drive overlooking Maunalua Bay. He had worked hard his entire life, seen men die and witnessed human suffering beyond imagining. He deserved the idyllic retirement Hawaii offered. Richard Monroe was at peace with himself.

But there are only so many times one can stare out over the magnificence of Maunalua Bay and the green sawtooth hills beyond before iridescent beauty morphs into nagging boredom. Especially for a man like Monroe, with his history of conquest and adventure, the need for fresh challenges and tests of will never really ever diminishes. Monroe said nothing, not to his closest friends or family. He simply held it in, reliving memories of tank charges and clearing enemy fighters from urban strongholds. He could almost smell the stink of war and hear its unmistakable racket as he stared at dark nimbus clouds that belched rain across the bay. In truth, Monroe was stoically miserable in retirement, not yet three months in duration.

His wife of thirty years suggested he get his recollections down on paper in the form of a military memoir. Initially, Monroe rejected the idea. Though he was a good writer, unlike most of his fellow officers and commanders, the very notion of revealing his inner thoughts and personal memories was distasteful. What changed his mind was Cindy's suggestion that such a book would be the perfect platform from which he could argue his broader points, the same ones that had cost him his career. The final chapter could detail in full his geopolitical beliefs and serve as clarion call of the real threats facing the United States. Motivated in this way, Monroe threw himself into the task of writing his memoirs with the same dedication, diligence, and hard work that defined his years in the military.

His book, *A Life in the Army*, was a mammoth bestseller, with almost nine hundred thousand copies sold. More importantly, the memoir and its reception drew the attention of a number of influential people in the party, a kind of unofficial nominating committee, that met with the general and convinced him to undertake a few exploratory visits to early primary states, where his speeches, written by Monroe himself, were met with wildly enthusiastic receptions. A groundswell emerged around the idea of a President Richard Monroe. Faster than anyone could have predicted, including Monroe himself, the retired general led a field of more conventional party candidates. Sensing an unstoppable bandwagon, several of his strongest opponents dropped out of the race, and Monroe cruised to an easy nomination in Philadelphia less than two years after being ignominiously sacked by the sitting president.

At every campaign stop during the general election, Monroe made the same pitch: left unchecked, China would be the number one superpower in the world and capable of dominating the US militarily. His stance regarding NATO and Russia were rarely requested by reporters and, consequently, rarely offered. Jobs and military security were the positions on which General Monroe staked his candidacy for president, and they were the positions that won him that office in an electoral landslide. His inauguration was greeted with great hope and a sense that US values had been reaffirmed. After a long period of chaos and upheaval in the nation's capital, the majority of voters believed that normalcy had returned to Washington. America had elected a decent, honest man to be their leader.

Almost a full year into his presidency, one punctuated with significant legislative victories as well as rancorous clashes with the opposite party and members of the entrenched Washington establishment, President Monroe sometimes walks the corridors of the White House residence late at night, gazing into the faces of the presidential portraits hanging on the walls. Privately, he is bewildered to be among their company, the nation's iconic founders. The Great Men. On these nocturnal strolls, observed by no one, Monroe longs to smell war again and hear the cacophony of battle. Who is he really, this specter on the silent second floor of the White House residence? Why him? How is it he came to live and work in this hallowed place? Of these musings and doubts, no one must know. Not Cindy. Not anyone. No one should know the truth. Not ever.

---

THE CIA OFFICE of deputy director, Intelligence Integration, is spacious and well-ordered. Framed photographs hang on the wall, images from James Odom's life's work in service to his country. Riding a camel in Saudi Arabia. Odom standing in the rubble of what was once the picturesque Old City of Mosul. Receiving an honor from Barack Obama. The office inhabitant's prized possession is propped in a corner, a Charleville musket, Model 1770, that was reportedly fired by a colonist rebel at the Battle of Bunker Hill. Visitors invariably are drawn to the historic weapon and are encouraged by its proud owner to pick it up and handle it to better appreciate its weight (ten pounds) and impressive length (sixty inches). Every Fourth of July, the gun is discharged at one Independence Day celebration or another and as such is always a showstopper.

James Odom, seated behind his desk with landline phone pressed to his ear, stares at the musket as he waits for a call to be picked up by its recipient. He ponders the human race's instinct for war, to settle all disagreements with violence and submission. These ruminations are not self-righteous or ethical judgments but rather simple observations of fact. All that he has achieved, his position with the agency and stature within the intelligence community at large, will not be taken from him without a fight. The undeniable fact that his needs dovetail with those of the nation renders his actions unassailable and pristine. His cause is virtuous.

The call goes through. A male's voice comes across the line. "Yes?"

Odom is somber. History is made with phone calls like this one. He must not ever forget the moment. Two words suffice. "It's time." He replaces the phone receiver in its cradle, stands up from his seat, and turns toward a coatrack standing next to the office door.

A few minutes later, the deputy director exits the building through the main entrance and, wearing a navy-blue duffel coat and astrakhan cap, hurries toward the parking lot. Despite clear, blue skies, Odom hunches over as if carrying a heavy burden over his back. The air has gone cold and the wind blows steady.

HAYLEY IS DRAWN to the protest in Lafayette Square, a spectacle that cannot be ignored. Normal human behavior has seemingly been suspended, replaced by temporary insanity and rule of the mob. The city police, joined by units from federal agencies, attempt to tame the beast, but it is too large and unpredictable. Barricades have been trampled, and demonstrators pour into the streets like supercharged, hometown fans onto a football field after a come-from-behind victory.

More phalanxes of police march into the fray. Hayley stands on the sidelines, watching the police go about the business of establishing order with a frenzy that matches the mob's fury. They swing their clubs and truncheons with crisp flicks of their wrist, relentless and methodical as seasoned farmworkers.

But the furious protestors, having submitted to their beatdowns at the hands of the Russian security personnel the day before, refuse to capitulate to the US authorities. They fight back with sticks, improvised weapons, and fists. Hayley watches, horrified by the violence. Somewhere a tear gas canister expels its noxious fumes. A mounted policeman swings his baton from high up in the saddle, clubbing heads. The screams of demonstrators who have been injured merge with the howls of their compatriots who avenge those injuries. Hayley shouts but cannot hear her own voice over the clang and blare of the riot.

It is a nightmare in daylight. The sight of a Park Police officer repeatedly striking a female protestor with his baton fixates Hayley. The woman has ceased

MONROE PAUSES IN the doorway of the Cabinet Room, where the Russian president and his clutch of advisors have gathered, and takes in the scene. The Russians are on one side of the long table, facing the Rose Garden windows, while Deputy Chief of Staff Rodgers and other aides wait for him to join them on the opposite side. The US president enters; the room instantly becomes quiet and alert. This long-anticipated and controversial meeting between superpower leaders is moments from commencing. Nothing is more important than its success. No sound or racket of the riot in Lafayette Square permeates into the room.

The new intern, Charlotte, enters unnoticed. She carries the president's all-important briefing book, significant in its leather binding and historic background. The young female intern scarcely breathes. Blood pounds through her vessels, head buzzing. Not in a million years would she have imagined this moment would be a reality. As instructed by Karen Rey, Charlotte has triple-checked the contents of the briefing book, compiled by the staff only within the last thirty minutes, and delivers it to the president's seat at the table opposite the Russian president. "Neither seen nor heard" was Rey's admonition an hour earlier and not difficult for Charlotte to obey. Her anxiety level is off the charts as she places the briefing book on the table.

"Who the hell is this?" Charlotte hears someone say, unsure who has said it and to whom it is in reference. She looks timidly in the direction of the president and is horrified to realize it was Monroe speaking about her! Karen Rey, standing next to POTUS, gapes at her like Charlotte is on fire, or worse. What would be worse than being on fire? Bewildered and ashamed, Charlotte cannot begin to find the answer to that question.

---

KAREN REY IS defined by her position as a senior aide in the West Wing. When she wakes up in the morning, she is an assistant to the president, White House Operations. When she goes to bed at night, she is an assistant to the president, White House Operations. When Karen Rey dreams, she dreams as an assistant to the president, White House Operations. Six months ago, at the prodding of her colleagues, Rey composed a profile on Bumble, the dating app, and dutifully fielded dozens of suitors before settling on a modestly good-looking lobbyist with thinning hair and dad body. A dozen desultory "dates" followed their first coffee. Sexual intercourse was achieved on two occasions but even in those interludes, Karen Rey remained, essentially, an assistant to the president, White House Operations. The lobbyist, understandably, grew bored with Rey's shoptalk and decamped for further, more productive swiping.

Job security is not a hallmark with any administration, but Peter Hall's shocking death has raised Rey's employment anxiety to a high pitch. A new chief of staff will want his or her own people for the most important West Wing positions. To shore up her defenses against this probable outcome, Rey has been waging a campaign to ingratiate herself with the president and make herself the "indispensable woman" in the West Wing. She has never gotten the sense the former general really likes her very much, and Rey frets she isn't "female" enough for the traditional-minded president. His eyes always seem to soften in the presence of Suzy Powell, the assistant to the president for presidential personnel, who has curves going in just about every direction but down. If she had the time and, more critically, the money for breast implants, Rey unhesitatingly would purchase them.

Sadly, bigger breasts won't help her now. POTUS is furious with her for exiling Hayley Chill, that sneaky little bitch, to the Library of Congress and has demanded the West Virginian be re-installed within the hour or else. Monroe's "else" needs no elaboration. Rey can no more easily imagine being fired from this job than a parent can imagine the death of a child. Several calls to Deb Spellman over at the Madison Building have achieved nothing. Hayley hasn't been seen in more than two hours and cannot be located. Calls to her cell phone go straight to voice mail. What can Rey do to find the missing intern? Call up the National Guard?

How the president could concern himself with the whereabouts of a single intern while Malkin visits and Lafayette Square explodes with riot is beyond Karen Rey's comprehension. Unless the intern is located soon, Rey is finished in the West Wing. She sits at Hayley's old desk in White House Operations and looks around the room. Asher Danes disappeared. Hayley Chill missing. Her future in shambles. If there were a loaded handgun on the desktop, Rey would blow her own brains out. To have come this far only to be undone by an undereducated, thin-lipped, taciturn hillbilly from God Knows Where, West Virginia, is too dismal a fate. In her desperation, Rey wonders if her two-fuck, ex–Bumble date would help in securing a job at his lobbying firm.

The landline on Hayley's desk rings, and Rey, shot through with renewed hope, answers before the second ring.

"Yes? Who?" she barks into the phone. On hearing the answer, Rey experiences euphoric relief. "Yes, dammit! She works here!"

---

WITHIN TEN MINUTES, Deputy Chief of Staff Kyle Rodgers greets Hayley as she enters the first floor of the West Wing from the stairwell.

"Well, I guess this is what they mean when they say, 'the worm turns,' eh Miss Chill?"

"I think this is exactly what they mean by that one, sir."

Hayley respectfully starts to walk around the deputy chief of staff, assuming he has more important things to do than chat, but apparently office gossip is significant enough.

"You would've enjoyed the look on her face when POTUS was asking after you."

"Yes, I imagine I would've liked that very much."

Rodgers works his imagination coming up with a

relatable image. "Deer in headlights doesn't really do it justice."

"Back home folks hunt for wild boar and such with a Moultrie feeder hog light. Something like that, I'm guessing."

The deputy chief of staff grins as he starts to move on, enjoying the image. "Yes. Something a lot like that."

When she arrives finally at the deserted White House Operations office, she stands in the open doorway, stopped by the sight of Asher Danes's empty chair. He hasn't returned any of her calls. All she wants is to know he is okay. There is no reason to think he isn't fine, well north by now and home in Connecticut by nightfall. But then she thinks of Homer Stephens and recalls the glimpse of Peter Hall through the pantry window, lying on his back on the kitchen floor. Death stalks all of them. Its specter increases her sense of isolation. Almost but not quite, she wishes she were home or, better, back at Fort Hood. Death is not what she fears but rather this arid loneliness, gnawing at her from within. She misses Asher's companionship.

"Well, there you are!" exclaims Karen Rey, standing in the other doorway, her voice too bright and shiny. "We were worried about you."

Hayley smiles lightly, adopting the persona required for the situation, dark thoughts packed into a box and put away for the time being. "Thank you, ma'am. Nice to be back."

"I can't believe you were caught up in all that craziness out there. Were you hurt? Shall I call the doctor?"

Hayley shakes her head. "Thank you. No, ma'am. I'm fine."

There will be no mention of her banishment to the Library of Congress. From this point forward, they will be best friends. Karen Rey's job depends on it. "Hayley, I wonder if you'd be available this weekend?"

"Ma'am?"

"POTUS is spending the weekend at Camp David. We could use your help out there. Asher would normally be on tap to do it, but he seems to have flown the coop!"

Rey's forced cheeriness threatens to shatter her entire face into a million pieces of bitterness and rage. If she can't retreat back to the safety of her own office in the next few seconds, the White House aide feels like she might kill this vicious bitch with her bare hands. Hayley, pretending to be unaware of the power she now holds over Rey, mercifully refrains from drawing the moment out. Vanquishing her West Wing nemesis is neither a priority nor of any real interest to Hayley. "Yes, of course, ma'am. It would be an honor."

The smile creasing Rey's face like an open wound disappears. "Caravan leaves from the complex at eleven sharp tomorrow," she tells Hayley before vanishing from the doorway.

------

THE PARKING LOT to the side of Andy's Crab House in Shady Side is again packed with black cars, SUVs with tinted windows, and a familiar Buick Regal TourX. Out on the bay, the wind pushes up a frantic chop across the water. A small-craft warning is in effect. The trees framing the property twist and heave in the wind. The louvered windows on the large, walled-in porch are closed with blinds drawn. What transpires inside the wood-frame building is meant to stay private and hidden from view.

Inside, the conspirators meet. Seated around a picnic table are the six men, all with grave expressions. Andy knows well enough to stay inside the kitchen. None of the men care whether or not their coffee is hot, their guts in the grip of fear and regret. Their business is grim, the stakes monumental. The world as it has existed all of their lives teeters on the brink. To do nothing risks becoming an anachronism. The decision facing them is one they didn't want to make and did everything they could to forestall, including the murder of a friend and sometimes colleague who had betrayed their collective interests. But to show ambivalence or empathy is weakness and not a habit of their tribe. Bravado is a mask, and stabs of gallows humor a better one still.

"I swear, if I have to watch the country led by this despot one more day, I'll take a gun to him myself!" Senator Cox mutters.

"Is that a campaign promise you can actually keep, Senator?" quips one of the other conspirators.

The senator raises himself up as tall as his faltering spine will allow. "I fail to see the humor in the situation, sir."

Odom gestures for quiet. He holds affection for none of these men and considers all of them his intellectual inferiors. But this is a democracy, or so they say. What was Rumsfeld's line? You go to war with the army you have. In James Odom's opinion, truer words were never spoken. He wishes he had been the one to say it first.

"Gentlemen, a show of hands. The operation can be approved only by unanimous vote."

Senator Cox quickly raises his hand, followed by the four other conspirators. Odom pauses, then also raises his hand. "So be it. Damocles is a go."

For a moment, there is an unnatural silence at the table. All of these men, including Odom, are rarely hesitant to talk. Over the course of four months, they have met here almost a dozen times to discuss the Monroe presidency and devise a plan to contain it. These discussions have been heated and marked by fear, obscenity, and disagreement. How could you expect less from a roomful of powerful, inside-the-beltway egomaniacs?

But with their momentous decision made, the men seem spent. A shadow of depression and emotional exhaustion has fallen on each of them, abruptly and unexpectedly. Those capable of reflection wonder how they got here and if a better man couldn't have devised a better alternative. Those not prone to looking inward simply feel numb and shove their broodings to less threatening arenas. All of them, however, experience a sudden passivity to which they are unaccustomed. Trigger pulled, they are reduced to the roles of spectators. All will be saved or all will be lost. There is no middle ground in the panorama of potential consequences.

Only a few seconds have ticked past since Odom last spoke, but those moments seem like eternity. One of the white-haired men stares down at his hands folded on the tabletop, hesitant to look the others in the eye. "God save the United States," he says quietly.

---

THE POTOMAC ANGLERS Association charges its members neither dues nor initiation fees. With total membership numbering eleven, the PAA meets every Saturday morning at the Whole Foods in Alexandria to discuss, over coffee and baked goods, nearly everything except fishing. They are all male, except for Susan Cho, and they are all over the age of sixty-five. The founders of the Potomac Anglers Association are Hal and Stan, and the most frequent attendees. What is generally understood but never discussed is the fact that Susan Cho is the best angler of them all, though the newest member, Terry Winch, just might give her a run for her money.

Hal and Stan had mentioned the possibility of taking a boat out last Saturday, but the weather had been poor all week—cold and cloudy—so that plan wasn't likely to be realized. The members of the PAA dislike going out on the river on weekends. Too many drunks. Too much trouble. It was enough to gather at Whole Foods on Saturdays and then watch sports on television on Sundays. Surprising to each of them, really, was

To settle their disagreement, they agreed to flip a coin. Stan, the natural born gambler, won the toss, and off they rowed, south toward the Key Bridge.

Hal set anchor a hundred yards north of the bridge. Stan lit a cigar. Hal threw his line into the water, having gotten his rig in order while Stan rowed. Settling back and enjoying the truly awe-inspiring view, Hal reflected on how intensely he loved his life in retirement. Thirty-five years spent in a tollbooth on the Dulles Greenway will give a man a keen appreciation for simple pleasures, such as fishing with a buddy from a Fletchers rowboat one hundred yards north of the Key Bridge. What fish can one hope to snag on the Potomac, within the sight of the nation's Capitol building? Striped and largemouth bass, shad, and catfish are the primary prey of a typical angler, but the members of the PAA count the elusive snakehead as their prized catch. Susan Cho has caught them all and in infuriating abundance.

But it isn't for fish any of them journey onto the river, with all members espousing a "catch and release" philosophy. No, their true, shared motivation is having the experience and companionship. Unspoken is the urge to feel the texture of life while they still can. They each can feel the hot breath of death on their shoulders. Time is short and life is sweet. Fishing is only an excuse to just stop and breathe. All that being said, the tug on a line was still a thrill, the connection with something *down there*, below the surface of the water and cloaked in murkiness. Such was his delight when Stan threw his rig over the side, watching the line carried south by the gentle current toward the bridge and when, to his eternal surprise, he felt that joyous and sudden pull.

"Holy shit, Stan! You've got a big one! Holy fucking shit!" Hal immediately starts to reel in his line so he can be available to help his friend with his catch.

"Goddamn, Hal. I can barely reel 'er in. This sucker's fightin' like a sonuvabitch." Stan, the stout-hearted fisherman, reels steady and true.

His rig secure, Hal peers into the water where Stan's line disappears taut into the murk. "Christ, I think you've got a snakehead, Stan! Holy goddamn, a snakehead! Wait until Susan Cho gets a load of this!" Hal fumbles for his phone so he can record the mighty feat for posterity.

Stan continues to bring the beast to the surface, the inexorable reeling-in like the work of a divine machine. "Let's just wait and see, Hal. Almost there." The pole bends almost in half. "Goddamn, she's a motherfuckin' fighter, this one!" The smile on the old man's face is one of unadulterated joy. It's the smile he wore fifty-seven years ago when he landed his first fish. Life is good. Life is so very good.

As the shape at the end of Stan's fishing line materializes from the depths, it looks neither like fabled snakehead or any other fish the men have plucked from the gentle Potomac. "What in the world is that?" Hal asks no one in particular as he gazes over the boat rail. "What the hell did you catch there, Stan?"

Stan cannot lift the object out of the water with his fishing pole. His line would snap from the weight and bulky shape of the thing. But he can see it with his own eyes now, hovering just an inch or two below the river's surface. He can read the label on the object from where he sits, plain as day: JANSPORT.

"That's a goddamn backpack, Hal," he needlessly informs his fishing buddy. "Some poor dummy lost their backpack in the river."

Hal leans over for a better look. "Holy shit, Stan. Look. There's a freakin' knife stuck in it. Like it's been stabbed!"

---

JAMES ODOM IS back at his office. He had called Sinatra from the car just after leaving Andy's. The operative received the go-ahead without comment. General plans are already in place, but the president's schedule shifts daily and the operation would not be truly set in motion until Sinatra has reviewed the immediate schedule in detail. He promises to get back to Odom as soon as he can give him operational details and an exact time of kickoff. That was only a couple hours earlier. Odom is surprised when he sees that Sinatra is calling again so soon.

"Received an interesting call from my contact with Metro Police," the operative informs Odom.

"I'm all ears."

"A backpack was recovered from the river by a couple old farts fishing. Our guy's knife was stuck in it."

"Yes?" Odom can't hide his excitement. The other conspirators had expressed a good deal of anxiety green-lighting the operation while an unidentified witness remained even a possibility. He allayed their fears with assurances his team would find the witness if in fact one existed. Privately, Odom worried the mysterious second passenger would emerge after the operation's successful conclusion and present a significant problem. That a lead had materialized from the bottom of the Potomac at the end of a fishing pole was a delicious twist of fate. He wished he could share his delight with someone, but Sinatra was an unlikely candidate. His operative was just too damn weird to relate with casual emotion or humor.

"Mostly emptied out by the currents and whatnot. Cops can't determine for certain it came from the car, having no way to tie the combat knife to our man. But there were some building keys. Henry House, in Rosslyn."

"Henry House? What the hell is that?"

"Intern housing. Only interns live at Henry House."

---

WALKING ON JACKSON Place, along the west side of Lafayette Square, Hayley can see city workers cleaning up the detritus of the earlier riot. Having gone from seeing the inside of a prisoner transport van to cruising the carpeted hallways of the West Wing, Hayley has experienced circumstantial extremes in a span of less than six hours that few can imagine. The phone call from Karen Rey informing her of the transfer to the Library of Congress seems a very long time ago. Ending the day once again stationed only steps from the Oval Office, Hayley might be tempted to believe her world restabilized. But hope can be a drug, the self-medication of the deluded and mentally lazy. She has a job to do and a clear path to completion of that mission. A whole weekend in the more casual environment of Camp David affords her the perfect opportunity to speak directly and in private with the president.

Her stomach hurts from not eating. The only food she consumed the entire day was after her run that morning, a small bowl of dry granola and fruit. Waiting for her at home, in total, is a can of tuna and an avocado. She's too exhausted to contemplate going to the store. Rest is what she needs. Close and lock the door behind her. Turn off the phone, television, and computer. Read nothing. And sleep. Of all the days since leaving Fort Hood, many of them difficult and long, this day had been the longest and most difficult.

The walk from her bus stop in Rosslyn to Henry House is less than ten minutes. Many of her neighbors are also arriving home from work. Cars are stacked up in the street, circling the block in the eternal search for an available parking space. Hayley only has to round the corner at Ode Street, walk the fifty or so feet to the walkway leading to the building entrance, then into the vestibule, up one flight of stairs, and stroll the few steps to her apartment door. She's almost home, her refuge. Approaching the corner, Hayley stops suddenly and shifts laterally, stepping off of the curb and crouching between two parked cars.

Every available parking space is occupied on the block. On both sides of the street, a large percentage of parked vehicles are SUVs. For that reason, Bishop had felt reasonably confident in his choice of stakeouts. One Cadillac Escalade with tinted windows draws no more notice than the GMC Yukon with tinted windows parked directly in front of it. Directly across the street is a Lincoln Navigator. Three cars forward is a Chevrolet Tahoe. Clearly, America loves its vehicles big. What Bishop could not have factored into his decision was Hayley's photographic memory. She has seen this relatively generic Escalade before, parked outside Scott Billings's house. She knows this vehicle and can easily recall its license plate number. Virginia plate, YHT-9919.

Somewhere she can hear the joyous howls of the neighborhood children playing in their yards in spite of the raw December air and early night sky. Blue shadows are cast out of the windows of surrounding homes and apartments by televisions tuned to favorite shows. Kitchens are being straightened after family dinners, the familiarity of early-evening routine like a comforting blanket. If Bishop had bothered to look back over his shoulder from the passenger seat of the Escalade and scanned the open space between a Ford and VW van parked at the curb behind where they'd parked, he would see only that: space. The object of their stakeout and pursuit, Hayley Chill, is long gone.

# 8

★ ★ ★ ★

## DAMOCLES

The J. Edgar Hoover Building, a cast-in-place concrete pile located on Pennsylvania Avenue, had outlived its natural life span and mediocre design more than a decade ago. Embracing its Brutalist architectural style with the bear hug of a professional wrestler, it inspires only dread and existential angst. Against the cold, gray December-morning sky, the headquarters of the Federal Bureau of Investigation stands as a stark monument to a bulldog of a man who led it for nearly fifty years.

Hayley sits in the lobby, having spent the night wandering from one improvised haven to the next. First, it was an all-night diner on Wisconsin Avenue. Leaving there after an obscenely satisfying meal of eggs, bacon, and pancakes, she walked what seemed like the length of the city, paying homage to deserted landmarks that seemed imbued with the spirits of their historic honorees in the cold hours after midnight. Alone, with ol' Abe staring down at her from his granite and marble throne, Hayley certainly knew the end of her rope when she'd found it. James Odom had somehow linked her to Scott Billings and was aware she was witness to their treasonous crimes. She had no doubt in her mind what the men in the Escalade would do if they found her.

If Hayley had learned anything in her life experiences and training, it was to be pragmatic. Every action involves a degree of risk, calculated or not. Standing in the shadows of the otherwise deserted Lincoln Memorial and shivering from the subfreezing temperatures, she fully appreciated her dilemma. Should she continue to keep her own counsel and risk her message dying with her or reach out again to a potentially untrustworthy authority?

How far the conspiracy spread throughout the federal government and its agencies was not for her to guess. But one thing was crystal clear: she needed rest in order to think clearly. Sleep-deprived, and with temperatures plummeting, Hayley found refuge at Union Station, that elegant confluence of Pennsylvania and Baltimore and Ohio Railroads willed into existence in 1903 by President Theodore Roosevelt. Collapsed on a varnished wooden bench and gazing up into that lusciously hypnotic Beaux-Arts geometric ceiling, she slept like the dead.

With first light came her decision. Hayley made

the call before seven a.m. and, as instructed, now sits here, under austere architectural expression, and better rested. Helen Udall exits the elevator across the lobby and immediately clocks Hayley on her bench. "Ms. Chill, thank you for calling and coming over straightaway."

"Thank you for agreeing to meet me, ma'am."

"Are you okay? Do you need some coffee?"

"I'm fine, Agent Udall. Thank you."

"It would've been better if you had spoken up before. You may recall, I asked you repeatedly if there was more to your story."

"Sorry, ma'am. First I had to get a better idea who were the good guys and who were the bad." She pauses, meeting the FBI agent's gaze squarely. "I'm just an intern and new in town."

"The FBI would be the good guys, Ms. Chill," Udall says dryly.

"I really wish I could be certain of that, ma'am."

"You're sitting in the lobby of the J. Edgar Hoover Building. Is there a more trustworthy place in the country?"

"We could ask John Callahan if he were still alive. I think it was an FBI special agent who helped Whitey Bulger kill him."

Udall doesn't particularly enjoy being called on her own bullshit. "Just an intern, huh?" she asks rhetorically. "You in the habit of disrespecting the people you ask for help?"

"Ma'am, I'm just trying to explain the motivations

behind my actions." Hayley wants to appear sincere. She knows Udall is potentially an important ally. A recognizable world teeters on the precipice. "I guess the thing is, you can only trust someone until you can't."

"Yes, and that cuts both ways, doesn't it, Ms. Chill?"

Hayley says nothing. She worries she has lost the FBI agent with her crack about Callahan and the Bulger scandal. She launches into the entire story, relating every detail from discovery of the boot print to Scott's attack, and wrapping up with her entanglements with James Odom and the hit team staking out her apartment building. Udall takes notes throughout Hayley's monologue, never lifting her eyes off the pages of her notebook. After Hayley is finished, the FBI agent spends minutes reviewing her own notes, tapping the end of her pencil against the side of her head with increasing excitement as she reads, before finally looking up to meet Hayley's anxious gaze.

As measured as possible considering what she has just heard, Udall says, "This is all very interesting, but . . ." She falters, finding it hard to continue.

"What?" Hayley asks warily.

"Frankly, I haven't been able to find any concrete evidence of wrongdoing in Hall's death. Our investigation was more or less concluded."

"So? I'm here. I'll do whatever is necessary. Make an official statement. Testify. Whatever."

Udall can only offer defense by way of a thinly veiled criticism: "I wish you had spoken up sooner."

"Ma'am, the president's life—"

"Is threatened probably fifty times a day, in one form or another. Everybody wants to kill every president. Monroe is no different. That's why we have the Secret Service."

"Agent Udall, the Secret Service, or parts of it, may be involved in this."

Udall seems unimpressed. "It'll take some time, Ms. Chill. My superiors will need convincing."

"What about the drugs you found in Peter Hall's system? I saw direct evidence of intrusion into the chief of staff's residence the night of his death."

The FBI agent is stone-faced. "Further investigation uncovered recreational drug usage in Hall's immediate history."

"A Secret Service agent on the president's detail tried to kill me, ma'am!"

"Wouldn't be the first time lovers quarreled, Ms. Chill," Udall reminds her with a slightly judgmental tone. If either of them knew Hayley's backpack had been retrieved from the Potomac, Udall would have all the hard evidence she needed to believe at least a portion of what the intern alleged. But that evidence had been inventoried the previous night at the Metro Police Department's Evidence Control Branch at 17 DC Village Lane, in the southwest, and placed alongside more than one hundred thousand other items. The knife and pack have zero chance of being connected to Scott Billings or Hayley Chill by the police.

The FBI agent stands up to leave. "Give me a day or two. Take a beat while I handle things on my end."

THERE IS NO time to absorb the whiplash of disappointment in Agent Udall's failure to act quickly. The sting of regret will diminish as the inevitable cascade of emotions and decisions forces its way to the surface of her consciousness. Pushed down, she stands back up. The way blocked, she reverses course and returns to where she has first come. This is her way, a mental toughness that defines her character. After a night spent literally on the street and wearing the same clothes she wore the day before, Hayley must make some stops before returning to the White House. Without looking in the mirror, she's certain she looks like hell.

After purchasing some necessities at Walgreens on F Street, she brings them into the bathroom there and does a reasonable job of fixing hair, face, and teeth. She finds a Forever 21 on the same block and ducks inside. Any clothing will do as long as it's a change of clothing. Swapping out of what she'd been wearing for the last twenty-four hours in the dressing room, she puts on the new outfit and places her worn clothes in the shopping bag with her toiletries.

Leaving the clothing store, Hayley heads toward the White House complex, only a few blocks to the west. She scans the streets for any sign of a familiar black SUV in a city where it seems only black SUVs populate the roads. The passenger vans will be leaving the White House for Camp David in twenty minutes. She cannot be late. In order to avoid danger that may be lurking on Seventeenth, Hayley loops north and approaches the White House gate from the west. At Seventeenth and G Street, she slips into Così, a quick-bite joint directly across the street from the EEOB and White House gate.

Before she risks showing herself, Hayley assesses her surroundings from the relative safety of the sandwich shop. After only a few seconds, she sees the hit team's SUV parked on Seventeenth across G Street. Hayley checks her watch. Less than five minutes remain before the vans are scheduled to depart. To her right, a stack of *Washington Post* newspapers with a headline reporting Russia's troop movements on its border with Estonia distracts her only for a moment.

A Metrobus rumbles south on Seventeenth, passing just outside the sandwich shop. With this last opportunity for safe transit, Hayley dashes out the door and, using the bus as cover, runs across the street toward the White House gate. Out of the corner of her eye, she sees the SUV lunge from the curb. Martin, behind the wheel, had spilled his cup of coffee when Bishop thumped him on the arm. "There she is! Go!" Were it not for a random black car ferrying two lobbyists to a late-breakfast meeting with a congressman from California and speeding northbound on Seventeenth, the operators would have intercepted their target in the middle of the four-lane street.

Ned greets Hayley with a warm smile as she runs up to the gate. "Saturday morning, Hayley? Don't you take any days off?"

Hayley glances over her shoulder at the black SUV skulking on Seventeenth Street, the scowling faces of the two men inside like Day of the Dead masks, and then turns back to her friend with a relieved smile. She shrugs. "Guess not!"

Hurrying up the drive toward the South Lawn, she hears a familiar roar and sees Marine One rise high above the trees and pirouette to the northwest. Lower-level staffers accompanying POTUS to Camp David are gathered in the driveway with their roller bags, waiting for the van. They watch last-to-arrive Hayley approach with no other luggage except for the Forever 21 shopping bag and predictably arch their eyebrows.

———————

MANAHAN ROAD, IN rural northwest Maryland, slices through small homesteads and woodlands. Many of the farms were sold off years ago and their pastures left fallow or sited for brick ranch-style homes. A quiet, peaceful area, it's unremarkable in every respect except for the proximity of Camp David, the presidential retreat, less than two miles to the south. The sheer anonymity of the area is one of the reasons why US presidents since FDR have used the compound as a retreat from the pressure cooker atmosphere of Washington, DC. No one else comes here.

Twin sport utility vehicles, both with darkly tinted windows, speed incongruously down the two-lane road where farm tractors and pickup trucks more typically travel. Manahan Road is poorly graded and several undulations in its surface necessitate lowered speeds, but the big black vehicles pay no heed to the driving conditions and nearly leave the ground traveling over some of those humps. With little deceleration, the SUVs screech hard into a turn and enter the gravel drive of a farmhouse that has been unoccupied for more than five years after its owner, an alcoholic grandson of a long-deceased barley farmer, emphatically committed suicide with both gun and noose. The doors of a barn a hundred yards from the main house are pushed open from within by Lewis, who stands to the side as the two SUVs drive into the structure with only a few seconds of brake lights flashing. Once both vehicles are inside, Lewis reenters the barn and pulls the big doors closed again behind him.

Within the dimly lit barn, the operators exit their vehicles and begin to unload duffels and backpacks. Sinatra supervises their work, smoking a cigarette. Bishop senses his team leader's gaze following his every move and feels his gut twist. For an operation of this magnitude, why didn't the clients hire someone who wasn't quite so, well, freakish?

"Bishop, c'mere," Sinatra calls out from near the front of the vehicles.

Bishop finishes stowing his duffel bag with the others and then approaches Sinatra, staying on guard for he's not sure quite what.

"Remember what you told me, after you braced the intern at her apartment?"

"No," Bishop says, lying.

"You said she didn't know shit."

"If that's what I said, so?"

"You were wrong."

The words land with a thud. "Okay," Bishop says lamely, very nervous now. Sinatra takes a long, dangerous pause. Bishop hasn't a clue what's coming next.

"Remember we *prayed* you were right."

Bishop remembers all too well. "Yeah." He can almost feel the cold metal of gun barrel end placed against his forehead. His mouth tastes acrid fear.

"Do you feel it, Bishop? God works in mysterious ways."

"Feel what exactly?" he asks casually, masking his terror. If he's going to die, he wants to go out with his dignity intact.

"The power of redemption at work." Through the blue cigarette smoke, Sinatra's eyes appear flat and already dead.

Bishop releases a short breath with the realization the psycho isn't going to kill him. He just wants to get this crazy fucking operation over with, take his half-mil, and fly back to Alaska. Shoot a grizzly bear if he fucking feels like it. Easier than killing a president, right?

"I sure do, bro. Feelin' it strong," says Bishop.

"Have you ever killed a woman before? A young, pretty woman?"

"No."

"Can you, Bishop? Can you kill a young, pretty

woman? Do this and provide living proof that the power of prayer and potential for redemption is greater than any one man's failings."

Bishop doesn't even have to think about it. What would he be doing with this crew if he had qualms about killing anything? Well, maybe a kid would be a tough nut to crack. Bishop makes a decision then and there not to ever kill a kid, at least intentionally. "Yeah, man, I'm down. Why?"

"Our client has informed me the individual responsible for Billings's demise is the intern you questioned. She will be at the operation location. It goes without saying her death is mandatory."

"You want me to kill her, boss?"

"Yes, Bishop, I'm assigning you that very special task. I'd like you to make sure that bitch ceases to exist."

Bishop gives it a thought and decides to push his luck, now feeling more in control of the situation. "Extra work means extra pay, dude. Fifty grand for the girl, five hundred for the president."

Sinatra nods, agreeing to Bishop's terms. Before Sinatra can make an offer to pray, Bishop turns tail and diddy bops back to his kit. Sinatra watches him go, taking a last pull off his cigarette then dropping it to the hard-packed dirt floor. He carefully grounds out the cigarette butt under his boot. His exchange with Bishop has left him depressed. Try as hard as he might, the men simply don't seem to like him, and Sinatra cannot figure out why. He suffered the same bewildering and unwarranted hostility from his ex-wife. What has he done to any of them but offer employment and companionship? If his religiosity is the problem, then there is nothing to be done. Jesus is his life, and his life is Jesus. Consumed with this brooding, Sinatra lights another cigarette and waits for emails from his real estate broker. He feels a headache coming on.

Something over two miles away, the White House van is checked through the secure gate leading into the iconic presidential two-hundred-acre retreat by heavily armed Marines. Given the military presence and a high-security fence that surrounds the entire facility, the one-hundred-plus contingent of Secret Service agents who typically protect the president while at the White House is vastly reduced to less than a dozen. Only six agents maintain constant vigil at the president's private cabin, Aspen Lodge, while the other six are posted at the "executive" building, Laurel Lodge. Privacy and seclusion are the operating principals of the presidential retreat at Camp David, making for the perfect atmosphere for relaxation, romantic trysts, or leisurely diplomatic talks.

The one-hour-and-twenty-four-minute drive via Interstate 270 from the White House complex to Camp David was routine. Chatter was at a minimum among the six passengers, all of them preoccupied with their electronic handheld devices. Hayley, however, kept her phone in her pocket. She gazed at the passing landscape outside her window for the entire trip, emptying her head of focused thinking as a form of meditation she'd developed while in the army. On long trips in loud and uncomfortable military transports, she discovered a quiet mind was the best preparation for the difficult tasks and challenges that lie ahead.

The van drops her off in front of a snug cabin nestled among the trees in an isolated section of the compound. A quarter mile distant from the president's retreat, Aspen Lodge, and the administrative center, Laurel Lodge, the single-room Linden Cabin is exactly what a mountain cottage should be, with its bare furnishings, knotty pine walls, and twin single beds. Hayley responds instantly to her quarters, feeling secure the moment she crosses the threshold, and experiences a surge of purpose and optimism. Despite setbacks and her current isolation, Hayley is convinced she can accomplish her goals. A presidential weekend at Camp David is the very best situation in which to communicate her message to Monroe.

Leaving her cabin and walking along the wooded path toward Laurel Lodge, however, a new anxiety begins to take grip. Immersed in the silent woods that engulf the retreat and its horror-movie seclusion, she realizes the naval installation is also the logistical ideal for a presidential assassination. If she were the commander of Odom's hit team, she would choose this place and time to execute the mission plan. Though the naval compound is thoroughly guarded by well-armed Marines, Camp David is no White House complex in the middle of a busy urban center. With planning and, most important, collaboration from select Secret Service personnel, Hayley estimates six men with special-operations military training could kill Monroe and escape with only medium-level risk.

This whipsaw of moods, from secure to unsettled, does not undercut her ability to perform. Infantry training has given her a deep reservoir of adaptability while dealing with unstable operational environments. She controls her breathing and, consequentially, her heart rate. The large, squat wood-and-stone facade of Laurel Lodge appears through the trees. As she approaches the unguarded building, she observes that not a single Secret Service agent stands outside the door. Hayley can't help but worry about the lack of security. The vibe is stunningly relaxed, nothing like the siege mentality of the White House.

She enters Laurel Lodge, which immediately impresses her as a woodsy West Wing, a perfect transfer of the signature frenetic bustle from its urban edition. Though fewer in number, the handful of aides present in the lodge go about every task, however mundane, with a sense that history is being made by their hands. Self-importance at every level of the administration, no matter how low, is in the West Wing's DNA. Consequently, when Hayley encounters Karen Rey soon after entering, the president's aide greets her with annoyed impatience before the intern has said a word.

"You're late. Did you take a nap or something?" Apparently, Rey's strategic resolution to be more ingratiating toward the star intern has withered under the greater pressure of an unquenchable antipathy toward Hayley.

"No, ma'am. Dropped my bag and came right over," Hayley assures her supervisor.

Rey wears a perplexed frown, as if suffering intestinal cramp, and heads off to whatever momentous duty she is undertaking on the president's behalf.

"Are these new Secret Service agents, ma'am?" Hayley asks after her, gesturing toward the security detail inside the lodge.

Rey stops and turns back toward the intern, irked. "What? I don't know. Maybe. Why?"

In the few minutes she spent walking up the path to Laurel Lodge, Hayley had brooded on how she might sound an alarm and to whom. No matter what, the president's life must be protected. There was no time to wait until she might be afforded the opportunity to deliver her message directly to Monroe. But she had to be careful, lest she be deemed a security risk herself. Hayley had surmised it'd be best to speak generally, withholding details of what she knows. "I'm concerned for the president's safety, ma'am," Hayley tells Karen Rey with a level of seriousness people in the West Wing have come to expect from her.

The senior White House aide regards Hayley with a mix of exasperation and contempt. "What?"

"I know it sounds crazy coming from an intern, ma'am, but I really have to question President Monroe's safety here at Camp David."

A long moment passes as Rey studies the intern with brow well furrowed, a frown carving her lower face to an almost comical degree. "Stand in a corner somewhere. And be quiet. Someone will find a use for you."

As Rey walks away from the vile West Virginian, that snake in the grass, she struggles to re-center her thinking on tasks requiring her immediate attention. But Hayley's words and her absurd mind-fuckery remain with her, inescapable and galling, like a too-loud car radio one lane over. Saddled with the intern by the president's farcical affinity for her, Rey curses her own fate. No matter what Rey does to push forward and keep focused, she hears the young woman's twanging assessment of a possible danger to the president, as if she knows anything about anything. Lord, what will deliver her from the loathsome creature that is Hayley Chill?

---

INTERSTATE 95 COVERS a distance of approximately twenty-three miles in length across Delaware. The interstate's first off-ramp in the state is, logically, Exit 1, DE 896, that, if taken in the northerly direction, leads to the University of Delaware and its host college town, Newark. Traveler motels crouch close to the four-lane State Route 896 just north of the interstate's cloverleaf on- and off-ramps, offering modest respite from the highway travel as well as beds for trysting college professors and their ambitious students. One of these motels is the Red Roof Inn & Suites, erected on the bones of that travel franchise of decades ago: an orange-roofed Howard Johnson's restaurant.

Asher Danes's Prius is parked in the lot, just outside the ground-floor room with a 112 stenciled on its door. Inside, Asher emerges from the shower and looks at his watch. It is 1:14 p.m. He had crawled out of his Red Roof bed thirty minutes earlier and taken a shower using Red Roof soaps and is just finishing rubbing his body dry with a Red Roof not-quite-plush white towel. He had exited the interstate yesterday evening, a little more than two hours after departing DC and still more than three hours from his parents' home in Greenwich, Connecticut.

What had prompted him to interrupt his trip? Fatigue, both emotional and physical, was a factor. In addition to general weariness, Asher dreaded seeing his parents and conveying to them the news of quitting his job at the White House. How to explain his reasons? While it's true his father had contributed hundreds of thousands of dollars to the party's preferred PAC and thereby secured Asher's position in the new administration, that amount of money meant very little to a household that enjoys a ten-figure annual income. No, it wasn't the money blown on Asher's aborted "Washington experience" that caused him a sense of paralyzing dread, but rather the awareness his parents would be deeply concerned about him and might once again lobby for his voluntary commitment to psychiatric hospitalization.

Indeed, it was a secret from everyone in Asher's life except his parents he had suffered what he likes to call his "pre–nervous breakdown" after the junior-year breakup with Mr. Lacrosse, an ugly night in which he cracked up on his parents' kitchen floor. Alarmed by the emotional disintegration of their only son, normally such a jovial young man, Asher's parents hustled him off for a two-week stay at New Canaan's Silver Hill Hospital. Equal doses of talking therapy and Lexapro were just the thing to get the boy on a better emotional track and back to Cambridge. Regardless of his apparent recovery, however, Asher's mom and dad have been vigilant of his every mood swing and "bad day." Fleeing from DC and his job there could easily trigger a second, more prolonged stay at Silver Hill.

Ten hours of uninterrupted sleep and some Red Roof complimentary coffee have failed to ease Asher's anxiety. In addition to dreading his parents' reaction to this latest muck-up is a renewed sense of guilt for abandoning Hayley Chill to professional assassins back in DC. Though he had initially had his doubts regarding the intern's warnings of a vast intrigue originating from the deep state, this despite his own complicity in that conspiracy, Asher cannot ignore the evidence that has piled up in quick succession. Inescapable was the harsh self-assessment that he had taken a most cowardly way out.

Checking out of room 112 and stopping at the Boston Market directly across the street for a truly abject take-out rotisserie chicken breast sandwich, Asher is torn with indecision. Should he continue north or return south? Facing him are two distinct choices that will result in two completely opposite destinies. He climbs back inside the Prius and points it toward Interstate 95, less than a half mile distant. Saturday-afternoon traffic is moderate. The on-ramp for north is beyond the overpass and south just before it. As Asher draws ever closer to choosing which direction and thereby deciding his fate, he has to chuckle. How ludicrous is life anyway?

---

JAMES ODOM GETS up on Saturday morning at six a.m., expending that extra hour out of a small kindness extended to his loyal wife. After decades of marriage, they are neither lovers nor much loved by the other. But what they do share is a level of grudging respect. They have provided for each other, nurtured one another in countless ways, and grimly persevered. As a result of that dedication to the marital bonds, anything but generous deference to the other's basic needs would be abhorrent. James Odom reveres his wife and therefore remains motionless as a corpse on his side of the bed for those sixty minutes after his own awakening.

After a black coffee and dry toast, he goes to the office for a few hours to catch up with the previous week's incomplete tasks. Odom relishes these quiet hours at Langley. Younger employees avoid the place like Chernobyl on the weekend, but old-timers like him can often be found shuffling down its corridors on a Saturday or Sunday morning, swapping small grins of recognition if not hellos. But this, of course, is no ordinary Saturday. James Odom is an old warrior with the battle scars to show for it, but even he suffers a mild case of the butterflies in these few hours before Operation Damocles changes the course of American history.

He craves to speak to his team leader before jump-off, aware the call is as pointless as a wish list left for Santa Claus. The team has its orders and has developed its plan. A call from Odom would only happen if the operation was being terminated. Rummaging through file folders and fretfully reviewing analyst reports from the depths of the agency's intranet Odom finds his gaze repeatedly falling on his modified BlackBerry KEY2. Like chieftains of drug cartels south of the border, he carries five such devices, and one is used exclusively for communicating with Sinatra. The operative answers after the fourth ring.

"I'm kind of busy here. Are you terminating the operation?"

"Certainly not," Odom assures him. "We're go."

"You've commissioned me to assassinate the president of the United States and you're checking up on me?" Sinatra asks with understandable incredulity.

"Christ, you're an asshole. Has anyone ever told you that?"

There's a long pause from Sinatra, and Odom fears he has unduly insulted the man. He hasn't met a trained killer who wasn't somewhat mentally unbalanced, thinking particularly of a murderous pederast he once had the unpleasant experience of hiring, but this one really seems to have more than several screws loose.

"Would you kindly refrain from taking the Lord's name in vain when speaking to me?" Sinatra's voice has the timbre and modulation of a psychopath on the verge of a bloody homicidal frenzy.

"Of course. My apologies."

"What do you want?"

"Are there any problems? Do you need anything?"

Sinatra expels a long-suffering sigh. "If I needed anything or if there was a problem, I would've called you."

Odom doesn't say anything, and he really doesn't know why. What's wrong with him? What's going on? He's run covert operations practically in his sleep or, at least, after a long nap. Why is he deviating from standard operating procedure here?

"What's wrong?" Sinatra asks with as much compassion as he can muster, which is very, very little. "You sound weird."

God, Odom thinks, even this murderous basket case can perceive he's cracking under the pressure. It isn't every day you kill a president, right? Think fast. Focus. Show some fucking backbone here! Whipping himself into a semblance of psychological shape, the CIA deputy director grasps the first straw that comes into sight. "Whose idea was the whole Rat Pack business? Yours?"

"I'm going to hang up now, if that's all right with you. My guys are going through their kits for the third time, as I demanded, and in two hours and forty-four minutes we're getting on with it."

Sinatra's recitation is every bit the therapy Odom requires in the moment. The terror that threatened to consume him subsides, draining back into whatever emotional swamp it flowed from. "Good, good, good. Okay. We'll talk after it's finished."

The operative says, "You won't hear from me again. Never call me again. Once he's dead, I'm breaking this phone into a thousand pieces and dumping them into the Chesapeake. If the money isn't where it's supposed to be six hours after the new president announces three days of national mourning, you know what happens."

In the moment, Odom can't fathom how the dynamic has changed between them. Perhaps he is getting too old for this business. "Needless to say, the money will be where you expect to find it and in the agreed-to amount."

"Excellent," Sinatra mutters, adding, "praise be to God."

He included this glorification like a final twist of the knife. Nonbelievers have such issues with displays of genuine faith, it gives Sinatra enormous pleasure to rub their faces in it. Indeed, Odom gives a little shudder hearing it. While there is no denying the man's capabilities as killer, the CIA deputy director cannot imagine anyone eerier.

"Goodbye, then," James Odom politely tells his operative, getting only the dead air of the call's disconnection in response.

HAYLEY SPENT MOST of Saturday afternoon in a small windowless room (again, most likely a converted janitorial closet) compiling briefing books and coaxing a recalcitrant Ricoh MP C2550 copier to comply with an acceptable efficiency. POTUS is holed up in the Laurel Lodge conference room with senior aides, teleconferencing with leaders around the world regarding the situation in Estonia. The scuttlebutt that Hayley is able to glean from those staffers coming in and out is that the blowback was extreme from long-standing European allies in reaction to US tolerance of Russia's aggressions. The leadership expected from America is MIA. To all of these detractors, the president expressed again his conviction the true danger was in the Far East, with China.

She walks back to Linden Cabin in the dark without seeing Monroe once the entire day. If Hayley wants to eat dinner, she needs to be at the small dining room at Main Lodge no later than 7:30 p.m., but it's been over thirty-six hours since she's bathed. A hot shower is more important than food, given how she currently feels. Turning on the water as soon as she arrives back at her quarters and stripping off her clothes in seconds, she sits on the closed toilet lid for several minutes and lets the billowing steam from the shower envelop her, coating her in a sheen of damp warmth. Emerging forty minutes later from the cottage, Hayley feels refreshed and optimistic.

The menacing woods that had earlier seemed to portend violence now recall the forests in which she cavorted as a child and teenager back in West Virginia. Throughout her childhood, the woodlands served as refuge from a dysfunctional adult world. Hayley and her friends inhabited those forested, rolling hills whenever released from confines of school and home, spirited forest goblins and fairies fueled by cheap booze and cannabis smoke.

Those were carefree times, and memories of them carry Hayley on her ten-minute walk to the Main Lodge and the dining room there. Most of the other staffers have finished their meals and retired to their cottages for the night. Apart from a couple of senior aides who would have nothing to do with the likes of an intern apart from barked requests for coffee or copying, Hayley has the dining room to herself. Through the open door leading into the kitchen, she sees Leon Washington, the chef from the West Wing's Navy Mess on Camp David duty.

The cook personally delivers her grilled cheese and split pea soup. "You just had to try one for yourself, didn't ya?"

"Leon, I've been wanting to get my hands on one of these bad boys since I first laid eyes on it."

"Well, dig in, girl. Don't mind me." He sits down across the table from her, dish towel thrown over his shoulder, the workday more or less done. "How you been?"

Dipping the corner of the sandwich into the steaming bowl of soup and savoring each bite, Hayley beams at Leon with primal gratitude. "Amazing."

"Your life or that sandwich?"

"Definitely sandwich," she assures Leon. "Only sandwich."

"Bad, huh?"

"Not what I expected exactly."

"Care to share? I'm told I'm a pretty good listener. Comes with having six kids and twice that many grandkids."

"Wish I could, believe me. It's complicated. Think I just need to keep it to myself for now."

"Okay. I can understand that. Know that you've got at least one friend in the joint, ya hear?"

Hayley's heart fairly bursts. "I really appreciate you saying that, Leon. I do."

"It's more than talk. Leon Washington is an old man you can count on in a jam, that's right."

Hayley smiles her thanks. She feels like she could almost cry. The battling welterweight champ of the entire Sixth Army has been brought to her knees by the gentle kindness of a sixty-two-year-old cook with yellowy eyes. With a life in which her elders have always disappointed her, in one way or another, Leon Washington has connected with Hayley and come through when she needs emotional support most. She has no words.

He pats her hand with his own, scarred by a thousand knife cuts and kitchen burns. "You hang in there, girl. God loves perseverance, because it sure ain't easy."

She walks back to Linden Cabin with spirits more buoyant than she had felt in weeks. Whereas her friendship with Asher was somewhat coerced, bowing to the sheer dint of Hayley's will, these five minutes of fellowship she's had with the cook nourish her to a profound degree. Actual human beings do inhabit this corrupted world. It had been too easy to forget that fact with her stay in Washington and in the hothouse of the West Wing. The shrouded woods that line the gravel path back to her little cabin seem like something out of a benevolent fairy tale. Night song of a female eastern whip-poor-will ricochets off the surrounding poplar and ash trees. A quarter moon shimmers in the black sky, casting shards of light on her trail home. God loves perseverance, indeed.

---

IT'S TIME. UNDER minimal lighting inside the musty barn, Sinatra watches as his team finishes preparations, almost ready to move out. Four of his men are dressed in black leggings, boots, and pullovers, skin-tight outfits that remind the team leader, a slight grin coming to his face, of murderous mimes. Three of the men—Lewis, Martin, and Lawford—have strapped large tactical duffel shoulder bags to their backs. Two others—Bishop and Davis—shoulder smaller backpacks. Only Bishop wears street clothes. Sinatra, dressed in tactical black clothing, carries a Sig Sauer P320 RX with optics in a chest-mount holster crisscrossing his upper torso Mexican bandito–style. If required, the weapon is readily accessible in what shouldn't be a high-action operation. Better to be prepared, however, for any contingency. Sinatra has survived countless combat missions thanks to exactly this kind of redundancy. The team leader checks his watch for the third time in the last ninety seconds. "Everyone ready? Quick-check your buddy."

They obediently scan the man next to them, up and down, front and back. Something as mundane as a loosely tied shoelace could upend an operation. They are silent and serious. There's no horseplay or pre-mission banter. No one can ignore the sobering momentousness of this particular operation. Each man gives Sinatra the "OK" sign.

"Let's move." He leads them out a door in the rear of the barn and into the night. They cross the back-yard of the farmhouse, uncut grass grown thigh-high, and enter the forest beyond, one man at a time swal-lowed up by the deep shadows of the great Maryland woodland. Approximately forty-four minutes later, they emerge again from the forest's edge, facing west and the outer boundary of the naval installation named after President Eisenhower's grandson. The nearly hundred motion-detecting sensors the team had passed in their hike through the woods approaching the presidential retreat had all been deactivated sixty minutes earlier. A little-used maintenance-access gate in the high-security fence in the middle of the woods had been conveniently left unlocked. Where the operators emerge from the trees had been carefully selected, beyond the sight line of a sentry position manned by four Marine guards on this eastern edge of the compound. Only open ground lies between the hit team and the first collection of structures on the property.

The men crouch on one knee and look forward, each wearing night-vision goggles that give them the appearance of cartoon aliens. They wait for the command from Sinatra to move forward. A low mumbling can be heard from behind them, and initially none of the men can make out the words. But soon the chant becomes clear and shockingly familiar.

"The Lord is with thee. Blessed art thou among women, and blessed is the fruit of thy womb, Jesus. Holy Mary, Mother of God, pray for us sinners now and at the hour of our death." Sinatra pauses in his slow and methodical recitation, waiting for his men to join him. Of course, none of them are willing to do so. "Amen," he adds almost bitterly.

The men say nothing. If Sinatra's prayer helps them achieve their mission goals, all the better. Even still, however, any mention of "the hour of our death" strikes them as pretty poor form. Sinatra stands up to a low crouch from a kneeling position and gestures ahead. "Let's do this."

---

SHE SITS AT the small wooden table by a window, rendered a black mirror by the dark night outside, scanning news reports on her computer, when she hears a knock at the door. Hayley is on guard when she stands and crosses the two-dozen feet from table to door. "Yes?" she calls through the door.

"Secret Service, Ms. Chill," comes the muffled reply. "It's Agent Christie."

Hayley pauses to consider her options. The operative clearly knows she's inside the cabin. Refusing to open the door will betray her knowledge of the man's true intentions. Her best hope is the element of surprise, gained by the fact that the operative doesn't know what she knows. Hayley opens the door halfway, revealing Bishop in his casual sportswear and Patagonia down jacket outside. She says nothing, waiting for the agent to speak.

"We're just doing an area check on all the cabins." He looks over her shoulder, into her little cottage. "Everything seems status quo here," he announces with a friendly grin.

"Yes, sir. Thank you. I'm fine."

"Mind if I come in for a sec. Frozen half-solid out here."

Hayley hesitates.

"Just a few minutes, I promise."

She reluctantly opens the door wider for Bishop to enter. He slaps his gloved hands together and hugs himself, making an elaborate show of warming up. She makes no offer of anything, simply waiting for him to leave but on her guard, every muscle attuned to defending herself from attack.

"Got the place to yourself, huh?" he innocently inquires.

She nods her head yes. Mute.

He gestures at the computer on the kitchen table. "What's the latest?"

"The Russian army has occupied Tartu and Narva," she tells him flatly, without emotion.

"Holy shit! No kidding? It's really happening! God-damn!"

Hayley doesn't share his surprise. "Yes, it's happening . . . whatever 'it' is."

"NATO?"

She shrugs. Wary. If Bishop clocks her apprehension of him, he doesn't show it. All is a lark.

"Well, if Monroe manages to get us all blown up, at least I won't have to pay off my car loan!"

"Always a silver lining." Hayley hopes by being just a couple notches friendlier, he'll leave. Is he trying to hook up with her?

Bishop points at the half-filled pot of coffee in the automatic maker she had brewed a half hour earlier, anticipating a late night. Tomorrow may be her last shot to deliver her message to Monroe, and she doubts sleep is a likely. "Maybe I'll cash in that rain check."

She looks at him blank-faced.

"When I interviewed you at your apartment? You offered me a cup of coffee."

"I did?" She honestly can't remember.

"Pretty sure you did." He says this with a smile.

Hayley relents, turning to retrieve the coffeepot from the maker. Glancing to her right, at the window next to the table, she sees the reflection of Bishop drawing a concealed 9-millimeter Beretta from a shoulder holster and taking aim on the back of her head.

With less than three seconds before her execution, Hayley grips the coffeepot in hand and pivots on the balls of her feet, flinging the glass container at his head. It shatters on impact and splashes hot coffee in his face and down his shirtfront. Bishop screams, momentarily stunned.

Hayley launches her attack, seizing her brief advantage. Two quick punches to Bishop's head dislodge the Beretta from his grip. Thus disarmed, he seems to recover his equilibrium and recognizes the precariousness of his situation. Equally trained in close-quarter combat and outweighing Hayley by at least sixty pounds, Bishop counters with a flurry of punches his opponent can only partially deflect.

Bishop comprehends Hayley is no slouch in martial arts. He picks up a ladder-back chair and throws it at her, then snatches up the other chair and throws that one, too. She is unable to block a flying kick that follows and is knocked down to her knees. Bishop is on her in less than two seconds, pummeling Hayley with punches to the head and back. Defenses softened, she cannot stop him from encircling her throat with both hands. Starbursts explode in her field of vision. Roaring fills in her ears. Her brain empties but for one thought: I am dying.

Beyond her reach by maybe six inches are the tools for the small fireplace at the center of the cabin's back wall. Too far to reach. Just too far. But God, in his benevolence, loves perseverance. Blessed are those who don't quit. She has a job to do. All her life, she has toiled to complete what is expected of her. She has fought and won every personal battle, no matter the odds. The pyrotechnics blaze in her vision, and she recalls her siblings on July Fourth holidays, frolicking in the dirt front yard with sparklers, the only fireworks the family could afford, under her watchful eye. Only fourteen years old, she bears the burden of the family's welfare on her shoulders. To this day, Hayley has lost no one. Not on her watch. God loves perseverance, because it's never easy.

Thinking she is as good as dead, Bishop leans in to apply even greater pressure around her throat, drawing close enough for Hayley to bring her right hand up and jam her thumb hard into his left eye. Wailing in pain, Bishop releases his grip from around Hayley's neck. She stretches now and grips the fire poker by the pointed end, swinging it around and clubbing Bishop against the side of his head with the heavy, wrought iron handle. Knocked out cold, his howls cease abruptly.

Hayley shreds the top sheet on her bed and uses strips of it to bind and gag Bishop, as well as dress the nasty wound on his head. She drags him into the cramped bathroom of the single-room cabin, wedging all six feet, two inches of his frame between the toilet and bathtub. Bishop slowly regains consciousness as she finishes the task, his eyes expressing pain and rage. She crouches down in front of Bishop and speaks without anger or judgment. "I know what you are and who you work for. I know what you're trying to do here. I'm going to stop it from happening." Her matter-of-fact pronouncement complete, Hayley stands and backs out of the bathroom, closing the door on Bishop's futile protest.

Odom's team of mercenaries would not have infiltrated Camp David for the sole purpose of killing her. Without a shred of doubt, Hayley is convinced an attempt on the president's life is imminent, if not over. There isn't a second to lose. Checking her phone, she tries to make a call but hears only an eerie, telephonic howl come through the line. Pocketing the phone, she grabs a jacket, jams Bishop's handgun into the back of her waistband, and hits the door.

The first breath of fresh, cold air clears her head of the fog induced by her near-choking. She starts sprinting up the path, heading through the woods toward Laurel Lodge. While she runs, Hayley discards useless anxieties that Monroe is already dead. If she were heading the operation, would she order Bishop to eliminate a secondary witness before taking out the target? Not likely. But any further hesitation to calculate those odds is unacceptable. She must act quickly, before Bishop's delay in returning raises alarm with the conspirators. Disruption of the hit team's operation is all that matters now.

As Laurel Lodge becomes visible through the trees, she's heartened to see it ablaze with lights. Despite the late hour, she is reassured staff and Secret Service will be on duty at the installation's administrative center. But no agents are posted at the entrance. Perhaps their presence outside is deemed unnecessary during off-hours. She enters the building but finds no one in the reception area just inside the front doors. Nor can she find anyone in the security office just off the entry hall.

Hayley continues through the building, checking each room for occupants. She fails to find a single person inside the brightly lit administrative center. Lights and machines hum with power. A steaming cup of coffee sits on the desktop in an administrator's office. Three televisions tuned to different network stations are in three different rooms. She can find not one living soul. A check of a corded phone confirms her suspicion—the line is dead. Undoubtedly, the entire installation is cut off from contact with the outside world. Whether personnel left under their own volition or against makes no difference. They're gone.

Hayley backtracks and exits the building. She is on her own. Odom's hit team is somewhere in the compound, and it's up to her to stop them. The wind swirling through the trees that surround Laurel Lodge is the sound of fear and isolation. The black night chokes out all light and hope. Loose rocks are piled on the edge of the path at her feet. Hayley bends down and retrieves a palm-size stone with a jagged edge. She grips the rock and squeezes as hard as she can, the sharp pain shooting to every point of her body. She squeezes harder, pressing through the pain and absorbing the rock's density. Pain becomes determination. Opening her hand wide, she sees the rock is coated with her blood, and she drops it to the ground, continuing to gaze at her hand and the constellation of small cuts and abrasions in her skin. She's ready to fight.

Running up the drive in the direction she knows is the location of the presidential residence at Camp David, she fixates on the single notion of saving Monroe's life, whatever the cost. The bright quarter moon that illuminated the woods after dinner has set and the night is cloaked in the blackest of blacks. Despite her light jacket, she doesn't notice an air temperature that nears freezing. Since leaving Bishop trussed up in her bathroom, she hasn't seen another living soul anywhere in the installation. She feels like the last human alive in the world.

The driveway dips and then seems to be swallowed whole by the surrounding woods. Hayley worries she has lost her way. Is she running away from the place where she is needed, rather than toward it? Nothing would be worse than getting lost now. Peering into the darkness that looms before her, Hayley thinks she sees a figure approaching and quickly, within moments, hears accompanying footsteps. She stops and prepares herself for a fight, retrieving Bishop's gun from her waistband and holding it down, against her right thigh.

The shadowy figure continues to approach, the occasional glow from cigarette end flashing in the darkness. Only when he is less than fifteen yards away does Hayley see that it is the Navy Mess chef, Leon Washington.

"You gonna shoot me with that thing?" he asks casually, gesturing toward the gun at her side.

"Leon," is all she can manage to say in the moment. Her relief on seeing a friendly face is enormous.

"What's wrong, girl? You don't look so good." He pauses, adding sardonically, "And then there's the gun."

"I need your help, Leon."

"If it's a midnight snack you're looking for, I'm your man. But I'm thinking that's not the thing."

She is reluctant to involve the cook. But does she really have any other choice?

"They're going to assassinate the president, Leon. Tonight."

"What?! Who?!"

"I don't know. Powerful people."

"Are you crazy, girl? What have you been smoking?"

"Nothing. No. This is happening, Leon. *Right now.*"

Leon stares down at the ground and shakes his head, trying to process the information. "Can't be . . . Just crazy."

"We've got to do something. We've got to stop this."

The cook's head snaps back up, gaze locking on Hayley's. "What's a chef supposed to do about it?" He laughs at the absurdity of the notion. "Doesn't the man have a whole Secret Service for that sorta business?"

"They're all gone, Leon. No one's here."

The old cook begins to grasp that she's serious. "Everybody? Where'd they all go?"

"I don't know. Right now it doesn't really make any difference. They're just gone, which means it's on us to stop something terrible from happening." She pauses, letting the full weight of her words land on Leon before continuing. "Please, Leon. There's no one else."

Leon frowns, and it's the first time she can recall

seeing the chef as anything but affable and good-natured. He dislikes being put in this position. Hayley can't possibly know the life Leon Washington has lived, the prejudice he has encountered his entire life, and the failure of politicians of every stripe to correct those injustices. Why risk his skin for theirs? But Hayley's earnest sincerity stirs something within the old cook's consciousness. It feels like a throwback to greater ideals, something that Leon knows to be patriotism. The cold nips at his cheeks. A breeze rustles dead leaves on skeletal tree limbs. What to do? There's no denying it. The old man is scared.

---

SINATRA LEADS HIS team in a running crouch around the pool and closes the final distance between the woods and the dark Aspen Lodge in seconds. There's no sign of the three Secret Service agents who normally man the command post outside the cabin. The operators hug the wall on either side of French doors leading out to the pool's patio and wait for a signal from their team leader. The desolate call of a whip-poor-will drifts across the open ground surrounding the building. It's 2:21 a.m. There have been no further communications from the CIA deputy director. Operation Damocles remains a go.

Sinatra hasn't been able to raise Bishop on the two-way radio. The operative is overdue from his assignment to eliminate the intern. Obviously, there is a problem, but so far it does not seem to have impacted their primary mission. He cannot see how the operational plan could have been laid out any differently. Once the president is dead, they could not possibly remain on scene a minute longer. Perhaps including the intern as a target in tonight's operation was a mistake, but Monroe's death may send her off the rails. Going back over his decisions, Sinatra can't see he had any choice. The intern's presence in the isolated compound was too good an opportunity to pass up.

There's little leeway with time. The supervising Secret Service agent, sympathetic to the cause, had handpicked the dozen similarly minded agents for duty this weekend, men and women who could be counted on to "disappear" at the right time. But that operational window, by necessity of short duration, was rapidly closing. If Sinatra doesn't get the men going soon, it will be too late to execute the plan fully, and they'll have to abort. If they abort, there will be no million dollars transferred to his numbered account at CIBC First-Caribbean International Bank in the Cayman Islands. If the million dollars isn't transferred, then he won't have the means to purchase a new-built home to rival the one his ex-wife enjoys with her new husband. And, the Lord knows, that is an outcome Sinatra is unwilling to accept. He pumps his right clenched fist, signaling his men to begin.

Within a minute, the five operators have donned their white containment suits and entered Aspen Lodge through the unlocked patio's French doors. The residence appears unoccupied. Where Secret Service agents would normally be stationed if POTUS were on-site, there is only evidence of someone having been present a short time ago. The president's security detail appears to have simply vanished, as if plucked from the face of the earth.

Sinatra checks his watch and silently gestures toward the end of the cozy presidential cottage, relatively unchanged since the Eisenhower years. Lawford hangs back to keep watch to the north side of the building, while Lewis crosses the living room to keep guard of the south side. Martin, Davis, and Sinatra continue deeper into the building, their paths through the darkened rooms illuminated by night-vision goggles. Stopping outside one of the closed bedroom doors, Martin crouches down and places his backpack on the floor. Withdrawing the components of the kill machine, he carefully assembles the insertion apparatus composed of boron-nitride nanotube syringe and glass reservoir.

Completing assemblage in less than ninety seconds, Martin looks to Sinatra and gives him the "OK" sign. The team leader grips the doorknob, pushing the door open. As he enters, the president's sleeping form is visible under the comforter. The other operators enter into the room, moving directly toward Monroe.

The president rises halfway from the bed, his facial expression reflecting bewilderment and indignation. "What the hell?"

The operators are silent as Sinatra and Davis fall on the president with brutal efficiency. Assuming the missing Bishop's task, Davis inserts the tip of the squeeze bottle into one of Monroe's nostrils and blasts two bursts of GHB. Unlike Peter Hall, who was almost immediately rendered unconscious, Monroe struggles against Sinatra's immobilizing hold for more than twenty seconds before succumbing. The team leader looks to Martin for explanation.

"Seventy-percent dilution. Undetectable within two hours postmortem."

Sinatra nods and checks his watch again. "Six minutes." He tilts his head to speak into the two-way radio mic. "Six minutes."

Lawford, standing on the pool patio just outside the French doors, keeps watch to the north side of the Lodge. "Roger that. North side clear."

Lewis, standing on the front porch, maintains surveillance of the south side. "Six minutes. South side clear."

In the president's bedroom, Martin makes final preparations to the insertion apparatus. "Six minutes is cutting it close."

Sinatra isn't opening the matter for discussion. "We're gone when they all return. That's the agreement."

Martin nods, laying out the insertion apparatus on the bed next to the unconscious Monroe. While Sinatra and Davis watch, he inserts the thin nanotube into the president's jugular vein and begins to feed it down the major artery. Davis, surprisingly squeamish for a trained killer, looks away. He hates this part.

On the pool terrace, Lawford sees a figure emerge from the gloom of the surrounding woods. Leon

Washington approaches Aspen Lodge from across the broad, open lawn. Lawford pulls his shoulder-mounted mic close to mouth. "North side. I've got eyes on unidentified black male approaching. One-two-five yards."

"One male?" Sinatra asks via his radio.

"From what I can see," Lawford responds, looking in all directions through his night-vision goggles.

Sinatra steps back from the bed and turns his head to the mic attached to his left shoulder. "Lewis?"

The operator on the front porch scans the surrounding area through night-vision goggles. "South side clear."

"Back up north side. Move!" Sinatra orders.

Meanwhile, Martin has finished inserting the feeder tube. He glances to Sinatra, who nods his go-ahead. With the aid of a Keplerian Loupe, the operator threads the micro-thin wire into the nanotube in Monroe's jugular vein and starts to feed it through the length of the insertion conduit, into the right atrium of the president's heart.

Lewis has joined Lawford on the terrace, where they both watch Leon Washington, who has stopped approximately seventy-five yards from Aspen Lodge and simply stands motionless there.

"What's with this fucking guy? Did he not get the memo?" Lawford wonders aloud.

Lewis shakes his head, uncertain. "Fucking shit show."

Lawford halfway raises his suppressed HK MP7 submachine gun. "Smoke him?"

Lewis shrugs. Into his radio: "Unidentified male has stopped seven-zero yards from location. Advise."

Sinatra observes Martin's final efforts to place the conducting wire into the president's heart. Into his mic: "If he comes any closer, take him out. We'll evac south and loop around through the woods." He checks his watch. "Bishop?"

"Negative," Lewis responds.

The rest of the house is quiet and deserted. Light spills out of the president's bedroom, cast by the bedstand lamp Sinatra had snapped on to facilitate Martin's work. The two operators on the pool terrace are visible through the French doors, gazing out over the north lawn, as Hayley enters silently through the front door on the south side of the residence. Relying only on the density of shadow to guide her inside the gloomy living room, she gets her bearings.

Inside the bedroom, Martin attaches the free end of the wire to the battery-powered device on the bed. Monroe moans, in a drugged stupor. The operator looks to Sinatra for a signal to proceed. The team leader nods. Martin reaches for the switch.

"Stop!" Hayley's voice comes from behind them. Martin, Davis, and Sinatra all look in unison and see the intern standing in the open doorway, gun held at arm's length.

"You wouldn't be holding Bishop's gun on us if

Bishop had done his job," Sinatra observes to Hayley, cool as a Zen master.

She ignores Sinatra, addressing Martin. "Put that thing down and move away from the bed."

Martin does no such thing. Doesn't take his eyes off her.

Sinatra wishes he could have a cigarette but can't afford to contaminate the kill site. "One of the first women to make it through basic infantry training," he tells Davis, gesturing at Hayley. To her, he adds, "I imagine you're pretty good with a gun."

"Sharpshooter badge. Forty for forty."

"Forty for forty? Now that is impressive." He pauses, chewing on his thumbnail in lieu of a smoke. "Are you prepared to die for your president, Ms. Chill?"

She points the gun at Martin. "Put it down."

"He won't respond to your command, only mine," Sinatra explains to her. Then he looks to Martin. "Finish it."

Martin puts hand to switch. Hayley tilts the gun barrel up a fraction and fires, bullet striking the wall just above the operator's head. Martin freezes, looking to Sinatra for guidance.

In his earpiece, Sinatra hears from Lawford outside. "What the hell's going on in there?!"

Sinatra is thinking of the best course of action. He tilts his mouth toward the mic. "Your unidentified male still stopped short of location?"

"Affirm that," comes Lawford's response.

Sinatra does not miss the flicker of anxiety that

crosses Hayley's face with the mention of an outside intruder. He understands immediately the significance and tilts his mouth to mic again. "Take him out if you don't hear from me in the next thirty seconds." A beatific smile creases his face as he looks to Hayley again. "Your friend for your president, Hayley? Is that a deal you're willing to make?" Hayley stares at Sinatra, her powder blue eyes revealing nothing.

On the terrace, Lawford checks his watch. Sinatra's deadline passes without word from him. The operative raises his weapon to take aim at Leon but then lowers it again. "Fuck" is what he says as he watches the woods light up with the beams of multiple flashlights, then erupt with two dozen men and women wearing dark blue windbreakers and carrying semi-automatic weapons.

★ ☆ ★ ☆

## 9

## HAYLEY CHILL

Sinatra hears Lawford's muttered obscenity over the radio but hasn't a clue what prompted it. Did his kill shot miss its mark? Did Lewis shoot first, stealing his kill? Did the unidentified male flee or hit the deck for cover? Whatever is happening on the Lodge's north lawn isn't his immediate problem right now. The advantage inside Monroe's bedroom still lies with him. The intern has no idea his men have encountered a problem outside. She has unwisely revealed her connection to the unidentified male on the lawn and her concern for him can be exploited.

He gestures toward the unconscious president. "This vain and arrogant man is worth saving in exchange for your friend's life?"

For most people, this might be an unbearable dilemma without clear choice. But for Hayley, there really is no other option. The president's life must be saved above all other considerations, including her own preservation. Such is her hard wiring. She takes even more emphatic aim on Martin's head. "Step away from the president," she orders the operative with a tone leaving no question about her conviction.

Sinatra shakes his head. "Sorry about your friend." He pulls the mic closer to his mouth. "Smoke him."

The order given, Sinatra gives the intern a look brimming with admonishment and a blessedly guilt-free conscience. A flicker of regret crosses Hayley's face as she imagines the death of her new friend. But Sinatra hasn't heard back from his operative with confirmation of a kill. He tilts his chin down toward the radio mic.

"Lawford?" He gets nothing back. Hayley, not privy to the radio's network, reads the look of concern on the team leader's face and experiences the first glimmers of hope.

"FBI! Inside the house, drop your weapons and exit with your hands in the air!" The voice, amplified by a megaphone not far outside Aspen Lodge takes root in Hayley's consciousness. The play of flashlights across the lawn visible through the bedroom windows confirms the voice wasn't just inside her head.

Sinatra hears and sees the same evidence of the FBI's arrival on the scene and reacts by quick-drawing the Sig Sauer from its chest-mounted holster, pivoting toward the president. Hayley doesn't hesitate in the slightest, shifting her aim from Martin to Sinatra and firing, the bullet entering Sinatra's head just above his left ear and exploding out the right with unquestionable result. As the team leader drops where he stands, Hayley coolly turns her aim back on Martin, whose right hand remains poised above the machine's switch.

"Raise those hands," she orders with a voice that quavers ever so slightly.

Martin obediently lifts his hands over his head as bulletproof-vest-wearing FBI agents flood into the room with weapons raised, followed a moment later by Agent Helen Udall. With one look at the unconscious president, nanotube inserted into his neck, Udall lifts a radio to her mouth.

"Get a medical team immediately!" The whoop and roar of an incoming helicopter engulfs the room as FBI agents force Martin facedown on the floor and clear space for an arriving medical team to administer to President Monroe. Udall looks to Hayley, who has placed her weapon on the floor and retreated to the far side of the bedroom. The FBI agent approaches the intern.

"Are you okay?" Udall asks her, taking note of Hayley's blood-smeared right palm.

Hayley has never killed anyone before. The shock of taking Sinatra's life is only beginning to reverberate. She glances at her hands and sees a tremor there, surprising her. But infantry sucks it up. Infantry shows no pain. Processing it all is for back home, after the mission is done. "I'm fine, ma'am." She has a more pressing concern than her own well-being. "The Navy Mess chef is outside . . ."

"He's fine. Not a scratch." Hayley is relieved. Udall puts the pieces together. "He worked with you by creating a diversion?"

Hayley nods. "He was very brave, ma'am."

Udall concurs with a caveat. "If you're calling that brave, what do we call what you just did?"

"My duty." Hayley isn't boasting, just stating a fact.

The FBI agent has encountered many selfless public servants in her career in law enforcement but can't recall one who possessed Hayley's otherworldly dedication. It's unnerving, and Udall takes a beat to distill her own accomplishments so as not to waver in the intern's presence. What is this vibe the young woman gives off? Udall looks back toward the unconscious president, the object of the military medical team's frenzied attention, to avoid Hayley's gaze.

"Ma'am, if you don't mind my asking, how did you know to come? This morning . . ." Hayley lets the sentence trail off. No need to remind the FBI agent of her refusal to heed a clear alarm.

"Asher Danes," Udall responds simply.

Hayley ponders Udall's response, reading into it all that wasn't spoken. Recalling that Asher had met Udall when the FBI agent had come to the White House after Hall's murder, it takes Hayley less than ten seconds to intuit what it all might mean. For the first time, she is caught off guard.

"Asher was part of the conspiracy," she says, mostly to herself.

Udall nods. "You seem to inspire unusual degrees

of courage in people, Ms. Chill. Mr. Danes's involvement was limited to his association with CIA Deputy Director Odom. Talking to me has put him in potentially serious legal jeopardy. No doubt, though, Asher's cooperation today will be taken into account if charges are brought."

Hayley is saddened by the revelation about Asher and even more upset for not having considered the possibility of his complicity before now. She wonders if she'll ever speak with Asher again so that he might explain why he chose to help Odom's cabal. She recalls when they first met, in the White House Operations office, and his words to her then. *Our hero arrives.*

Not particularly a connoisseur of irony, Hayley shoves the words into a small box and files them away in her memory, having no use for them.

———————

VIRGIN ATLANTIC FLIGHT 4690 departed from Washington Dulles International Airport three minutes after its scheduled departure of six a.m. Sunday morning. Seated in the first-class cabin, Senator Taylor Cox breathes a measured sigh of relief as the wheels lift off the tarmac. For obvious reasons, his travel plans were made in haste. Like all the other conspirators, he had not slept a wink the night before, waiting for news from James Odom. The first inkling of disastrous failure came when Cox heard from another conspirator with contacts in the bureau. That very early warning gave several members of what will come to be dubbed the Shady Side Cabal some wiggle room to make their hasty getaways.

Taylor Cox has survived countless Senate battles and election challenges. He is a warhorse who doesn't bolt at the first exploding shell or a superficial wound. But the inevitable exposure of his involvement in a presidential assassination attempt is a legal conflagration he has neither the desire nor the stamina to endure. The only option he saw available to him was the ignoble reality of spending the rest of his life as a fugitive from justice. Within thirty minutes of learning of the operation's collapse, Cox had packed a bag and was in a black car headed to Dulles.

Landing around eight a.m. at JFK, his plan is to connect with an Emirates flight to Dubai. The US doesn't have an extradition treaty with UAE, and the senator has many powerful friends, including the emir of Umm al-Qaiwain, Sheikh Saud bin Rashid al-Mu'alla. Cox is confident he will avoid prosecution if he can set foot in the Emirates. Like many of his senatorial colleagues, he has long maintained a numbered bank account in Switzerland, courtesy of friends in private industries and allied governments. With more than six million dollars in reserve, financially he ought to be fine.

His flight lands at JFK without incident, and Cox takes a tram to the Emirates airline terminal. A few passersby recognize the senator and greet him enthusiastically. As he strides down the gleaming concourse, Cox ruminates on the end of this sort of public adulation and awe. In the UAE, he will be just another pale, rich Westerner living in quiet anonymity. So be it. Such a fate certainly is better than if he had chosen to remain in Washington. The thought of even one night in jail is enough to make Cox sick to his stomach. Death would be better than incarceration.

The senator only has his one carry-on bag. Gripping it in his right hand, he hurries toward his gate. The Dubai flight is scheduled to depart in less than thirty-five minutes. Though he has seen at least a dozen airport security agents, members of the TSA, and uniformed armed National Guard soldiers in the two terminals, none have given Cox even a second glance. It would seem he has lucked out, with the FBI failing to roll up the major conspirators in the first hours since the failed assassination.

When Cox comes within two hundred feet of his gate, at the farthest end of the terminal, he sees several FBI agents, wearing their tacky windbreakers, standing around the gate's counter. Panicking, Cox stops and reverses direction.

The shouts from farther up the concourse are immediate and emphatic. "Senator Cox! Stop!"

Looking over his shoulder as he runs, the sixty-three-year-old senator sees the FBI agents giving chase. They are young and athletic, while he is old and not. Engaged in a footrace he cannot possibly win, Cox looks right and left for other avenues of escape. The federal agents in pursuit continue to shout for the senator to stop. People in the concourse stop and stare at the old, white-haired man in the luxurious Burberry double-breasted cashmere coat staggering in one direction and then another, his face racked with dread, thwarted in his escape.

The seven FBI agents approach at a dead run. They are less than forty feet away when Cox almost collides into a Port Authority police officer just emerging from the men's restroom. As the policeman begins to apologize to the clearly disoriented man, and before the FBI agents have again shouted for the senator to halt, Cox grabs the officer's gun from his holster and turns it on the FBI agents.

"You stop! You stop!" Cox shouts somewhat childishly at the hard-charging FBI agents, who comply. All draw their service weapons and train them on their august suspect.

"Stop! Just stop!" Clearly, the senator has lost his senses, a complete disassociation from the great man he was only minutes earlier. His brain has mostly stopped functioning in a rational sense. Reality is fractured. The noise and thundering inside his head has made him utterly deaf to the shouted exhortations and demands of the FBI agents and Port Authority police officer. He spins in every direction, pointing the gun at whoever threatens to approach.

"Safety's engaged! Safety is engaged!" The Port Authority police officer is shouting, but in the chaos and screams of passengers in the terminal, it's doubtful the FBI agents hear him. The cop edges closer and closer to Senator Cox, reaching for the gun. More shouting. More screams. The FBI agents are almost within arm's reach of Cox, who has been pulling on the trigger all the while, to no effect. He hasn't fired a gun in more than thirty years, having been taken to a DC firing range by a lobbyist for his thirty-fifth birthday, but he realizes the problem with firing must be the safety latch and blindly disengages it, turning the gun on the man closest at hand, the Port Authority cop.

Before Cox gets off his shot, first one and then all of the FBI agents fire their weapons, killing the senator instantly with two shots to the head and five to the upper torso. The force of the fusillade throws Cox on his back, his arms and legs spread-eagled. He will be buried in six days back home in North Carolina, in a family plot next to his wife's grave. His three adult children will attend. Members of the news media, quarantined outside the cemetery gate, will outnumber the mourners. Few words will be spoken over Cox's grave. Not even the flag at the local US post office is lowered to half-mast for the dead senator. The woman who succeeds him in Congress is an ardent supporter of President Monroe and will be put on the short list of vice president contenders for the second term.

————————————

JAMES ODOM RECEIVES word of the mission's implosion approximately seven minutes after Sinatra was shot dead by Hayley Chill. Intelligence has been his entire professional career, and he takes pride in his ability to gather it. He even knows it was Hayley Chill who not only killed his operative but also had inspired Asher Danes to expose the conspiracy to the FBI. Recalling his first impressions of the intern and his decision not to recruit her, Odom's biggest regret is that he did not have her eliminated. Instinct is everything in the espionage business. His gravest error, then, was in this instance failing to act on his intuition.

He does not bother contacting the other conspirators. No doubt they will learn the truth on their own and in due time. Unlike Taylor Cox, the CIA deputy director has no intention of running. Attempting to assassinate the president was, of course, a calculated risk. The only honorable recourse is to accept the consequences with dignity. Naturally, Odom is aware of the senator's attempt to evade arrest even before the authorities undertake pursuit of him. Odom isn't surprised. The senator, like most politicians, is a weak man whose narcissism makes him far too predictable. His flaws outweigh his good qualities by too large a percentage. If only Odom's fellow conspirators were made of the right stuff, perhaps the outcome would have been different.

Long after midnight, Odom walks through his stately old house in Falls Church, where he has lived for the past thirty years, pausing several times to examine the mundane personal objects that have defined his adult life. His wife sleeps, blessedly unaware of the tectonic shifts their lives will undergo in just a few, short hours. Framed pictures on the walls testify to an adventurous life filled with professional and personal achievements. All of these material objects will be scattered to the winds, but memory of this expansive life will remain foundational and intact.

He stops in the kitchen and spontaneously decides to make an omelet for himself. Pulling the ingredients from the refrigerator—eggs, mushrooms, green onions, cheese, peppers—the CIA deputy director gets to the pleasant work of preparing a delicious, simple meal. Halfway through the task, just when it all really comes together and timing is particularly critical, his wife appears in the doorway.

"Honey, what are you doing?"

"As you can see." He is just sautéing the onions, peppers, and mushrooms, and they are at that perfect degree of doneness that requires addition of the eggs.

"It's almost four a.m.," she needlessly tells him.

"Are you hungry? This will be a spectacularly scrumptious creation."

Odom's wife laughs lightly, enjoying her husband's rare carefree demeanor. "I am, actually. It smells delicious."

Without pausing from the intricate operation at the stove, Odom gestures with his spatula. "Grab a bottle of chardonnay, the Mâcon-Villages should work nicely, and take a seat."

She does as she's told. Sitting informally at the kitchen island, perched on stools they've owned for almost four decades, Odom and his wife enjoy the aromatic dish he's prepared and the wine while chatting pleasantly about this and that. They discuss banal items of household business, nieces and nephews, the weather and sports scores. They chatter about incidents from their past, health issues, and the flavor of mushrooms encased in lumps of fried egg. They talk about everything except the future. Artfully, the CIA deputy director steers their conversation away from anything having to do with the hours, days, and years to come. His wife's heart brims with happiness. It has been years since they've felt anything more than a gratifying fondness for each other, and for many that is plenty enough. True intimacy had ended ages ago. With affairs of the heart, really could it not be so much worse?

When they have finished their meal, Odom clears the counter of their dishes, dumping them in the sink with the fry pan and cutting board. He wordlessly takes his wife by the hand and leads her back to their bedroom. While she lies back down and falls immediately halfway back to sleep, he goes into the bathroom and takes a pill from a barely touched prescription bottle purchased four years earlier. Returning to bed and lying beside his wife, Odom gently caresses her shoulders, neck, and back. She floats in that wonderful state of half-wakefulness. Before too long, Odom feels his cock stir and fill with lifeblood. His wife feels it, too, and surprised, turns to face her husband.

They fuck like they haven't fucked in decades. Odom's wife is sixty-five but that doesn't stop her from wrapping her legs around her sixty-eight-year-old husband, pulling his thrusts toward her with ecstatic strength even she didn't know she still possessed. She can't remember the last time she experienced a real orgasm, but when it comes, Odom's wife screams a cry of pure delight and gratitude. The Bearded Man grins on hearing her joyful howl, hoping any insomniac neighbors might also be a witness to their ardent love-making, and gives release to his own pleasure. Coated with a sheen of sweat and out of breath, Odom and his wife clutch one another out of divine exhaustion. It takes many minutes for their heart rates and breathing to diminish to normal rates. They kiss then, tenderly, and make love again.

Odom wakes up just after dawn and gets out of bed. His wife, he knows, will sleep for hours more. One of his oldest contacts at the bureau had texted overnight. Odom knows precisely how many min-utes of freedom he has left. He shaves, showers, and gets dressed. It's Sunday morning and most of his top people will be home. He calls each of them. All are aware of the attempted assassination at Camp David, of course. Whether Twitter, MSNBC, the *New York Times*, or your run-of-the-mill political blog, the dis-cussion is 100 percent assassination-attempt coverage. The earliest theories hold that the conspiracy, given the ease with which the hit team was able to infiltrate the installation, involved what has come to be known as the deep state, but none of Odom's lieutenants suggest their boss might be involved, at least not to his face.

Odom eases the potential awkwardness of these phone conversations by casually admitting to his com-plicity. In response, his lieutenants are speechless.

What can possibly be said in response? Odom explains to them all the motivations behind his actions, laying out the danger Monroe represents to the nation. Lest they worry, Odom assures each of the men and women working under him they will in no way be implicated in the conspiracy. The paper trail he has artfully left behind in the event of his unmasking will lead investigators only to those persons who were actually involved. The phone calls end haltingly, with Odom's people unsure how to respond or say goodbye. The CIA deputy director makes these farewells as succinct and painless as possible, quickly signing off with a chipper "best of luck" and encouragement to "keep up the fight."

The not entirely anonymous phone call comes just before eight a.m., coincidentally only moments before the shootout at JFK. His male caller informs Odom the FBI will be knocking on his door in less than five minutes. With little time to spare now, Odom performs a "fatal" hard drive delete on his one computer that matters and then stands up from his home office desk for the last time. He walks briskly to the master bedroom and wakes up his wife. As kindly as possible, he informs her of the broad strokes of what has transpired and what is to come. She says nothing in response and later, to friends, she will confess to having been surprised by none of it. In the years to come, she will remember their last night together with heartfelt nostalgia, and those memories will prompt her to visit her husband once a week, every week, until she dies from a heart attack fifteen years to the hour of her last orgasm, when she came with the glorious ecstasy of a college girl.

Odom kisses his wife on the forehead, stands, and turns when the knock downstairs reverberates through the house like the chains of Jacob Marley's ghost. He walks down the stairs and straight to the door, pulling it open to reveal the FBI agents who have come for him on the other side.

"Deputy Director James Odom?" an agent asks him.

"I am James Odom," he confirms.

"You need to come with us, sir."

Odom nods and takes a step out of the foyer of his house, outside and under a crystalline blue sky. The air is cold but without wind, not uncomfortably so. "Yes, I do," he tells no one in particular.

Before proceeding down the steps, he looks out over his yard, crowded with FBI agents. Fortunately, there are no news reporters yet. The intelligence community takes care of its own, even in its disgrace. Odom's gaze does find the intern, standing off to the side next to a middle-aged black woman who couldn't give off more of an FBI vibe if she tried, and locks on her. As he is led down steps to the walkway, the CIA deputy director gestures toward the young woman from West Virginia, whom he has come to respect more than anyone else in a very long time. "A word with Ms. Chill, if you please? Just a moment," he assures the agents escorting him.

The FBI agents look toward Udall, who gives her assent with a subtle nod. Up above, Odom's wife stands in the window of their bedroom and bears witness to her husband's arrest by federal agents. So handsome, her husband, she thinks. He has always carried himself as a man. She wishes he had bothered to wear a coat or that ridiculous Russian hat. Odom's wife starts to cry now. The scene below is like a painting she has seen someplace but can't remember where. The first neighbors have appeared in their doorways. A dog begins to bark down the block.

Odom stops in front of Hayley and Udall. The intern stares at him with nothing but keen curiosity. Udall has apprehended all manner of criminals, from mob bosses to gunrunners, but this is her first federal official. Odom's arrest is bigger than Petraeus's, Jesse Jackson Jr.'s, or Oliver North's. Hell, this is bigger than Aldrich Ames.

Operation Damocles will be plenty enough on which to make her bones and retire, of this she has no doubt. In fact, Helen Udall will put in her papers three months after the Sunday morning they take down Odom and accept a position of head of security for China Petroleum & Chemical Corporation, the largest corporation in the world, receiving a multimillion-dollar annual salary. It will be an adventure relocating to Beijing and even more so as a black woman. Her newfound wealth and power will afford her a lavish lifestyle, a genial Irish boyfriend, and a measure of happiness she never enjoyed under vastly different circumstances in Washington, and all due to a certain White House intern.

"I really wish I hadn't waited to recruit you, Ms. Chill," Odom admits with a look of chagrin.

"Or you could've not tried to assassinate a president, sir," Hayley suggests.

Udall mistakenly thinks she needs to protect the intern from the CIA man. "Don't even begin to suggest you did it for God and country."

Odom ignores the FBI agent, in his snap appraisal a working stiff possessing only modest intelligence and investigative skills. Gaze remaining locked on Hayley's, he stares deeply into those blue eyes, trying in vain to unlock the secrets that lie behind them and decides they don't exist.

"Tread lightly, Ms. Chill. Know your enemies better than you know yourself." With that wisdom imparted to a young woman with whom he has fallen a little bit in love, he looks to the FBI agents holding him by either arm.

"Let's get going, then."

---

Hayley did not return to the West Wing for the entire week after the incident at Camp David. Her days were filled with interviews in windowless rooms at the FBI headquarters and in the down-market motel where she had been sequestered. The federal authorities from various agencies exerted enormous influence to protect Hayley's identity out of fear for her safety. Her story was vetted and rigorously corroborated, at every level and from every direction. No detail went unexamined by the top investigators of the land. Everyone associated with her was thoroughly interviewed, from her first-grade teacher to the young female congressional interns who lived down the hall from Hayley at Henry House. Not a single aspect of her story failed to check out. At a time when the trustworthiness of nearly every federal appointment, contract player, or elected official was under suspicion, Hayley Chill rang as genuine as her soft West Virginia twang.

In these early days, Hayley was reduced to a more passive role than she was accustomed. Her astonishing ability for recall was a subject of wonder by many of her interrogators. But the long, laborious interviews were more exhausting than any physical or mental exercise she had undergone in the past. The agents allowed her to venture out for her morning runs, accompanied by a minder, of course. Just before dawn, the cold air sharp in her lungs and nostrils, running with a feeling of release and celebration of her physical body, these were the minutes of that time in which she actually experienced something akin to contentment.

She wasn't distraught over killing the as-of-yet unidentified man who threatened the president with a Sig Sauer. The assassin's death was the unavoidable consequence of saving Monroe's life. What else was there to consider? An army psychologist had told Hayley she exhibited a form of mental rigidity, arising from her earliest childhood traumas. The suggestion was that her low tolerance for uncertainty pushed Hayley to find a quick answer without bothering to look for the right answer. At the risk of only confirming the shrink's analysis of her, Hayley terminated the session early and never went back.

Whether or not Hayley was "closed off" emotionally had little bearing on the FBI's investigation. After seven days of nonstop interviews, she is cleared to return to the White House. Much of the federal government remains in the thrall of rumor and innuendo. The FBI itself is unscathed. Not a single agent or director of that investigative agency is found to be sympathetic to the Shady Side conspirators. Among the five thousand agents in the Secret Service, exactly twenty-three agents are revealed to be complicit to varying degrees, and suffer consequences commensurate with their levels of involvement. More than a hundred conspirators are ferreted out from the ranks in the intelligence community and in Congress. Other agencies undergo vicious purges as well. Old scores are revived and at times settled with the slightest suggestion an adversary was party to the conspiracy. Lives and livelihoods are ruined overnight. Hayley's morning bus ride seems a fractured reality. The city has been altered, irrevocably thrown askew, though the other passengers on the Metrobus can't possibly know of Hayley's role in the explosive events that have convulsed the United States of America.

Even Ned, the Secret Service uniformed officer at the Seventeenth Street White House complex gate, doesn't seem to be the same person. As Hayley approaches, he appears tense and on edge. Half of his fellow officers are unfamiliar and obviously new to their positions. Where had the previous officers gone? Hayley had heard rumors that the social media accounts of federal employees at every level of the government were analyzed for evidence of disloyalty to the administration. Personal cell phones were apparently scrutinized as well. For the sake of thoroughness, the purge was more widespread than the conspiracy could have ever been.

Hayley smiles at her friend as she has on dozens of previous mornings. "Morning, Ned."

He takes her ID card and scrutinizes it as if today were her first occasion to enter there. Hayley watches him, repressing a glib comment. Ned returns her ID and gestures.

"Proceed, thank you."

Hayley is slightly taken aback by Ned's formality and is momentarily flustered. Unable to make eye contact with her friend, she inputs her code and receives the green light to proceed to security scanning. As she moves forward, Hayley hears him quietly speak after her.

"I'm sorry, Hayley. It's . . . different now."

She turns back toward him and nods, sympathetic. "I know."

Hayley perceives a changed West Wing within moments of entering its ground floor, initially by clocking the sheer reduction of people inside the building. Those staffers who survived the purge remain on edge, paranoia and distrust the underlying dynamic of all interactions either within or outside the West Wing.

Like the entire federal government, the Monroe administration staggers forward but under a siege mentality.

Staffers are aware of Hayley's heroic actions at Camp David, in spite of the news blackout. As she walks the hallway and climbs the stairs to the first floor, White House personnel regard her with a mixture of awe and fear. Her public persona is almost mythical and superheroic, a mixture of Joan of Arc and the X-Men's Rogue. Before Camp David, Hayley had been something of an outlier. Now she is utterly unapproachable. No one says a word to her in the entire journey from the West Wing's entrance to the White House Operations office on the first floor.

Asher is gone, of course. He has been charged but released on bail, confined to his luxurious condo on Water Street. His mother has moved temporarily from Connecticut to be with her son. Asher's father has hired the same lawyer who defended Bill Clinton when he was impeached. The case will crawl through federal courts over the next four years. With Asher's full cooperation, federal prosecutors ultimately offer the disgraced White House aide a deal in which he will plead guilty to an assault charge under US Code Title 18, Section 111, that prohibits "assaulting, resisting, or impeding" officers and employees of the United States while engaged in or on account of the performance of official duties and be sentenced to time served. As a convicted felon, Asher will no longer be able to vote, let alone run as one of the nation's first openly gay presidential candidates. To his parents' immense relief, he will obtain an MBA from Harvard and join a hedge fund soon thereafter. It will take years, but Asher eventually will find true love with a wildly successful television celebrity chef and marry. Though he'll never speak again with the intern who altered his life's path so dramatically, Asher and his husband will name their first and only daughter Hayley.

Her first order of business once arriving back in the West Wing is to venture down to the Navy Mess takeout window. In the early-morning hours after the attempted assassination, Hayley had been kept apart from Leon Washington as FBI agents interviewed them separately. From Camp David, Hayley was driven to the Hoover Building and placed in what was termed "protective custody" for the following week. Consequently, she had no opportunity to communicate with Leon, or anyone else for that matter. Hayley repeatedly asked after the one individual who had been of incalculable assistance in saving the president's life but was told only the cook's situation was still a subject of FBI investigation. It was an absolute imperative for her to check in with Leon Washington before anything else.

The old man's face lit up upon seeing his fellow presidential savior.

"You packing? Was beginning to get used to the idea of a 'life of danger.'"

"No, Leon. Once was enough for me." She pauses to shift the mood, her face reflecting a genuine concern for her friend. "You okay? The FBI . . . ?"

The cook interrupts her with a gesture, waving off

her concern. "In the beginning, they weren't too sure about me. I wasn't necessarily the president's biggest fan." He laughs. "Maybe now that I saved his bacon, he'll do something about my brother's health care!"

"I'm pretty sure the president's grateful for your help that night, Leon," Hayley assures him before moving on.

After straightening up the office for an hour, Hayley sits at her desk and waits for further instructions. Her only communication with Karen Rey since Camp David has been in the form of emails assuring Hayley that, despite the momentous events of the past few weeks, her internship in the West Wing would continue. Rey had survived the purge and, in many ways, benefited by it. Her record and loyalty to the president were unblemished. Like most of the dozen staffers on-site at Camp David that fateful weekend, Rey had been snug in her cabin a half mile from Aspen Lodge and blissfully unaware of the drama unfolding there. Hayley would learn only after the fact that staffers were expected to remain in their accommodations after nightfall. This standard sequestering of personnel was an important element in the conspirators' scheme, as were the military personnel's routine orders to steer clear of the president's cabin. The dozen Secret Service agents who had withdrawn from their assigned posts that night remain in jail for their treasonous activities, as does their supervising agent.

Karen Rey walks into the White House Operations office shortly before ten a.m. She doesn't quite know how to interact with Hayley, who is undoubtedly the most powerful intern in Washington, DC, and, by extension, the world. Technically speaking, Rey is Hayley's supervisor. In reality, the intern could probably have Rey booted from the complex with only a few words to the president. The senior White House staffer's resiliency crumbles under the strain of Hayley's newfound domination. Within weeks, Rey will leave the White House voluntarily and spend several months unsuccessfully searching for a comparable position elsewhere in the federal government. Within a year's time, she will move away from Washington, DC, and try her luck in California. To the surprise of the few friends she keeps in Washington, several powerful digital economy companies pursue Rey for her experience with federal regulators. A job with Uber will land her a salary in the high six figures, a more West Coast–casual wardrobe, a venture capitalist boyfriend, and a disconcerting but mild addiction to Adderall. All things considered, life will seem to have taken a promising upturn for the ex–White House aide when, four years after leaving Washington, her self-driving Tesla X crashes into the back of a US mail truck at sixty miles per hour, killing Karen Rey instantly.

On this January morning, however, a life outside of the West Wing still seems unimaginable. Rey surprises herself with her willingness to capitulate in the face of Hayley's astonishing rise. How can you not respect this remarkable young woman? The smile on the senior White House staffer's face is almost genuine when she

return to the White House but under the condition he would spend four additional days confined to the executive residence. Monroe, his own boss, had remained on the White House second floor for three days before returning prematurely, this morning, to the West Wing.

Hayley's gut clenches with nervousness and she immediately floods her brain with positive thoughts to counter these worries. She will handle this challenge, or she will blow it. Fretting only makes matters worse. Uncertainty is a fact of life. The best way to cope with the unexpected is a calm mind and exertion of willpower. Even if she is only an intern and he is the president of the United States, what she knows to be true is what empowers her. She's ready.

Hayley stands up without further word from Rey, following her out the door and into the Outer Oval. The president's personal assistant, sitting at her desk, gestures to Karen Rey.

"Go ahead in. He's waiting."

---

RICHARD MONROE IS seated at the *Resolute* desk when Rey enters the Oval Office, with Hayley Chill following her supervisor inside. He's intently reading a briefing report from the CIA and continues to do so for a number of seconds longer, while the women stand respectfully across the room.

Finally, the president finishes his reading and looks up from the papers on his desk, toward Rey and Hayley standing by the couches. "Ah, very good." Monroe stands. "If you don't mind, Karen, I'd like to have this be a private meeting with Ms. Chill."

Rey wordlessly pivots and retreats from the office, closing the door behind her. Standing and moving out from behind his desk, Monroe indicates one of the couches that face each other by the fireplace. "Please, have a seat."

"Thank you, Mr. President." Hayley sits on the couch with her back to the Rose Garden. Monroe sits in the armchair, his back to the dark fireplace.

"Well, needless to say, I felt compelled to take a few minutes out from my first day back in this office to personally thank you, Hayley. You've had a remarkable internship here at the White House, I must say."

For a moment, Hayley says nothing but instead simply looks to the president with an enigmatic expression. Despite being the most powerful man on the planet, Richard Monroe finds the experience unsettling. And, with a couple more seconds of her silence, the president becomes irritated. "Yes?"

Hayley opens her mouth and, in fluent Russian, tells the president, *"It has been an honor to serve my country, sir."*

The muscles in Monroe's face freeze, forming an expression of bewildered astonishment and, momentarily, fear. He recovers quickly and then, with anger, thunders at her, "What the devil?" He starts to stand up from his chair.

"Sit down, sir," Hayley orders with a very firm tone, adding in Russian, *"Na lovtsa I zver' bezhit."*

The president appears to not know what Hayley has said, halfway between sitting and standing erect.

"'Speak of the devil, and he appears,'" she translates for him. "That's how the Russian proverb goes, does it not, sir? You're the native speaker after all."

Monroe slowly sits back down. For a long moment, he only stares at Hayley. Finally, in Russian, he asks, *"Who are you?"*

"I am an intern in the White House Operations office." Switching to Russian, *"I am a person who knows the truth."*

"Truth? What truth?" Monroe asks indignantly.

In Russian, Hayley lays it out for him. *"Your parents were agents of the KGB, entering the US under false passports in 1958, the year after you were born in Moscow at the brand-new Kremlin Hospital. Your father enlisted in the US Army and continued his military career for thirty years. You were raised as a typical American boy, but in the privacy of your home, you were groomed as a Soviet mole. Your admission to West Point in 1976 was the primary mission objective and culmination of your parents' KGB careers. The rest, as has been said, is history."*

Monroe seems shell-shocked. The ground beneath his feet has turned to quicksand but he still musters a shadow of indignation.

*"Where is all this nonsense coming from?"*

*"The people I answer to have taught me many things, including the truth about you, Mr. President."*

Monroe is utterly defeated, his secret exposed. With resignation, he asks, *"Are you Russian?"*

Hayley shakes her head no. "West Virginian, born and bred."

Monroe tries to make sense of it all. He can't and never will. "What do you want?"

"Is that all, Mr. President? Only what I want in order to keep your secret?"

The president says nothing, calculating his get-away.

Hayley switches back to Russian. *"You will never escape. Your career as an agent for Moscow ended when I entered the room."*

Monroe can only blink and stare. He realizes this game has cost him his freedom, if not his life. *"Why did you not let James Odom and his cabal kill me if you knew?"*

*"The people who trained me and placed me here have other uses for you, sir."*

Monroe is clearly perplexed. "Odom? Senator Cox?"

Hayley dismisses the conspirators with a slight toss of her head. "The 'deep state' is more interested in their own careers and positions of power than the state of this union. I represent those individuals who have served our country in the past, most of them no longer in those offices. Former presidents and directors, retired senators and Supreme Court judges, with ties still to the government and other clandestine agents like myself. A deeper state you might call it, sir, interested only in the preservation of the best example of a democracy the planet has ever produced and its Constitution."

Monroe takes all of this in. He now knows what will be demanded of him if he does not want to spend the rest of his life in a military prison. "You want me to be a double agent for this 'deeper state,' operating against Moscow."

"You will be working for the United States, sir," correcting him, though her voice has lost its harder edge.

Monroe calculates his fate. Work against his mother country? Impossible. There must be a way for him to return to the land of his birth. The operation was over. It had been, by any estimation, a success. Monroe's performance exceeded even the best-case scenarios of his KGB handlers, rising to the upper echelons of the US Army. Then, by simple good fortune, the highest office in the land became available to "Richard Monroe," making him the most successful mole in the history of espionage.

Then Hayley dashes all such hope of escape. She reads his thoughts as if they're printed on his forehead. *"You know better than I, Yuri Sergeev, the office of president of the United States is a gilded cage, a cage that is strong and inescapable."*

The president sighs, acknowledging the veracity of her statement. *"Your Russian is very good for a West Virginia girl."*

"I was recruited for the position I have today, sir." She smiles with the memory of it. "Training was not without its rigors."

"No one would suspect an intern, no matter how good an intern she might be." He shakes his head in admiration of the tradecraft. "Were you sent to protect me or to turn me?"

*"One and the same."* Switching back to English, she adds, "No one must know the truth, lest Moscow know the truth as well."

Monroe gives it some thought. It seems like many long minutes when in actuality they sit in silence only for another fifteen seconds. In Russian, he tells her, *"I will do what your 'deeper state' wants of me."*

Hayley nods. "Once you've finished your term, and your work for us, life as a former president is not so bad."

*"Yes, yes, I can see that now. We are in agreement, then,"* he says, the deal closed.

In that moment, the door leading from the Outer Oval is pushed open and Karen Rey reenters the room.

"Mr. President, your cabinet is ready for you, sir." Rey is all too ready to separate POTUS from his favorite intern.

As Monroe stands to his feet, he gives Hayley the slightest nod before turning toward Karen Rey. Transforming before her eyes in an instant, he resumes the iconic countenance of military hero and popular US president. "Yes. Let's get rolling."

With upright stride, the president follows Rey back out the door into the Outer Oval on his way to the Cabinet Room. For just a few seconds, before being shooed out by the president's assistant and shown back to her intern's windowless office, Hayley sits on the couch in the silent Oval Office. Motionless and meditative, she imagines the men of history who have toiled in this exact place, from John Adams to Russian mole, Richard Monroe, and she can almost smell the sweat of their collective fears, the grunt of ego, singularly male and entrusted with the grave task of steering this majestic ship, these United States, through tempest after awful tempest.

# 10

★ ★ ★ ★

## THE BEAR

*One year earlier*

Without seeing what she is seeing, Hayley gazes out the window from her seat as the Greyhound bus passes through the outskirts of Killeen and enters the on-ramp of Interstate 14, heading east toward I-35. Leaving hadn't been an easy choice, the army being the engine of her escape from a low-wattage life of underachievement, unwed pregnancy, and cascading addiction. The comfortable routine of military life, its hidebound structures and hierarchies, created the cohesive and functional family unit absent in her upbringing. And Hayley had left all of that behind, voluntarily and with relatively short deliberation.

The Man in the Blue Suit had approached her three days after her boxing match with Marcela Rivas, stopping her in the produce section of the PX. By all appearances a civilian, he inexplicably had complete access on base. Blue oxford shirt, double monk leather shoes, and deeply tan, the Man in the Blue Suit broke the ice by congratulating Hayley on her fight. It was obvious to her their encounter was no accident and consequently put herself on guard. But the Man in the Blue Suit possessed a gravitas, the words he spoke direct and having weight. "What would you say to the opportunity to pursue a higher purpose in life, Hayley, one in which service to your country is paramount?"

"I'm doing that already, sir, with the army."

"What I'm suggesting would be of a greater commitment and even higher service than the army."

For a number of seconds, Hayley simply stared at the Man in the Blue Suit with a perplexed expression. What was this? The two of them stood next to a bin of peaches. Across the aisle were stacks of gleaming apples and pears. Other service people pushed their carts past Hayley and the Man in the Blue Suit, going about their shopping same as always.

"I can tell you're thinking, 'Who the hell is this guy?' My name is Andrew Wilde. I was in the military myself, the Marines, for seventeen years. After that, I spent several years in the intelligence community. Andrew Wilde, of course, is not my given name. I was in the Marines, though. That much is true."

"Are you being obtuse on purpose, Mr. Wilde?"

He smiled with real affection for Hayley, having developed that affinity for her long before this day, while being one of several individuals working up her background dossier. There was much to admire in what Wilde discovered about Hayley, and even more to inspire a rooting interest in her. "Let's meet again, dinner off base perhaps might be best, and I'll explain more completely what I'm proposing."

"I'm busy, sir."

"Get unbusy. This is important." Not even with her years in the military had Hayley been addressed with such command.

Wilde selected a Red Lobster in Round Rock, fifty-three miles to the south of Fort Hood, as a venue for dinner. Their privacy was reasonably assured. Both Hayley and Wilde ordered seafood salads and sparkling water. Wilde, or whatever his real name was, did almost all of the talking. First he laid out the general outlines of the group he represented, describing a loose affiliation of individuals who shared lifelong government service and extreme patriotism. Most were retired from those official offices, which included former presidents, Supreme Court justices, NSA and CIA directors, senators, and military brass. None maintained those powerful positions at the present time, thereby guaranteeing their motivations were pure and absent the typical self-serving incentives of their active counterparts.

There was no name for this group. Nor was there a leader or hierarchy. Few of them had ever met one another, their identities hidden behind avatars and pseudonyms. Communication between participants and conferences in general were facilitated by ultra-secure, cloud-based intranet run from a server farm in north central Canada. Membership to the group had been closed for more than two years, coinciding with the rise of Richard Monroe's political career. Though the group had no name, Wilde and other members referred to themselves as Publius, a nod to the Federalist Party formed by Alexander Hamilton, James Madison, and John Jay in support of the not-yet-ratified US Constitution. The essence of their effort and entire reason for being was the protection of the historic document and its tenets, no matter the origin of any threat to its preservation.

Hayley did not ask what all of this background information had to do with her. Wilde moved quickly on to that topic without her prompting. She had been prescreened and selected for inclusion in a corps of similarly capable individuals who could be called on to act, always covertly, as agents of Publius, operatives to combat current and future threats to the nation and its Constitution.

"I'm not exactly sure what it is you're asking me to do, Mr. Wilde."

"Put in your papers immediately. Your discharge will be approved within thirty-six hours, I can tell you with complete certainty. You'll then join other agent candidates at a facility in the Northwest, where you will undergo extensive training to prepare you for future operations. I'm afraid that's all I can really tell you right now, Hayley."

For several moments, she said nothing in response. Then she asked, "How soon do you need an answer, Mr. Wilde?"

"Now. Tonight. If you say no, you'll never see me again. We have confidence in your discretion should you decline to join us." He paused long enough to take a drink of water. Then he carefully placed the glass on the table again and locked his gaze on her. "Is that your preference, Hayley? The army? No doubt you can and will do great things there."

"Less great things. Less vital service."

"Yes."

Her answer was firm and immediate. "I will put in my papers first thing tomorrow, sir."

If he was surprised or inordinately pleased by Hayley's decision, Wilde did not betray it. He merely nodded and gestured to their server for the check. "A taxi is waiting outside to take you back to Fort Hood." He stood and very nearly departed without further word or a goodbye. But then he thought better of it and stopped, hands gripping the back of his chair as he looked down at Hayley across the table.

"I told you that you'd never see me again if you chose to stay in the army. I didn't tell you the same would be true if you chose to join us. Publius has no face. We have no names or positions. For obvious reasons, the entity, such as it exists, is diffuse and rigorously compartmentalized. My job as agent recruiter takes me all over the United States and overseas. Consequently, I'm perpetually on the move. Remember always you have joined an extensive network of citizen patriots whose power lies not in their positions but in their beliefs. America as an idea can be weakened but never defeated. I've very much enjoyed getting to know you in this brief time. It's been my honor to do so. Your efforts on our behalf, while never to be officially recorded, will have every bit the impact of the country's greatest heroes."

Somberly, Hayley nodded in acknowledgment. "Thank you, sir."

Wilde turned and strode out of the restaurant. Hayley watched him go. Visible just beyond the glass doors, a yellow cab idled at the curb. The server came to clear the table and informed Hayley the bill had been settled. On the hour-long taxi ride back home, the West Virginian briefly wondered whether she had made a mistake. How could she ever be certain the shadowy organization she had agreed to join actually shared her same values? How could she perform any due diligence if the individuals giving the orders were hidden behind virtual personae and aliases? Whatever the training she had just agreed to undertake in order to become a covert agent for Publius, Hayley decided an additional priority, of equal importance, would be investigating the identity and true motivations of those individuals she was now obligated to serve.

---

NINETY-SIX HOURS AFTER pulling out of the bus station in Killeen, Texas, a different Greyhound bus drops Hayley off at the depot in The Dalles, Oregon, one of the more charming bus stations she has seen in her transcontinental trip. A black passenger van is waiting to collect her. Climbing into the rear of the van, Hayley is gratified to discover she is the only passenger. The driver, a young black man roughly her own age, doesn't say a single word to her. Road weary, Hayley welcomes the lack of conversation over the course of the eighty-minute drive south.

The landscape in eastern Oregon is dry, brush-covered rolling hills and rugged. In slightly under an hour, the van leaves the two-lane state highway 197 and heads east on an unmarked, intermittently paved road. After seventeen miles through a desolate moon-scape, they arrive at what is clearly a recently con-structed training camp, complete with prefabricated barracks, classrooms, fitness center, and mess. Fir-ing range and athletic-training fields have been con-structed by leveling out a few of the surrounding hills and ravines. There isn't a proper tree for thirty miles. Any available shade is provided by awnings or hoisted tarps. The date is September 3. The heat is sharp and piercing, totally unlike the soft, moist sauna of Texas. In the days, weeks, and months ahead, a new Hayley will be forged in the furnace of this brutal geography, creating an alloy stronger than its components. Only later will she learn the name given to the spot by state maps is Bakeoven.

Hayley meets the other agent candidates in the mess hall at the evening feed. Thirteen men and women, between the ages of twenty-one and twenty-six, sit at three cafeteria-style dining tables. Similarly recruited from various military and intelligence agencies, they all share an intense idealism for country. Like military pilots in the 1960s chosen for the Gemini space program, the Publius agent candidates are driven by an acute desire to push the envelope, however vaguely their superiors have described that mission. Leaving all notions of military-themed teamwork behind them, competition between the agent candidates is keen, a fact Hayley discovers before she has taken a seat in the mess.

"Sorry. You can't sit there," an athletic, female agent candidate tells Hayley as she is about to sit at the only place available at all three tables. Since the earliest days of the training camp's existence, April Wu, a computer science major who graduated from West Point near the top of her class and was recruited from her position at US Cyber Command, has enjoyed an undisputed domination over the ranks. The other candidates continue to eat but watch the unfolding exchange with mild interest.

"Why not?" Hayley asks.

"Because you're new and you don't know shit."

Hayley, holding her meal tray out before her, considers the other agent candidate's statement for a brief moment and then starts to sit anyway. April slides over, effectively taking up two places.

"Uh-uh," she tells Hayley. "Prove to me you know shit."

"I don't have to prove anything to you," Hayley says.

"Proof positive you don't know shit."

Hayley looks to the other ACs seated around the

table, their mildly interested expressions clinical and waiting to render judgment.

"Don't look to them for help. They don't know only a little less shit than you."

Hayley turns her gaze back on her tormentor. "Move before I shove this tray up your ass."

"I'm definitely intrigued to see you try," April tells her.

Hayley walks to the end of the table and places her tray on some open space there, returning to where April sits. Her nemesis has casually resumed eating her vegetable stir-fry as if having nothing to fear from Hayley's impending attack. Hayley reaches to haul April off the bench seat from behind and, with seemingly no passage of time, finds herself on her back with the other AC astride her in a shockingly painful submission hold.

"Like I said," a grinning April whispers into Hayley's ear. "Doesn't know shit."

Hayley grits her teeth against the pain.

"Tap out," April orders her.

Hayley isn't about to do any such thing. "Ever hear a pencil break?" she asks. Before the other woman can answer, Hayley wrenches her right hand free, grasps the index finger of April's left hand, and yanks back hard. The metacarpal bone fractures with an audible crack that causes everyone at the table to wince and groan.

April rolls off Hayley, grimacing against the pain but refusing to so much as whimper. "Sounds pretty much like that," Hayley tells the other agent candidate before standing to her feet.

HAYLEY SITS IN the air-conditioned prefab building kitted out as a classroom. An instructor leads the agent candidates through intensive Russian language instruction. Seated at a desk beside Hayley is April Wu, whose index finger has been in a splint for the past two weeks since being fractured. Both women, like the other agent candidates, are completely focused on their instructor. In addition to physical fitness and combat training, other class topics in the coming weeks and months ahead will include criminal law and procedures, advanced criminal investigation, human psychology, interrogation techniques, criminal profiling, and presentations on government and federal policies and procedures. The rivalry between Hayley and April that commenced in the mess hall continues in the classroom. Only one candidate will be selected for the first mission, and the competition for that honor is intense. Five of the ACs have emerged as clear contenders, including Hayley and April, of course. Their grasp of the Russian language is already better than all of the other agent candidates. When the instructor asks for someone to read out loud, in the original Russian, a difficult passage from Mikhail Sholokhov's *And Quiet Flows the Don*, Hayley and April vie strenuously for the instructor's attention. In this case, Hayley is selected to read the passage, and her recitation seems flawless, winning the approval of the class instructor.

When the class ends and the candidates head for

the door, however, April gives Hayley a personal critique on her reading. "You're heavy on your reduction of vowels in the unstressed position, dumbass. Unstressed 'o's are pronounced either as 'a's . . ."

". . . or as a very weak reduced sound, depending on the position in the word," Hayley finishes for April. "What you're failing to acknowledge, hotshot, is that Muscovites tend to reduce their 'o's even more. I'm guessing our potential contacts will be something more urban-centric Russian than the average provincial schoolmarm."

April isn't about to give up so easily. "You're a lost cause, Chill. I locked this up the day I arrived. Second in my class at West Point and US Cyber Command's 2019 Best Warrior Soldier of the Year. Face the facts, mental case, I'm simply a higher-caliber human being than you."

Hayley isn't rattled. "And here I thought you were going to thank me for being considerate enough to break the finger on your left hand."

April responds by shooting Hayley's legs, lifting her up and then slamming her down on the floor of the mobile classroom. They grapple furiously there, the few candidates still in the room continuing out the door because this sparring between April and Hayley is a regular thing. The West Virginian finally gains control of her rival, who stops trying to pass her guard. Both of them are winded from their exertions. "Are you trying to fight me or fuck me?" Hayley asks between gasps for air.

"Is there any difference?" a winded April asks in response.

"Hate to break it to you, baller, but I'm straight."

"Then I guess it is fighting that we're doing here."

Hayley smiles at that one. She releases her submission hold on April and helps her rival to her feet. The two young women continue out the door. April is in a more conciliatory mood. "You're not a half-bad ground fighter. And maybe you know how to reduce a fucking vowel in Russian, I'll give you that much," she tells Hayley as they walk across the sunbaked grassless quad surrounded on all sides by prefab buildings. "But I'm still coming out on top. Whatever the mission, I'm their operative."

Hayley grins and gives her new friend a wink. "Second at West Point, second at Bakeoven."

It's the middle of September. There isn't a cloud in the pale blue sky. The temperature is ninety-four, with low humidity and even lower wind speed. Hayley has been on-site for two weeks. In response to Richard Monroe's official nomination to be his party's candidate for the president of the United States in late August, the Dow Jones Industrial Average dropped more than five hundred points. Three dozen major newspapers have run editorials condemning Monroe's nomination, but during the same twenty-four-hour period, in more than ten thousand "news" stories hosted by the complete spectrum of social media platforms, his opponent is accused of crimes and misdemeanors ranging from Satan worship to child murder. Very few Americans, whether civilian or within the government, realize it, but the country is under attack in a manner far more profound than at Pearl Harbor on December 7, 1941.

---

AFTER SEVERAL MONTHS of intensive training and instruction, as well as continuous physical and psychological evaluations, only six agent candidates remain of the original fourteen. Three males and an equal number of females comprise an accomplished corps of prospective covert agents ready for assignment. April and Hayley stand out even among this elite group, excelling in every single quantifiable aspect of physical and psychological evaluation. Their intense rivalry continues albeit under friendlier auspices. In fact, Hayley has grown as close to April Wu as anyone in her entire life. Though the other four agent candidates continue to strive for selection in the first mission, each knows they are really competing for third position.

Indications that a facility-wide meeting is afoot are apparent from the earliest hours of the first Monday in March. Winter in central Oregon is every bit as harsh as summer, with relentless winds and freezing temperatures. An unmarked helicopter lands just after dawn, not a completely unusual occurrence at Bakeoven, but the presence of several armed private security guards is remarkable. The six agent candidates assemble in the classroom just after ten in the morning. Moments later, facility personnel enter the room as well and find a seat.

Instructors, analysts, facility supervisors, and medical staff are all present.

Soon after the facility's entire resident population has gathered in the classroom, the door opens, and two men and one woman dressed in business clothes enter the room, somber as undertakers. The older of the men, introducing himself with the obvious pseudonym of "Mr. Jones," starts speaking, focusing on the agent candidates. He has their full attention. The young people realize their moment has come. One of them will be selected for a mission destined to be of enormous national importance. Jones gets directly to the point, informing the assembled recruits that a high-ranking figure in Washington has been determined to be a Russian mole. He will not identify the individual to the group; for obvious security reasons, only the agent candidate selected for the mission will be briefed with that privileged information. Mission details are also left unspecified, with Jones stating merely that the newly minted agent will be tasked with the difficult job of "turning" the Russian mole into an intelligence asset for the United States.

The reaction in the classroom to these frustratingly vague assertions runs the gamut, from irritation to stunned disbelief. Some of those present, both candidates and staff, raise their hands to request more details, particularly regarding the identity of the Russian mole. Having anticipated their frustration, Jones deflects their demands by driving home his primary theme. "Make no mistake, ladies and gentlemen, we are at war. And it is a war we are losing. Our enemy is relentless, brutal, and will not stop its attack until he has utterly destroyed us. We must not lull ourselves into the false belief the Russian Bear can be reasoned with or is capable of mercy. The Bear only knows one thing: to kill his prey and feed off its carcass. He is a vicious, remorseless beast and one which we have every reason to fear. But, with guile and cunning, we can prevail against the Bear. We can fight him, blow for blow, if we employ the same weapons he uses to undermine us. We can win this war."

When Jones finishes speaking, the rush of questions resumes. Who is the mole? Is the Washington heavyweight an elected or appointed figure? Is he or she in the military or a member of the intelligence community? Jones deflects all of these questions, with the firm conviction he has told his audience all they need to know. Some of the agent candidates betray their irritation with Jones but then back off, not wanting to hurt their standing with the organization. Hayley has remained quiet through the entirety of this question-and-non-answer period but raises her hand after the others have expended themselves and grown compliant.

"How do we know you're who you say you are?" she asks Jones.

Jones stares quizzically at Hayley. "Elaborate, please."

"Everyone associated with this group, one that we've agreed to join and serve as operatives, remains behind a veil of anonymity and pseudonyms. How do we know *you* aren't actually the Russian moles and your target the true patriot?" The emphasis she places in the "you" of her question has the swing and heft of a cudgel.

Jones appears momentarily thrown by Hayley's query. Neither he nor his two colleagues have cogent responses. How can they prove the true nature of their motivations? They speak quietly among themselves at the front of the room while a murmur rises from the attendees. April, seated at a desk next to her friend, leans over for a private word. "Are you fucking crazy? Say goodbye to your chances for first mission," she surmises. With a crooked grin, she adds, "Thanks, I guess."

Jones turns back toward the classroom, having finished conferring with his colleagues. "The agent candidate makes a good point, with the only question that needed to be asked. How can I, standing before you, be trusted? Am I who I say I am, and is what I've told you the complete truth? To that end, we request you continue your training. My colleagues and I will return at a date very soon and provide all the verification necessary to accept what I've presented here today as fact."

With that said, Jones and his two colleagues depart the classroom with a clutch of the facility's senior management. Within a couple of minutes, those still inside the classroom can hear the helicopter revving its engine and lifting off. Everyone files out of the building to continue with the day's normal schedule. Hayley shrugs off April's attempt to join her out the door, staying seated at her desk instead. Within moments, the West Virginian is alone in the classroom with only her thoughts as

thousands of fallen warriors before him, Tommy's body was returned to the US by way of the air force base in Dover, Delaware, and then delivered home by van to Lincoln County.

There was no question of his funeral service being anything but closed casket. Linda Chill had been told simply that it would be best for the family if her husband's remains were kept from their view. Linda, hollowed up by grief and fear, agreed without complaint. The only member of the entire extended family having an issue with this decision was Hayley. Not quite yet nine years old, young Hayley fervently wanted to see her beloved father one more time before saying goodbye forever.

Late the night before the scheduled service and burial, just after midnight, Hayley sneaked out of her house and bicycled two miles through dark streets to the one funeral parlor in town. Breaking into the building wasn't difficult, involving nothing more than shattering the glass of a rear window and climbing inside. Opening her father's casket was only slightly more difficult, the massive wood lid having been screwed shut and sealed. Hayley located a screwdriver in the funeral parlor's workroom and, with the aid of a step stool, proceeded to remove all thirty-two securing screws.

Hayley pushed the lid up and revealed the casket's contents to the grim half-light of the storage room. Remains are exactly what she found, in the truest sense of the word. Handsome, charismatic, and always-smiling Tommy Chill had been shredded to nothing more than a grotesque array of bloody, raw body parts stowed in a half-dozen plastic collection bags. Bone, gristle, and torn flesh were the residue of the father Hayley loved and adored. Rather than grief, however, Hayley experienced an uncontrollable rage that invaded her body like alien spore and commanded her to destroy everything within eyesight. By the time the police arrived, much of the entire interior of the funeral parlor and its furnishings were a complete ruin. The only object that remained untouched in the child's chaotic destruction of the funeral parlor were her father's remains and his casket.

There was exhaustive talk of criminal charges and reform school. Given her age and the circumstances, however, Hayley was ordered by juvenile court to undertake extensive psychological therapy. The greatest punishment by far was being kept home from the funeral. Just as well, Hayley ultimately decided, as she came to view the vengeance she wrought upon the funeral parlor as the most fitting farewell to her dad. From that point onward, Hayley's path deviated from that of her peers. That awful night taught her the value of violence as therapy. With maturation, she came to sculpt that ferocity into controlled action, more thoughtful and directed. Violence is life, she had decided. Directed violence is a directed life. Enlistment in the army, therefore, and all that lay beyond it was the only natural course for a natural-born hellion.

Hayley recalls that night with conflicting emotions. Losing her dad was the worst thing ever to happen to her. But viewed from another angle, the cathartic release ignited by her father's death was the spark for everything that has gone right in her life since that time. As she stands up from the student desk in the prefab classroom of an unnamed training camp in Bakeoven, Oregon, she walks toward the door with a roaring conviction. If she is a loaded gun, she needs to know who will be pulling the trigger.

———————————

THE AGENT CANDIDATES hear the helicopter approach two days later as they're prepping for a twenty-mile hike through the surrounding eastern Oregon outback. Facility staff enter the barracks and draw all the blinds and block the door as the chopper is heard landing in the quad. After a few minutes have passed, the ACs are instructed to continue with their preparations for the all-day march. One of the instructors approaches Hayley and tells her to put down her pack and follow him out of the barracks. April and the other four agent candidates stop what they're doing and, with slack expressions, watch Hayley follow the instructor out the door. The West Virginian shoots a glance over her shoulder at April before closing the barracks door behind her.

"Motherfuckingfucker," April mutters with a disappointed grimace. Each agent candidate understands the significance of Hayley being pulled from the group. Just like that, the contest between them has become one for second position.

Hayley follows the instructor across the quad, past the helicopter, and into the classroom. Entering, she stops in the threshold when she sees the two people seated in the first row of ridiculous student desks. The man, close to sixty-five years of age, had been president of the United States when Hayley was a teenager. Governing for two terms of impeccable leadership, unmarred by scandal, he had rescued the nation from devastating financial crisis and ushered in an era of unsurpassed prosperity. Even with his retirement from public life, the former president is a national figure of such upstanding moral rectitude and ethical vigor that nomination for sainthood doesn't seem entirely far-fetched. The elderly woman sitting next to the former president is similarly recognizable, a retired Supreme Court justice who, while diminutive in physical size, possesses a gigantic legacy for landmark decisions affecting the lives of every single citizen in the nation. Her integrity is unimpeachable. Both smile easily as Hayley continues to remain frozen in the classroom doorway.

"Good morning, Hayley!" the chipper former president greets the West Virginian. "Mind closing the door behind you? My friend here was just complaining about the cold, in total contrast to the so-named Bakeoven."

The retired Supreme Court justice casts a sidelong look at the former president. "Throw me under the bus, why don't you?" She looks back toward Hayley. "Come in, dear, and have a seat. We promise not to bite."

Hayley enters, the instructor who had led the way silently withdrawing from the classroom and shutting the door after him. The stunned West Virginian is alone with her dignified visitors.

"Kinda shocking, huh?" the former president guesses, good-naturedly.

Hayley nods her head. "Just a little, sir."

"Well, that's perfectly understandable. But spend a few minutes with us. You'll come to see we're regular folks, just like you."

"I'm not sure anyone in this room can be categorized as regular folks, Mr. President," the retired Supreme Court judge cracks.

The former president laughs. "Maybe so, maybe so."

Hayley doesn't let her guard down, not nearly relaxed as the two visitors. "If I can make an easy deduction, both of you are here to lend credence to what 'Mr. Jones' had alleged two days ago."

"I suppose that is rather obvious, isn't it?" the former president confirms. He continues, "Our only power is in our legacy and our commitment to the Constitution of the United States and its preservation. Publius is the organization that has formed around those ideals, and you and the other agent candidates are the manifestation of its commitment to action."

Hayley says nothing, busy absorbing everything the former president has said.

"What my wordy politician friend is trying to say, dear girl, is we need your help because we're too damned old to help ourselves." The former president winces at the former Supreme Court justice's all-too-accurate assessment of their viability, or lack of it.

"Are you thinking about taking this act out on the road, by any chance?" Hayley asks, warming to the relaxed dynamic in the room.

"We were thinking a YouTube channel might be the ticket," the former president offers.

The former Supreme Court justice cuts to the issue at hand. "You must be curious as to the identity of the Russian mole in our government, Hayley."

The somber nature of the moment prompts Hayley to merely nod her head in anticipation of being a privileged recipient of this secret.

"Your target is President Monroe," the former Supreme Court justice tells her. "He is an agent of Russia's Main Intelligence Directorate, their CIA, born in Russia but raised in our country for the sole purpose of penetrating its most sensitive institutions."

As that bombshell reverberates in Hayley's brain, the former president provides more details. "A trusted covert agent placed deeply within the Russian intelligence agency and handled by one of our associates during her career with the CIA passed along top secret information regarding Monroe's true origin soon after his election to president. My understanding is the GRU man was paid a million dollars for that information, since corroborated by several additional trusted sources."

The former Supreme Court justice asks, "Are you

quite satisfied with the integrity of our motivations, Hayley? The situation is dire. We'll leave it to one of our operations colleagues to explain the broad and finer points of your mission."

Hayley reacts, surprised but not surprised. "I am the selected agent candidate?"

"You are," the former president assures her. "There has been little question of you being our choice since the first day you arrived."

"I am honored, sir." Hayley's modesty is genuine.

"I suggest we are the ones who are honored by your selfless sacrifice, Hayley," the former jurist informs her.

"What I don't understand is, why not just let the proper agencies handle this?"

"The proper agencies cannot be trusted to act within the confines of our beloved Constitution, my dear. In fact, at this very minute, certain figures in those agencies are preparing a possible assassination of the president." Hayley reacts to this revelation, unable to mask her shock.

"You see, Hayley, in some ways, a lot of the folks back in Washington can be expected to act with only marginally less self-interest than our foreign adversaries," the former president suggests.

"Also, clever members of our strategic planning committee foresee better uses for Mr. Monroe than with a bullet in the back of his head or in jail," the former Supreme Court justice elaborates. "An illegitimate president can be a weapon turned back on those who deployed him against us."

Hayley says nothing, processing all that her distinguished visitors have told her. The former president stands up, with difficulty, from the confining student's desk. "Can't believe we make young people sit in these torture devices."

The former Supreme Court justice gets up with much less trouble. "You should try planking, Mr. President. Changed my life."

The former president guffaws. "That'll be the day. Next thing you know, my wife will be after me to take up hot yoga." Both of them move toward the door while Hayley stands respectfully motionless with averted gaze. "C'mon, Hayley. We may be retired, but you've got places to be."

She has no idea what he's talking about. "Sir?"

"You're coming with me and Madam Justice. The chopper will take us to a private airstrip and a plane for back east."

Hayley still hasn't quite caught up. The former Supreme Court justice beckons with a sympathetic gesture. "All of your things have already been stowed on board, dear. It's time."

But even with these icons, destined for the history books, Hayley isn't blindly obedient. She stays rooted in place. "The other agent candidates won't ever have the confirmation they need if we leave before they've returned." The two older people seem temporarily flummoxed by Hayley's intransigence. Hayley adds, "With all due respect, Mr. President, Madam Justice, they deserve to be told whose side they're fighting for."

The former president gestures toward a surveillance camera in one corner of the room's ceiling. "You just told 'em, Hayley. The last few minutes of our meeting here will be played back for their edification."

She looks toward the camera, embarrassed, only now remembering that all of their classes were video recorded. Sheepishly, Hayley follows her two distinguished visitors out the door and across the quad to the waiting helicopter. She falls into step beside the tall, rail-thin former president hunching his shoulders against the cold wind blowing down from Canada. "They tell me you'll be continuing your training in Virginia. The plan apparently is to insert you directly into the West Wing," he informs Hayley with the appropriate amount of seriousness.

"The West Wing? What's my mission?" The enormity of her task is just beginning to become clear to her.

"Oh, you just need to protect the man from assassination and then convince him to work for us." The former president gives her a wink. "Piece of cake, right?"

Hayley doesn't say anything in response but pauses before following the other two into the helicopter, looking down at her feet and seeing a jagged rock just to the side of her right foot. Reaching down to take hold of the stone, she stands again and takes in the camp she has rarely left in the last several months. Each way station since leaving home, whether in the military or since her discharge, has transformed her, an evolution that feels far from complete but profound nonetheless. It occurs to Hayley as she steps foot onboard the helicopter and sits in the jump seat between a former president and a former Supreme Court justice that she has learned all she possibly could in this windblown, desolate place.

The engine coughs to a start and whines as rotors begin to lazily turn, then faster and faster, clouds of dust swirling outside the windows, and then they're aloft. Crew members help the more distinguished passengers don headphones, but Hayley rebuffs the offer. She prefers turning off her mind in the roar and whoosh of the chopper. The aircraft rotates, bearing west and to an ill-defined future. Is she anxious? Not much. She has prepared herself, trained and conditioned every part of her mind and body for the challenge to come. Everything is possible. The Bear is at the nation's throat. He is a vicious and brutal beast that will rip the country apart, left unchallenged and unchecked. Without a doubt, the brute has bloodied its prey, and the end may seem near. But Hayley remains steadfast and fearless, thinking to herself, They just think they're winning.

---

SITTING IN THE roaring helicopter for a short, forty-five-minute ride to a private airstrip outside Portland, Oregon, the former president muses on the strange place in which he finds himself and, by extension, the nation, too. He blames himself for not seeing the threat until it was too late. Perhaps he could let himself off the hook by blaming the intelligence he was provided in the closing days of his administration, but such a rationalization mitigates his regret not one bit. This business he and the others have undertaken on behalf of the nation is the only recourse. He prefers action to self-recrimination, which achieves exactly nothing.

He glances to his left and briefly takes in the young woman sitting next to him. So much will be riding on her untested shoulders. Perhaps they are asking too much of her. More clever minds than his have determined that the current plan, while far from foolproof, remains the best option for reversing the terrible gains made by America's enemies. It is harrowing to think that a twenty-four-year-old West Virginia woman without a college degree will determine the fate of the nation.

The former president glances down to the young woman's hands and sees her right fist is clenched so hard the knuckles are white. He finds himself transfixed by the fury of her clenched fist, shocked to see the faintest trickle of blood seeping from between two fingers. The former president starts to say something but stops himself, realizing with astonishment that he is intimidated by this young woman and not the other way around. Here is only more reason for confidence in their selection. Hayley Chill will be more than equal to the task assigned to her. More sobering, however, is the former president's awareness the nation faces even graver threats than a Russian mole residing in the White House. As the helicopter churns west, he mutters a silent prayer for the young woman sitting beside him and her safekeeping. Her country needs her.

# ACKNOWLEDGMENTS

★ ★ ★ ★

I would like to thank my amazing editor, Emily Bestler, for her wholehearted support. Emily and her intrepid assistant, Lara Jones, as well as the whole team at Atria Books, have been a godsend. Thank you, Emily, for being this new author's lifeline.

No words of acknowledgment are equal to the gratitude I have for my film and television agent of three decades, Jordan Bayer, whose ferocious and unwavering support of my creative efforts has been nothing short of a miracle. Jordan, you are so much more than simply my agent. You are my very good friend.

I would like to thank my book agent, Ann Rittenberg, and her unbeatable team at the Ann Rittenberg Literary Agency, Rosie Jonker and Imogen Jenkins. Were it not for Ann's boisterous enthusiasm for this book and unerring instincts for finding it a home, I might not be a published author today.

To my fellow Hollywood trench fighter, Douglas

Steinberg, who led the charge outflanking the enemy and first suggested I fill the page with words "that go from margin to margin," a most heartfelt thank you. Lunch is eternally on me, Doug.

I would also like to acknowledge my far-flung and lifelong pals, Wesley Harris, Jim Woodside, Joe Pomar, Brian Allman, Marty Gross, Andy Lerman, Harry Steinway, and Tom Christie. Good buds all, you guys have made the time between writing jags a most enjoyable alternative.

Christie Ciraulo was kind enough to proofread the manuscript. Thank you.

Gratitude must be expressed for my late lawyer, J. Franklin Stewart, a true southern gentleman whose generosity was a legend in the industry and very much appreciated. Rest in peace, Frank. I miss you.

And, finally, I would like to salute a wise and anonymous critic of welcome brevity who said a book had to be about something to be successful. I pray I've been equal to that task.

# ABOUT THE AUTHOR

★ ★ ★ ★

**CHRIS HAUTY** is a screenwriter. He lives in Venice, California, with his feral cat and a Triumph motorcycle. *Deep State* is his first novel.

Turn the pages for an exclusive look at
Chris Hauty's new thriller

# SAVAGE ROAD

# PROLOGUE

**H**ayley Chill exits the Oval Office through a door that opens onto the Rose Garden and must pause to admire the absurd perfection of the weather outside. Balmy sunshine and the brilliant green of the executive mansion's grounds are a stark contrast to the bedlam inside the West Wing on this dreadful day. The twenty-seven-year-old White House staffer— flaxen hair and powder blue eyes notwithstanding—is unnoticed by Secret Service and FBI agents driven into a frenzy by the unfolding crisis. Wait until the full story comes out, Hayley muses as she walks up West Executive Drive. America won't know what hit her. But the pandemonium has provided Hayley with a welcome diversion. Weighing on her mind as she leaves the White House complex, most likely for the last time, is the awareness she will be on a list of those held accountable. Failure of national proportions will demand a host of sacrificial lambs.

Hayley catches up with three housekeepers—two Filipinas and a Latina—as they exit the security gate at

Seventeenth Street, on the west side of the Eisenhower Executive Office Building. The residence staff members were the first to be released by the Secret Service.

"I'm looking for Alberto Barrios, one of the president's valets. Have you seen him today?"

The Latina housekeeper nods and points across Seventeenth, indicating a man on foot, just turning the corner at G Street and heading west.

"Alberto," the housekeeper says.

By the time she has jogged across the bustling avenue and rounded the corner at G Street, Hayley sees Barrios has already advanced halfway up the block. The Cuban, tall and broad-shouldered, walks with a brisk pace. Hayley increases her gait to narrow the distance between them. She hasn't a coherent plan or strategy. Barrios must be apprehended, at the very least. Stopping him before he flees the country is all that matters.

What is the extent of the man's training? Is he armed? Where does he intend to rendezvous with his compatriots? These questions stay unanswered as Hayley follows Barrios up the mostly quiet side street. The skills she developed in the US Army, as one of the first female graduates to earn the blue cord, kicks into gear. Intercepting the Cuban well before he makes contact with his associates is an absolute imperative. By any means necessary, she must detain him long enough for the police to arrive. Careful to maintain a discreet distance from her target, Hayley retrieves her phone and dials 911.

"Hello. What's the nature of your emergency?"

Hayley covers her mouth as she speaks into the

phone. "A man and a woman are fighting on the sidewalk. Twenty-one hundred block of G Street."

"Ma'am, do they have any weapons?" the operator asks.

"The man has a gun." She sees Barrios crossing the street in the middle of the block. Has he detected her pursuit? Into the phone, she says, "Please send the police. Quickly!"

Hayley disconnects the call before the operator can request she stay on the line. Pausing on her side of the street, she observes her target entering the GW Delicatessen. His turn toward the store is abrupt. Not natural in the least. To prolong the hope that Barrios is unaware of her presence would be a dangerous indulgence in wishful thinking. The real chase has begun.

As Hayley crosses the street, she considers the possibility that the deli has a rear exit, one that will provide the Cuban an escape. She could continue to the end of the block with a plan of intercepting him on Twenty-second Street. But Barrios could be watching from inside and exit through the front door once she's around the corner. Hayley calculates that her best chance for success is to follow him inside.

She imagines how the next few minutes will unfold. Violence will come. Blood will be spilled. Hayley has been here before. The experience has always been the same. There is a flattening of sound. Colors become over-saturated. Time is elongated, certain to be followed by a sudden lurching of events into hyper-speed. Instinct is a pivotal factor in these situations. Training. Muscle memory takes over, as well as the brute willpower to prevail and survive. She pauses at the threshold of the convenience store, to breathe and modulate heart rate. Her eyes take in everything. Ears detect every sound, however minuscule.

Now, Hayley tells herself. This.

Pushing the glass door open, she enters the cramped delicatessen. Occupying a narrow storefront, the owners have maximized the limited space with high shelving that runs the length of the interior. A female cashier restocks the shelves directly behind a checkout counter, to the left of the entry door. The Cuban operative is nowhere in sight. As Hayley makes her way toward the back of the store, she notes the absence of surveillance cameras. Did Barrios, familiar with the store, select this location for that reason? Hayley feels the hairs on her forearms go up.

The deli counter at the rear of the store is deserted. Looking past the refrigerated case displaying an array of meats, cheeses, and salads, Hayley clocks the rear emergency exit door she intuited would be there. Weighing the likelihood that Barrios has fled, Hayley considers her next move. A restroom to the right of the rear exit offers another possibility. Checking the door, she finds it unlocked.

Every instinct sounds an alarm. Hayley puts herself in Barrios's shoes. He thinks he can take me. She pauses to look over her shoulder, to the deli counter behind her. A magnetic strip over the prep counter is easily within access, offering an array of long knives. She quickly discards the thought. Instead, Hayley trade desperate blows. Their fight is ferocious but not long in duration. Barrios cannot exploit his larger physical size. Can't extend the full reach of his punches. Hayley brings force to bear with the understanding that she made the correct decision in rejecting the choice of a long knife from behind the deli counter. Her spiked fist is equally devastating and much more maneuverable. Her agility overwhelms the Cuban. Hayley inflicts far more damage on him than she receives.

Barrios isn't the first opponent to underestimate her. Being sold short has been an undercurrent in Hayley's life. Her gender, family background, and West Virginia accent have all played into her status as an underdog and not one she encourages. But she won't hesitate to exploit that poor judgment. They just think they're going to win. Barrios laid his trap, miscalculating the advantages of Hayley's smaller size in the cramped toilet. The error is a catastrophic one. He failed to foresee the sheer ferocity with which his pursuer would wage close-quarters combat. Who would? Her destructive force is freakish and, in that way, completely unpredictable.

As she slams her spiked fist repeatedly into his face, Hayley recognizes one unavoidable fact: the Cuban will not be taken alive. Barrios will fight as long as he is physically able. The longer their brawl continues, the greater his odds of success. Though Hayley has gained the upper hand, the ultimate result of their fight is not predetermined. She could die here, in this fetid toilet.

She drives her elbow into the man's head. The blow causes him to drop his knife. Hayley retrieves the knife from the floor and, holding it close to her body, buries it in the Barrios's chest as she stands up straight with knees locked. The Cuban struggles for a few moments as she drives the blade deeper into his thoracic cavity and then goes limp. He falls backward, sitting comically on the closed toilet seat. The blare of a siren signals the approach of the police, summoned by Hayley's call to 911.

Winded and delicately spritzed with her adversary's blood, she withdraws her phone from a pocket. After snapping a photo of the dead man on the toilet, she quickly exits the bathroom. Standing again at the rear of the long, narrow storefront, Hayley can hear the cashier ringing up a sale and chatting with an unseen customer.

The past days have posed a dilemma, with rapidly unfolding events forcing her to choose between the worse of twin evils. Duty-bound and genetically unable to shirk her responsibilities, she has thrown herself against the country's inexorable creep toward the precipice. There is no time to lose. With Alberto Barrios's death, she has given the United States a slim chance to avert a domestic catastrophe. Turning right, Hayley Chill, a covert agent for the "deeper state," exits the delicatessen through the rear door.

# CHAPTER 1

## THE LIVES WE SAVE
## TEN DAYS EARLIER

**W**ednesday, 8:25 a.m. Kyle Rodgers, a bespectacled black man of expanding girth, is waiting for Hayley when she walks through the office door. His coveted position as president whisperer and sounding board landed Rodgers with premium real estate on the West Wing's main floor. Richard Monroe's chaotic first two years as president culminated with an attempt on his life. The wholesale purge that followed those chaotic events spared the genial and eminently capable senior advisor. Among several outstanding attributes, Rodgers is notable in Washington for having gained his influential position without having made bones of anybody.

He is as good a boss as one can expect in the White House's pressure-cooker environment. For that indisputable fact, Hayley Chill esteems and admires Kyle Rodgers.

The feelings are mutual. His office is the best run in the building, and he has his young chief of staff from West Virginia to thank for it. The secret machinations of Hayley's superiors in the deeper state—a clandestine association of former presidents and Supreme Court justices, retired directors from the intelligence community, and other discharged heavyweights of the government establishment that calls itself "Publius"—placed her in the West Wing twenty months ago as an intern. But it has been by the sheer dint of her extraordinary skills that Hayley is where she is today: fifty feet down the carpeted corridor from the Oval Office.

"Thank god you're here," Rodgers says, without looking at her. "Today is going to be insane." He mixes sugar-free Red Bull with coffee at his desk, his go-to breakfast.

Hayley's meteoric rise from humble intern to the chief of staff for one of the president's key advisors generated widespread acrimony among the other West Wing staffers. The army veteran—possessing only an associate's degree from a two-year community college and an accent particular to people from the Appalachians—is widely considered by her peers to be undeserving of her fantastic success. Hayley Chill has dealt with this poisonous envy all her life and unfailingly turns it to her advantage. But the exertions of holding down two, high-pressure jobs—as White House staffer and covert agent—has taken its toll. Twenty-hour workdays are the norm.

Wearing a Jones of New York knee-length, dark blue skirt, a tie-front silk blouse, and sensible shoes, she drops her knock-off tote on the couch. "What's up?"

Rodgers scans his computer screen for Monroe's daily

schedule, a detailed, minute-by-minute rundown available only to West Wing staffers. "Okay. First off, we—"

"—need to get the president up to speed on the *LA Times, Washington Post* and *New York Times* hack." Hayley read reports on her way into work. Coordinated cyberattacks hit computer servers at printing plants across the country. The nation's major newspapers managed to get the day's editions out, but only after significant delays.

"Yeah, I heard about that," Rodgers says absently, taking a sip of his energy drink concoction. Glancing toward his young chief of staff for the first time since she'd arrived, he clocks Hayley's slightly haggard countenance. "What happened to you?"

She got only a few hours of sleep the night before. Hayley spent most of her Tuesday at the Library of Congress; the president's speechwriters required material for Monroe's address to workers at an auto plant in Ohio on Wednesday, and the job was tasked to Kyle Rodgers's wunderkind. A two-hour workout—six sets of a circuit of exercises that included timed pull-ups, crunches, and push-ups, followed by a twelve-mile run—followed a nine-hour stint at the library. After a quick dinner, Hayley put in several hours compiling a detailed weekly report on the president's activities for her superiors in the deeper state. Naturally, she squeezed in another workout this morning before coming into work.

She disregards her boss's question. "Has there been any attribution yet?"

"Who do you think?"

"We can't always blame Russia, sir. Other players

out there have the same capabilities. North Korea, for instance. Tehran."

Rodgers shrugs and turns his attention back to his computer, reading through an email to the president's chief of staff and vice president one last time before sending. He had joined Monroe's presidential campaign just before the start of the primary swing, proving indispensable in tailoring the candidate's message for early contests in Iowa and New Hampshire. A veteran of numerous national and state-level campaigns, Kyle Rodgers possesses the highly desirable ability to distill a politician's incoherent and insecure ramblings into network-ready sound bites. Married to his college sweetheart and the father of four-year-old twin girls, he is a pessimistic optimist. Rodgers recognizes humanity is on a collision course with its stunning idiocy. Simultaneously, he believes in the restorative powers of a competent executive branch. Bolstered by that conviction, Rodgers sets himself apart from ninety-eight percent of the other political wonks in town mired by their jaded nihilism.

Hayley persists. "Communications working on a statement?"

"The president will continue treating these low-level, nuisance attacks on private sector institutions as a non-government matter," Rodgers says by rote. He checks his watch. "I'm heading up to the residence to talk to the big guy." He hurriedly loads files and briefing books into a large leather satchel. "Don't forget. The Rose Garden thing has been moved to 9:45."

"Shutting down the printing operations of the three

national daily newspapers seems something more than a nuisance, sir." Hayley adds, with greater emphasis, "You might even call it a direct attack on the First Amendment by one of the nation's historic enemies."

Her boss doesn't seem overly concerned. "Well, if Moscow really wants our attention, they'll just have to turn off the lights at the Pentagon."

"Y'all know they can do that, don't you?" Hayley shouts after her boss as he heads out the door with his satchel. Of course, Kyle Rodgers is well aware of the capabilities of Moscow's cyber army. They match those of the United States. Soldiers at Cyber Command could turn the lights off in the entire country of Russia with a few clicks on a computer keyboard. But having that power is a far different matter from exercising it. The consensus in Washington is a cyber Mexican standoff will continue for the foreseeable future.

With a cascade of pressing concerns requiring President Richard Monroe's attention, Rodgers offers only a raised middle finger as he heads up the corridor. He thinks the world of his chief of staff but finds her to be galling as hell at times, too.

---

WEDNESDAY, 10:10 A.M. As he strides down the West Colonnade, accompanied by a Navy chief in full dress uniform, President Monroe's affinity for the Rose Garden is easy to understand. The outdoor location has been an effective tool for White House communications for decades, used as a backdrop for welcoming other world leaders, staging of official ceremonies, signing significant pieces of legislation, and non-campaign campaign events. More so than his predecessors, Richard Monroe has deployed the French-style garden adjacent to the Oval Office as his preferred venue for presidential stagecraft. With chiseled features and a hawk-like profile that wouldn't be out of place on Mount Rushmore, his looks are perfect for the iconic setting.

The president steps down from the colonnade, turns to face the one hundred plus invited guests— members of his cabinet, assorted dignitaries, military brass in dress uniforms—and blasts them with his trademark grin. A career soldier before winning his first and only political campaign for the president of the United States, Richard Monroe led a tank charge across the sands of Kuwait in Operation Desert Storm. Later, as a major general and commander of the 1st Armored Division, he drove the tyrant Saddam Hussein from Fortress Baghdad in Operation Iraqi Freedom. His obvious strengths, commanding presence, and unassailable integrity have been the perfect tonic for a nation torn by division and political polarization.

Everyone stands with the president's arrival, the electricity in the Rose Garden super-charged by his charismatic presence. Monroe smiles good-naturedly. This morning's event is one of the "good" ones, a time of celebration. After a wet and cold spring, the weather in the nation's capital has finally turned. Bright, warm sunshine bathes the proceedings in magnificence. The president is relaxed, and his casual attitude goes a long way to putting all in attendance—especially the Marine in blue dress uniform who accompanied him from the Oval Office and now stands at attention beside him—at ease. Monroe gestures with both hands. "Thank you, everyone. Please, sit."

All those assembled before the podium take their seats, while aides and staff members to either side of the garden remain standing.

"Thank you again, everyone, for coming out for today's event. It gives me enormous pleasure to be here today to honor one of America's finest and a true hero, US Navy Chief Edward Ramos. The Medal of Honor is the highest award our great nation bestows on an individual serving in the Armed Services of the United States. Chief Ramos receives this award, the Medal of Honor, for conspicuous gallantry at the risk of his life above and beyond the call of duty as a Hostage Rescue Force Team Member in Afghanistan in support of Operation Enduring Freedom on November 9, 2012."

Generous applause washes over the president and his invited honoree. Hayley watches from the sidelines, standing next to Kyle Rodgers. She listens to the president's speech and reflects on her extraordinary journey from an impoverished childhood in West Virginia to the White House Rose Garden. The deeper state plucked her from the army's infantry ranks, trained her in covert operations, and infiltrated her into the West Wing as an intern. Hayley fully appreciates the enormity of her responsibilities.

After Monroe finishes his speech and has draped the medal around the war hero's neck, the assembled crowd remains seated while the president and Ramos turn and retreat to the West Colonnade. A trio of Secret

Service agents follows at a discreet distance. Kyle Rodgers and Hayley Chill, having ducked out from the ceremony moments from its conclusion, wait near the French doors leading into the Oval Office as the president approaches with his honored guest.

Monroe exchanges small talk with Chief Ramos as they stop in front of the West Wing staffers. "Well, the weather couldn't have been better for the occasion."

The war hero is understandably stiff in the presence of his commander in chief. "Yes, Mr. President. Thank you."

"So very grateful for your service, chief." Monroe gestures toward his top advisor. "Mr. Rodgers will show you the way out of here. Kyle?"

Hayley looks to the ground to avoid Rodgers's startled expression. He's not used to being dismissed in favor of his much more junior chief of staff.

"Yes, sir. Of course," says Rodgers. He indicates the way back up the West Colonnade. "Chief, after you."

CWO4 Edward J. Ramos and Kyle Rodgers walk off, leaving the president alone with Hayley outside the French doors that lead into the Oval Office. They remain there, rooted in place, avoiding whatever prying eyes or electronic ears might be lurking on the other side of those doors.

"What do you want?" Monroe's voice is flat and hostile. That he hates the young woman with the powder blue eyes is abruptly clear. His transformation from charismatic chief executive to an angry old man is instantaneous.

Hayley absorbs the president's aggressive hostility

with cool aplomb, glancing over her shoulder to ensure the president's protection detail, posted at different points on the colonnade, is out of earshot.

Turning back to Monroe, she says, "You read my message earlier. Otherwise, you wouldn't have saddled Kyle Rodgers with the task of the lowliest aide."

"I'll flag the dead drop when I go upstairs again before lunch . . . Okay?" The man's bitterness doesn't befit his station. Hayley ignores it.

"Ask them if they know anything about the cyber-attack on the newspapers' servers last night."

Monroe smolders. He cannot bear taking orders from the twenty-seven-year-old female. By all appearances, he has no choice but to do so.

"Mr. President?" Hayley prods him, desiring only one thing: his unquestioned compliance.

"I'll ask them, goddamnit." His voice is a low growl of frustrated rage.

"Good. That's why you're here, sir, remember? Instead of a federal prison."

Monroe's lip curls as if he's on the verge of a bestial snarl. But he remains silent.

"Очень хорошо. До тех пор." Hayley's Russian is flawless, spoken only with the slightest American accent. Very good. Until later then.

The president of the United States looks over his shoulder, confirming their privacy. He grudgingly says, "До позже." Until later.

Monroe turns and reenters the Oval Office, where a scrum of subservient aides meets him. Hayley Chill remains just outside the door, watching him. Inside that hallowed space, Richard Monroe is the leader of the free world, the face of the greatest democracy that humanity has ever achieved. But Hayley—and only Hayley, in these precincts—knows better. Since before her arrival at the White House as a covert agent of the deeper state she has known the truth. Richard Monroe is a Russian mole, covertly entering the US with his parents as a one-year-old and since then under orders of the Main Directorate of the Russian General Chief of Staff. Moscow's corruption of America's highest office represents the most successful operation in history until Hayley Chill flipped Richard Monroe and, as his handler, uses him to undermine Russia.

Message delivered, and anxious to get other pressing tasks, she turns away from the door and nearly collides with a female Secret Service agent. Hayley experiences a sharp, stabbing fear. How long has the agent been standing so close behind her and the president? How much did she hear?

The expression on the woman's face is stern, even for a Secret Service agent. Her eyes are accusatory.

Stepping aside, Hayley begins improvising a response to the inevitable inquisition. Why is she speaking Russian with the US president?

The agent peers through the glass door, into the Oval Office, and then looks to Hayley again. Her expression softens, culminating in a friendly smile.

"It never gets old, does it?" she asks.

Hayley effortlessly masks her relief, returning the other woman's smile. "No, ma'am, it never does."